In the Arms Of the Spiral

C. Rhalena Renee

2nd Edition

Books in the Spiraling Past Series

In the Arms of the Spiral
In the Song of the Beloved
In the Chambers of the Nautilus
In the Dance of the Web

In the Arms of the Spiral

Copyright © C. Rhalena Renee 2021

1st Edition: Copyright © C. Rhalena Renee 2017. Published by Craigh Na Dun (An imprint of Ravenswood Publishing).

Names, characters and incidents depicted in this book are based on the author's personal experience and people she knows in the different realms. Any resemblance to actual events, locales, organizations or persons, living or dead, is based on the author's personal experiences and has been used with permission/personal consent.

All rights reserved. No part of this book may be reproduced or transmitted in any form or by any means whatsoever, including photocopying, recording or by any information storage and retrieval system, without written permission from the author.

GilGaia Publishing
Ellensburg, WA
Printed in the USA

In the Arms of the Spiral
TESTIMONIALS

When one of the tribe reclaims their true voice, it is a gift to us all. This book is one of those songs, crafted to guide us all home to embodying our authentic knowing.

Mellissae Lucia, author of The *Oracle of Initiation*; creator of the award-winning *Oracle of Initiation* deck; and creator of *Santos & Signs: Holy Intermediaries for Sacred Journeys.*

C. Rhalena Renee crafts a beautiful story, which radiates back and forth between the past and present in a mysterious magic. This mystery cannot be understood without the power of community coming together for rituals, and healing. The circle of friends in this book discovers how impactful their choices are, and how the denial of what truly is - can hold one hostage. Uncovering the stories within the mystery and beyond what is stored in their cellular memory, the circle begins to see how the threads are woven together. Until this happens, they are held back from being their full selves.

These characters teach us that when we surrender to embrace the wholeness of who we are and work together, we can heal the past and the present. One cannot happen without the other! This book is a way shower of how you can merge the past with the present and find healing.

Kris Steinnes, Founder, Women of Wisdom Foundation
Author of the best-seller, award-winning book, "Women of Wisdom - Empowering the Dreams and Spirit of Women"

To my ancestors, from whom I inherited my gifts; to my Teachers, who helped me develop those gifts; and to Elan and my other allies, who walk with me between the worlds.

Acknowledgements

William Smith and Martha Duskin Smith gave me the use of their beautiful home as I conceived the story and created the first draft of this work.

Cynthia Mitchell edited that first draft and gave me the confidence to keep writing.

My dear friends - Robert Wade, Mellissae Lucia and Suzy Wenger – provided feedback, and endless support, which helped the story mature. I thank you all from the bottom of my heart.

Finally, I am in deep gratitude to Jennifer Moultine, whose editing made me a better writer. Her questions, kudos, and insights brought both depth and sparkle to the final manuscript.

Preface

Stepping into prayer, setting intentions, doing magic - these are all powerful ways to let the Universe, God, Goddess, Spirit know what you want to create. And when you enter into any of these mystical pathways, you open yourself to experiences you can never guess at.

The book before you began as a personal bit of magic. I woke up one morning to the realization that I had made my life too small. I wanted more, but what? I'm good at goal setting and manifestation magic - which are useless if you do not know what it is you wish to create.

I knew that I wanted to use my gifts and talents well and to offer them in service to the world. I knew I needed to let myself dream about different ways to offer my work. Yet, as I began to dream about possibilities, I kept running into reasons why I couldn't pursue them. I needed a way to bypass these limits that kept blocking me.

For me, writing is a beautiful process of letting my imagination run freely and then editing it to perfection. I decided to use story as a tool for moving beyond what I considered my current reality. Anything can happen in a story; if I need something, I just write it in.

Along the way I get to try on different versions of myself; to create situations and circumstances that tickle my fancy; and to meet intriguing characters and engage with different aspects of my own nature.

So I began.

I created my ideal setting where I offered the work I love to do. The story was, of course, strongly based on the details of my everyday life – details that were integral to the story that finally emerged. But along the way, something else happened.

Magic has a way of serving your heart in ways you cannot imagine. Watching it unfold is part of the fun, but you have to let go and let it take you.

Take me it did! For a long time, I struggled with the fact that the emerging book was not really about me. Key elements of my life remained constant: I am a Teacher, Healer, psychic and lover of circles. The land I love stayed in the story. Yet the details of my life kept shifting. Characters I've never met became deep friends, lovers, family. Stories intertwined and teachings revealed themselves.

At times I felt more like a reporter than a storyteller. I was guided by intuition, but also by the needs of the emerging characters and the story they embodied. I attempted to take my personal self out of the story, but the magic wouldn't allow it.

It wasn't until after I published the first edition of *In the Arms of the Spiral* that I truly understood what was happening. In writing these books, I am traveling between the worlds and discovering an alternate reality where a version of myself understands teachings that this reality's version has not yet learned – or doesn't have access to.

Looking back, I see how long this alternate reality had been beckoning. Whispers of the soul, flashes of insight, intense journey work, voices calling me to remember – these had been happening for over a decade.

I'd been living my everyday life as a Healer and Teacher, but always with a sense that there was more for me to do and a "someday" waiting just around the bend.

I often felt I was preparing for a life I couldn't ever live and for a time when I could finally reveal all that I had come here to do. I felt the hand of Spirit bringing people and situations into my life that would take me to that "someday". Even the discontent, which led me to the writing magic, had the mark of Spirit in it.

Long ago, I surrendered to the call of Spirit, so there was nothing left to do but follow; I entered into co-creation with Spirit, discovering an untapped talent for journeying into other realms.

In those realms I experience different freedoms. I've found new guides and teachers and fallen in love with a circle of characters whose stories overlap my own.

Removing me personally from the story was simply not an option, because the story was both my healing and a new way to offer my work. I was becoming a StoryCatcher, gathering stories and teachings our world is hungry to receive. This work has become a powerful tool of magic for creating the bigger life I had been sensing.

Passing along the lessons and insights that have been part of this journey has resulted in "The Spiraling Past" series. The characters in the circle, for the most part, keep to the other realm except when they reach through to call me back to the story.

Through our adventures, challenges, and friendships, we teach principles of living in balance with nature, of seeing the Universe as an abundant source of allies, of using practical magic. We explore metaphysical concepts experientially. We weave healing and joy into the world.

Each time I wanted to pull myself out of the story, Spirit would not allow it. Pulling that thread, it seems, would unravel the tapestry. Being guided in my personal life through the story was vital to me becoming the woman and StoryCatcher I am today. My new circle in the other realm helped me to see how I focused on my work to the exclusion of a personal life in both realms. A very juicy love interest stepped into the story to give me a taste of how much a partner could enrich my life and my work.

The unfolding story helped me to step into what might be an ideal rhythm for me as a writer. I discovered that my joy in writing had become a passion and a way to explore new ideas for sharing my gifts and talents. Through this "exercise in magic" I was stepping into the life I wanted to live and embodying it.

I became a writer and now have several projects on the table. I've also entered into love relationships. My life has become much bigger and I enjoy offering my gifts and talents in exciting new ways.

Magic always brings with it a surprise or two. Just like prayer or setting intention, you send out ripples into the world. Watching how those ripples manifest in one's life, and embracing the magic of it, is essential. Those ripples remind us how intricately we are woven in co-creation with Spirit.

I still struggled with the story initially being *for* me, but no longer being *about* me. The central character, which started out as me, had moved beyond me in my everyday world. She certainly informed and inspired me in my everyday life, but her life is not mine and it did not seem right for her to carry my name.

I do not want my readers to feel the same confusion or unrest about the me that isn't me – or to believe these stories are autobiographical. I resolved this issue by changing the central character's name. I changed it several times only to feel the story refuse to continue.

Finally, I chose a name that is similar to mine in this realm. This change, although significant to me, did not disturb the story. I felt no objection from Spirit.

So, my dear readers, I invite you to step with me into this realm of story. I dearly hope that the characters you meet will inspire you and inform your life - as they have done for me. Finally, I ask that, like me, you return to your everyday life inspired and informed, but celebrating who you truly are in the here and now.

Cailleen Renae exists only between the worlds in the realm of story. C. Rhalena Renee lives on the everyday plane and enjoys the life she continues to create.

Bright blessings,
C. Rhalena Renee

Characters in Past/Present

*Names in parentheses indicate reincarnated characters.

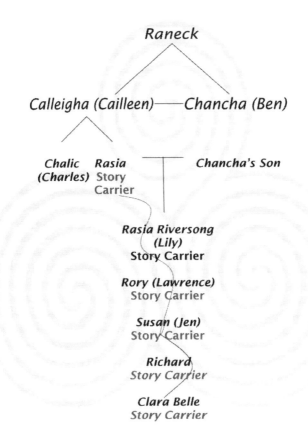

Characters

The First Three (who created the disharmony in past life)

Calleigha –Senechal (shaman/song healer) of the tribe, who challenged headsman and was banished; mother to Chalic and Rasia; married Raneck's son. Reincarnated as Cailleen, the witch, healer and teacher.

Chancha – headsman of the tribe, banished Calleigha and helped create disharmony. Reincarnated as Ben Hodges, friend of James, husband to Camille, father of Lily.

Raneck – Senechal (shaman) of the tribe, who's blindness led to upheaval in the tribe; trainer of Calleigha; Grandfather of Chalic; Great grandfather of Raisa; great, great grandfather of Raisa Riversong.

The Circle of Five (current time)

Cailleen Renae – reincarnated Calleigha, Healer and Teacher; apprenticed Lawrence, Jen, and Charles.

Charles Murphy – Herbalist, Healer, Teacher, dreamer, psychic and music producer; apprenticed with Cailleen; Teacher to James; the reincarnated Chalic, son of Calleigha, grandson of Raneck.

Jen Arante – Artist, psychic and oracle; apprenticed with Cailleen; soul twin of Lawrence; Teacher of Lily

Lawrence MacDougal – Lawyer, photographer, journeyer; apprenticed with Cailleen; soul twin of Jen; partner of Yvonne.

James McEwan – Retired Cop, neighbor of Cailleen's, college friend of Ben's, uncle to Lily, student of Charles.

Other Major Characters

Ben Hodges – Father of Lily; married to Camille; college friend of James; the reincarnated Chancha, headsman of the tribe, who banished Calleigha.

Camille Hodges – Wife of Ben, mother of Lily, friend of James.

Lily Hodges – Daughter of Ben and Camille; the incarnated manifestation of the original three, who created the imbalance; the reincarnated Rasia Riversong, a story carrier; great granddaughter of Raneck; granddaughter of Chancha; daughter of Rasia, niece of Chalic.

Yvonne Eriksen – Legal assistant, partner of Lawrence, friend of circle.

Elan – exists between the realms, guardian of the crossroads.

Songs

Song is a vibrant thread in the weaving of this story. Many of the chants and songs that came forth in the writing have not yet been recorded. Those that have been recorded and other songs that are referenced are listed below for you. I hope you'll listen and let the music add a texture to this story.

Cailleen and Charles often do SpiritSong. For an example of a SpiritSong, listen to: *SpiritSong – Gratitude* by Coleen Rhalena Renee **https://www.youtube.com/watch?v=lAOnlvPpP9s**

Chapter 8:

Spirit Love by Coleen Renee *youtube.com/watch?v=SCL9L-oIVpc*

Chapter One
Dreams & the Past

Until one can see the beauty in a dream, one doesn't yet truly understand it. Cailleen Renae knew from experience the depths of this truth. She discovered long ago that the courage to explore a dream may seem daunting, yet with a little time and patience, even the most nightmarish one became a treasured gift.

Dreams fascinated her. She loved the textures of each kind: precognitive dreams, ancestor dreams, collective dreams, lucid dreams and ordinary dreams. She thoroughly enjoyed letting them reveal their secrets.

But now she was puzzled. A dream would not let her go, nor would it fully reveal itself. She could recognize the textures of all the different kinds of dreams, yet this one's secrets eluded her. It was becoming a torment.

***

One would not have guessed at the clashing emotions rippling through Cailleen as she lay quietly in bed, her breath barely noticeable. Cailleen had a particular gift for lucid dreaming. The current dream was showing up more and more frequently of late. She could narrate it as it happened:

Intense eyes demand my full attention, drawing me across time and space. I sense great power behind those eyes and sense the fear that so often accompanies and isolates such power. Vague memories of love mingle with the command and challenge in those eyes. I shiver with the power and uncertainty they evoke in me. My heart races.

A vast landscape opens before me and I am alone, surrounded by barren hills and deep crevices. It feels empty, but I am glad to have a break from the power of those eyes. As my heart beat returns to normal, the eyes pull me back again into that other realm. I can almost remember the one they belong to. It's like a tickle in the back of my mind. I feel deep respect and a strong loyalty to him.

Suddenly, something shifts and my memories become crystal clear. Pain pierces my heart.

"Teacher," I gasp, "Grandfather!"

"The time to meet your vows looms." He commands me, "prepare yourself and remember."

He speaks no other words, but his eyes fill with emotion.

We are transported back through centuries of time to when I was exiled. I feel bereft and notice that the memory of my exile brings him great sorrow. Closing his eyes, he releases the sorrow with a long exhale. Then hope sparks with the raise of an eyebrow and power erupts from his eyes.

I flash on a memory of that same look filling his eyes on the morning of my initiation as a Healer and Carrier of Song. It was glorious to feel his pride in me, to feel proud of my own accomplishments, and to stand on the precipice of my life as an acknowledged healer. I had no idea how quickly my life would change.

By sundown on that same day, I was banned from my tribe, no longer allowed to do my work among my loved ones. My heart breaks and I want to leave this dream. Grandfather holds me in his vision to help the memory of my banishment play out. I remember:

Grandfather walked me to the edge of the land we had protected together. We knew every inch of it. The land was as much a part of our life, love, and magic as the people whom we were trained to serve were. His words at our parting came back to me:

'You will survive this cycle of banishment and return to me after a full turn of the wheel. Meet me as the Grandmother's face hides. Together, we will walk again upon this land we have promised to guard and serve. Chancha can refuse you your place of honor as Healer and Carrier of Song within the tribe, but he cannot take away your gifts and power, nor the mark laid upon you by Great Spirit. Your vows were made to Great Spirit through me as witness and priest.

'You may refuse to return, Daughter,' he acknowledged. 'You have that right. I pray that the work we share and the need of the people will call you back to us. I have seen you in the fullness of your power and I tell you now, a time will come when your vows will be fulfilled.'

Suddenly Grandfather's eyes flame with an intensity that brings me physical pain. He banks those coals quickly, just as he did when the head tribesman banished me out of fear and jealousy.

My eyes fill with tears as the last memories play out. Grandfather nods in recognition of my renewed memory. I now see his full face. It pulls my body into another vision for a few moments.

I sit in circle with the tribe around a winter fire. The smell of smoke, close bodies, fur wraps and food from the cooking fires comfort me and ground my memories. Even as I settle in and begin to search out other faces, I feel the vision fading.

'Not here in this time, meet your vows in your own time. You must remember and meet *them. Much depends upon you doing so. The time for re-balancing the wheel is upon you. Go in power, blessed daughter. May your feet walk in beauty.'*

"May your feet walk in beauty, Grandfather," I call back to him as the dream dissolves.

Cailleen begins to stir in her bed as the dream leaves her. Originally, the dream came to her as a vision during a ritual with her students. They were celebrating Spring Equinox and it came to her during a meditation. The speed and intensity of the vision took her so deep, she had trouble coming back to her own reality.

It made her uncomfortable thinking about that. Cailleen shifted and stretched a bit wanting to free herself from the tentacles of the dream and come back to her own present. But the dream pulled at her. It must be recurring for a reason. Knowing that it's best to follow when Spirit keeps taking her to the same place, Cailleen sank back into bed again and returned to the time of that first vision.

Grandfather in his great power had reached across centuries of time and halfway around the world to bring it to her. After the vision came, she had felt the awakening of memory in her body, and did not know what to do with it. She'd felt no awakening of skills. She felt awakened power, although tapping into its depths seemed beyond her.

Was that still true, she wondered? No, she didn't think so. She had grown in her power and her skills. Was that why the dream returned so often now? She could feel its intensity growing. It was starting to distract her throughout the day, like a dog whining for attention. Something was coming. She could feel it. She could also feel something, or someone, underneath the dream - something hungry and unbalanced.

Chapter Two
Names

The alarm sounded and she was relieved to leave the dream and get on with her day. She didn't use alarms as a practice. Dreamers need to dream and an alarm will chase a dream away faster than a flame will consume paper – leaving tiny unsatisfying remnants on the edges of your consciousness. Her work required an unscheduled life, free of alarms and overburdened calendars. However, this recurring dream was taxing her and some days she had specific commitments. Her life moved at a slower pace, but she kept busy enough between writing, teaching, gardening and living in tune with the seasons on her land in Eastern Washington.

Today she was headed for Yakima to work with young girls, who were preparing for their transition into womanhood. In many ways this was her favorite aspect of the work she did. It was an honor to be present with young people, witnessing their lives as they straddled a crossroads or discovered the living spiral of their lives. These girls were not children and not yet adults, but they were hungry for "more". Many of them had no idea what "more" meant, but Cailleen was always happy to work with the hunger that motivated taking action to create change.

She also enjoyed seeing the healing and shifts in relationship between the young girls and their mothers, aunts, grandmothers or sisters who sponsored them. As each sponsor witnessed the walk of their young girl taking her journey, she also renewed her own sacred journey. The spirals were all connected.

The ceremony that concluded the formal working with the young girls always brought a feeling of deep connection that extended beyond the women gathered. This first rites celebration was designed in part to acknowledge that all women are sisters. It anchored the teaching that each woman is sacred. Cailleen looked forward to that moment of recognition in their young eyes. Today she would meet the young girls and welcome them into the journey.

She arrived early at the retreat center and walked through the gardens and groves. Atop a hill, the retreat center looked over a vast valley. Cailleen liked to spend time with the ancestors and tell them of the young girls seeking initiation. She walked to the sacred pool where each of the girls would be cleansed and blessed during their ceremony. Yolanda, the owner, always kept everything well cared for while leaving it as natural as possible.

Cailleen followed the path that wandered to each of the directions: east, south, west, north, and then spiraling into the center. As she circled, she remembered when she, herself, was young and uninitiated. She liked touching in with her naive and expectant younger self. In the center, she stood at the altar rock and spoke the names of the girls who were gathering. She lit incense and offered prayers of gratitude for their coming and whispered encouraging words for their journey. Finally, she asked that she be a clear and loving guide for them.

Hearing chimes ring and the sound of drumming, Cailleen knew the circle was gathered and it was time for her to meet the young girls. She walked with purpose to those waiting in a yurt.

As she entered, the intensity of the drumming increased. Cailleen smiled as the girls and their sponsors turned expectantly toward the entrance. She knew they needed to feel a sense of sacred holiness from her so that they could feel it in themselves. She was also aware of the awe that rippled through the room and sent a silent prayer that someday those gathered would recognize that she, Cailleen, was no more or less special than each of them was. But for now, she would play the part they expected of her.

She settled into her chair, taking a moment to arrange the folds of her burgundy dress and black shawl. Then, with eyes closed, she took several deep breaths until she felt the room ripe with anticipation. She smiled. She opened her eyes and looked at each woman and girl in greeting.

"Welcome girls! I'm so happy to meet you and work with you as you prepare to become young women. I want to thank all the mothers, sisters, grandmothers and friends who have come here to support and witness for these young sisters.

"Rites of passage mark not only the lives of the individuals who come to receive them, but also of the community to which the participants belong. I want to take just a moment to talk about these important events generally.

"Throughout time, humans have created rites of passage to mark the end of one phase of our lives and the beginning of another. With experience you may one day see these moments as turns on the sacred spiral that holds you.

Some rites of passage are quite simple while others may take years of training and preparation. Baptisms and marriage are examples of two rites of passage we still practice regularly. One welcomes a new person into a community and the other ties two adults together in love and commitment. Each is a very important moment to witness and celebrate. But what about all the time and vital life stages between and beyond these two?" Cailleen paused and waited for them to consider.

"In recent times – perhaps the last 50 or 60 years," Cailleen went on to explain, "we have failed as a culture to provide significant rites of passage for our young people. I won't go into how this came about in our times. I do want to point out that this same time period has seen an enormous increase in teen suicide, pregnancy, drug use and depression.

"Rites of passage mark our passing from one stage of life to the next. Without this sacred acknowledgment we become lost. You see, we long for these moments. If we are not guided to and through them by those who have gone through the same experiences before us, we search for something to replace them. An unguided search often involves inappropriate activities and harmful consequences. I want to express my deep gratitude for all the sisters, mothers, aunts and grandmothers here today, who are gifting our young girls with this experience – and of course, with your own presence.

"And I am also deeply grateful for each of the young girls who are gathered with us. I choose to dedicate time here with you because I believe your transition into womanhood holds great importance for you, for me, for our communities, and for the world. I want to provide you with tools for moving into the next phase of life with as much ease and awareness as possible. It is my duty and my great privilege to help guide you – to teach you to dance on the spiral of life.

"Rites of passage include aspects of mystery, personal power, commitment and acknowledgment. They must be witnessed. The participants must be prepared and sponsored.

"So, we begin our journey together."

Cailleen rose and circled the space, lighting a candle in each of the cardinal directions. Banners hung from the wall of the yurt in reds, pinks and purples. A "red tent," she noted – a beautiful reflection of the blood that connects all women.

A massage table sat ready along one wall. Pillows, candles, singing bowls and sacred objects from many spiritual traditions sat on the floor and on small tables around the edge of the room. Cailleen enjoyed doing the sacred work of women's mysteries in a yurt. It suggested a cave or womb. Yet, with such a simple structure, it also seemed part of the environment that surrounded them.

As she circled the yurt, Cailleen sang to the *Grandmothers*, the women who came before her. She asked for their blessings and guidance. When she felt their presence, she moved to her place among the circle of pillows. She allowed a small part of her power to surface and be felt by the circle. Then, speaking for herself and the *Grandmothers,* she began:

"Girls, we will do our very best to share with you what it means to walk as women in our world. We will gift you with tools, challenges, advice and story. I will begin with a story right now. This is the story of my name. Next week, you will each share the story of your names. Names have power in them. Without the knowledge of the story and meaning of your name, you cannot hold or wield its power."

Cailleen paused again looking around the room at the faces of the young ones waiting for her guidance. For the most part they were open and curious. As usual, some were cautious, some guarded and one carried a mask of indifference. Most of these girls had never experienced a rite of passage and could not fathom how one could possibly affect their lives in any significant way. Cailleen almost preferred working with these girls rather than the girls who simply did what they were told and sought to be the most "successful" at the rite of passage. She knew the process of preparation had great power to shift any one person, including the facilitator.

Cailleen nodded at Jen, a graduate of her wisdom school and now a friend who came to assist. As Jen dimmed the lights, Cailleen cast her awareness to encompass the space. It was easy here in this sacred yurt. It was always easier to do this work in a place where sacred work happened on a regular basis. She cast her awareness outside the yurt for a moment to be certain they were secure and free of potential interruptions. In that moment, she mentally sent a call to her spirit guides to guard and protect. She brought her awareness back into the circle and shifted her body to settle in for the session. She heard the rustle and movement of other bodies and pillows as the girls and women in the circle followed her lead.

Taking a deep breath, she looked around the room into each face. Yes, they were ready to listen. A couple more deep breaths and they would all be in sync with each other – sharing breath and the rhythms of their bodies. This moment was vital. It taught them without words that all women are sisters with shared experiences and responsibilities. Awakening to this mystery sweetened the air in subtle and powerful ways. Cailleen smiled and began.

"My mother's people come from Ireland. Her people in Ireland stay close to their traditions, to the land and to the magic that surrounds them. They are a people of story, music, mystery, laughter and sorrow. They believe in Faeries, the Little People, and their own ability to know what cannot be seen. My mother knew that I would be the most Irish of all her children. And so, I needed an Irish name. What better than being an Irish Cailleen, which means girl?

"I have an older sister whose name is Sarah May. My mother wanted our names to rhyme. I'm not sure why. But she looked and looked for a middle name to rhyme with May, that she liked. One day she was chatting with the neighbor down the street. The neighbor was telling a story about her daughter, Peanuts. Since my mother spent so much time considering names, she was curious about this daughter's name.

"Where did you get your daughter's name?" my mother asked. "It's quite unusual."

'Oh my,' the neighbor exclaimed. 'We didn't name her Peanuts. That's her nickname. She was wrinkled like the skin of a peanut when she was born. The nickname stuck. We named her Renae.'

"My mother immediately liked the sound of it. It's been Sarah May and Cailleen Renae ever since. "

Cailleen's voice indicated this was just the beginning of her story, but she paused here to let what she'd shared sink in.

This was Jen's favorite part. Cailleen could use a pause better than anyone she ever saw. She knew just how long to hold it for each group and also how to bring them out of that silence. Sometimes she sang them, sometimes she taught them a chant, sometimes she simply continued the story. Jen was learning this magic by assisting. She anticipated a song with this group, but no particular song suggested itself to her.

Cailleen began with a very long low note that seemed to come from deep within her.

I am Cailleen.
I am Cailleen
Cailleen Renae

Cailleen moved into a Jana Runnals' chant that speaks of the long memory of women. She'd personalized it. Jen smiled. Along with every other woman in the circle she found herself leaning forward in anticipation of what was to come.

"As I got older," Cailleen began, "I studied anthropology and history and discovered a few more things about my name. Cailleen in Irish Christian traditions means 'woman of God'. I have always had a strong spiritual nature, so the name fits me. In studying more ancient Irish tradition and language, I discovered that –'een means, young, little or small. Caill- comes from the Calleigh or the hag. So, my name dubs me a little haglet, or a hag in training."

Several groans of empathy and maybe even one of horror moved through the circle.

"Now, I heard those groans," Cailleen smiled. "But don't worry. The word, hag, has been altered to mean an ugly old nasty woman. I assure you I am not training to be *that*. There will not be any nasty tricks or harsh words as we prepare you to walk as strong women in the world.

"No," she continued, "in earlier times, the hag was the wise woman and healer. That, I proudly claim to be training for. It will take at least a lifetime. And I promise to pass along as much wisdom as seems, well – wise.

"You might be wondering about Renae. Well, it happens that I also carry a significant amount of French blood in me. Renae is a French word meaning reborn. This also fits me. I have moved a lot and changed careers several times until I finally found healing and teaching as my life path. My name also reminds me that each day – each moment really - offers an opportunity to rebirth oneself.

"I am. I am Cailleen Renae, haglet reborn. I share with you my name and in the sharing I reveal a bit of myself and with it, my power. I trust you will hold it with care."

Another silence filled the room as Cailleen looked into the eyes of each girl and woman. In that look she communicated that she had indeed gifted them with a part of herself and that she expected and trusted they would indeed hold it with care. Jen remembered when she'd received that look herself. For her it was a calling to awaken to her own power as a person, to acknowledge that what she did actually mattered. She felt Cailleen's eyes on her again. She looked up and Cailleen nodded. That was her signal to gently raise the lights. As she did, Cailleen drew in a large breath. As she exhaled, she released the intensity of the room. Then she repositioned herself on her pillow and smiled at the circle. This was the smile from the everyday, more accessible Cailleen. She still sat as priestess, but the cloak of great mystery no longer enfolded her.

"Cailleen?" one of the girls asked.

"Yes daughter," she responded.

"What about your last name? Do we only share our first and middle names?"

"I see you pay attention to details. It's a very good question. One you must each answer for yourselves. Healers and wise women belong to the entire community in a very special way. I released my family name when I chose to step into my name and become a hag. I have since added several middle names, which I have also not shared with you today. I have revealed to you what seemed right and appropriate both for you and myself.

"You will also choose what to reveal to the group of sisters next week. If you look around the room you will find women who took their husband's name when they married, others who did not, and still others who kept their own name and added their husband's name. Names are important. They tell the story you wish to be revealed about yourself. Some of you will ask to add a name at your rite of passage ceremony to help you carry a new part of yourself out into the world. Some of you will not feel that need. Each of you must decide for yourself. Wherever you go, it is best to know from where you came and to know where you currently stand.

"Now, let's take a quick break and when we come back, you will briefly introduce yourselves in whatever way feels right for you in *this* moment."

Chapter Three
Stories & Secrets

After her long day of teaching, Cailleen examined her reflection in the mirror. She appeared calm and content. Her long dark wavy hair hung loosely around her shoulders, its silver threads adding a shimmer that cascaded down and danced in the evening light. She began and ended most days sitting here; simple moments in beauty to set her intentions for the day and to reflect back on its events.

Cailleen picked up her brush, then put it back down, reached for the lavender balm in the fanciful blown glass bottle, which her sister had given her, and put that back down. The restlessness of her hands gave her away. She felt anything but calm or content.

Looking at herself in the mirror, she shook her head.

"It's no good," she said to herself. "You can't pretend the dream hasn't returned and you can't deny you've made no progress in deciphering what it wants from you.'

Cailleen stood and went to her closet. Meeting Kate tonight for dinner would be a good distraction. She caught her reflection in the full-length mirror. Average height, good Irish skin, wide hips and lots of soft curves. She'd always been a large woman who appreciated her own curves. She wouldn't mind being a bit smaller, but she never wanted to be skinny or angular. That simply would not suit her. A little more height for more effect in her flowing tunic and scarves would be a real plus. But overall, Cailleen Renae was comfortable with her body.

The phone interrupted her thoughts. As she picked it up, she heard chaos on the other end: giggles from her nieces, a barking dog, running water and her sister's slightly frantic voice.

"Hang on, I dropped the phone," she laughed.

"Emily." Cailleen smiled. "How are you?"

"I'm good. I called to tell you I was going through some of Dad's boxes and found a recording of his grandmother telling stories. I knew you'd want to hear it. It's in an envelope with your initials on it. I don't recognize the handwriting. Just says, 'Recording of Clara Belle story for C.R.'. It might not even be for you, but I can't think of anyone else in the family with those initials. Odd, isn't it?"

Emily rushed on.

"Anyway, I knew you were having dinner with Kate so I sent it along when I had coffee with her this morning. Odd that we're both seeing her in the same day, and on the day I found the envelope. Well, you can hear the chaos here. Jennifer, don't pull the dog's ears! Gotta go, love ya."

Cailleen shook her head and chuckled fondly. Emily always seemed to be doing five things at once.

***

The Kittitas Cafe provided a relaxing environment in historic Ellensburg. It was a 20-minute drive from Cailleen's home on the Teanaway. Cailleen anticipated a long leisurely dinner and an intimate conversation with Kate. Although Kate and Cailleen lived within fifteen miles of one another, they only enjoyed the rare evening together. Kate's husband, John, was out of town and their daughter, Fern, was at a sleepover. Tonight, was theirs.

Kate stood tall and willowy in her well-tailored wool skirt of dark chocolate brown and a buttery cashmere sweater with matching wrap. Her hair was short and despite a windy evening, every strand was in place. She waited for Cailleen with a composed and rather serious expression on her face.

Cailleen walked in with a gust of wind behind her. She ran her fingers through her long curling hair in a way that made one think she was just adding a final touch to the work of the wind. Both hair and billowing clothes settled in place around her yet seemed ready to dance with another breeze, if chance brought it. She wore silky slacks and a sweater in a rich navy blue. Over them she wore a duster of silver blue decorated in a playful border of embroidered leaves.

The two women turned towards each other and the magic could not be missed. Kate's movement revealed jewelry that seemed to come alive. A fiery amber necklace caught and reflected back the candlelight from the tables. As she hugged Cailleen, gold bracelets jingled. As much as Kate seemed to come alive, Cailleen seemed to calm and settle. They linked arms, leaned into each other and turned at the approach of their favorite waiter, Terry.

"Welcome ladies," he greeted. "Just the two of you tonight?"

"Yes, Terry," Kate answered, "it's girls' night out."

"Well, let's seat you in the corner over here so you can talk your hearts out with little or no distraction. Will you be starting with your usual tonight?"

"Please," the women said in unison.

"Where's John off to?" Cailleen asked as Terry left to get their drinks.

Kate's face fell immediately. Cailleen reached over and squeezed her hand, then waited.

"He's gone back to Colorado to see his mother. She's not well. He thinks we might need to move there. I feel selfish, but I love my life here. Fern is settled and happy. John has his work and really good friends. You've probably guessed that life hasn't always been easy for John. His childhood was rough. He's the only one of his family who seems to have moved beyond it. But each time he visits he gets pulled back into their dysfunction. It takes him a week or more to recover from a visit. I can't imagine moving there even for a short while. I wish we could just leave the past in the past.

"I tell myself it's for her ease that I hope she passes quickly. But I can tell *you* the truth. I dread the thought of moving there for even a short time. Can you tell me if you sense anything specific about the situation?"

Cailleen held Kate's hand in both of hers and went within to connect with the other realms. "I see you and Fern here. I cannot see where John is. But I can tell you that whether she lives long or passes quickly, John will have to face the ghosts and lessons of the past." She opened her eyes and looked directly at Kate. "And you, my dear friend, will be gifted with a basketful of lessons as well."

"Oh sure, tie a pretty bow on it," Kate said with a smile but her lips trembled.

"You'll be OK," Cailleen assured her. "You have really good friends here, too. You might need to call heavily on them. And I know you, my friend; you will want to chart something. So tomorrow I'll email you my traveling schedule and ask Emily and Charles to do the same. You call Everett, Alice and Miranda. Chart who's in town and when so you'll know who's most likely to be available at any given time."

"You joke, but you know that's exactly what I'm going to do," Kate responded. "Here's to a well scheduled crisis!" Kate lifted her glass and both women burst out laughing.

Terry took his cue and walked over to take their order. Two hours later, after excellent food and companionship, the two women walked out arm in arm.

"I needed that," Kate whispered.

"So did I," Cailleen confirmed. "Where did you park?"

"Just around the corner on Main."

"Me too."

"Good, I need to give you a bag from Emily. She said she thought you'd want it ASAP."

They walked to their cars and Kate handed Cailleen a gift bag. Inside was an envelope with a cassette tape inside it.

***

As soon as she held the cassette in her hand, Cailleen felt that knowing "click". Something important was happening. She felt as if she was holding a key in her hands. A key to what, she didn't know. But the tingling along her scalp was the same sensation she felt during the recurring dream of the last few years. She felt caught up in the power of a spiral dance. She took several deep breaths and opened the window to the cool night air. She needed to drive.

Her classic Volvo had a cassette deck, but Cailleen knew it was best to listen at home in her study where she'd be surrounded by her elemental objects. She would light some candles and maybe a fire. She'd pour herself a glass of port – no, better make it Irish whiskey. Then she'd sit at the table in the center of the room with a journal and listen to her great, great grandmother's voice and stories.

Why was she so sure this would be a pivotal moment? She simply knew, just as she knew she'd been meant to hear this tape. The stories it held had been passed down from generation to generation, preserving information that somehow, she knew she needed.

As she pulled up to her house, she saw Charles' Saab parked by the garage. She could tell by the flickering light that he had already lit a fire. Charles had always been particularly tied to Cailleen psychically. Did he sense the importance of this moment? Is that why he was here? She wasn't sure if she wanted any company right now. She was usually thrilled to see Charles, but at this moment he felt like a distraction.

She sighed with resignation, then shifted her expectations to make room for him. She gathered her purse and the gift bag with her grandmother's tape. As she walked to the door, she wondered if the gift bag was a good omen. Gifts aren't always wanted and often not appreciated, she said to herself.

Cailleen opened the door, expecting Charles and a big bear hug. But only warmth and silence greeted her. She walked to her study and peeked in. The soft light of the fire was joined by a scattering of lit candles. On the table in the middle of the rug was a round glass table. On the floor next to it sat a bottle of port and a bottle of whiskey. On the table was a note. Cailleen threw her coat onto a chair, kicked off her shoes, sank into the floor pillows, poured some whiskey and read the note.

Darling,
The last thing you may want tonight is company. Then again, you might want the ear or shoulder of a good friend tonight or tomorrow.

Do what you will, love. I'm making myself at home upstairs. If you need or want me at any time, come and get me. Otherwise, I'll see you tomorrow.
Charles
P.S… couldn't tell whether you'd need the port or whiskey. They don't mix well, so don't do both. Kisses!

Sweet Charles. Of course, he would know. She sat smiling, letting his love give her courage.

Cailleen began gathering what she would need: a cassette player, pen, journal, a honey cake for grounding, and tissues. She sat them on the table and arranged the pillows so she would be facing north, the place of the ancestors.

Going to the north side of the room, she touched the picture of each of her grandmothers. She'd come to trust their guidance over the years. She smiled at the knowledge that they were more accessible to her now than when they were still living. She chose a piece of jade from the shelf and circled to the east.

She picked a sprig of rosemary then lit a cone of cedar incense. A silver vial of clary sage oil nestling between the lavender and sage plants called to her. She put a drop on her third eye to open her senses and closed the drapes to eliminate distractions. There was no moon in the sky tonight she noticed – a dark moon; a clean slate.

She continued around to the fire. It made such a cozy, warm and safe room. She stood meditating for several minutes letting the fire burn away any hesitation, fear or expectations that would hinder her clarity. Then she let the flames mesmerize and pull her back to the time of her great, great grandmother. She'd seen pictures but had never met her in this lifetime.

"I've come to hear your stories, Grandmama," she whispered. She heard the creaking of a rocking chair and felt welcomed.

Cailleen pulled her mind out of the mesmerizing flames to move on to her task. As she did the scene shifted and Grandfather's eyes floated before her and his words came back to her, "The time to meet your vows looms. Prepare yourself and remember."

"I have not forgotten your message," she answered. "If you are here now, perhaps I will be gifted with some more information tonight."

Cailleen took a taper, lit it in the fire, chose a candle from the mantel and lit it. Carrying the candle with her she circled to the west.

Willow's quilt on this wall always brought her a sense of peace and tranquility with its seals and mermaids. Tonight, the silver threads sparkled like sun on the water and she felt blessed by Yemaya, Poseidon and the Selkies. On the table below it a tin of Irish sod drew her attention and she picked it up to represent the West.

Cailleen placed the jade, rosemary, candle and tin on the table in corresponding directions of North, East, South and West. In the center, the place of Spirit, sat the tape from Clara Belle, her grandmother. She held her hands over the table feeling the items connect and the sacred energies shimmer.

"By Earth, Air, Fire and Water I create this sacred space centered in Spirit from which all things come," she chanted, "and to which all things return. May the work I do here serve my highest good and the good of all my relations. I begin with open heart and clear intention. I ask the Ancestors for guidance and the Goddess Hestia to witness as I reconnect with my past and seek to understand more fully that which is hearth and home to me. So be it!"

"Clara Belle, speak to me," Cailleen beckoned as she settled comfortably among the pillows and pressed the play button.

The first sound she heard was a reel-to-reel tape. The recording was a bit scratchy. She hoped she would be able to get a clear enough message. A man's voice began:

"This is Richard Jeffries, grandson to Clara Belle Springfield, who is with me today in a recording session of her life and stories. It's late summer in the year 1948.

"Grandma, you've told us stories of your childhood, marriage to Grandpa, your children, life in Ohio and stories your grandmother told you. I have one last question and I hope you'll forgive me for not asking it years ago. I never understood it, frankly. But before he died, Papa made me promise to ask this question of you. He said you carried a family mystery that only a few ever heard. He said some were to hear it and some were to simply pass it on. I would know which it was for me. I think I am meant to pass it on."

'Yes Richie, if it was yours to hear you would have asked years ago,' Grandma confirmed.

"I'll keep the reel going and leave you to tell the story. When you're ready for me to come back just pound your cane on the floor. I'll listen for it." Richard said.

"Yes, that will do nicely," Grandma said.

She cleared her throat and Cailleen heard her settling in for a long story.

"My name is Clara Belle Springfield. I heard this story from my grandfather. He heard it from his Grandmother and she heard it from her father, who heard it from his grandfather. At least every two generations the story is passed onto someone. Sometimes, the person who is to hear the story is charged to change it.

"When I was 60, I felt I'd failed the family, myself and maybe even the world because I had not succeeded in resolving this story. But lately, I've begun to suspect that I have done my part. I feel complete in my life now that I am telling this story. Once I've finished with it, I think I'll find my way home to my dear Harold pretty quickly.

"The story can only be resolved in the right time. We do not know exactly when that time is. Each, in his or her own time, has carried the story. Some carry it with the intention of seeking to resolve it. Some carry it only to pass it along. You will know which wrung of the spiral is yours in your time.

"I thought at one time that it would be best to tell everyone. It seemed to me that the more people working on resolving this story, the better.

"The story was wiser. Each time I attempted to tell it something prevented me from doing so. I understand now that this is a power story.

"I remember Grandpa telling us that some stories could only be told at certain times or to certain people. If told to the wrong person or told out of time, the story lost its power and could be lost altogether.

"A few years back I was growing tired and I worried this story would die with me. I considered once again telling the story to the whole family. But that night Grandpa came to me in a dream. I remembered his warning. And so, I waited until finally on the day of my death Richard asked me to share the story.

"And you my dear Grandchild – for that is what you must be – are probably tired of waiting. You must be anxious for this old lady to stop rambling and actually tell you the story."

After a brief fit of coughing and the sounds of swallowing followed by the rattling of a teacup on a saucer, Grandma Clara Belle continued.

"In each telling, there is the possibility that the teller added something inconsequential but distracting or failed to pass along vital parts of the story. Still, I believe that somehow, what's meant to be heard and told, will be.

"Long ago, when people dwelled together in small tribes and lived on the land in harmony with the other creatures of Mother Earth, our ancestors were a tribe of hunter-gatherers living in what we now call northern Europe. They lived inland in a beautiful valley hidden among the hills, except in the summer months when they camped by the sea.

"Our totem was the Bear. We depended on Brother Bear for our survival. Like bear, we lived in warm caves during the long winter and among the forests and streams in the warmer months. We knew where to find the best berries and fish. Bear skins kept us warm in winter. Bear fat lighted our way in the dark times. Bear meat and bones provided food and tools.

"We always loved the arts and our tribe produced the best wood and stone carvers as well as storytellers and singers. Summer gatherings eagerly awaited our arrival and we did well in trading. This made us a very proud people.

"In the time of Raneck, the Senechal, and Chancha, the Headsman, tragedy befell our people. That tragedy has rippled out into my time and yours.

"Wars, people throwing other people into ovens and stripping them of their dignity; it breaks my heart to see such atrocities. The harmony must be restored.

"You are a granddaughter, I'm certain. I've sensed you in dreams and loved you dearly. You have a sweet spirit that is often unsettled and hurt by the ways of the world. Bless you, child. You have the strength to bear the story and perhaps to change it. Now, where was I? Ah yes, the tragedy:

"Calleigha, another sweet-spirited child, showed early gifts as both a Healer and a Song Carrier. She keenly observed everything around her. She sensed people's truths and could sing them into wholeness. In those days, song was used for healing, hunting, finding food and more. The Healer and Storyteller- we called them Senechal – had great power: often as much as the Headsman, sometimes a bit more, sometimes a bit less. The balancing of these powers could be challenging.

"Calleigha was an apprentice to Raneck, the Senechal. Teaching her was such a joy, for she not only had great talents, she had curiosity and a hunger to serve. Raneck often felt that he was not teaching her so much as reminding her of what she already knew. Calleigha's beauty caught many a young man's eye. But she had no interest in such things.

"Chancha, the Headsman, was wise in the ways of hunting and tribal leadership, but lacked the ability to judge people's hearts. He depended on Raneck for such things. It was Raneck who noticed each child's heart path and made suggestions as to how he/she might best serve the tribe.

"Chancha saw the value of Calleigha as a woman and was enthralled by her beauty. As she came of age, he told himself the Senechal would offer her to him in marriage and the two would lead the tribe together.

"However, Raneck was also enthralled with Calleigha, as a student and future Senechal. Calleigha was not just any apprentice. She was born with knowledge that was beyond Raneck and he felt she needed full initiation in order to completely access her gifts. She was ready to commit herself to the Land, the tribe, and Spirit. Raneck wanted her to mature into her role while he still had many years left to guide her.

"He was so certain of her path and of his role in helping her walk it that he could not see any path others might consider for her. Everyone had the right to choose their own path. Raneck already knew what her choice was. But his blindness to the desires of Chancha cost everyone dearly.

"As Calleigha's coming of age ceremony approached, no one was surprised when Raneck declared that something special for Calleigha and for the tribe would be announced. As the day drew near, Chancha and many of the tribe's people anticipated a marriage agreement.

"When the day came, Raneck proclaimed that Calleigha surpassed the requirements and training and he would initiate her as a Senechal at the full moon. His heart was bursting with pride as he spoke of how admired their tribe would be when they arrived at Summer Gathering with two powerful Senechals.

"Pride kept Chancha silent. He would not let the tribe see his dashed hopes. The radiance on Calleigha's face at the news told him he'd never had a chance to wed her. He saw clearly for the first time where her passions lay.

"As the days leading up to the ceremony passed, Chancha grew annoyed and then fearful. This child – now a woman with ever-increasing power - could present a challenge. Two Senechal and only one Headsman presented another concern. He thought on the relationship between Calleigha and Raneck, and how close they were, like father and daughter or maybe even lovers. That thought planted a seed of jealousy that quickly turned poisonous. Raneck could consecrate her and make her a Senechal, but only Chancha, as Headsman, could allow her to serve that role in his tribe. That he would not do!

"Three days after her initiation ceremony, Raneck formally brought Calleigha before Chancha to offer her services and be accepted as an adult. Chancha refused. His refusal shocked the tribe and people started grumbling and protesting. Calleigha in her youthful ignorance quieted the people herself and challenged Chancha.

"On seeing the power she had with the people, Chancha felt certain he was right. He objected to her challenge. She argued and in the heat of her own passions she challenged him again. He saw his own fall and the doom of his tribe if he lost face. He banished her from the tribe and insisted she be gone by sunset.

"Every heart in the tribe was broken at this pronouncement. Chancha had followed tribal law to the letter, but had broken spiritual law by denying a qualified adult the right to serve her tribe according to her skill and passions.

"Harmony was shattered and Calleigha was cast out for a year and a day. If she survived, she could return and ask to be accepted into the tribe as an adult, but never as Senechal.

"Calleigha survived. She returned to her teacher, to the tribe and to the Land she'd pledged her life to at her ceremony. She lived a half-life among them, practicing her skills only occasionally and in secret. She married Raneck's son, giving him a grandson and granddaughter. Her heart never healed from the devastation of being denied her work and Calleigha died young.

"That, sweet child, is our family story. And the theme of rejecting our gifts or being rejected because of them has followed us through each generation. Look at our family tree and you will see failures with great talent as often as you see respected artists and craftspeople. If you dare take a closer look you will also find leaders oppressing the people. It is all unresolved pain. It started with the assumption of one man, the blindness of another man and the ignorance of a young woman. The carelessness of only three people created ripples of pain for our family and the lives we've touched. They did not resolve it in that lifetime, and the imbalance will continue through time until they do. We are all held in the arms of this particular spiral.

"Here in my time, a handful of people have initiated great horrors. Never think that only one or two cannot make a difference. World history and our family history disprove this. Remember this, for you have the greatest opportunity to resolve this story and bring some harmony back into the world. It matters what one person and one family does. But I think you know this, dear child. All the Carriers before you have known this. I believe it's what identifies each of us as the next Carrier.

"I am tired now and need to take a rest," Grandmother concluded.

Cailleen heard the pounding of a cane on the floor and Richard coming into the room.

"Grandmama, how are you doing?"

"I'll need a rest before I finish – just a short nap."

Cailleen stopped her own recorder when she heard Richard stop his reel. She had never felt so heartbroken or lonely in her life. Her blouse was damp from the steady stream of tears that, even still, rolled down her face. She remembered it all; she'd lived it all. The burden of responsibility overwhelmed her and she felt cold. The fire was now just a few glowing embers. She considered going to bed, but knew she wouldn't sleep until she'd heard everything her grandmother had to say.

Cailleen got up to stretch and to rekindle the fire with more logs. She knew she was not here in this room when Grandmama told the story. She'd traveled to her back in time and then further back to that first village, to her own son and daughter. She loved them so much – all of them.

Cailleen felt the all too familiar anger at not being accepted and not being able to do her work in this lifetime. At times it became unbearable. Now, she understood why. The pain was so old, and it grew rather than being tempered with time. She also now understood the need within her to do something particular, something that would make a big difference in the world. She'd never been able to touch it until now.

Now she knew what, but not how. How would she resolve this?

Cailleen felt the heat of the fire warming her bones again. She'd returned fully to her body and now walked around the room a bit. She grabbed her wool shawl and hugged it close to her for comfort. She fingered the amulet around her neck, a gift from Charles. He said it helped her connect with him, if she needed to. She felt it warm instantly under her fingers and feared she might wake him with her thoughts. So she tucked it inside her blouse and walked back to the fire.

She knew she was simply procrastinating. But why? She was not afraid of what else Grandmama might say. No, she would listen to Grandmama as long as she could. She just didn't want the tape to end. She knew it was silly to think that by not listening she could keep Grandmama with her longer. Grandmama had left the planet decades ago. Still, even the scratchy recording could not lessen the vibrancy of her voice. Cailleen knew that when Grandmama finished what's on the tape, she died. And she wasn't ready to lose her. She could listen to the tape over and over, but it would not have that surprisingly lifelike quality after this first time.

As Grandmama had talked, Cailleen felt pulled in by her voice and the creaking of the rocking chair. The rhythm mesmerized her and took her into a trance. She could smell her lavender and rose perfume and see the papery texture of her aged, but strong hands as they rested on the arms of the chair. The room she sat in smelled green, the green of early spring.

The fire popped, bringing Cailleen back to the present. She stared at the flames and promised herself that she would return to the tape in a few minutes.

"Get on with it," she heard. "I really do not have much time left and I have a lot to say to you."

Cailleen turned with an expectant smile, but Grandmama was not in the room. Disappointment moved through her entire body.

"I'm sorry, child. I do not have the energy to materialize. I must have come to you while I napped. Did I disturb you?"

"No, Grandmama," Cailleen responded, "you did not disturb me. But I do wish I could hug you or hold your hand. It might seem silly since we've never actually met, but I've missed you terribly."

"You have a lovely room here," Clara Bella said. "I see Hestia still has her place in the family. The quilt is truly beautiful. Is that my lace doily? You've kept it very well. I'm so glad. You're not drinking port and good Irish whiskey together, are you?! Oh, please tell me you do not cotton to excessive drinking. So many of our family have lost themselves, their fortunes, and their family in a bottle. Best to use that stuff in moderation, if you must use it at all.

"Yes, Grandmama. I mean no, Grandmama. I do not use alcohol excessively. Charles put it out for me."

"Oh, my dear. Such a sweet boy. Your own grew up to be quite the man in all his lifetimes. I visit from time to time," she said as her voice began to fade. "I think I must return now or I will not have the strength to finish my work. Come to me, if you can, Love."

"Yes, I'll come right away, Grandmama," Cailleen assured her. She pulled out her amber again and held it until it warmed in her hands. She focused on Charles and entered his dream just for a moment to tell him she would be doing some traveling and he should come check on her in a bit. She felt his agreement and retreated.

Cailleen drank some water, then focused on the dancing flames to induce a light trance. Then she pushed play and waited. The sound of the spinning reel drew her deeper into the trance and as Grandmama's voice began,

Cailleen found herself seated at the foot of her rocking chair with Grandmama patting her head.

"There's a good girl. I knew you'd come. I've told you the story, but so much remains to be shared – things you need to understand. Compassion for everyone will be vital. Know that although three were key players, the entire tribe bears responsibility. No one stepped forward to resolve this situation.

"The Headman can banish someone, but anyone could have called for discussion. No one did. It might not have changed much, but it might have. Calleigha could have apologized. Raneck could have suggested another way to resolve the conflict as Chancha expected he would. And Chancha could have offered Calleigha a way to redeem herself for challenging him. He had 13 moons to create a way before she returned. For such a leader, that should have been enough time.

"Our tribe, our family has so much pride. Generation after generation it has proved a challenge. And these stories of being rejected, of no one standing up for us – they have followed us through time. Calleigha chose ultimately to be a victim of the situation. She had great power and didn't use it. You can change that. I believe in you and in your ability to change it."

Cailleen looked up at that moment and caught Grandmama's eyes. A shock of recognition jolted her to her feet.

"Raneck!"

"Yes, child," Raneck nodded, "I have returned to speak to you through your grandmother. All the players continue to reincarnate. You and Chancha are reborn. I can still travel through time and space. I have kept you both close, offering assistance as I can and as you will allow. So many chances we've had to reweave this story. So much heartbreak we have endured.

"It broke my heart to escort you to the edge of our village when you were banished. I had such hope when you returned to us. Then you left us again by giving into hopelessness and heartbreak. I died four turns of the wheel after you left the planet. Our village was left without an experienced Senechal. You were young, heedless of the delicate power structure in our tribe and you lacked compassion for Chancha. But how I loved you. My son loved you, your children loved you and the people loved you.

"Chancha loved you. Did you understand that? Did you understand that his service to the people as Headsman was as sacred as ours is? He knew that two powerful Senechals and only one Headsman would upset the balance in the village, particularly when one was so young and headstrong and the other so enchanted by the first. I was blind and I failed you.

"I knew your power was great and I dreamed of what we could do together. But your power should have been tempered with experience before your ceremony of commitment. I feel that power still within you. You feel it too, but will not open to it. You must find a way. I will help you all I can."

Then he left and Cailleen saw her Grandmama's eyes again.

"Granddaughter, it remains to you now to do what you can to resolve this tragedy and heal our pain. Do not let yourself be overwhelmed by this task. I will look over you as best I can. I see that several will come to help you. I also see you will be offered more than one version of this story. Use your heart and intuition more often than your head. Remember your task is ultimately to re-balance power. Do not get lost in the personal aspects of the story. Whatever you do will make a difference. Act from love as you wield your power. Know that your actions will ripple into the past as well as into the future. May you walk in beauty."

Those were Grandmama's final words. She took one last shuddering breath and left her body. Cailleen held her hand and helped her pass to the other side with song. The words, Dream Me, echoed in her head from two voices: Grandmama's and Raneck's.

"Cailleen! Cailleen! Come back to me. You're so cold. You've got to come back now!"

Someone was slapping her cheeks and chaffing her hands together. It was so distracting. She was in the middle of something important. Who was bothering her? She tried to tell them to stop, but didn't seem able to speak. She tried to open her eyes, but they felt so heavy.

"Goddess Bless! Open your eyes. Don't leave me again," Charles pleaded.

It was the anguish in his voice that brought her back.

"Where would I go," she whispered? She felt drops on her face.

"Is this water torture you're doing here?" she asked.

Charles emitted a sound that combined laughter, anger, fear and frustration. Then he shook her, then cradled her and rocked her while he cried with gale-force emotion. Charles was a large bear of a man and his body warmed her quickly.

"You were worried," she said with surprise. "I was with Raneck and Grandmama. They wouldn't harm me."

"I know who you were with," Charles shouted. "I could feel him. I could feel your love for him. I could feel you following him. You should have learned to be more careful than to follow where he leads. It killed you once. I won't have it again. I won't have it!" He squeezed her tightly and held her again for several long minutes.

"I'm sorry," he finally said. "Here drink this whiskey and have a honey cake."

Cailleen meekly did as she was told. She knew the wisdom of it and really did not have the strength to refuse him at this moment. As the whiskey shocked and warmed her insides, she nibbled at the honey cake. Charles was stoking the fire and throwing more wood on it. It had died down again. She looked around and saw that sunlight was peeking through the drapes. She'd been gone a long time.

"I'm sorry. I didn't know I'd been gone so long," she offered.

"Quite," he clipped coldly. "I'll make some tea and bring you some solid food." With that he stomped out of the room.

In the kitchen Charles put the kettle on and filled the teapot with water to warm it. He put another pan on to boil and poured oats and dried fruit into it. He chopped walnuts and put them into two bowls, then waited for the water to do its magic.

He loved this room. In here, Cailleen was most accessible. She didn't wear her Teacher, Healer or Priestess hat here in the kitchen. Well, at least not when she was cooking or having a casual meal. He looked around at all her special touches. He'd helped her find and lay the cobalt blue tiles with the dancing herbs that made the back splash behind the sink. The blue and green jars of herbs and dried fruits and vegetables spoke of her connection to Mother Earth. He laughed when she wanted cedar rafters put in so she could hang and dry her flowers and herbs. But he loved the look and smell they brought to the kitchen. She turned the pantry into a half bath when she moved in. Then she put shelves up on every available wall. They were her pantry, she said. She liked seeing the bottles of spices and all the food she canned in their colorful jars, so she surrounded herself with them. Fresh herbs grew in the bay window above the sink. He nearly got a hernia helping move that big old farm table in. They spent hours sanding and refinishing it. It was the center of the kitchen now. She kneaded bread and chopped vegetables while visitors sat around drinking and chatting. She laughed and sang in this room with a joy and freedom he didn't see in her anywhere else. Here in this kitchen, she was once again the mother he'd lost such a long time ago.

The kettle boiled and Charles emptied the teapot, threw in chamomile and oat straw, and then filled it with boiling water. He stirred the oatmeal and turned off the burner. While the tea steeped, he got down her tray and smiled. The tray was one of her surprises. It depicted a feast and if you looked closely you noticed that everyone was naked and some were in rather compromising positions. She said it helped her recognize which of her guests were awake. Feeling more composed now, Charles lifted the tray and headed to the study.

While Charles puttered in her kitchen, Cailleen opened the drapes and cracked the window open. It was chilly on this mid-October morning. The oak leaves had fallen and squirrels were busily collecting acorns. A deer was nibbling at leftover lettuce in her garden. She'd told them they could now help themselves to whatever they needed. In the next week she'd have to turn over the soil and plant the winter cover crop. Her pumpkins sparkled with dew. A large crow was trying to perch himself among the corn stalks without much success. He flew to the fence post and cawed out a morning greeting. Starlings and quail were busy at the feeder. Rosey, her clumsy old golden retriever, was no doubt still snoring on the kitchen rug. She liked to sleep in most days, which also suited Cailleen. Her little family was intact. She sighed contentedly.

The porch swing should probably be taken to the back of the barn for the winter, she mused. The front of the barn she had remodeled into a workshop space and healing room. She liked not having to travel far for her daily work. She had one more book tour in a couple weeks and then she was home through February. Life was seasonal and she insisted that her work life would be seasonal too. No matter how they begged, she did not leave her hearth and home to travel in the winter. Winter was meant for introspection and quiet projects, not running from city to city promoting books or teaching workshops. She only allowed them to talk her into two short book tours each year: one in the spring and one in the fall. Summer was for gardening and harvests. Winter was for dreaming and writing, and reconnecting with herself.

Samhain, the day marking the beginning of the Celtic New Year, came in two weeks. The veil between the living and the dead thinned and the ancestors became more available on this plane. This year she knew she'd be spending a lot of time talking with the other side. She only hoped Charles would forgive her in time to be with her for it. She sighed and turned to the center of the room just as Charles came through the door with a loaded tray.

She quickly cleared the table of the night's paraphernalia. She and Charles sat on the pillows and began unloading the tray in a familiar rhythm. While she poured tea, she felt his scrutiny. When she looked at him, he simply nodded his satisfaction that she was now fully back and seemed none the worse for wear.

Ease began to move between them again as they ate. Neither spoke. They both knew Cailleen needed time and sleep before she was ready to talk. Charles also needed some time to make a few decisions. Revelations would be made today.

Chapter Four
Connections

Charles made sure Cailleen was securely tucked in and had drifted into a deep and restful sleep. While she'd showered, he'd put fresh linens and pillows on her bed. He knew she occasionally put clary sage on her pillow to induce dreams. Today, she needed a sound sleep. He placed a sachet of chamomile and lavender under her pillow, closed her heavy drapes so no light would awaken her and cast a circle of protection, which he anchored with his personal stones. He thought she might be angry that he'd taken such precautions without her leave or assume that he did not trust her to take such precautions on her own. But she'd said nothing.

Charles thought it wise to take a short nap himself, but he was too wound up from the last few hours. He sat on the chest at the end of his bed and sorted through what he would say to her when she awakened. Truths would have to be shared; knowledge would be important in the next few weeks – particularly if the danger he sensed was real.

Over the years, people made up lots of different stories about his relationship with Cailleen. A few thought they were both gay and used each other as cover. Some thought they were lovers, some assumed they were siblings, others simply that they had an unusually deep relationship for a man and a woman. They had been lovers and siblings many times in past lives. What no one had suspected, including Cailleen, was that they had once been mother and son – a very long time ago. After the events of last night however, it was time she remembered him from that life.

He got up and paced the room. He needed to move. He considered going for a run, but didn't want to leave Cailleen until she woke up and he could assure himself once again that she was all right. His fear of losing her was too fresh.

Their first life together occurred so long ago, yet the pain and unfinished business continued to follow them. For some reason Cailleen had never seemed aware of that lifetime. But last night changed that. When she caught up with herself and went over the details in her mind, she would remember or work it out. Grandmama had practically told her.

Charles was feeling very thankful that he'd listened to his knowing. Yesterday morning he'd awakened with a sense of foreboding and knew Cailleen could be in danger. Once his morning business was finished, he kept a psychic line open to her. He sensed she was edgy about something and that he might be needed. So, he left Seattle and headed over the mountains.

The world considered Charles Murphy a savvy businessman with an uncanny sense of timing. His first big success came in the form of Whitney Dooley, songwriter and vocalist. The moment he listened to her haunting tones, he knew she could be famous. He also knew she needed very specific care so she didn't crash and burn in the music industry.

Whitney was the keystone that opened his life to its true purpose. Something about her triggered his innate knowing and gifts. With her, he simply could not ignore his intuition and she called forth the protector in him. He'd been a junior producer for a big-name recording label when they met. But Whitney didn't really trust anyone but him. The company decided he might as well get his feet wet with her and learn the fullness of artist promotion. They, of course, wanted him to get massive exposure for her with as much stage and screen time as possible. But Charles knew that would not work with or for Whitney. Her voice and music were elusive as well as haunting and had a tenderness that was irresistible. Her public presence should match her music.

Charles fell in love with the idea of treating artists uniquely and promoting them in line with that uniqueness. When Whitney suggested he quit and become her manager, he jumped at the opportunity. They became inseparable. Their working relationship grew to friendship and then love. A quiet wedding was followed by six months of blissful retreat. Then Whitney died in a car accident on the way to lunch with a childhood friend. Charles was devastated. Fans held vigils for Whitney all over the world.

It was Whitney who had brought Cailleen into Charles' life. A brief news item mentioned that Cailleen would end her book tour with attendance at one of Whitney's concerts. Whitney was a big fan and had called Cailleen's publishers to invite her backstage after the concert. He would never forget the first words Cailleen said to him.

"Does she know how big of a protective shell you put around her? And does she know you feed her energy throughout her performance? In fact, do you know?"

He'd been stunned. He hadn't really known consciously, but once Cailleen mentioned it, he could not deny it. He can't be certain if it was her words or the sound of Cailleen's voice that triggered and opened his own memories to the past.

Cailleen and Whitney became close friends. Cailleen was one of the few people invited to the wedding. After Whitney died Charles leaned on their friendship, and through the grief process he learned to tap into his memories and hone his skills. Charles knew Cailleen offered her home and guidance as a distraction for Charles. And the same intuition that guided him with Whitney would not let him refuse Cailleen's offer. Now it was Charles' turn to be there for Cailleen.

Charles stopped his pacing and sat down again. He looked around this room, which he'd first slept in five years ago. He remembered walking in and thinking the room could have been designed specifically for him. He liked to think that subconsciously Cailleen *had* created it for him. The idea comforted him, especially when he felt frustrated that she didn't remember their life together as mother and son.

She'd decorated it in colors that suited him: rich greens and browns. The Celtic spirals carved along the top of the headboard and a circle with two cranes on each end spoke of his past. Cranes were one of his totems in all his lifetimes. At the foot of the bed sat a large trunk inlaid with burnished copper on both front and lid depicting scenes of the Fey in forest and meadow. Against the wall opposite the bureau sat an antique pharmacopoeia filled with bottles and tins holding herbs and stones – the perfect piece for an herbalist. He kept at least half of his stock of herbs here as most of the herbalist work he did was in service to their work.

He smiled at memories of their work together and he noticed that he no longer felt so anxious. He walked into the bathroom. It also seemed made for him. Thick towels of deep green hung on a turquoise rod that flared into shell spirals at its ends. On the wall hung an arrangement of Lisa Langel photographs of the Olympic Peninsula, with its magical forests leading to the water's edge. Bowls of seashells, sand dollars and river stones were placed ascetically on counter and shelves. Tiles depicting scenes of water nymphs and mermaids interspersed with solid deep greens and blues surrounded the large tub. The entire bath evoked a timeless mystery and playfulness that was neither masculine nor feminine yet allowed for both.

The tub beckoned to him and Charles did not resist. A long bath would soften the edges of the night's experience. He had not intended to be drawn into Cailleen's journey. He was simply checking in on her psychically. The pull of the journey grabbed him before he could stop it. It had endangered both of them and he knew Raneck had played a part in that. Raneck had always meddled and manipulated other people's lives. Some things never changed.

Charles felt his anger swirling again – anger at Raneck for playing his usual tricks, and at himself for allowing it. And he had to admit (at least to himself) he was angry with Cailleen for being oblivious to Raneck's tricks. She'd had a blind eye when it came to him. Charles would have to be careful when he spoke to her about it all.

Before he sank into the balm of a hot scented bath, he picked up the phone and called Jen and Lawrence. Years ago, they'd all made a pact to call each other if ever a need arose in any of their lives. Cailleen might or might not feel the need, but Charles could use the support and comfort of intimate friends, particularly ones with healing and psychic gifts. The four of them worked well together, even from the beginning.

Jen and Lawrence had a bond you would only expect with twins. The two of them met in first grade, and except for the occasional family vacation, they had spent almost every day together since. In their early 30's they bought houses next to each other. They considered buying just one house, but feared it would not leave enough space in their lives for finding partners, marriage or children.

Jen had a steady string of relationships with very interesting women – some flings, a few that lasted longer. Lawrence however was looking for that one woman to have his children and share his life. Yvonne walked into his life about a year ago. They fit well together as a couple, and also with Jen. Time would tell.

Charles dialed Jen, who answered immediately. He told her something was up and it would be good to see everyone together for dinner tonight. She agreed and offered to bring a lasagna she was dying to make. He then rang Lawrence, explained that the matter was a bit private, and suggested he come alone. He asked him to bring the dessert and rang off.

He checked his watch and estimated Cailleen would sleep for at least another couple of hours. He wanted to be as prepared as he could for whatever lay ahead of them. Not knowing what was ahead made it difficult to prepare. He decided to try to get more information between the worlds.

He lit candles, added scented salts to the running water for cleansing and grounding, disrobed, and sank gratefully into the hot soothing water. He let himself drift and move into a light trance.

Charles called on Archangel Michael to guard and protect him and on Raphael for healing. He asked his totems, the Cranes, to help him stay in the place of love as he worked his way through the tangles and knots of so much time and so many personal agendas. Archangel Uriel, he called upon to help him find clarity. And finally, he welcomed brother Bear, the totem of his family.

He needed privacy for this work and did not want to get pulled into Cailleen's dreams or Raneck's manipulations. He also did not want to leave

Cailleen totally disconnected from him. So, he called on his old friend, Crow. Since his infancy, Charles had an affinity with crows. They were always with him and cawing to let him know who was near. He asked crow to watch Cailleen and to alert him, if she should wake or be in any danger.

Most people had no understanding of the dangers of psychic journeying. One could be pulled along the psychic currents and get caught in undertows or simply become lost. With strong links – such as blood, emotion or common history – the pull could be fast, deep and disorienting. If one stayed away too long in these out of body experiences, the physical body became endangered. Without proper protocols such as grounding and protective measures, the journeyer could become vulnerable to other psychic forces. Shifting between the worlds too quickly could cause physical, emotional, mental, psychic and spiritual pain. Although Charles had a strong gift for journeying, that did not make him less vulnerable.

The training Charles chose to do with Cailleen after Whitney died was indeed a gift. Occasionally, it was also a burden. His awakened gifts brought him a sense of purpose and peace. Yet, there were times when he simply wished he didn't know. These moments were always fleeting, however they served to keep him aware of the costs of the gifts he carried. It also reminded him of how precious the ties he'd forged with Cailleen and his classmates, Jen and Lawrence, were. Years of traveling together in the everyday world and between the worlds created a strong bond. He trusted them as he trusted Crow, Bear, Crane and the angels who worked so closely with him.

With Raneck in the psychic field, the long night, and the emotional terrain he was about to traverse, Charles was taking no chances. Before slipping into the tub, he'd set a protective circle and set chimes to ring in 30 minutes. Rosey sat watch on the other side of the doorway. She knew to bark if he did not rouse when the chimes went off. Michael and Crow were on guard.

Asking for clarity, he slipped into a deeper trance. Crow followed and Charles welcomed him with both gratitude and relief. He found himself walking down a familiar path. Crow flew ahead, cawing to announce their presence. Charles chuckled to himself.

"So, you didn't come to help me," he laughingly chided Crow. "You came for Elan's honey cakes!"

Elan's house could barely be discerned as separate from the forest in which it nestled. Over the years the two seemed to have melded into each other's edges. Charles first met Elan in one of his early journeys and he often found himself at her hearth when he needed clarity and guidance.

Now, as he walked the path to her house, he considered that first meeting with Elan. He was so young then and pretty new to the craft. He wondered if it was pure luck running into Elan, or if she'd sought him out. He'd have to ask her that sometime.

Like him, Elan traveled between the worlds. Unlike him, her work was guarding the path between the worlds and giving guidance to travelers of the *good way*. She only recently spoke of her work to him. Perhaps she knew what was coming and wanted to prepare him.

"Charles, dear boy," she had begun. "I will tell you something about my work. You know that my role is to guide travelers on the good way. The good way refers to the path each individual walks – the one that keeps him or her on purpose and serves the world best. Many have asked me how to avoid the "bad" way. It makes me sad to see travelers clinging to such duality. People can step off their path without being "bad". In fact, stepping off the path is necessary at times. It helps one better define what their good way is. There are many ways, but the one that suits you best is your good way.

"There is actually a network of pathways that gives us access to each other along the web. Points of crossover are opportunities for great power and service. At these points, the co-creation available becomes so potent that travelers without sufficient preparation can become lost to themselves and their service. You must remember this Charles. Intentions can become inverted or skewed. It takes courage, focus and grounded intention to successfully co-create at these power points. Many of the most atrocious events in history are examples of those who came to these points of power unwilling, unprepared, unfocused, or with a lack of true courage or intention.

"Everyone can sense these crossover points. Fear of these places of potential keeps many travelers hidden in the "safety" of their homes where they never have the opportunity to tap into the wonder and mystery of their gifts and talents. They carry the illusion that doing nothing will keep them safe. But the spiral keeps moving no matter what they do.

"They forget"- Elan stopped and looked him in the eyes for emphasis- "that inaction is a choice that carries as many consequences as any action does. Inaction simply offers others the opportunity to create your world. And you know that the odds of someone else creating a world, which truly suits you, is very small. Conscious and considered action must be taken," she said with a final nod at him.

Elan was timeless. She lived in the physical world somewhere, but Charles never learned where or even when. He did learn to trust her wisdom and guidance. Today, as he approached her forest home here between the worlds, he smelled heavenly soup and fresh baked bread. Elan waited for him. She sat snuggled in a wool shawl with Crow perched next to her. They both seemed to ask him, "What took you so long?"

"Greetings Mother," Charles said as he sank to one knee and bent his head for her benediction.

"Greetings, Son" Elan answered as she put a wet and noisy kiss on his forehead.

They looked deep into each other's eyes, asking and answering the question, "How goes it with you?" Satisfied with what they saw, they stood together and arm in arm walked into the cottage.

"Come," she commanded him. "You look tired, hungry and worried. The soup will meet your hunger and lift your tiredness. The only thing to do about your worries is to unburden yourself of them. Go ahead. Sit them in the basket on the hearth and place the lid tightly on it. Then come and eat. When you're nourished, we can take them out and get a good look at them."

Charles smiled and did as he was told. The soup smelled of rosemary and garlic. Carrots, green beans, tomatoes, potatoes and corn floated in an almost blue-green broth, which revealed the presence of nettles. Nettles, the mother plant, contained almost anything a body could need to replenish itself. Fresh butter on hot oat bread cheered his heart as well as filling his stomach. Only here between the worlds did he enjoy the richness of fresh butter.

Elan filled his cup with hot tea. "Oat straw and chamomile to calm you." She walked to the hearth to stoke the fire and hummed absently to herself as she tidied the place and allowed Charles to finish his meal.

When she sat in her chair and the cat jumped to her lap, Charles took his cue and moved over to make himself comfortable in the adjacent chair. A tree frog hopped on the windowsill next to him, croaked a few words of wisdom and hopped off into the trees.

"So," Elan said at the sight of the frog, "you need some help deciding whether to live in water or on land?"

"I expect so," Charles nodded. He stroked his well-trimmed beard and hesitated. He was unsure what to say. His questions involved many lives and personal stories that weren't his to tell.

"Open the lid on the basket, Charles. Let's see what pops out," Elan suggested.

Charles understood that a physical action would mirror any mental action that might be needed. So he leaned towards the hearth and lifted the lid of the basket. In doing so he upset the balance of the chair and fell noisily to the floor. He looked both shocked and confused. Elan only nodded her head in understanding.

"I see," she said. "Specific stories cannot be revealed here. I fear it will be a busy day for me." Elan slipped into a trance and in a faraway voice continued.

"You approach a crossover connection with a particularly strong power potential. You have, of course, been here before. Three other travelers have also been at this place. The three have approached together before but were unable to stay connected and activate the power. They came so close and their memories of almost touching it are filled with pain, regret, sorrow and… yes, I sense fear and disappointment. You have never been here with them – at least you have never been here with all of them at the same time.

"When the veils between the worlds thin, you will meet. You must prepare them as best you can. And you must resolve your own emotional discord before you can do that. The time has come to reveal what you know to your Teacher and friends. Cut away illusions and re-forge your blades. Choice and power await."

Charles felt a warm tongue on his cheek and heard a whining of distress. Then he became aware of a symphony of chimes and a chill on his skin. He opened his eyes and was startled by Rosey's big brown ones staring back at him. He lifted his hand to assure her.

"Good girl," he crooned as he scratched behind her ears and then moved down to that sweet spot just behind her haunches. She barked happily, then went through the doorway to settle herself comfortably on her rug again.

He turned on the hot water and the Jacuzzi jets to warm his body. He scrubbed himself to bring warmth to his skin and to bring himself fully back into his physical body. As he did so, Charles felt a certainty to the path ahead. He would tell Cailleen all he knew. And he would trust that she could handle the emotions it would bring up for each of them. Jen and Lawrence would be on hand for first aid and perspective, if needed.

He jumped up out of the tub with a vitality he hadn't felt in days. Elan's a wonderful witch, he chuckled to himself. She could calm, fortify and confuse all in one visit. But Charles did not really feel confused, he discovered. He didn't fully understand the message she'd channeled for him. But he felt a sense of certainty.

Charles thanked the guardians and totems, opened the protective circle, snuffed the candles and threw on jeans and a sweatshirt. Downstairs he made tea, toasted bread and heated soup. Then he headed upstairs to wake Cailleen.

Cailleen felt the warmth of the afternoon sun on her face and slowly surfaced from a deep and restorative sleep. She stretched for a moment then began to snuggle back into the warmth of flannel sheets and a down comforter. She heard the snap of fingers a second before Rosey jumped on top of her and began thoroughly washing her face with a very large and wet tongue.

"Rosey! Get down," she laughed. "Who let you in here? Down girl. Down!"

Rosey jumped down and Cailleen emerged from under the covers to see Charles smiling with delight. He cocked his head, checked her face and energy field, and then turned on his heel to walk out of the room. "Lunch is on the table in 5 minutes" he called back. "Don't be late or I'll eat all the black currant jam myself."

Charles was certainly bossy and sure of himself all of a sudden, she thought. She reached her toes out and slipped them into her pink furry slippers. On the way to the bathroom, she caught her reflection in the mirror. Not too bad, she thought – especially considering the long night. Maybe Charles seemed sure of himself only in comparison to her own rise in uncertainty. What was she supposed to do now?

Last night's work raised more questions than it answered. She now knew the family secret and the source of many trials she'd experienced in this lifetime. Grandmama charged her with resolving the family's past. But what was she actually supposed to do? And how would she go about it? She couldn't take Charles, Jen or Lawrence into her confidence. It would require revealing the family secret. Yet could she do what she needed to do without them? They would not cooperate if she tried it alone. They'd sense something was up and hound her until she included them.

She could take the offer to teach in England for a fortnight. They would not be suspicious if she left them behind for a business trip. The teaching job only asked her to teach a one-hour class each day. The rest of the time was hers. She could arrange to leave tomorrow. The offer just came in yesterday and she hadn't really had a chance to speak to any of them about ordinary things yesterday. She'd ask Charles to take her to the airport after lunch.

With a plan in mind she felt more prepared to face the day. She dressed, ran a quick brush through her hair and added a touch of color to her lips. The lipstick made her look a bit pale, so she added mascara and blush. Dressed with a woman's basic armor, she headed to the kitchen and a much-needed lunch.

Charles was sitting at the table spreading jam on his toast when she walked in the kitchen. When he saw her he got up and filled two bowls with soup and brought them to the table. They ate in companionable silence, each lost in their own thoughts. Charles broke the silence before Cailleen.

"I had a dream last night I'd like to tell you about. And I had an interesting visit with Elan an hour or so ago. Shall we walk or go into your study? Or if you don't mind, I could make another pot of tea and we could talk here in the kitchen. I need to make a salad and some bread for dinner tonight. Jen and Lawrence are coming for dinner."

"Jen and Lawrence called?" Cailleen asked. "I didn't even hear the phone ring."

"I rang them, actually," Charles explained. "We don't really have a lot of time. Samhain is only two weeks away."

Cailleen's hopes of eluding the three of them were dashed.

Charles began heating the water for another pot of tea. He chose his own special blend of chamomile, mint and a dash of ground ginger, and added it to the pot. With the tea steeping he cleared the table to help him clear his thoughts.

"When you sent me your psychic message last night I was dreaming. When I answered you back, I was pulled into your journey. It happened before I could prevent it. You didn't wait for my acknowledgment and when I reached out to assure you that I was on duty, I was suddenly with you. You didn't notice."

Cailleen was stunned. First, because it seemed he now knew the family secret. And second, because she *hadn't* noticed someone had entered her journey. To be that unaware on a journey could mean danger. Of course, she had set safety protocols with calling the Elements and casting a circle. Still, why had she not noticed his presence?

Her thoughts were suddenly jumbled. Charles had followed her on a journey without invitation. He was chastising her. Why *hadn't* she noticed a new presence on the journey? He was angry with her. Maybe it was because he was so close to her? He knew the family secret!

Charles did not need a psychic connection with Cailleen to read the thoughts racing across her face. He waited for her to catch up and in that moment knew their relationship had changed forever. But he couldn't take it back and he did not want to.

Cailleen could actually feel the tables turning on their relationship. She was the one who was now lost and Charles stood steady as a rock. In fact, on an energetic level, he had grown both taller and deeper. The brown and green auric colors that always surrounded him grew richer and from within him a startling light shined. She was reminded of the scene in the *Lord of the Rings* when Gandalf is revealed to Aragorn, Gimli and Legolas after they think him dead. And like for Aragorn, Gimli and Legolas, in Cailleen's heart fear was quickly replaced by overwhelming joy.

Memory took her to another time and place.

Her son stood before her glowing with pride and power. He was 12 years old. His father had taken him from her hearth at the dark moon after his first successful kill. He could now provide for himself and a family. He no longer belonged at his mother's hearth. And so, his initiation into the men's mysteries began.

When he left, she began crafting a man's belt for him. She beaded it with the sacred symbols of their tribal totem, the bear. She'd added a personal touch by weaving into the design two cranes, his personal totems. As she moved into the rhythm of the bead work, she felt the ancient powers moving through her. She could not prevent it. They were hers and she'd promised to use them to serve her people. She'd not been allowed to do that, but she would not withhold such power from her son. She could not withhold anything from him in that moment.

For thirteen turns of the wheel, she'd kept her powers under wraps. She'd only used them minimally on rare occasions when someone needed help and Raneck was not available. She'd held herself apart from her children so they would not appear as threats to Chancha. He had taken away her right to use her precious gifts. They were such a part of her. Yet she had to hide her true self or risk banishment. In effect, Chancha had taken her children from her. She couldn't reach them from where she had to hide. They never knew the true her.

When she'd returned from her banishment, Calleigha was physically fit, but during her year of isolation she'd refused to let herself feel or think about her situation. She'd survived, that was all. She returned numb and without a place in the tribe. When Raneck suggested she become his son's partner and the mother of his children, she did not object. He said it would give her a place in the tribe and as the mother of his grandchildren she would always have his protection.

Calleigha became an ordinary woman doing ordinary tasks. She loved her children as all mothers do, but only in the silence of her heart. When people knew what you loved, they could take it from you.

Chalic had always been a dutiful son and she had been a dutiful mother. But in this last task she would dare letting her love for him move through freely and grandly. The magic of both her power and her love flowed through her and into his belt of manhood. When he returned from his initiation, she would put it on him and then send him forth to walk his path as the man he had become.

Chalic returned from his initiation walking proudly and the village gathered behind him as he approached his mother's hearth. The reserve he'd always carried in his mother's presence was a heavy cloak on his shoulders. He stood outside waiting for her to come and clothe him one last time. When she came out and their eyes met, he saw his mother for the first time. She had dropped her own cloak of reserve and her eyes shown with pride and love. Chalic's heart broke open and his cloak of reserve fell.

Calleigha stood before him a little taller than the village could remember seeing her. She fastened the belt around his waist and the power of the belt and the physical contact of putting it on him opened a psychic link they had always shared but never guessed was theirs. In that moment, Calleigha got her son back.

Neither son nor mother heard the gasp of the crowd as they saw Calleigha and Chalic being lifted off the ground in a circle of light. Only the two of them, and of course Raneck, noticed the transference of power from mother to son and the activation of gifts within Chalic. He grew tall and deep as the power surged in his young body and aligned his energy pathways with the Universal source of power.

When the exchange ended, both mother and son collapsed and lay still as death. Raneck gasped and groaned with despair. He rushed to their side and sang songs to keep their spirits in their physical bodies. He ordered women to boil water and bring him his medicine bag. He had men carry the two into Calleigha's home. He covered them with furs to keep them warm. He brewed special teas and rubbed a balm into their bodies.

They both survived the night, but the next day Calleigha chose to slip away to the ancestors. She knew her daughter, Rasia, didn't really need her; she spent most of her time with the headswoman, learning the ways of leadership in the tribe. Calleigha had passed her power onto her son. She hadn't meant to, but it was done. Raneck would continue to train him and the tribe would have a medicine man when Raneck returned to the ancestors. That was the only way she knew how, in at least a small way, to serve her tribe as she had promised to do. And now, Calleigha simply could bear no more pain; she quietly crossed to the other side, leaving this life forever.

"Mother!" she heard Chalic call to her. But she wanted to turn away. Seeing him robed in his power filled her with pride and broke her heart all over again. She couldn't survive feeling that power and knowing she was forbidden to use it. She couldn't do it anymore. It took her so long to close it off and now she'd gone and opened the door again and she would never have the strength to close it.

"Mother!"

"No," she cried. "No!"

"Come back, damn it!" Charles demanded. "Where the hell have you gone? I can't come after you. You've got to come back!"

Rosey started barking and crows started cawing. Charles gently slapped Cailleen's cheek. She made no response. Her skin was pale, her pulse was slowing and her body was limp. He rubbed her hands and feet. Still, he got no response. He couldn't even reach her on a psychic plane. He felt abandoned and he began to panic. He crooned gently, "Mother, come back to me." He demanded fiercely, "Damn it, Mother, come back!" She seemed so lost to him. The little boy in him just wanted to cry, but the trained healer and psychic knew to ask for help.

"Archangel Michael, I call on you for assistance. Let your sword point her way back to me. Archangel Raphael, please keep her safe on this journey back to the present."

Charles felt their presence and began to feel their warmth and love surround him.

"If you wish to bring her back to this time," they told him, "use the name you use for her in this time. Return to this time yourself and stop straddling the past and the present. Call her, gently. Sing her back."

Charles heard their words and brought himself more fully into the present. He called Rosey to sit next to Cailleen and keep her warm. With a new task at hand, Rosey calmed and settled. Charles began singing, his baritone growing in strength and power.

"Cailleen, Mother, Priestess, Healer —
I call you to my side.
Release the past and follow my calling
to the pulse and rhythm of our present's tide.

Teacher come, Healer come,
Priestess, Mother, come.
Cailleen, Cailleen, Cailleen, Cailleen

Feel my heartbeat and my love,
feel me holding you fast.
Return to the present and the call of my heart,
only here can you heal the past.

Teacher come, Healer come,
Priestess, Mother, come.
Cailleen, Cailleen, Cailleen, Cailleen."

Charles chanted her name and let his calling spill forth and grow solid. It surrounded and enfolded them until her breathing strengthened and she began to stir. He continued singing until she opened her eyes and reached out to hold him tight.

"Chalic," she cried out, then burst into tears. They held each other tightly, rocking and patting each other in comfort.

That's the scene Jen and Lawrence walked into ten minutes later. They each had a premonition that they were needed much earlier than dinnertime. They left work early and headed out to Cailleen's.

"They know," they said in unison, then went into action without another word. Jen went to the study for brandy and a smudge stick. Lawrence put on the tea kettle then ran upstairs for blankets and hot water bottles.

In ten minutes, Charles and Cailleen were huddled next to each other on the couch with hot water bottles on their tummies, blankets around their shoulders and a strong cup of tea laced with brandy in their hands. They kept touching each other's hand and shoulder and face as if to make sure the other was real and actually sitting there.

Jen and Lawrence went to the kitchen to fix dinner and talk about what they needed to do next. Lawrence called Yvonne and told her there was a bit of a crisis and he would just see her tomorrow.

Chapter Five
Revelations

"What took them so long?" Jen asked tensely. "The strength of their psychic connection suggested significant past lives together. We saw that practically from the beginning. They were finishing each other's sentences by the end of our first class five years ago. Why have they never pursued it? If they had, they might have been a bit more prepared for whatever happened today. They both look stunned – and stupidly happy. I've never seen them so pale. I thought my heart would stop and you'd have three people to rescue."

"Jen," Lawrence said patiently, "take a breath. They're OK. You're OK. And we've had this conversation before. Doors to the past and windows of connections open in their own time. I think their past might have caused them to fear knowledge of their connection. Of course, I don't really know anything and am probably full of crap. But we'll not learn anymore until we all sit down over a delicious lasagna, a fresh salad, and this very tempting garlic bread – I found it in the freezer. I'd love to open this Cabernet to go with it, but I think we might need clearer heads tonight."

"More tea?" Jen suggested.

"I'll put the pot on," Lawrence answered. "Go gather our travelers and let's feed them. Then we'll force them to tell us all their secrets."

"I think we knew their secrets before they did," Jen said as she headed for the living room.

Jen and Lawrence shared a love for words, lots of them. They talked fast and long but somehow, within the rhythm of conversation, they informed, comforted, challenged and teased each other. The more worried they became, the more intense their dialogue grew. Their conversation on the way to Cailleen's would have stunned even the most loquacious.

Jen moved quietly into the living room. The glow of the fire brought some color into Charles' face and brought out the red tones in Cailleen's hair. It amused her to see them huddled in blankets and hot water bottles here in the most formal of rooms. They rarely came in here except for formal business receptions, which were part of the expectations of Cailleen's work. Jen called it Cailleen's "public face room." Cailleen called it her "just so" room – everything tidy and clean with absolutely no clutter.

The furniture was sleek enough to be chic and soft enough to be comfortable. Matching couches in rich cream brocade with accent pillows in mauve, sienna and forest green framed the large conversation area. Two high backed chairs and a loveseat in rich earth tones flanked the hearth for a more intimate conversation. An antique writing desk sat in the corner always looking as if Cailleen had just left it in the middle of a brilliant plot. The shelf above it featured first run copies of each of her books. The art of local abstract painters hung tastefully on the walls. Sculptures that merely hinted at whimsy were perched on corner tables and on the mantel. This was the only room in the house done by a professional decorator. Cailleen went in after the decorator was done to insert a few objects that her more mainstream fans would not particularly notice but her pagan followers would never miss. Crystals sat next to the decorator's creative bowls of potpourri. A handmade broom sat in a quiet corner. A candle etched with the triskele, a Celtic symbol of three spirals, sat on a corner shelf. Playful ornamental plant sticks with gems, copper wire and Elementals were scattered among the plants.

One of the formal couches currently held Charles and Cailleen. Jen laughed to herself at the incongruity of the two of them all tousled and rumpled here in the center of this perfect room. Her gaze caught their attention. Still holding each other's hands for comfort, they looked at Jen questioningly.

"Dinner is ready. Can you two manage the walk to the kitchen on your own?" Jen asked.

"We're fine," Cailleen replied. "Just got a bit disoriented there. A good meal will put us to rights. Charles?" she asked to confirm he was ready.

Together they stood and linked arms with Jen as they left the room. They both now needed some buffer from the intensity of their shared experience and the new information they'd gathered earlier. After dinner they would have to decide what needed to be done and who they could include in the story. For now, they were content to simply eat a meal with friends. They entered the kitchen to find Lawrence rushing around, almost frantic.

"There you all are," Lawrence greeted in a voice laced with speed and anxiety. "Just in time. I've heated a bit of minestrone as a start. Grab a hunk of bread and I'll bring it right over to you. We have a harvest salad with apples and walnuts to follow and then Jen's lasagna. Yvonne sent along a box from our favorite bakery. I haven't had a chance to see what treasure it holds, but I'm sure it will get us through coffee after dinner. Can I get anyone anything else right now?"

"How about a little peace and quiet. It's time for *you* to take a breath, Lawrence. Everyone's all right here. Come, sit, and eat your soup. Chill, darlin'," Jen commanded.

Lawrence laughed at himself, brought the soup to the table, and took a seat. "It's just a bit disconcerting to be the ones taking charge." He looked quickly at Cailleen, who simply smiled and nodded.

They all held hands around the table, grounded in each other's presence, and gave thanks for the food and each other. Over dinner they chatted about jobs, family, friends and some ideas about celebrating Samhain.

"After dinner," Jen and Lawrence chorused together. "Go ahead," Jen nodded at Lawrence.

"After dinner," he repeated, "we have a couple of dreams to share with you. We know you've had a rough afternoon, but it seemed to both of us that they were important. Do you think you can take any more information in today?"

Charles and Cailleen glanced at each other and understood the other would be happy for a brief distraction before telling their friends they simply could not share the events of the last 24 hours.

"Why don't we clean up the dishes, then hear the dreams over dessert and coffee," Cailleen suggested.

They took dessert and coffee into Cailleen's study. Charles had lit a fire and rearranged chairs in front of it. Yvonne's gift box held an assortment of eclairs, tiramisu, mini chocolate cakes and berry tarts. Jen opened the box and let out an exclamation.

"You'd better keep her, Lawrence," she shouted. "She either has a problem with decision-making or knows our penchant for sweets when we're in the midst of something. Either way, she's a gem. I get dibs on an éclair."

After making their choices, taking a bite and sinking into the pleasures of well-crafted treats, they decided to finish dessert before they shared dreams. Well sated and comfortable in each other's company, they sipped coffee and settled in for stories and planning.

"I'd like to share my dream first," Lawrence said. "I dreamed it two nights ago. I wrote it down and emailed each of you a copy of it. I think I can tell it in full without notes, but we'll check them later to make sure I included everything. Lawrence closed his eyes to help remember.

"In the dream I was about 10 years old. I lived in the country on a farm somewhere in what I guess to be Northern Europe. A gentle rolling landscape with a hint of salt air lay before me. Behind me I felt an old forest – the trees held a heightened sense of awareness. Beyond the forest were mountains in the distance.

"I was barefooted, wore short pants and a tunic made of rough but sturdy homespun cloth. My hair was tied back with a leather string. I remember feeling alive and vital and carrying a strong knowing of my place in the world."

"It was really quite something to feel that, you know," Lawrence said looking to the three of them. "I think I feel confident in my place and comfortable in my body in this life. But it doesn't even compare with what that 10-year-old felt. It might have been his youth and innocence, but I think it was more about the time and the simplicity of life. He could see his past and his future; they lived with him. His grandfather and now his father had worked this same land for decades and he and his children would continue that. He knew the trees in the forest behind his home. I don't mean he recognized the species – he knew the individual trees on a personal level. He knew under which ones the pigs would find truffles. He knew which tree had given its limb for the hoe he held in his hands. He also knew the other plants and animals in that forest. They were family and their spirits flowed together. I'll never forget that feeling. It actually makes me ache deep inside. If it wasn't for Yvonne, I might just go back there and stay."

"Thank goodness for Yvonne, then," Jen said coolly.

"I'd take you with me," Lawrence cajoled. "You know I can't live without you."

"OK, you're forgiven," Jen replied. "As you well know, it's not easy for either of us when one or both of us are in a romantic relationship. I love Yvonne and think she's very good for you. But this one little bitty part of me wants you all to myself. Unless, of course, some juicy goddess of a woman is in my arms."

"Goes without saying – the door's been closed in my face on more than one occasion," Lawrence said with a laugh. "But you're forgiven. Now, do you mind if I continue with my dream?"

"Sure go ahead. It's about time you stopped digressing. Clearly Charles and Cailleen are on tender hooks," Jen teased.

Cailleen and Charles both sat listening as the "twins" bantered and teased each other. It felt familiar and comforting to watch them. The coziness of the evening among friends eased their fears and soothed the edges of unanswered questions. They have could easily drifted off to sleep, if given the opportunity. The sound of their names roused them.

"Yes, Lawrence, please finish your dream," Cailleen requested. "Although with the intensity of your experience it may have been an out of body experience. You may have dreamed yourself into one of your past lives."

"The thought occurred to me," Lawrence confirmed. "It felt real enough." Closing his eyes again, he continued.

It seemed to be about this same time of year. Haystacks stood tall in the fields and the air held a slight chill. I saw my grandfather coming toward me across the field and waved to him. He walked slowly these days, so I put down my hoe and headed to meet him.

I'd been watching him carefully ever since the Hag had come to me in a dream. Two nights earlier at the dark moon, the wise woman walked to my side and then stumbled. I helped her steady herself and asked her if she needed my assistance. "Not me," she whispered. She walked to the other side of the fire, where Grandfather sat sharpening tools. She looked at me, then down at Granddad and then back to me. My mother called to me and I turned to answer her. When I turned back, the Hag was gone. I went over and asked Granddad who the Hag was. He had not seen her. Dreams need deciphering and I kept waiting for this one to make itself clear. But the passage of a couple days had not offered illumination.

"May your feet walk in beauty, Granddad," I called as I neared him.

"The beauty remains, but I'm afraid the walk turns to more of a stumble," Granddad replied. "But I'll not complain, Rory. Your sister made oat cakes, so I thought I'd bring you a few. You work hard and I'm proud of you."

"Granddad, my heart pounds with joy that you would think of me, but you should save your energy for more important tasks than filling my ever-hungry belly," I said.

"I need to speak to you about something quite important," said Granddad. "I think you know that I shall not be with you for much longer. I'm sad to leave you, boy. I truly am. But I'm just as ready to rest these weary bones.

"I just talked with your ma. I can't tell you of what we spoke except to say she has a task before her, one I hoped to be around long enough to help her through. She will need help and I've come to ask you to do that for me. Are you up for the task?"

"Of course, Granddad. The Hag told me to help. I would help you in any case, but I certainly cannot deny both of you."

"The Hag?" Granddad questioned.

"Yes, she came to me when the moon was dark. I did not understand what she wanted at the time. But as you spoke, I could feel her over my shoulder again. What is it I am to do?" I asked.

"Just watch your mother, my Rory," Granddad said with a pleading voice. "And mind that she doesn't catch you. She's a proud woman, who thinks she needs no one's help. But she'll need you. And if you just happen to be there when she does and you go along with her as if you've been in it together from the start, she'll allow it. She'll need courage, son. And her pride and love for you will help her rally it."

"This task she has to do, will it be dangerous, Granddad?" I asked.

"No, not dangerous — at least not in the way I think you mean," he replied. "Our family carries a great burden that one of our ancestors laid upon us centuries ago. Every now and then, someone in the family has an opportunity to resolve an old conflict and relieve us of this burden."

Cailleen and Charles sat up in their seats, their bodies leaning forward in anticipation as the dream unfolded. Lawrence stopped at their movement. When they said nothing, he continued.

"How can I help her if I don't know what her task is?" I asked of Granddad.

"It is enough that you know your task. I have carried the story. That was my task. Your mother has an opportunity to change the story — that is all you need know of her task.

But also know that each time an opportunity comes to shift the story, the person charged with doing so receives the gift of someone to help. As the carrier of the story, I have learned a bit about each attempt. Always at least one helper comes forward. The person charged with the task, however, has not always allowed help. Pride is a difficult ally. We could use less of it in this family.

"Just keep your heart, ears, and eyes open and you'll do fine Rory." He patted my shoulder. "You'll do just fine. I think I'll take a nap under that singing willow by the creek."

Granddad rocked his way to his feet and then walked carefully to the creek. I watched him until he disappeared among the trees.

A gentle burden now sat upon my shoulders, but I seemed to have grown wider shoulders during the talk with Granddad."

Lawrence finished and the four of them sat in silence for several minutes, each person digesting the details of the dream. Jen stood up and went to warm her hands near the fire. A chill moved through her as she heard Lawrence's dream. The feel of his dream resonated so closely to that of her own. She knew it was more than coincidence they had dreamed them so close together. Although they had shared dreams on occasion, Jen had never felt this eerie sense of another presence. She wondered if Lawrence felt it.

"If you don't mind, I'd like to share my dream before we talk over Lawrence's." She paused a moment. "No objections? Great."

In my dream I live in a big city – maybe New York or Philadelphia or Chicago. It's the 1920s or thereabouts. So much energy just buzzes around me. I'm pretty sure it's before the Crash. Everyone feels optimistic and bigger than life. They survived World War I and feel indestructible. No, no that's not right. They behave as if they feel that way. There's a vulnerability to all the buzz.

I'm running from something. And my heart nearly breaks from grief. I hear the words, 'I'm too young' over and over inside my head. I duck into a gin joint where several people greet me. The bartender just hands me a drink and winks at me. I seek out an empty table in a dark corner and drink my gin.

Tall dark and handsome glides over to me, lights a cigarette and hands it to me. I take it and glance up at him with a weak smile. "What's wrong doll?" he asks. I'm surprised at the quickening of my own pulse at his obviously cheesy come on. I'm also incredibly attracted to him, a guy.

So, I figure this is probably an out of body experience and that I should just tuck my current self away a bit and go with it.

"Come on, doll, tell Fred all about it," he says as he runs his hand up and down my arm.

"I just need a moment to myself – that's all Fred. It's been a couple of tough days."

"I heard your Grandmother died. I'm sorry to hear it. But she didn't leave you destitute or anything did she, toots? Don't worry if she did, Fred here will take care of you. I'll take real good care of you."

Despite his practiced charm I saw right through him and just wanted to get away. I tossed back the rest of my gin and headed for the door. I planted a smile on my face, laughed a bit too loudly, waved at everybody I knew and escaped out the door and into the cool night.

A tall man grabbed my elbow and I swung around to stare into the concerned face of Neville, the boy next door.

"You can't fool me with that fake smile," he said. "What's wrong, Susan? Why are you walking out here at night without an escort?"

"Neville, I didn't see you in there. I didn't come with an escort. I just needed to get out and, and… I don't know. I needed some air or something," I answered. "I'm fine. Please don't worry."

"I won't worry if you say not to. But I will escort you wherever you're going. Home, maybe?"

"No Neville, anywhere but home. I'm too young and probably too weak to be at home right now. Can we walk to the river? I'd love to feel a fresh breeze and have enough quiet to think."

"Sure, let's go to the river. Where's your wrap? Never mind. Here, wear my coat across your shoulders. You're trembling, you know."

"No, I didn't notice. I guess I am cold. Can we not talk?"

Neville and I walked along the promenade and down to the river. We found a bench under a tree and sat next to each other. Neville put his arm around me in an almost brotherly way.

"I'm here to help you in whatever way you need. I've appointed myself your guardian for tonight, but I'm open to a longer-term commitment," he offered.

I felt so trapped by it all. My Grandmother and closest confidant had died just two days ago. On her deathbed she had revealed a family secret that I had to now carry and try to resolve. But I could not tell anyone else about it — no one. I was so ill prepared for such a burden. I'd lived my life to entertain, and be interesting, and look gorgeous. I certainly did not need a well-meaning neighbor who was half in love with me following me around, insisting that I let him help me. It was all too much."

"That's when I woke up. I had tears in my eyes and an overwhelming sense of shame. Somehow, I know I never followed through. I put the burden onto someone else without ever even trying. I chose to stay the party girl and my heart is broken. This heart in this body, standing here before you, is broken," Jen sobbed.

Cailleen stood and went to Jen. She wrapped her in her arms and held her while she sobbed out her grief and shame. "Let go," she soothed. "Let it go." Cailleen waited for Jen to quiet down and then sat her in the chair next to the fire. She kissed the top of her head, then walked to her own seat. After a moment's pause, she simply said, "I think, my dear, you may have another chance at it."

They spent the rest of the evening hearing Cailleen and Charles speak of their experiences over the last few days. The two of them had carefully avoided too much detail. The ground seemed a bit rocky and the steps ahead uncertain.

When finished with the tales of the last 48 hours they all decided to go to bed and look at everything fresh again in the morning. Cailleen and Charles exchanged a look that said they would be talking, just the two of them, before breakfast.

As Cailleen slept that night she wandered through a forest. Her feet seemed to know the way to wherever she was going. The ancient gentle trees reminded her of a place she knew well. An owl hooted above her in the cool, clear night. The wind caressed her face and she undid her hair to let it fall freely. She experienced sublime joy in the simplicity of the wind blowing through her hair. For her it was like plugging in all her antennae and becoming one with the forest. She felt very sensual and her entire body was attuned to the world around her. Soft mosses beckoned her touch, as did the sharp spines on a ponderosa pine cone. Her body swayed with the rhythm of saplings in the wind. She inhaled the fecund earth, sharp pine, and the sweetness of ripened berries. She waded barefoot through the bubbling stream and bathed in the light of Grandmother Moon in her fullness. She heard a gentle voice singing the happy song of a woman wrapping up her tasks of the day.

Cailleen followed the sound of that song, knowing she had come to speak with this woman. The song led her to a path that led deeper into the forest and into a grove of ancient oak and sycamore. She was delighted at the sight of sycamores. The moon was brilliantly reflected in their bark and seemed to light the circle. She still missed the magical sycamores of her childhood home. Sycamores were not native to her current home in Eastern Washington.

When the moon reached her peak, Cailleen heard flutes from among the trees and stars of light twinkled at her. After a few moments, the scent of honey and apple blossoms filled the air as a dozen or so Faeries emerged and climbed the small hill that stood in the center of the grove. Cailleen had not noticed it until now.

The woman who sang linked her arm through Cailleen's and together they joined the circle at the top of the hill. A fire now flamed and Cailleen could see they were in what was left of a dance on the hill. Thirteen stones stood equidistant apart except for the opening in the south, through which they had just passed. The air shimmered and Cailleen turned back toward the opening.

"Please stay," the woman beckoned. "We delight in having you with us on this glorious night."

"I…? Thank you. But I did not ask permission to enter. I will do so and then return," Cailleen explained.

"Wood Pigeon, you are of us and need not ask permission to enter your own home. But do as you will. I'll wait here for you."

Cailleen exited the dance, then turned and faced the threshold. She had nothing in her pockets to offer. Why had she gone into the forest unprepared, she wondered? She combed her hands through her hair and gathered three long strands, which she wove into a circle. She hung the circle on the branch of a currant bush in offering. Then Cailleen asked and waited for permission to enter from the Ancestors of Place. An unseen door opened and Cailleen passed through it into the dance once more. With her sight clearer now, she returned to the woman's side and greeted her with respect.

"Merry meet, Mother."

"Merry meet," *the woman answered with a smile.*

"You called me by the name, Wood Pigeon. How is it you know me by that name?" Cailleen asked.

"Because, dear child, I gave you that name." At that the woman briefly kissed Cailleen on the third eye and whispered, "Remember."

And Cailleen did remember: the procession at Avebury in 2003 when she first heard that name in this lifetime; the Serpent Mound in 2006 when she journeyed under the Mound and found herself back in Avebury; Red Rock State Park south of Sedona in 1999 when the ancient tree took her to a previous life; lying flat on her back in a hospital when she was 6 years old, and then, planting the family garden all by herself when she was 12 years old - all portals to other times and other lives.

Cailleen sat up in her bed with eyes wide open as she considered the implications of the teaching in this dream. She'd been so afraid to enter too deeply into her past lives and the information available to her through such travel. She feared she'd be lost and would not want, or be able, to return. But the last two memories were when she was a child and "untrained" in journeywork. She didn't even know she was traveling, and yet she returned easily enough. Not that she wouldn't take certain precautions, but "dammit," she thought to herself, "I've been making things way too hard and this is an important part of my work."

If a better time to do this work emerged, she'd be very surprised. As she thought more about it she remembered the skill with which Raneck moved through time and space and lifetimes. She, his prize student, probably had talents to match. This insight explained so much.

Her mind wandered back to her relationship with Everett years ago. He had represented nothing she sought in a partner – at least not in this lifetime. He was a stodgy philosopher with a major drinking problem who smoked like a chimney. Even in the midst of the relationship her head had told her it made no sense. He was not what she needed or wanted. But the link and the attraction were undeniable. She eased into the relationship with very little resistance. Two months later when his alcoholism was obvious to everyone but himself, she'd ended it. He had quickly become selfish and abusive to those around him.

At the end, and even after the relationship was over, Everett regularly visited her psychically, especially late at night. She'd be working into the late hours and suddenly his scent filled the air and she could feel him in the room with her. She'd had to place rigorous shields up to keep him out. It wore on her nerves and drained her both physically and emotionally. As a result, it interfered with her work. Maintaining protective shields all the time began to affect her other relationships as well as her ability to make good choices. She had to do something.

He was unaware that he was psychically traveling. She considered psychically repelling him for a moment. But it just wasn't in her to do anything that could potentially harm someone psychically. She knew from past conversations with him that asking him to stop would have no affect; he didn't believe in such things.

Instead, she decided to do her own journey and figure out the source of their connection. She found herself in a long corridor with many doors. She immediately understood the doors to be lifetimes she had shared with Everett. Only one door was opened and she moved to that door. At her approach, the door opened a bit wider and Cailleen could feel the pull. She felt memories stirring and a sense of a deep and profound respect and love.

She put her hand on the doorknob and moved to pass through to this other lifetime. Archangel Uriel stopped her with a gentle hand on the shoulder. "There is nothing you need through that door. Close and lock it. Its reality bleeds through to this lifetime. Your business with him was completed. He wishes to hang on, but it will not serve you. Close and lock the door. Return to your present time."

Cailleen felt the strength and joy of their relationship in that time. She also saw clearly now that it had very little to do with the reality of him or their relationship in the now. Now knowing the source of the pull and the attraction, she found the strength to close and lock the door.

The psychic visits stopped. The experience taught her quite clearly how much the past could bleed through and affect the present.

Time and space had always been pretty fluid to Cailleen. And because of that, she'd feared being lost. This wasn't, she told herself, an unreasonable fear. But this morning's dream and the awakening memories that resulted, suggested she had the skill she needed to do it safely. Tomorrow, she told herself, would be soon enough to explore it all further. She drifted back to sleep.

Chapter Six
Allies

Several hours later Cailleen awoke to the sound of geese flying overhead. She felt rested and calm. As she stretched and slipped out from under the covers, she remembered threads from her dream last night. "I think I shall be doing some traveling," she said to herself. "But first, some tea!"

She threw on her thick flannel robe of deep purple and pulled on a pair of thick wool socks. Then she padded quietly toward Charles' room sending a psychic call ahead of her. She opened his door to find him stretching one arm and scratching his belly with his hand. She noticed that instead of rolling her eyes at the big rumpled, unshaven man scratching himself, she found herself smiling with motherly pride at the strong, confident man before her. "Blindness of a mother!" she thought.

"I was just thinking about getting out of bed and making my way to your room. Pull up a chair," Charles said as he tied his robe.

"I could use a cuppa," Cailleen said. "Let's go down to the kitchen or take tea into the study."

"Sure, let's go to the study. We need to talk before Jen and Lawrence start asking a lot of questions. They contained themselves last night, but I don't think they'll last much longer. We gave them a bit of a scare. Do you want to make the tea or light the fire? We can lock the door and settle in for a chat," he said in a voice that warned her he would not be pacified, distracted, or put off this morning.

"I'll make the tea," she said, and left the room with a regal air about her. Before going downstairs however, she stopped in her room to gather her journal and Mellissae Lucia's deck, *The Oracle of Initiation*. She took the time to put her rings on her hands and run a brush through her hair. This was not to be a cozy talk and she wanted her tools with her.

On her left hand she wore the golden amber, a ring she had made from an amber bracelet she'd inherited from her great, great grandmother on her father's side. She had earrings and a necklace, but it was the ring she had empowered. It represented her inherited gifts and she wore it when working with any magic. On her right hand she wore a claddagh ring and a snake of transformation on her pinky.

By the time Cailleen entered the study, carrying the tea and some scones on her favorite tray, she felt ready to get down to business and begin setting plans as well as boundaries for the work ahead.

Charles had thrown on a pair of navy blue sweats that highlighted his strong physique. Broad shoulders tapered down to a narrow waist, toned gluts, and well-developed thighs and legs. He looked strong and solid rather than hard. He was the kind of man you can sink into when you need comfort, yet he never seemed soft. Cailleen sometimes wondered why she'd never been attracted to him sexually. Their life as mother and son was just too close to the surface in this lifetime, she guessed.

He smiled and took the tray from her, placing it on the floor next to the table and sinking into the pillows. He'd gathered stones for clarity and grounding, which sat in a copper bowl on the table. His journal lay on the floor next to him, and she saw he wore the medallion of his bear totem. Charles fingered a small black silk bag on the table next to the copper bowl. She watched as indecision moved across his face. Then he took a cleansing breath and handed her the small bag.

Someone had made the bag by hand from raw silk with a fine leather thong to close it. She felt the chain of a necklace through the silk. She opened the bag and let the necklace slither out and into her waiting hand. She held a round disk made of antler about the size of a quarter. She turned it over and found a delicate carving of Bear and Otter playing in a river with songbirds flying around them. In her lifetime as Calleigha her mother had given this to her. Originally, it was not on a chain but on a thin piece of leather dyed with woad. She remembered her mother putting it on her on the day she was initiated as a Song Carrier and Healer.

"Wherever did you get this, Charles? It should have been buried with me. Why do you have this in your possession?" Cailleen demanded in a confused voice.

"That has been in my family for generations. It is guarded carefully and passed down from generation to generation. It was given to me about three years after I became your student. I meant to bring it for you to see a long time ago. But I kept 'losing' it. I don't think the Fey meant for you to have it until now. I found it in my bag when I was looking for socks this morning.

I've never opened that bag. But I have seen that necklace before in a dream. I took it from my mother's body when she died and I hid it. I remember thinking that she would need it someday and that I needed to keep it safe until I could return it to her - when she was ready to fulfill her promise."

"Thank you for keeping it safe. Hold it for a bit longer, will you?" Cailleen put the necklace back in the bag and placed it in Charles' hand. He nodded and drank his tea.

Cailleen stood and went to the window to watch the birds at the feeder. She fingered the stone at her neck and spoke softly.

"I have a dilemma. I seem to have inherited a family secret, which I am honor bound to keep secret. I have been charged with resolving an ancient struggle without revealing its details. On the other hand, sitting before me is the reincarnation of my son, who in this life seems to know the secret. And upstairs are two dear and trusted friends, who I know are intent upon helping me with this charge, who also seem to know about the family secret. I know in this lifetime they do not know the secret. But Jen's dream seems to indicate she knew it in a past life. Lawrence knew *of* it, but I think not the specifics. Yet if Jen knows, Lawrence certainly might, as they have no secrets from each other. The question is how much do you know, and how much am I allowed to reveal of what you don't know?

"This is my quest and my charge" she continued. "None of you can do it for me. But the information from the dreams seems to indicate I need your help and that I should not let pride get in the way of accepting it. And yet, I hesitate to put all my cards on the table, so to speak.

"I brought my friend Mellissae's cards down to guide me. I'd like to pull some cards before we proceed."

***

Jen slowly came to consciousness as the autumn light filtered into the room, warming its peach and burnt orange tones that flowed throughout the room. Such a feminine room really did not suit her on an everyday basis. But she always claimed this room when she stayed at the "manor." She smiled to herself. Cailleen was not suited to a manor. But this large converted farmhouse had the feel of a manor. The bedrooms were spacious with touches of luxury. Two had their own bathrooms, two had fireplaces and one had a balcony. The balcony overlooked five acres of gentle landscape with a river, small forest, three gardens and what Cailleen called the "wild area." Most of the barn she'd remodeled into a healing studio and classroom. She left the back of the barn for gardening tools, lawn mower, and other such things. Recently, she'd transformed the old hayloft into a ritual space and put solar panels on the roof for power.

When Jen first started studying with Cailleen they met in her study. Cailleen remodeled the house first, using a bedroom for her healing studio. Jen remembered sitting in some of the rooms as a class project. They would listen to the room and ask what would suit it. They'd each journal their perceptions and then compare notes over tea. The first time they did it, she'd been amazed at how similar the perceptions were. It was one of the most important lessons she learned from Cailleen: everything has life and purpose and preference. As they moved from room to room in the house, she developed the ability to tune in to the unique character of each room. The communications became clearer with each experience. They also walked the land itself and opened to its messages. And Jen became attuned to how the individual parts blended into the whole. When each was listened to, all could be served well.

Furnishings in this room were simple and functional, but seemed to have been chosen for their texture as much as anything else. The drapes and the upholstery on the chairs had a nubby texture. The frame of the queen-sized bed had a bisque finish that was stressed, giving it interesting shadows and lines. A chest in the same design sat at the bed's foot. Antique lace flowed over the matching dresser and night table. The big down comforter of golds and reds looked almost fuzzy, like the soft skin of a peach. Pillows on the bed, chair, and the floor beneath the windows and in front of the fire were covered in contrasting shades of soft peaches, golds, deep reds or oranges. Everything in the room evoked softness and warmth, except the sculptures of the blue herons and the abstract in brushed pewter on the corner table. The coolness of these three pieces made the contrasting softness palatable. It tied the feminine room up with a deep sense of strength. The walls featured paintings of strong and inspirational women in circle - with children, in the garden, and in council.

In this room Jen felt like she sat in the company of all the Grandmothers who came before. Their love and wisdom enfolded her, made her strong and encouraged her to meet whatever challenges lie ahead. She always slept well in this room and woke up gently and deliciously.

Today she knew she could have a bit of a lie in. Charles and Cailleen would need some time to talk together. Yvonne was arriving early to join them for breakfast and to take care of dinner so the four of them could do whatever work presented itself. So she stretched under the covers and then rolled over and sank back down for another half-hour.

A bit later, the crunch of tire wheels on the gravel driveway brought her back to consciousness. That would be Yvonne. Jen got out of bed then walked to the window to wave at Yvonne and to breathe in the fresh morning air. Winter would be here soon enough to discourage opening to the great outdoors. She saw Yvonne point to the front door and then dash into the house through the kitchen.

Yvonne was good for Lawrence, she thought. She took care of a lot of little details, but never let him assume she was responsible for doing them. Yvonne carried herself with grace and ease. She looked like a model with her long limbs, great cheekbones, thick blonde hair that danced when she moved, deep green eyes, and just the right amount of muscle definition. With her looks and slow, sultry laugh, one never suspected Yvonne's practical nature. A salt-of-the-earth woman, she knew what she wanted and how to hold on to it when she had it. She wanted Lawrence, and he wanted her right back.

Jen preferred her women softer, curvier, and bigger than life. She'd had a major crush on Cailleen in the first year of her apprenticeship. But then she got distracted by Johanna, and then Desiree, then Barb and Mitch (they were such fun together), and finally Pricilla. Pricilla wasn't really her type, but intrigued her well enough for a couple of weeks. Suddenly, in the last couple of months Jen wanted more in a relationship. She was getting too old for passing intrigues. Since she didn't know what that meant, she hadn't seen anyone at all for a while. Maybe seeing how happy Lawrence and Yvonne were made her think she was missing something. "Well, you're certainly missing sex," she said to herself as she walked back into her room. "Better get going or you won't get that bubble bath." A quick bath, then she'd pop down to the kitchen to grab coffee before dealing with her hair and dressing. A perfect morning!

***

In the study Cailleen sat at the table with Charles, shuffling cards. "I chose Mellissae Lucia's *Oracle of Initiation* deck. She designed it specifically around initiatory journeys and the awakening power of ancient alliances. I think that's what we're dealing with here, at least for me," Cailleen explained.

She laid out three cards: *The Gateway of Balance, Resonance,* and *Discriminate.* The energy of the cards themselves, with their archetypal images, emanated both comfort and challenge.

"*The Gateway of Balance* seems obvious; balance is what I am to attempt to achieve and I stand on the threshold. Let's look at the other two first.

"*Ah, Resonance,*" Cailleen smiled. "I have certainly spent a lot of years teaching others to develop sensitivity to finding what resonates for them and to learn to trust it. This is a good reminder for me. I have been using my head to try to make decisions about how to proceed. We know the mind can really distance and distract us, creating false impressions and even illusions. Last night when Jen and Lawrence shared their dreams, something about it all did *not* resonate and it wasn't the dreams themselves. There's something suspicious, maybe the timing?" Cailleen shook her head to avoid getting distracted.

"What does resonate is that this is *the* time for me to do whatever I am to do to resolve the past and bring about a new balance.

"*Discriminate.* Hmm? This tells me that not only is it time for clarity, but that I have exactly what I need to achieve it. I can move quickly and concisely through things without being overwhelmed. I operate in the world at a deeper, wider and clearer level now.

"These two cards tell me to trust my training, my experience, my inner knowing. I am prepared for whatever comes at a very basic and powerful level. *The Gateway of Balance* is the house of regeneration and the harmonious heart. It tells me to offer resolve and receive alignment.

"Charles, what, if anything, do you want to add? Are you picking up anything I've missed?"

"It's important to remember that what feels like blindness is not always so. Look," Charles directed, "at the image on *Discriminate*. A feather and shadow cover the eyes, suggesting perhaps that all the pieces cannot be seen clearly with the eye. But her hand and arm seem to be catching illumination from out of the air. The overall feel of the card is certainty and power. The *Resonance* card, by the way, looks like you when you're traveling between the worlds. You start that process with the knowing of who you are in your essence. In other words, you know what resonates most clearly within you. That is how you find your way back. You can trust that. You will find your way through *this* maze.

"And, the card feels like a chastisement for me," he continued. "My own fears have led me to trust in your skills less than I should. I apologize and will do my best to put those fears aside.

"*The Gateway* card is pretty clear," he continued. "I noticed you gave the words "receive alignment" more energy when you spoke about it. I do believe you are to make alliances – another way of receiving alignment – on this journey. You've received at least one caution about refusing the help of those who have been sent to you."

Cailleen responded, "I have also been given a couple warnings about revealing the secret. So, I will ask you now to tell me specifically what you know," Cailleen requested. "That way I do not have to tip toe around details that you already have knowledge of."

"OK, I'll tell you what I know. I will do so with whatever emotions come along with it. I want you to know how I feel about what I know. It may help me to let go of some of my fears. That is my intention, to let go of any attachment and fear as I reveal my story. Here goes:

"You were my first mother on this planet. I came, in part, to bring you comfort and to help you heal your pain. I failed. We failed. You never found a way to open to me. You closed yourself to your power and to everything else around you. What I can't remember from that life comes to me in dreams. For the last five years I have been dreaming pretty regularly about that lifetime. And I've been wondering why you've seemed to have no knowledge of it. I wondered if it was blocked from you or if you were blocking it? I never mentioned it. I guess I felt I'd finally found a close relationship with you and I didn't want to risk it.

"In that life, I was very well taken care of in the village. I was 'the golden child.' Grandfather watched me like a hawk, looking for signs of power in me. He began apprenticing me at a very early age. I enjoyed testing my wings and discovering what I had within me. It was tainted, however, by Grandfather's hunger. I watched him every night as he watched you at the fires. He loved you certainly. He also felt deep regret and anger about the loss of your power. Then he would always turn to look at me with calculation and hunger. I avoided him as much as possible. And I'm sorry to say, I also avoided you. He wanted me to reach you and to awaken you to your power. I had no particular interest in that. I wanted my mother. I wanted to hear her sing and to see her walk in joy.

"I heard so many stories of you as a child and young woman. I was told of the time you walked the land and sang the waters when you were only five. That was the year of the drought. What water the village had was polluted by a dead carcass upstream. You went missing for three days. Your parents and the entire village were panicked. There was no sign of you; it was like you vanished. On the morning of the fourth day, you glided into the village. Your feet were not touching the ground. You sang as you entered. Your parents ran to you, but Grandfather stopped them. He could see you were in a trance. He knew it would endanger you if you were brought out quickly. You looked at the Headman with a faraway gaze, then began walking to the stream. You looked back at him once. He followed you and the entire village followed after him. You stopped at the edge of the stream and raised your hands and your voice. You seemed to gather the song in your hands, then stepped into the stream and released the song into it. Light flowed up and downstream. You ended your song on a note of triumph. Then you turned to Chancha's father, the headsman, and, with the sweetest smile the village had ever seen, simply said, 'the waters run clear.' You offered him a gourd and then fell to the ground in exhaustion.

"The headsman ordered Chancha, his oldest son, to carry you to your parent's lodging and stopped Grandfather when he followed. 'What does this mean, Senechal?' he asked Grandfather. 'The waters run clear,' Grandfather replied. 'The child speaks truth. I can feel the vibrancy of fresh water again. Would you like me to drink to show you her truth?" Grandfather asked. "No," the headsman commanded. "A village cannot survive without its Senechal. I will take the first drink." Chancha, who had just returned, stopped him. "Father, let me take the first drink. A village needs its headsman." With great pride, the headsman nodded his approval. "Don't wander, Senechal, you may be needed," he said. "I shall be with Calleigha," Grandfather replied as he walked toward the lodging.

"Grandfather entered the lodging in great haste. He'd been gathering his power as he walked from the stream. As he entered, everyone stepped aside in fear, except your mother. Ninu, Charles recalled, could never be intimidated when it came to the safety of her family. "Ninu," Grandfather spoke gently, "Calleigha is in great danger if her spirit has not fully returned to her body. I must sing her back and it may take all my power and concentration to be successful. I need you to step away so I can use my skill." Ninu stepped back, but not away. She trusted more in her love for her daughter than in the Senechal's skill. But she could love her from a couple feet away easily enough.

"Grandfather began singing and everyone settled in for a long healing. But after just a few minutes his song ended. His power still enfolding him, Grandfather turned to her parents. "This child is fully intact. Let her sleep. Wake her at nightfall, then feed her broth. I will bring you a tea. You will be sure she drinks it all throughout the day tomorrow. At the new moon, you will send her to me. I claim this child as apprentice to the Senechal."

"Ninu told me later that her heart clenched in fear at his pronouncement. It was in that moment, she explained, that you lost your name and became set apart as 'the child' in the village. You began to disappear in that moment, for no one except your mother called you Calleigha after that day. You were the child, then the Senechal, then the Banished One and finally, 'She who returns.' At 5 years old you realized your power and potential. You were loved and a little feared. You were no longer an everyday part of the village. Grandfather replaced your simple childhood games with training to become his replacement.

"I asked him once when he first realized your power was greater than his. It was a dangerous question and I only dared it when I was angry at him. I braced for his rage, but he simply said, "when she didn't need me to sing her back."

"Cailleen, I lived in the village where this story you're trying to resolve began. I was your son. I was born after the banishment, but I knew the details as if I had lived them. Your story was the favored one around the fires for at least three generations.

"Only once after your banishment did you show your full power. You used it to make me a belt for when I became a man. You hid yourself for three days. The village could hear you singing and they grew hopeful that you would fully return to them. You came out when I arrived to present myself to you as a man and no longer a boy.

"I had never seen you in your power. You shone like a star and I felt my power shine in response. As the village watched us, they say we rose off the ground together. When you placed the belt at my waist, I felt the fullness of your love for the first time in my life. I found my mother and she glowed with beauty and power. You transferred that power to me. The ecstasy and pain of it were overwhelming as it flowed through me. I lost consciousness.

"When I awoke, Grandfather told me that you had also collapsed. You were weakening with the day. Despite his objections, I went to your side. You roused as I spoke your name. You looked upon me with great love and in that moment, I also saw the depth of the sorrow you had carried for so many years. And then your face became so peaceful, and you just slipped away from me. I tried to sing you back, but your spirit refused. "It is complete," your spirit whispered. I left the village that day and did not return for a full turn of the wheel.

"They took you from me, so I took what you had given me from them. During that year, we spoke in dreams and you taught me things that Grandfather could not. You taught me to hold onto my humanity and to not separate myself from the village in an everyday way.

"You told me to find a mate to love with a passion. You told me your humanity had been trained out of you and when you were no longer able to use your power freely, you had nothing left. All your mental and emotional skills were tied to the use of your power. You were left with a physical body to birth children and tend to chores and a spirit that dwindled. You told me you were not brave enough to find a way to walk in both worlds.

"That was the regret of your life. You had never found a way to reach your children or your husband. You loved them dearly, but could not find a way to be truly with them. 'I gave you my power,' you said. 'Now I give you my hard-won wisdom: walk with your power and your humanity in equal parts.'

"I never planned to return to the village. But in the darkness of the thirteenth moon of my isolation, you came to me in a dream. You asked me to fulfill your promise to be Senechal to the village. You commanded me to return at the fullness of the moon. On the eve of the full moon, you came to me in spirit form and performed the rite that made me Senechal. As a Senechal and my mother, you had the power and the right. You gifted me with the staff and amulet that were the outward signs of the Senechal.

"After our ceremony I felt healed and complete. I acknowledged my own desire to return to the village and serve them as I had been trained to do. I learned well from your story. When I entered the village, I ignored everyone and went straight to Chancha. I explained to him what had happened to me. I asked to return to the village and offered when Grandfather died to step into his role as Senechal. I vowed to him that I would only step into that role when Grandfather was no longer able to carry it. Until that time I offered myself to him as hunter and warrior. I then asked him to consider finding me a worthy mate when the time seemed good to him. Chancha agreed. Over the next three years, we came to understand each other well.

"After seeing Chancha, I went to see Grandfather. I still felt anger toward him for his blindness and his manipulations of people's lives. In my year of isolation, I vowed that I would not let him manipulate mine any longer. I entered his lodging an arrogant and stubborn man. I expected to find the same within. Instead, I found a gray-haired, bent, old man. I still sensed his power, but he no longer carried it like a royal robe. My guard was still up, though. I had seen his glamours before and knew that he could shift as quickly as a serpent striking.

"'Chalic,' Grandfather spoke in a voice that crackled with age, 'I heard you'd returned. I see you finally found time for your mentor and the head of your family.' His voice held disdain and to Chalic's surprise, it also held hurt.

"I told him, 'I belong to no family now. I have been initiated as a Senechal. I belong to the village and presented myself to Chancha, the Headsman, when I returned. The village does not need another power struggle. I have learned well at my mother's feet this last turn of the wheel.'

"'Your mother is dead, Chalic! She taught you nothing while she was alive,' he sputtered bitterly. 'Why would she bother with you now? She has not returned even in death. I cannot find her and I am a Senechal of great power. What power do you hold that you could find her when I could not?'

"I told him, 'The power of a son's love. It's a simple power of humanity and no rigorous training is required. These are the lessons she taught to me: to hold my humanity as precious as my other gifts and never to deny it. Her inability to connect with her humanity killed her long before her last breath. She learned this lesson herself in her last act. The priestess within her placed a belt at my waist, and the mother within her showered me with love. That was the height of her power. She opened to it and let it flow between us. Even though her body could no longer hold its fullness, she let it flow and gifted me with it. She does not regret that moment. She does regret not having fulfilled her promise to the village. She sent me to do that for her and she initiated me so that I could. I have explained this to Chancha, and also pledged myself to him as hunter/warrior until such time as you are no longer able to fulfill your duties as Senechal.

"You have mentored me. You are my grandfather. I will provide for your physical needs as is my right and duty. I will assist you if you need it and as Chancha permits me time from my duties to him. Is there anything you need at this time?" Chalic asked.

"'Such pride in your bearing and in your speech,' Grandfather replied. 'You think you have surpassed me, your mentor. It's about time. You've been trained to do so. You've been sired to do so. I was robbed of the opportunity to combine the fullness of my power with the fullness of your mothers as two Senechals. How glorious that would have been. But I found another way. I talked your mother into marrying my son. The power doesn't run strong in him, but the potential is there. Rasia is your father's daughter. But you, you are your mother's son and my grandson. You are the combining of our powers. See that you honor it by carrying it well. I need nothing from you. Go sleep with your hunters.'

"Grandfather continued to weaken slowly over the next few years. I made sure he was taken care of and helped him when he would allow it. Toward the end my heart softened a bit toward him, but I don't know that I ever forgave him for his part in your story. Before he passed, he called me to his side. He explained that when I left the village he had fallen ill and was not certain he would survive. In my absence he charged Rasia with carrying the story and passing it through the generations to be healed. Now that I had returned, he asked me to take on that charge. I refused, saying it was in good hands.

"He begged me to take the charge, arguing that Rasia had no real power. I told him she had great love and that was very powerful. Each day when I visited him, he would rant about how the power balance had been disturbed and must be resolved. I tried to console him with tales of our time together during my isolation. I told him you did find a way to use your power and that I was fulfilling your commitment.

"He said it wasn't enough that one of the three might have resolved her life - all three had to come to resolution at the same time. 'The child is gone,' he kept saying. And his refusal to use your name hardened my heart again.

"In his last few days, he was no longer lucid. He kept speaking about the crossroads and only three opportunities. 'I cannot rest until it's complete,' he kept chanting. At the end I began the song to carry him safely to the other side. As I began, he blasted me with the last bit of power he could gather. It was strong enough to render me unconscious. I woke to the entire village in a panic. They heard a scream, which the crows took up. When they entered Grandfather's lodging, they thought both of us were dead. Chancha quieted them and went to our bodies to check. Grandfather was dead. I was unconscious. I came to later that day, but it was too late.

"The old man manipulated me even at his own death. Without the death song, his soul was not carried to the other side. He would wander the earth without rest. The village people knew he would be tethered to them and bring hardship if something was not done. My first act as Senechal would not be the simple releasing of a spirit to the other realm. Instead, I would have to call up all my powers to protect the village in these first days of his death. Until Grandfather's soul was separated from his body long enough to lose the attachment to the physicality of this lifetime, he was a danger to the village. It took great power and all my concentration to keep his soul from tethering itself to the village. Rasia helped by feeding me the power of her love. And in her loving wisdom she kept after Chancha to find me a mate. She told me later that she actually picked Elthia for me and made it seem like Chancha's idea. Rasia became mate to Chancha's eldest and when Chancha died, she became Headswoman. That was her destiny, and she carried it well. I thought you'd like to know that."

"I'm glad," Cailleen murmured. "Thank you. Thank you for everything. Thank you for not failing me. Not now and not then."

Charles looked at her sharply. "Don't try to make me feel better. It won't serve either of us, not really."

Cailleen reminded him, "Chalic taught Calleigha the power of a mother's love. It was allowing that love to flow into her power as a Song Carrier that freed and healed her. She taught you the importance of carrying both equally. But she did not learn it herself until the moment she put the belt on you. You called forth that love from within her. It was a power moment and she opened to it. She would not have risked it for anyone else. You allowed her to taste her own power once again. She died knowing she passed it on through you. I dreamed about that moment two nights ago. I remember it, now.

"After Calleigha's death," Cailleen continued, "she came to you and you allowed her to teach you and to initiate you as a Senechal. You have yet to initiate an apprentice, Charles. You cannot begin to know the joy and honor it brings. I know this from this lifetime. You, Jen, Lawrence and all the other students who have worked with me have brought so much joy and purpose into my life. Those sacred moments of knowing and initiation are priceless. I would not trade them.

"As you spoke of your initiation as a Senechal, I relived the joy of that moment. It transcends time. Thank you, my Chalic. And thank you for carrying out my commitment to the village. Through you, I found a way to fulfill it. I birthed you twice in that lifetime. I gave you life but was unable to embrace the new role you gave to me as a mother. Through me you became a Senechal and you gave me back the life I had hoped to fulfill."

"But Mother, I lost you," Charles countered. "You finally became my mother and it killed you. I got your power, but I lost you."

"No Charles," Cailleen said softly. "You found me and we spent a full turning of the wheel together. And thousands of years later, you sit here with me drinking tea and sharing power. That moment may have cost me my physical life, but it created a bond between us that neither time nor distance can sever. Be at peace now. We have some work to do."

Outside, a car crunched through the gravel, a door closed, and they heard Yvonne shout a hello. A moment later the front doorbell rang.

"I can't think why Yvonne didn't come through the kitchen. She's family." Cailleen stopped him as Charles rose to answer the door. "Stay and gather your thoughts. I will let Yvonne in. Then I'm off to take a bath and do some thinking. Let's do breakfast in about an hour. If Jen or Lawrence don't beat me to it, I'll cook."

***

Still dressed in her wool socks and fuzzy purple robe, Cailleen threw open the front door to give Yvonne a welcome hug and tell her she could just come in when she visited. But when the door swung open, instead of Yvonne, she stood face to face with a strange man.

Cailleen instantly became aware of her apparel, and closed her robe more tightly around her soft curves. Her hand went to her hair and then to the amulet around her neck. She stood speechless. Before her, stood a man in his early 50s. His dark, thick hair with silver streaks and a slight wave had been messed by the wind and it softened the hard lines of his face. He was a thinker. She could see that. His face wasn't beautiful as much as interesting. A tiny scar below his left eye drew her attention and when she looked into his eyes she nearly drowned. She heard her own intake of breath and then felt Charles' hand on her shoulder. The stranger's eyes of deep blue held the depth of the deepest sea. They shifted from her face up to Charles'.

He extended his hand to Charles with a smile, but his eyes crinkled with irritation. Charles shook hands and at the same time gave Cailleen a bit of a shake to bring her back from wherever she had gone.

"James McEwen," the stranger said. "I've just rented the bungalow down the road. I think you're my nearest neighbors. Thought I'd drop by and introduce myself. I understand the bungalow's been empty for a while. I'm not clear where the boundaries between the two properties lie, and I wanted to make sure I didn't trespass.

"Shelly at the post office suggested it might be best if I made my presence known as you have 'interesting and private goings on up here.' I'm not sure what she means by that, but she seemed pretty convinced I should follow what she considered basic protocol. I'm new to the area and decided it best to follow her advice with an explanation. I see I've called too early. I'll just go on back to the bungalow." Realizing he was rambling, James stopped and waited.

"Charles Murphy," Charles said formally. "This is Cailleen Renae, author, Teacher and Healer. Her work is not particularly conducive to chatty neighbors dropping by on a regular or an unannounced basis. Some of the locals don't understand the nature of her work. They have unfortunately been turned away when they showed up for a casual chat during a class or healing session." Charles ended his introduction abruptly and looked askance at James. James nodded and turned on his heal.

"Please, Mr. McEwan," Cailleen called.

"James," he said as he turned back to her. She almost lost her ability to speak again when he turned those eyes on her. This irritated her, so she shook it off and focused on his chin.

"James. We've actually been up for a couple hours. We had a lot to talk about this morning over tea. Please come in. We'll make another pot and you can have a cuppa, unless you'd prefer coffee."

"I really just stopped by to introduce myself. I'll let you and your husband get back to your morning," James responded with great formality.

"Don't be ridiculous," Cailleen almost snapped. "We have no trouble sending away unwanted visitors, as you know. We should know a thing or two about each other as neighbors. Assumptions can be dangerous. My dear *friend*, Charles, will take you to the kitchen. I'll be down in five minutes. We were about to make breakfast. You'll join us."

With that, Cailleen moved to the stairs with a regal bearing. No stranger was going to come to her home and discomfort her with his assumptions and formality. She'd get dressed and come back to shower him with gracious charm. Then she'd tell him where the boundaries were.

Charles raised an eyebrow as the *queen* dismissed them. He always enjoyed it when she became irritated enough to pull out the royal act. Unsuspecting mortals were usually slayed by her charm and sent packing before they realized what happened. He was going to enjoy breakfast, he thought. He didn't much like James' arrogance or the way Cailleen seemed to feel threatened by him. He wondered why she'd invited him to breakfast.

James watched as Cailleen left them. She glided away with a regal grace, but he had the feeling she was stomping away in irritation. He sure didn't need this, he thought. He'd come to do a job and to check up on her for an old friend. He'd sensed her power before she'd opened the door. Her beauty floored him. Blues eyes and wide impish smile sparkled on creamy skin surrounded by tousled waves of hair that streamed down her back. She had such a loving welcome on her face, until she saw him. Clearly, she expected someone else. Her eyes went right to his scar and then she looked right through him. He'd felt naked by that glance and his heart had stopped. Then the cavalry came in and he was snapped back into reality.

Charles was more than a dear *friend* and he made sure James was aware of that. The hair actually stood up on the back of his neck when Charles extended his hand in greeting. Nothing would be casual at this breakfast. He wished he could escape without losing face. But James McEwan didn't have a cowardly bone in his body. So, he squared his shoulders and prepared to play nice. At least he'd have an opportunity to learn more about this woman healer and her cohorts.

"There's a hook for your coat by the door there," Charles pointed. "I'll put coffee and tea on."

"I'm happy with tea," James offered. "No need to make anything special for me."

"A couple of other guests have a great need for coffee in the morning. So, if you don't mind," Charles said, "I'll go ahead with the coffee."

Just then Jen breezed into the kitchen in her bathrobe and with a towel around her head.

"Heavens, Charles!" she accused. "You might tell a person we have company!"

"Didn't know myself," he muttered. But Jen had already left the room. "She has no manners at all until after her first cup." Then, without asking James to sit down, he went about gathering things for breakfast. He left the silence for James to break.

James knew he was being deliberately ignored. Charles carried himself well and comfortably. He seemed the sort of man who would be comfortable in a boardroom, a high society social event, or in the family kitchen. Currently he was putting the screws to James to see how he'd handle himself.

The kitchen door opened and a golden retriever rushed at him with tail wagging madly. A large, friendly looking man and the gorgeous woman who'd directed him to the front door followed closely behind.

"Rosey," Lawrence laughed, "not everyone wants to be your friend. Get down! Didn't know we had company. I'm Lawrence," he smiled as he extended his hand. A stocky framed man with red wavy hair and piercing blue eyes, Lawrence left no doubt of his Scottish heritage. He gathered the blonde woman into his left side, a sign that she belonged to him. "This here is Yvonne."

Yvonne nodded and smiled. "We almost met when I arrived. I'm sorry I didn't get your name at the time, but I'd just driven for over two hours from the city and finished a large coffee on the drive," she laughed.

"James McEwan," he offered. "Nice to meet you both, and you too, Rosey," he said as he bent down to give her a proper greeting.

Cailleen entered the kitchen in time to see James bent over scratching her dog's ear. Rosey's eyes were in the back of her head and her tongue hung out the side of her mouth. At least Rosey liked him, she thought. Then again, Charles was playing guard dog, which pretty much put Rosey out of a job.

James glanced up at the sound of her entrance and then returned his attention to Rosey. She's nervous, he thought. She was worrying the edge of her scarf. He also noticed she dressed very well for a casual breakfast with friends. She was sending him a message.

So, out of politeness, he took in every inch of her, while pretending to focus on the dog. She wore a soft purple tunic with an ethnic design at the sleeves and hem. A scarf in deep red was draped around her neck in some mysterious fashion that women used. Amethyst and silver earrings peeked out from behind her hair, which she left hanging softly about her shoulders. The same amulet she'd worn earlier hung just above the hint of cleavage revealed by the neckline of her tunic. She wore brushed cotton slacks of a deeper shade of purple. On her feet she wore a sturdy pair of walking shoes instead of the designer shoes he expected.

James smiled to himself. Her message was subtle yet clear: she wore the colors of royalty, the style of a confident, well-respected woman with some flair, and the surprise of functional shoes. "Don't type cast me" was written all over her. She was complicated, interesting, and not to be taken lightly. He began to wonder if the nervous worrying of the scarf was feigned.

"James, have a seat," she invited with a gracious wave of her hand, then she turned away in dismissal. "Yvonne, so lovely to see you dear." She gave her the hug she had intended earlier and gave Lawrence a cheeky wink. "I smell coffee and see the tea is just about ready to steep. Everyone, sit down. I'll see what Charles has started for breakfast and give him a hand. Talk amongst yourselves."

At the sound of footsteps on the stairs, Charles poured a cup of coffee and added milk and sugar. As Jen popped back in, Charles handed her the cup and received a very noisy kiss on the cheek. James got his message. Charles knew these women well and was prepared to take care of them. James deliberately rose and introduced himself. Jen offered her hand. He took it and instead of shaking, turned it and kissed it gallantly.

"My apologies for startling you earlier," he said with as much charm as he could muster.

Jen curtsied in response. Lawrence raised his eyes as Charles glared and Cailleen quickly turned her back on James. Yvonne giggled nervously.

"I'm Jen," she said. "I'll talk more when I've finished this cup of morning nectar." With that she sat down next to Yvonne and leaned toward her in hello.

Yvonne's thick dark blond hair seemed to reach out and caress Jen's jet-black tresses. James shook his head at the fanciful idea. These people seemed to be enchanting him. Jen was slightly taller than Yvonne and their athletic bodies seemed to comfortably settle in together. After a brief moment of contact they moved apart. Their actions were very sensual; it suggested a deep comfort and familiarity.

Jen caught James noticing them and lifted her lips in a small smile. James noticed the smile and interpreted it as her believing that he found their actions arousing. But he found nothing sexual in it at all. They were both beautiful women: Jen was more lithe and dark, while Yvonne was softer, even though she had a more solid bone structure - an Indian Princess and a Valkyrie. James shook his head again at the fanciful direction of his thoughts.

A brief and uncomfortable silence fell until Cailleen dropped an egg and Rosey barked with glee at her fortune. James immediately rose to assist. Jen and Yvonne nodded their approval. Charles yelled at the dog. Cailleen drew her hand back as if she'd been burned when James accidentally touched her as he tried to grab the shells before Rosey gobbled them up.

Jen clapped her hands with joy. "Isn't it fun to have guests for breakfast, Charles?" she teased. Lawrence lifted his hand from Yvonne's shoulder and slapped Jen playfully.

"OK," she said, "I'll be good. But it might take another cup of coffee," she quipped as she pushed her empty cup toward Lawrence.

"While you're up can you grab plates and silver?" Cailleen requested. "My famous frittata is just about perfect and it looks like Charles has the fruit salad under control. The scones smell like they're about ready, too. Yvonne, you'll find cloth napkins in the drawer behind you. Jen, can you grab jellies and jams from the pantry?"

In an amazingly short time, everything was on the table and everyone was seated. They're a team, James thought. They've known and loved each other for a very long time. You could tell it by the way they moved together like a well-rehearsed dance. Yvonne was newer to the group. She played but stayed on the periphery – except with Lawrence and Jen. Cailleen reigned here and she'd just made her point abundantly clear. Charming and gracious, but a fortress not easily entered. The boundaries were drawn and acknowledged. Now they could enjoy a delicious breakfast.

An hour later, James left the group with permission to wander the forest at will - and an invitation to visit again, if he called first. Rosey walked with him to the edge of his property and barked in dismissal. "You too, Old Girl?" James shook his head and continued to his bungalow. He'd noticed it was conveniently supplied with an entire shelf of Cailleen's books and CD's. He'd spend the afternoon sorting through them. He turned at the sound of Rosey's bark in the distance. On the hill looking down at him stood Cailleen, her hair and scarf blowing in the breeze. He stood his ground and looked back until she bent and threw the stick Rosey dropped at her feet.

Chapter Seven
Weavings

Cailleen could feel the group waiting for her, but she needed a bit of time to herself. She would not spend it considering their breakfast guest. He wanted something from her. But that mystery would have to wait. She needed an action plan for the quest that had been laid upon her. She wandered to the boulder overlooking her valley and sat listening to the forest, hills and stream. Magpies chattered nearby. A hawk looked down on her from a yellow pine. Then a flock of geese flew low over her head, honking wildly.

They were changing positions in mid-flight. Geese fly for very long distances, often into the wind. They rotate their positions. When the lead goose tires, it shifts back to a place of more ease letting another goose lead the flock. With this gift of their medicine teaching, Cailleen rose and walked back to the house.

She passed Yvonne coming out as she walked in. "Going to do a little retail therapy and pick up some things for dinner. I'm cooking tonight. I'll be back in a few hours," she called behind her. Yvonne worked hard all week as a paralegal for a prominent Seattle law firm. She liked her work, but she worked with people who were very intense and focused. On the weekends, her bliss was wandering through a farmer's market or exploring tiny shops in small towns where no one knew her.

She'd found Lawrence during one of her wanderings. He actually rescued her from a woman trying to walk three dogs on a busy sidewalk in Magnolia. Yvonne had her hands full of packages when the dogs tangled their leashes around her. Lawrence calmed the woman and the dogs, and then extricated

Yvonne from the tangle. "You must be magic," she laughed. He smiled a crooked smile and said, "You have no idea." They shared coffee and have been together ever since.

Lawrence was indeed magic and practiced it as a spiritual tradition. Yvonne was a little curious, but mostly left him to it. She was happy he had something he loved and special people to share that love with. She was thrilled at how easily they accepted her as part of the group without pressuring her to join in their work. This weekend, she had the bonus of spending time with Lawrence's little family and also having this delightful shopping time to herself.

As Cailleen came back into the house, her friends rose and began heading to her study. "Stay," she said. "I feel the need of the comfort of a warm kitchen. Is there any tea left?" Lawrence rose to fill her cup and put more water on for a new pot. Jen left and came back a moment later with paper, pens and her tarot deck in hand.

"What's on the agenda this morning?" Jen asked.

"Let's start with an overview of what information we have," Cailleen replied. "Then I'll tell you the three steps I see that must be taken. We'll see where that takes us."

As tea was being poured, Cailleen gathered the elements in the center of the table. She'd learned long ago that things went more smoothly when they took a moment to recognize the elemental help available to them at all times. She went to the pantry and grabbed dried kelp for the West, cornmeal for the North, lavender for the East, and cayenne for the South. She set a small plate in the center of the table and poured each of the elemental substances in their corresponding directions. Then she took her finger and made a circle through the piles to remind them that all things are connected. The circle then represented the Center. She returned the containers to the pantry and grabbed some rosemary leaves. When she turned back to the table, Lawrence was placing four small candles in each direction. She nodded at him to light them.

"Welcome East," Lawrence began as he moved clockwise lighting each candle. "We thank you for the inspiration and clarity you bring. Welcome South. We thank you for the healing and playfulness you bring. Welcome West. We thank you for the cleansing and transformation you bring. Welcome North. We thank you for the wisdom and guidance of the ancestors."

Lawrence held his hands out and everyone clasped hands at his prompting. Before joining hands, Cailleen placed the rosemary leaves in the center of the plate and said, "Rosemary for remembering our purpose and help in remembering from the past what needs to now be revealed." With their hands clasped now in a circle, Lawrence concluded, "Welcome, Center and Spirit. Thank you for the deep connection and support you bring. Blessed be." They all responded, "Blessed be," and took their seats.

"Charles and I talked this morning," Cailleen began. "We both know the entire story, otherwise known as the family secret. Charles was my son in the lifetime where the story began. He has been dreaming it for the last five years. I am bound it seems by tradition to keep the story secret. I have received two warnings not to reveal it. I have decided to honor that tradition."

She looked at both Jen and Lawrence and registered both their disappointment and their acceptance.

"The dreams you each received also indicate that you are allies in this quest," she continued. I thank you for coming here today. You are not bound to this quest, however. I want to make that clear."

"But you'll let us help? I know I'm supposed to help," Jen declared. Lawrence patted her hand, then looked at Cailleen. "Me too," he said.

"Again, thank you," Cailleen smiled. "I'll take whatever you can give freely. I don't know what you will be allowed to do and I don't know what I'll be required to do myself.

"Here's what I do know. Jen, your dream suggests that you were charged with this same quest in another lifetime. Although I think perhaps you misinterpreted your role. I feel certain that only three people – we'll tell you more about them, later - and their reincarnations are able to complete the quest. I am one of the three. I do not believe you are, Jen. I think instead you were to pass the secret onto the next generation. As it has been passed to me, I assume you did that. However, you may have also been sent to help whoever was charged with the quest. In either case, you do have access to the family secret. I cannot tell it to you, but you can recover the information yourself from that lifetime. But I am not sure you really need the information in order to help me. Charles?"

"You are right about the three needing to be the ones to resolve the past," he said. "I have never sensed any of the three in you, Jen. Cailleen is one of them. The soul of the second never passed to the other side. I was at his death and know that for certain. He cannot be reincarnated. The third I knew quite well and his resonance does not match yours. But I do feel certain you have a part to play. You have been given another chance to choose to play it. I'm happy to have you with us."

"Does this resonate with you, Jen?" Cailleen asked.

"Yes, it does," she agreed. "And I feel relieved to be playing a lesser part."

"Smaller perhaps," Cailleen corrected. "But all parts have equal significance if without them the task cannot be completed."

"Lawrence, it seems clear that you are also sent to help in this quest. And if my pride gets in the way of allowing you to do so, I trust you'll find a way around me. You seem to be the clearest individual here, at least in terms of emotional attachment. We may need you most of all." Cailleen extended her hand and squeezed his as he laid it in hers.

"So, we have a band of questers - only one of whom is charged with completing the quest," Cailleen continued. "Something bothers me: the coincidence of your dreams and the revelation of my quest seem to me just a little too neatly tied together. It's possible that a powerful shaman has interfered. It is unclear to me whether this is help or hindrance. But I'd like to ask each of you to set protective shields whenever you sleep or do journeywork."

Cailleen paused for a moment to reflect on what Charles had shared with her this morning about Raneck. She had not remembered him as particularly manipulative. She did acknowledge that she had removed herself from so much in that lifetime that she may not have noticed it. And Raneck may have changed after her death. Her heart told her to trust Charles in this. With a deep breath, Cailleen nodded to herself and opened her eyes. Looking directly at Charles, she continued.

"The shaman that I suspect is one of the three. He has a history of manipulating people for his own purposes. I do not believe at this point that we can assume he is clear enough to know whether or not he is causing harm. He has an agenda that may or may not serve us, so let's be cautious." She looked around the circle now for comments.

Jen and Lawrence looked from Cailleen to Charles. Charles closed his eyes and silently asked the Cranes to help him stay in the spirit of love and compassion. Then he said, "I agree. We cannot trust in his ability to be clear or that his agenda will serve us. Although we both have knowledge and experience of him, we cannot know how centuries of holding on to the earthly realm has affected him. I cannot fathom why he chose not to pass through to the other side. I simply do not know what powers he may still possess or how controlled they may be. It might be best if he doesn't know we're even aware of him."

"I want him to know I am aware of him," Cailleen said. "It feels like the time to have all the cards on the table. From now on, however, our conversations and work will be done within a sacred and protected circle. Let's take a break now and meet in the study in about 30 minutes. We'll set our circle in there and leave the kitchen to Yvonne. I'll make some sandwiches for later. Do we want more tea or shall we make do with water?"

Cailleen left Jen to set a protective circle as she considered what must be done to start on this quest. Of course, she reflected, the quest was begun generations ago. But her part in this lifetime required some thought. As she waited for Jen to complete the circle, she glanced out the window and saw the geese once more. "OK," she whispered to them, "I get your point." She walked outside to get some fresh air.

Raneck saw her walk outside the protection of the house. She needed him. He was sure of it. She used to have such power. She could have that kind of power now, but she still refused to use it. He was disgusted by the waste.

And Chalic, it seemed, had found his beloved mother. They deserved each other! Neither of them understood the discipline and sacrifice that was necessary to meet the vows of a Senechal. He'd met his. He'd sacrificed more than anyone should expect. Yet here he was, stuck between the worlds; not fully embodied and not crossed over into the spirit world.

It has been too long, he thought to himself. I cannot hold myself together without tapping into other energies. Pure energies are not easy to find. He'd found one source, but she was very inexperienced.

Raneck watched Calleigha wander through her garden, carelessly brushing her hands through the rosemary bush and inhaling deeply. "Yes," he whispered, "remember who you are, your power, your inheritance." Maybe, he thought to himself, if he could tap into her energy, they could finally be together and do powerful magic. He licked his almost lips and felt rage at not being able to finish their work together.

The rage only weakened him. He could feel himself fading away. He didn't even have the strength to approach a semi-powerful witch in this time. He needed to go draw strength from his source.

Cailleen shivered and glanced around her for the source of the disturbance she felt. Rosey, who had followed her into the garden, stood on point with her hair raised and a low growl in her throat. "Come on girl," Cailleen said, "let's go back inside." Rosey barked her approval and headed to the house.

***

Jen completed the circle and nodded at the other three. "What's next?" she asked.

Cailleen and Rosey wandered into the study just as she asked. "I took a walk after breakfast to do some thinking and that's the question I asked. What's next? The geese answered me. As you know, geese shift the leadership position as they migrate. The goose at the lead works the hardest and those in the back work the least. As the leader tires he or she drops back and lets someone else take the lead. I think they have given this medicine to us for this quest. And although I anticipate I will be required to take the lead most often, I also anticipate dropping back when I need to.

"I have a question to throw out to you," she continued. "As I mentioned earlier, the coincidence of the dreams seems contrived. But I believe the information within the dreams to be valid. When I spoke about the shaman I suspect of interfering, I felt a very strong and slightly threatening presence. Did any of you feel anything?"

"Yes," Lawrence affirmed. "I found myself looking over my shoulder as I gathered things for our session here. I don't feel threatened so much as watched. Within the circle I do not feel it, but I sense he waits."

"I feel uncomfortable in my skin," Jen agreed. "But I would have that response as a result of Lawrence's discomfort. I'm not sure I perceive anything distinct from what I feel from Lawrence."

"I not only felt it, I can identify it," Charles declared. "Raneck, the

Senechal, watches. I remember well the feeling of being watched by this particular shaman. He knows a crossroads is upon us and this may be the last opportunity to bring things back into balance. He will manipulate us to do things his way, if he can. He had great power in his time, and perhaps still does. As I said before, we cannot trust his clarity, nor can we assume he has our best interests in mind."

"He must want it all to end," Jen said sympathetically. "Hundreds of years is a long time to hover neither here nor there. I also think his powers *are* limited. He can trigger dreams, but can he enter them? I felt no such presence in mine. I wonder what his role in all of this is? We cannot simply banish him, not if he has a part to play. He has a choice to make and I think we need to help him make it. What stands in the way of his clarity?"

"Pride and hunger," Cailleen and Charles said together.

"Are you sure you're clear when it comes to him?" Lawrence asked them.

"A fair question," Cailleen answered. "I loved him. He was my teacher and mentor. He helped me to develop and use my power as a Healer and Song Carrier. He saw my power and longed to combine it with his. It blinded him to other important matters. He initiated me too early and as a result I was banished. He never got over the loss. He keeps trying to recoup it. I truly believe he meant no harm and I suspect he won't stop until he can correct his mistake. And, he still may be holding on to the hope of combining our powers. That may be where the danger lies."

"I agree he is dangerous," Charles whispered. "I may even be convinced that he *meant* no harm. But harm he did and he must pay the consequences. He held the leadership and the power; he must bear the responsibility."

"Perhaps that is exactly what he's been doing for hundreds of years," Jen suggested. "I have been taught by my Teacher," she continued, with a glance at Cailleen, "that things are seldom as complicated or as simple as they might seem. Every story has many sides and we often operate from more than one motive. He has an undeniable part in this story. Shall we see him as ally or enemy? I feel he is an important ally, although perhaps a difficult one."

"You make a point," Cailleen conceded. "You also have an ability that neither Charles or I have to be detached about his role. He may be able to be more detached about you as well. What do you think about doing a little psychic research? You have access to the story and him through your past life. Can you and Lawrence do some journeying to get a clearer picture about his role?"

Jen and Lawrence did their "twins communication" and then both nodded. "We can give it a go in the next couple days," Jen promised.

"Good," Cailleen said. "I would like to transcribe the tape from my Grandmother that started all this and compare it with the dreams and visions we've all had. I think that perhaps looking at them all together will reveal more clues. We know where two of the three are in this lifetime. I am one and we know that Raneck is hovering and aware of the timing. Any thoughts about the third?"

"I wonder about James," Lawrence said. "His arrival on the scene is interesting, at least. Breakfast held its fair share of intrigue and secrets. They almost floated on the air around us. Who is this guy?"

"He is not Chancha," Charles declared. "Stubborn and flawed he might be, but I trust Chancha. I don't trust James McEwan."

Jen shook her head. "Guys and testosterone – gets in the way of common sense."

"Well, that's helpful," Lawrence answered. "If you're so smart, teach us, oh wise one."

"Just stop being watchdogs and use your eyes," Jen suggested. She walked over and stood behind Cailleen, then gently massaged her shoulders. She sensed that Cailleen would need not magical, but emotional support around James McEwan. The sparks between the two were obvious and it would be interesting to see what they were all about.

Lawrence and Charles looked at each other and shrugged their shoulders. "Do you know what she's talking about?" Charles asked. "No idea," Lawrence answered. "She's raised the *girls only* wall. That's impenetrable," Lawrence answered.

"Cailleen, you haven't said anything. What are your thoughts?" Charles asked. "I know you feel threatened by him."

She squared her shoulders in an unconscious pose of defense. "He surprised and startled me this morning. I was expecting Yvonne at the door. I didn't like facing a stranger in my fluffy purple robe and wool socks. I was mad at myself for not feeling his presence through the door before I opened it. That's all," she said firmly. "I am not threatened by James McEwan."

"You certainly went to a bit of trouble to put him in his place, my queen," Charles snapped. Cailleen blushed at the truth in his statement.

"James McEwan is arrogant and likes to make assumptions" she responded. "I find it irritating when strangers come to my home with such attitudes. I can tell you that I have never met James McEwan in this or any other life. I also can tell you he wants something from me and I mean to find out what that is sooner than later. I do not like being checked out and judged. That's what I feel from him. Other than that, I find him a distraction from this work. He has no part in it, so I sent him packing."

In a faraway voice Jen spoke. "Do not dismiss this man. He has several parts to play."

"What?" all three asked in unison.

Jen stood slightly slumped against Cailleen's chair and unaware of her surroundings. She had a faraway look in her eyes. The intense focus of the other three brought her back to the present. With a slight shake, she stood up straight, and walked over to her chair.

"What?" Jen asked in her normal voice.

"She was channeling," Lawrence interpreted. "Jen, you just said, 'Do not dismiss this man. He has several parts to play.'"

"Oh," she said, sitting down. "Well, we'd best not dismiss him then."

"I'll take a walk to the bungalow before dinner and get some answers," Charles said. "You want to come, Lawrence?"

"No, he doesn't," Jen declared, shaking her head at them both. "You will both stay here. Cailleen will go talk to him when the time is right," she said with a secretive smile.

"I suppose I should be the one to do it," Cailleen admitted. "He's my neighbor, and this is my quest. If there's time, I'll walk down before dinner. Before that, however, I would like a little more information. Jen, can you tap back in to whoever spoke through you?" Cailleen asked.

"I can try." Jen focused and slipped into a trance. After a few moments she opened her eyes. "I'm getting nothing," she said. "Did you pick up anything, Lawrence?" she asked.

"Nothing," Lawrence said.

"Let's see if the cards can shed any light on my new neighbor," Cailleen said as she shuffled and then laid out three cards. "*Gathering, Awakening* and *Commitment.*"

They all looked at the cards, each contemplating their meaning.

"Gathering what? Awakening who, or to what? Commitment to who or what?" Lawrence wondered aloud.

"His presence has already affected us," Jen said simply. "He made Cailleen gather herself in an unexpected way this morning. He awakened the protective nature of our boys here," she said waving at Charles and Lawrence. "And, I think it's interesting that he has entered our little world at the same time that all our relationships are changing. This always brings up questions of commitment and levels of commitment."

"None of that has anything to do directly with the quest. At least, not necessarily," Charles said.

"Not necessarily," Lawrence agreed, "however, he's also shown up when the three seem to be gathering, when Charles and Cailleen have awakened to their past life relationships and when we are all being asked how we will choose to commit to this quest."

Cailleen walked to the window. She could feel windows getting ready to open within her. Some of the windows felt familiar, but one very big window had been nailed shut and never opened. She both feared and longed for this opening. Something told her that James might be the one to open it.

Looking toward where his cottage sat, she sighed. "The bottom line is that he showed up on my door as I am being called to gather my allies, awaken to a new power in my gifts and make some kind of commitment. None of it is very clear at this time, but I cannot dismiss the timing, nor my strong reaction to his appearance. It seems Mr. McEwan does play a part. This is not convenient." She continued to gaze in the direction of the cottage. She wasn't sure if she wanted to reach out, or to turn her back to it. She sighed again.

Charles and Lawrence looked up in confusion. They had never seen Cailleen so uncertain, nor had they seen her wistful and maybe a little afraid. Charles wanted to just wash away the doubt and make her smile again. Lawrence searched for some solid advice to offer.

Jen smiled. Cailleen looked downright womanly – wistful, almost weepy and softer than she'd ever seen her. James McEwen enters stage left and shifts the texture of the entire play, she thought dramatically. Time will tell, she thought, but it looks as if Cailleen is in for a new kind of adventure. Jen was delighted to have a front row seat.

***

After a break for sandwiches and fresh air, the four gathered back in the study. They sat in silent contemplation, each lost in their own thoughts, for about 20 minutes.

"I think we should visit Elan," Charles suggested. "This is Cailleen's quest, but we are most powerful together. I wonder even if we have been called together in this lifetime for this specific purpose. Our roads have crossed and the path before us is unclear. A visit to the one who guards the paths and guides the journeyers seems timely. What do you all think?"

They all shook their heads in agreement.

"Twilight or midnight," Cailleen asked. "We might as well take advantage of a crossroads to travel to the crossroads."

"Twilight will be warmer," Jen suggested. "I assume we'll go to the grove?"

"Twilight it is," Cailleen said. "I'll go down and visit my new neighbor and tell him to stay clear. Let's all get some rest and meet at twilight in the grove."

"I'll ask Yvonne to delay dinner," Lawrence said, smiling at the thought of seeing her again and hearing about her day. She'd have new treasures to show him.

***

The afternoon sun felt warm and comforting. Cailleen paused for a while to soak in the October brilliance. She inhaled the fecund smell of plants returning themselves to the earth after the harvest. Some people thought it depressing to see the plants dying, but Cailleen felt great hope in their surrender to the cycle of nature – life, death and eventual rebirth. They took their energies back into the earth so that in the spring new life would flourish once again. This is why she loved being a witch. The deep connection to the cycles of nature made her aware that all things live and die in a constant cycle of transformation. The quest ahead of her was another turn in that cycle. She spread her arms with hands extended in a position of acceptance for all the abundance surrounding her. She spun slowly around in acknowledgment of this abundance and of her willingness to continue walking with the cycles of Nature.

A leaf fell from a tree next to her and she watched its flight. Gravity pulled it to the earth, then the air lifted and spun it in a spiral. Gravity pulled again and the leaf surrendered, then turned another spiral as it continued to earth. Wind came to lift the leaf high again in a beautiful spiral dance. Gravity took the leaf again, but it fell to earth in the arms of the spiral.

Cailleen saw a message from the elements in this spiral dance of the leaf. She would let her friends be the gravity that grounded and called her home. She would dance along the spiral of her past and present, allowing the journey to be graceful. She would do her best to stay out of resistance and let herself be transported where Spirit led. She thanked the tree for the gift of its leaf and tucked it in her pocket to place on her altar as a reminder. With a nod of completion, she pulled her cloak more securely around her.

She continued now toward the forest, greeting the trees as she went. They moved in welcome and she let the wind embrace her. The wind brought her news of berries yet to be picked over by the birds and of a new resident in the area; the smell of the fire from the bungalow announced James' presence. But just in case she missed that, the crows and ravens were excitedly cawing out the news.

Cailleen drew herself in and put up an energetic shield around her body. She didn't like doing that in her forest, but it was necessary in an unknown situation. She approached the bungalow from downwind. She wanted an opportunity to observe James undetected if at all possible. And she got her chance. As she approached, she heard the sounds of chopping wood and walked to the back of the bungalow.

James wore jeans and a t-shirt. He'd been at it for a while. His coat and blue flannel shirt had been discarded next to an impressive pile of split wood. The muscles in his body gathered tension as he inhaled and then let go in disciplined force with his exhalation. With each exhale, he swung his ax down, splitting through a log. He smiled at the satisfying sound of ax splitting through wood.

Cailleen watched for several minutes as he continued chopping. He had a great body for a man his age – for any age. And he moved with a grace that mesmerized her; such fluidity in all that strength. She couldn't deny she found him physically attractive. Since he wasn't drowning her in his eyes or irritating her with his arrogance, she quite enjoyed him. He looked in his element. So she just leaned against a tree and watched. She didn't want to interrupt his momentum, she told herself.

James knew he was being watched. The hairs on the back of his neck rose and he opened his senses to define the intruder. He used his inhale as he prepared to swing his ax to draw in any scent. The scent of roses and nag champa tickled his nose. Cailleen was here. It irritated him that he already recognized her scent. No, that wasn't surprising. They didn't call him the wolf at the police station for nothing. It irritated him that her scent got under his skin. He didn't trust it. He couldn't afford to trust her. He was here to do a job and someone's life was at stake - three lives were at stake. He couldn't let them down by letting his guard slip because he found the woman, he was investigating, attractive.

He bent to pick up a piece of the split wood and turned to throw it near the place where he could feel her standing. It landed within inches, but she didn't flinch. She held her ground. Damn she looked sexy, casually leaning against a tree as if it was an old friend. After reading some of her writing, he thought it just might be an old friend. She didn't flinch from the toss but she also didn't raise her guard quickly enough. He caught the desire in her eyes and stance before she veiled them. He might as well use it, he thought.

James swung the ax over his shoulder and sauntered towards her. He stopped near his shirt and coat. With a quick nod he acknowledged her, then turned away and set the ax down. He grabbed a bottle of water and drank deeply, then leisurely put on his flannel shirt. He threw his coat on top of the wheel barrel loaded with wood, grabbed its handles and headed toward the back door. As he passed her, he nodded toward the bungalow.

"I could put on the kettle if you're staying," he said with warmth and openness.

She didn't speak but followed him, wondering what he was playing at. Gone was the arrogance and formality. Instead, she found a sexy neighborliness. Had he just posed for her so she could admire his physique? She was pretty sure he had. He was wasting his time if he thought he could play her.

As she stepped into his tiny house she was overwhelmed by his presence – all male. He smelled of sweat and wood smoke and All Spice. He smiled a lazy smile at her.

"Not as big and fancy as your place, but it suits me for the time being. I'm going to go change out of this damp shirt. Back in a minute," he said as he put the pot on to boil.

She hadn't realized she was holding her breath until he left the room. "Damn, he's good," she thought. But two could play this game. She draped her coat on a chair and then started putting together things for tea. A woman making herself at home in a man's kitchen could undo him. She started humming softly under her breath for added effect.

She was pouring water into the teapot when he returned. Her back was turned and he allowed himself a moment to simply watch her. Her movements were functional, efficient, and very feminine. He let his eyes travel down her body and they rested on her full, round buttocks. She moved it in time to the tune she was humming and he was instantly aroused. He walked silently toward her and stopped a few inches behind her.

She froze for a moment, then forced herself to relax. She wanted to see how far he'd play this game. She let her breath come out a little ragged and then moved a fraction closer to him. She reached for the tray with the intention of turning nonchalantly and taking the tea to the table. But he was faster. With one smooth move he lifted her hair and softly kissed the back of her neck. She heard herself purr and eased back into him.

James put his arms around her and gathered her in. He inhaled the scent of her and nearly lost himself. With more control than he thought he had, he reined himself in. He spun her around, kissed her on the cheek in an almost brotherly way, and pushed her gently toward the table.

"Thanks for filling the pot," he said sweetly, as if no sexual tension had passed between them. "I can offer you some cookies, too, if you'd like."

She'd nearly stumbled when he nudged her toward the table. She felt like a mouse being played with by a very large cat. By the time she sat down she'd regained her composure, but her Irish was up now. She would not be played with like some silly schoolgirl. She smiled sweetly at him, but there was steel in her eyes.

"Thanks, but the tea will be fine. I just came by to tell you the grove in the forest is off limits tonight at twilight as well as on Samhain in two weeks, and well, on full moons, too. We often do work in that spot and guests are not welcome. I'm sure you understand."

"Certainly, no problem," he agreed. "Sugar?"

His agreeableness irritated her. But she was in his home and she would remain polite.

"How are you settling in?" she asked.

"Well enough," he answered. "I have to adjust to a bath instead of a shower, but it'll do."

Small talk! She despised small talk. But she might as well use it to her advantage, she thought.

"You didn't say at breakfast what brought you to this valley," she said.

"No one asked," he smiled.

"I'm asking now," she smiled back.

"I had a tough couple of months and decided I'd earned some time off."

"Time off from what?"

"I'm a police detective, semi-retired actually. I officially retired from the force about a year ago, but I keep getting called back in when they need an expert."

"And what is your expertise?" she asked.

"It's not an area of police work so much as a particular talent. They call me *the Wolf*," he said, then paused. "I can scent out a trail and almost always find what I seek. They call me in on difficult cases, or when a suspect seems particularly wily. Once on the trail, I don't stop until I find what I'm after." He paused again and she held the silence.

"But now I'm away from it all and enjoying the fresh air and peace." He stood up at that and took his cup to the sink. "I have a lot of wood to stack before it gets dark. If you don't mind, I'll get back to it."

"I have things to do myself," she said. "Thanks for the tea."

"You're most welcome." He smiled that lazy smile at her again and then held the door for her.

She walked to him slowly and turned to face him squarely. She treated him with a slow smile and a lift of her eyebrows and then turned on her heels with a cheery, "thanks again." As she stepped out the door, he grabbed her and kissed her hard. Then he turned the kiss into a slow, sensual exploration of her mouth and his hands went to her hips. He pressed her against the door. He ended the kiss, whispered "my pleasure," and then walked over and started stacking wood.

When she could walk without stumbling from weak knees, Cailleen glided back into the forest and returned to her own house. She took her time so she could regain her composure. She knew three sets of eyes would be looking for her when she returned. Four sets, if Yvonne was back from shopping. To avoid those eyes, she went to the front door and then up to her room. Being surrounded by highly intuitive and psychic friends had its drawbacks! Sometimes privacy could be an issue. She wanted to keep her encounter with James private.

Yvonne waited as Charles watched for Cailleen's return. When he stirred, she went with him to the window. They watched Cailleen emerge from the forest and walk to the front of the house. Charles moved to intercept her. Yvonne stopped him.

"How did you and Whitney find privacy when Cailleen was around?" she asked him. The mention of Whitney's name stopped him cold. He turned to her in question.

"What do you mean?" he asked. "Cailleen never intruded between us."

"You might do the same for her, Charles."

"I don't understand what you're talking about."

"She likes him, Charles. Cailleen likes James McEwan. I'm not sure she's fully aware of it yet, but she likes him."

"How could you possibly know that?" he demanded.

"I've got eyes, haven't I? You don't really need psychic powers for this one," she said.

Charles turned and looked to Jen, and then to Lawrence, who looked as confused as Charles felt. Then a light bulb clicked on over Lawrence and he nodded as he said, "Oh, I get it."

"What do you get?" Charles asked.

In unison Jen and Lawrence said, "Yvonne's right. Let her be."

"This is private and they don't need a physical or a psychic audience while they figure things out," Jen continued.

"Give her space, brother," Lawrence pleaded.

"But we don't know who this guy is or what he wants from her," Charles argued. "He's a wolf and he's hiding something. Besides, she doesn't have time right now to deal with romantic distractions."

"Charles, how do you know this isn't part of her quest," Lawrence countered. "Cailleen seems quite content in her work and she has us. But haven't you ever wondered why she doesn't have a partner? Maybe it's not her path, but maybe she focuses too much on her work and responsibilities. Maybe she needs to find out which is her *good road*. If James is here to facilitate that question it would be in alignment with the cards. Think about it: *Awakening* her to romantic possibilities, asking her to *Challenge* her levels of *Commitment*. I could be way off, but what if I'm not?" he asked.

"I don't know what to do." Charles replied, pacing. "My instincts are to guard her, but that may just get in her way. When in doubt, do nothing. That's the Healer's rule. So, for now, I'll do nothing. I'm going to go take a nap," he said, and left the room.

"Nice work, love," Yvonne said, then reached up to kiss Lawrence. "Shall we get a nap in too?"

"Sure," Lawrence smiled and walked with her to their room.

"That wasn't as much work as I anticipated," Jen said to herself. "Nap time for me, too."

***

James finished stacking the wood at the back of the house. Despite all the physical activity of the afternoon he felt restless. Emotions seemed to surround this case and he didn't like it one bit. A good investigator kept emotions out of his work. But he knew going in that he couldn't escape an emotional aspect to this case.

This wasn't a professional case but a favor for an old friend. Ben's daughter, Lily, was wasting away, and the doctors could do nothing. Camille, Ben's wife, saw Cailleen on some talk show and wanted to ask her to do a healing on Lily. Ben couldn't stand the idea of some charlatan raising her hopes and taking money for doing it. When Ben said no, Camille fell apart. She couldn't just sit by and do nothing, she told him.

Throughout Lily's illness, Camille had been a rock. She shed tears and lost her temper now and then, but she'd never collapsed in a puddle of tears and cried for what seemed hours. Ben couldn't stand that either. So he called James to have a drink and asked him to check Cailleen out as thoroughly as possible. James suggested a colleague instead, but Ben said he wouldn't really trust anyone else for this. James had a nose for detecting cons, and he knew Lily and cared about what happened to her. If James trusted this woman, Ben would feel much better about asking her for help.

"What if I don't trust her?" James asked him.

"I'll probably ask her to help anyway," Ben told him. "But I'll watch her every minute and I'll sue her ass for fraud if she harms Lily or Camille."

The pain and pleading in Ben's voice pierced James' heart, so he agreed to do what he could. When he found out she lived over the mountains near where he went fishing with his dad every summer, James decided to take a few weeks and get away. When he rented the bungalow next to her property, he thought it was a perfect cover. He could get neighborly and really see who this woman was. He hadn't counted on encountering a protective pack. Charles acted the guard dog at breakfast, but he had no doubt that Jen and Lawrence, and even Yvonne, would bare their teeth, if necessary.

Suddenly he felt way too close to the case. A bit more distance might have been helpful. But he couldn't change that now. And he couldn't change the fact that Cailleen pulled at him like no woman had in a very long time. And he'd acted like a teenager who couldn't control his hormones. She deliberately baited him and he'd fallen for it. He'd been a calculating ass and she got the best of him. Now he'd have to apologize. If she shared their encounter with the pack, he'd have to do more than that.

He'd deal with that later. Right now, he had to do something proactive on the case. He'd make dinner and work his way through more of her books. He felt better with a plan, and walked into the house with purpose. But his senses were assaulted by her scent as he entered the kitchen. It reminded him of the taste of her lips - sweet and spicy. He could feel the curve of her hips under his hands and the softness of her breasts as he'd pulled her into him. She hadn't resisted. She was taken aback, but stood her ground. Self-preservation was the only thing that made him pull back as her response to him flared. The thought of Lily made him allow Cailleen to walk back into her forest.

James was quickly acknowledging that Cailleen had some real power. But people with power often abused it. He'd been around her for only a few hours and already felt a pull to do things out of the ordinary. It wasn't like him to play with a woman. He felt dishonorable and just a bit slimy. He didn't really do anything out of line, specifically. He just felt out of control with this. And he'd never felt out of control on a case. It must be something she was doing. Was she manipulating him? Without a doubt she'd been testing him. That was clear and he didn't like it one bit.

Her scent disturbed his senses, her eyes were bewitching and the way she moved made his mouth water. To be fair, she wasn't the first woman to arouse him in such ways. Perhaps she was just a woman. No, he'd never believe that. She was extraordinary. But that didn't mean she wasn't manipulative. It was her vulnerability under all that power; that's what moved him. He sensed that she needed him, but in what way? Why did she have to complicate matters? He didn't want to like her. He wanted to observe her and report back to Ben. He wanted to do his job and move on. But, move on to what? He needed something new, something interesting in his life. He didn't want complicated.

"Damn, I don't need this right now!" he shouted to the room. Then he grabbed his coat and stormed out the door. He had to do something productive, so he decided to scope out the forest and find the grove he was asked to avoid. Who knows, there might be some clue to who and what she really was. He didn't know which way the grove lay but guessed she might have walked past to check the area during her walk. So he followed her scent and picked up her trail. "I *am* part wolf," he laughed to himself.

James found a path and followed it into the forest. He didn't really know what to expect. All the Hollywood scenes of witches and worse flashed through his mind, but he set them aside so he could be objective. With senses alert, he continued.

The forest thickened and eerie shadows were cast in the late afternoon sun. But the overall feeling of it was peaceful. James stayed alert but relaxed his body more. Crows and ravens announced his presence as he continued along. He heard the scurry of small animals and saw fresh deer tracks. As he crossed a stream, the path rose gently before him. On the top of a hill, he saw an opening in the forest. Here the trees became watchful but not threatening. He slowed his steps to take in everything.

Serene beauty greeted him as he stepped into the grove. It took his breath away. He stood under a circle of eight large cedar trees whose branches created a loose canopy overhead. Sun, star and moonlight would easily find their way into the circle. A circle of large river stones lay within the circle of trees. In the North a decaying tree stump sat. Several saplings grew out of the stump, and in its hollow, crystals sat among moss. In the West sat a larger stone with a shallow dish that held rainwater. In the East stood two poles with feathers and bells tied to them. The poles were about three feet apart and seemed to be the entrance into the circle. In the South was a fire pit outlined with red rocks. Another larger fire pit sat in the center of the circle. River rocks inside a circle of handmade stepping stones defined this one. Each handmade stepping stone seemed to be made of plaster and was decorated with shards of glass, semi-precious stones, imprints of leaves, and other odd bits. It looked as if some were made by children. Together they spoke of love, connection and community. The stones were set carefully into the earth about a foot apart.

James did not step inside the circle. It felt like a kind of church to him, only deeper and older. He also felt a gentle watchfulness in the grove and he didn't want to offend anyone. He didn't know the protocols for entering the circle, so he remained outside it. He didn't know what "work" they might be doing here tonight but it was already getting cold. He saw no wood for a fire.

Partly as a token apology and partly to secure his role as a good neighbor, James walked back to his cottage to get some wood. He didn't know where this case would take him, but he'd learned long ago to smooth things out as you went along.

His mother taught him that as a young boy. When she was diagnosed with terminal cancer, he hadn't taken it well. He skipped school. He blamed his dad for not protecting her. He was mad at everyone and was making a mess out of his life. He remembered the shame he felt when she called him to her bedside the day she returned from the hospital.

The memory brought back the scent of her sick room. The acrid smell of medicines mixed with the overly sweet smell of flowers that friends and family sent. To this day, that scent made him immediately feel like a helpless 13-year-old boy. He could face down a criminal with a gun more easily than he could face a sick room. And now, Lily was sick.

But he didn't want to think about Lily right now, or how ill she was. He didn't want to feel helpless now, any more than he did when his mother was ill. He still missed her. Because he had always loved and adored her, he remembered her with deep reverence and treasured the gifts she gave him, including the lesson to clean up your messes as you go.

She had looked at him with love and understanding. She took his hand and smiled. She told him how difficult she knew it was to adjust to the changes in their lives. And then she got that no nonsense look on her face. "You can't go around making everybody else suffer, just because you are suffering. This is difficult for all of us. We'll have to be gentle with each other and ourselves. When we act inappropriately and hurt people's feelings, or act out in other ways, we have to make amends for it. It's best to do it as quickly as possible – best for you and best for those you've hurt. Now, talk to me son. Let's work out the feelings and then you can get on with sorting the rest of it out."

They talked until his mother couldn't keep her eyes open. She explained how she got sick and that it was not his father's fault. She told him that no one could protect her from cancer. She had it and they would just have to deal with it, together. She urged him to apologize to his father as soon as possible, because if she didn't make it, they would be the only family either of them had, and she didn't want to leave this world worrying about how they'd get on.

After she fell asleep, he sat there for a while and considered all the messes he had made in the last week. Admitting them to himself was the first step. He squared his shoulders and stepped into manhood that night.

He entered his father's study and simply said, "I'm sorry Dad. I know it's not your fault that mom's sick and I'll try to be more helpful from now on. I think I'll go do my homework and then write an apology note to my teacher."

His dad didn't speak. He embraced James and held him fast for a moment or two, taking the strength he offered. Then he chucked him gently under the chin in their familiar way and nodded. From that point on, they were in it together. Together, father and son navigated his mother's death, the funeral, picking up their lives, the teenage years, college, his decision to become a cop,

Dad's retirement and the other ups and downs of life. Today, he missed his dad even more than he'd missed his mom when she passed.

Now, the only family James really had was Ben, Camille and Lily. His life as an undercover cop didn't really lend itself to creating family and deep friendships. He felt lucky to have such a deep friend in Ben and happy for the little family they made together.

As he emptied the cart of firewood up by the grove, he admitted to himself that witnessing the close ties of Cailleen and her friends had touched a deep need in him. It was time for him to create a different kind of life. Maybe the time in his cottage in the woods would give him some answers. He had to look like a man on vacation to maintain his cover, so he might as well put the time to good use.

He also had to admit, he was becoming quite curious about Cailleen and the work that she did. He never would have imagined himself delving into such a world. But here he was. His natural curiosity and his experience doing undercover work would help him explore this new territory. He felt confident.

James walked around the grove one last time and then headed home feeling calm and lighthearted. He might have stayed longer if it wasn't so close to twilight. The beauty of the place both opened his heart and helped him release the last pain of losing his parents. There would be other times to enjoy the grove. He would ask about the protocols of the circle so he might come again without fear of doing something inappropriate.

This time he was prepared for Cailleen's lingering scent in the cabin. He couldn't resist inhaling it, but it didn't stop him from making dinner and continuing with his research. He fell asleep within minutes of opening her next book. An hour later the sound of drumming and singing woke him.

***

Dressed in comfortable warm clothing, Cailleen walked the path toward the grove just before twilight. As she neared, she heard Jen and Charles discussing a fire. They had not entered the grove yet.

"I thought I heard you say you were bringing some wood for a fire," Jen said.

"I didn't think of it," Charles replied.

"Hold on, I'll see if I can get Lawrence before he heads up," Jen said as she concentrated. "Too late, he's almost here and he says Cailleen's just ahead of him. We might as well wait and we can all decide what we want to do. Let's see if anything else needs to be attended to."

They walked into the grove and right behind them entered Cailleen and Lawrence.

"Merry meet," they said to one another.

"It seems the faeries have anticipated our need," Cailleen said and pointed to the pile of firewood stacked just outside the boundaries of the grove near the south fire pit.

It seems they now use wheel barrels," Charles complained. "The tracks lead back to the bungalow. I thought you told him to stay away from the grove."

"Perhaps what they use, Charles, is thoughtful neighbors," Cailleen replied. "I did ask him to stay away from the grove, at twilight. Twilight is here and James is not. Shall we begin?"

They each went to the pile of wood for a few logs. James had also put smaller kindling and a tin of matches next to the split logs.

"Very thorough as well as thoughtful," Jen said as she picked up the matches and kindling.

"I brought matches and a candle," Lawrence offered. "Shall we put the fire in the center and the candle in the South, or the other way around?"

"Small fire in the center, I think," Cailleen answered. "I'd like us to be sitting in each of the directions and we might all need the warmth of the fire. Lawrence, I see you brought your drum. Would you sit in the East? Jen, I think you should probably sit in the West, where emotions flow. Charles, would you take your *bear* self to the North? I'll sit in the South."

They built the fire and gathered their blankets to each of their respective places. Within minutes they were set. Cailleen slipped into the role of high priestess for this journey.

"Please begin drumming to ground us, and when we're centered call in the East, Lawrence. Since we are here to visit Elan and to understand this crossroads, let's call in the Elements in that manner: East to West and then North to South. We'll sing in the Center together and then I'll walk the circle to seal the sacred space."

Cailleen nodded to Lawrence and he began a slow deep drumbeat. After a few minutes he changed the rhythm and called to the East.

"East, element of Air, I call to you now. Hear this sacred drum and be with us in this hour. Bring to us clarity and inspiration as we travel between the worlds. Be welcome, Air," Lawrence beckoned.

"Be welcome, Air!" the four responded as they felt the air stir around them.

"West, element of Water," Jen called. "I beckon you now. Join us in this sacred work. Help us flow with focused intention. Keep us grounded in our emotions and wash away impediments to our work. Be welcome, Water."

"Be welcome, Water!" the four spoke as gentle drops of condensation fell from the trees.

"North, element of Earth," Charles called in a deep voice. "We gather here among your sacred trees. Ground and protect us as we travel to the crossroads in search of truth and illumination. Come. Support us in our work. Be welcome, Earth."

"Be welcome, Earth!" the four spoke. They felt the roots of the trees weave a supportive net below them as the eight cedar trees encircling the grove became an active part of the circle.

"South, element of Fire," Cailleen called. "Light our way as we travel to the crossroads. Illuminate the path we must take and keep our bodies warm until our return. Be welcome, Fire!"

"Be welcome, Fire!" the four spoke as Cailleen struck a match and lit the candle.

Then Cailleen stepped to the center and lit the kindling. "Here we stand in the twilight - in the Center where East meets West and North meets South. Here, we welcome Spirit."

Cailleen led them in the *Spirit Love* song.

The love that flows through me to you,
That flows through you to me,
Is the Spirit that moves through all things.

After singing the song three times, Cailleen stood. She circled round to stand in the East, and moving clockwise, she sang:

Guardians of the East, inspire and illuminate,
Guardians of the South, transform and heal
Guardians of the West, cleanse and rebirth us,
Guardians of the North, protect and seal.

Cailleen continued around the circle moving just past the East point again to complete the magic circle, which lay inside the sacred circle of trees. Then she turned toward the Center and her three companions. She raised her hands up, drawing the energy of the circle up over their heads and beneath the canopy of the trees. Then she lowered her hands, drawing the energy down to the roots below them, until they stood in a protective sphere.

"The circle is cast in perfect love and perfect trust. We stand between the worlds. What we do here is not affected by the worlds, but ripples out to heal and transform. Blessed be."

"Blessed be," the others answered.

Cailleen took her seat again in the South, next to the fire. Each of the four added a log to the fire and then settled comfortably in their blankets.

"Charles, please lead us in this journey," Cailleen requested.

"Focus your breathing," Charles directed the group. "Send your grounding chords down into Mother Earth and let them branch out, sending a root to the other three in the circle and to the protective tree roots beneath us."

As they moved into trance, Crow cawed above them. Charles smiled.

"Brother Crow offers to lead us. Follow your breath as we shift from this forest to Elan's forest. Smell the oak, hickory and sycamore leaves and hear the bubbling stream nearby." Charles' voice faded as the air shimmered. The four found themselves in the other realm standing on a wide path in a hardwood forest. Crow cawed and flew down the path. They followed.

Up ahead they heard a woman singing an evening song. Charles, who was in the lead, picked up his pace. Across the stream and up an incline they walked. Around a bend they saw her old cottage, which seemed part of the forest. In front of it an old woman sat on a log. She met them with a smile as they approached.

"Merry meet," she greeted.

"Merry meet, Grandmother," they responded.

"Charles, you've brought friends with you. How nice!"

"I am preparing them as you directed, Elan," he replied, sinking to his knees for her blessing. She kissed him on the top of his head, then rose to greet the others.

"Jen, your brave and kind heart will lead you well. Release the past and its regrets." She patted Jen gently on her cheek.

"Lawrence," Elan said, taking his hands, "I see you have found love. You wear it well. Cherish it in both places," she said as she turned to include Jen in her gaze.

"Charles, you come to me much lighter than when I last saw you. You have laid down your burdens. Now you must release your worry. She is stronger than you could ever imagine. Don't tether her with unnecessary emotion."

"Cailleen," she said gazing deep and long into her eyes. "I have waited for you. It's been a long time since we last spoke. I have guided you between the worlds and have watched you on your *good road*. Walk with me a moment." She took Cailleen's arm and led her along a trail into the forest.

"Elan, I cannot see the path I am to walk," Cailleen said. "Can you guide me?"

"Of course, child. That is my purpose. You are quite adept at identifying and pursuing a path. This time, however, the path has found you. He brings you the third and offers you the opportunity to heal the past and balance the present."

"James?" Cailleen asked with surprise.

"James," Elan confirmed.

"He's not Chancha. I'd know if he was."

"No, Cailleen, he is not Chancha. He will bring Chancha to you.

Bringing the three together at this time is only part of the task," Elan continued. "Learn from the past, but look to your present and future to heal it. Look, the others await us," Elan pointed as the path took them back to her cabin.

Elan stepped ahead of Cailleen and spoke to the other three. "Remember, this is not your quest. You cannot solve this for Cailleen. You can help or hinder her. A protective circle can also stifle or crowd what it protects. Remember, risk often results in great reward.

"I can tell you that whatever happens on this quest, you will not lose each other," she continued as she pulled Cailleen forward into the group. "You have more work to do together than what's involved in this quest. I cannot tell you more except that you will have to trust in each other's power and strength. That means allowing each other to stumble and regain balance."

Elan turned to go into her cabin, then turned back. "I would offer you tea and honey cakes, but I'm afraid other travelers have need of me. Merry meet."

"Merry meet," they replied as the forest shifted and they smelled the cedar of their own grove once again.

Charles checked to make sure everyone had come back safely from their journey, then began breathing deeply. When he heard everyone breathing deeply along with him, he directed them to pull their roots back up, and into their bodies once again. They each opened their eyes and began to move their limbs to come back fully into their physical bodies and to warm themselves. Cailleen remained quiet, so Charles continued directing them.

They opened the circle giving thanks to each of the Elements. They scattered the cooling embers and covered them with dirt, then returned the tin of matches to the stack of wood. In silence, they returned to the house where Rosey and Yvonne greeted them with delight.

The kitchen smells made their mouths water. Elephant garlic, olive oil, balsamic vinegar, and rustic bread accompanied an antipasto plate of olives, peppers, zucchini, carrots and tomatoes.

"You're a wonder," Lawrence said as he picked Yvonne up, swung her around and then dipped her.

"Well, the pay's not so good," she teased, "but the benefits get better every day."

"Very touching," Jen said. "However, you're endangering your woman by blocking our way to the food. Step aside, lover boy!"

Yvonne blushed and pushed Lawrence away playfully. "Let the plebeians by," she laughed.

"Everyone, sit down and start with bread and the antipasto," Yvonne directed. "I'll put the Portobello mushrooms and asparagus spears on the grill. The risotto is just finishing up. There's red wine and lemon water. Does anyone need something else?"

"It's lovely. Thank you, Yvonne," Cailleen said. "You've put a lovely end on a very long day. I appreciate it."

"Oh, I'm sorry. I forgot to tell you. Your publisher called. He's at home until about 8:45 and says he needs to speak to you tonight."

"Tonight? What could be so important? What time is it now?" Cailleen asked.

"A little after 7. You have time to enjoy your dinner first. Sit," Yvonne commanded.

Cailleen did so immediately; she was happy to let someone else be in charge. The others followed suit, and soon the kitchen was filled with chatter and compliments to the chef. When everyone started to slow down, the group looked expectantly at Cailleen.

"OK, spill it," Jen invited. "What did Elan say to you on your walk?"

"She confirmed that James is part of the quest. Through him, it appears the other players in this quest will be gathered."

"You walked together for longer than two sentences worth of information," Charles blurted out. Jen kicked him under the table, Lawrence elbowed him and Yvonne frowned.

"Sorry," he said graciously. "I don't mean to pry. It's just that I don't have anything to do to help you on this quest. I need a job."

"I could use someone to help compile all the dreams and stories," Cailleen replied. "You're the only other one who knows the family secret. What about it?" Cailleen asked. "Are you game?"

"Bless you. A tangible task within my grasp is all I ask," he said with obvious relief. "I'll get to it first thing in the morning."

"Thank you, Charles," Cailleen said. "I better go call Deacon and see what he wants."

She left the room and returned ten minutes later looking pale. She walked to the shelves and grabbed the brandy and a snifter. At the table she poured herself a glass and sipped. "I'm being investigated," she explained.

"Who's investigating you and for what?" Lawrence asked as he immediately went into lawyer mode.

"Deacon doesn't know. An agency called asking for information about me. He didn't return the call. He wanted to talk to me and to his lawyers first. He said it could be nothing, but he sounded worried. He doesn't want me to accept any speaking engagements or make any public appearances until he gets some answers. 'Just keep a low profile,' he said, then rang off."

"It's not really bad news, yet," Yvonne consoled. "Why get upset until you hear more?"

"It's not the conversation so much as the timing," Cailleen said. "This feels like it relates to the quest and it doesn't feel good. The quest, the dreams, James showing up, and now this – it just seems like a lot to sort through, that's all."

"You think James has something to do with the investigation?" Jen asked.

I think I'll make it an early night," Cailleen said, leaving her brandy and going up to her room. Yes, she did think James might have something to do with it. When an investigator moves in next door on the same day you find out you're being investigated, it begs the question. But she couldn't answer it or any of the other questions that were raised that day. She needed sleep.

Tomorrow, she'd find answers. As she washed her face and brushed her teeth and hair, she consciously let go of any details of the day that she no longer needed. This was her usual practice before going to sleep. Today, she was particularly grateful for the relief it brought.

While Cailleen prepared for bed, Charles made a few phone calls. He rang Sgt. Pruit of the Issaquah Police Department first. Then he rang Jessie, an old friend of Whitney's who was a writer for The Seattle Times. Pruit and Jessie both agreed to see what they could dig up on Detective James McEwan. Jessie promised to also keep her ears open for anything about someone investigating Cailleen.

Charles would know nothing until tomorrow at the earliest. He was tempted to simply intrude on James and intimidate some answers out of him. But he knew three women, who would think he was a Neanderthal for doing it. So, he didn't.

Jen was not as prudent. She sensed something moving into the field of their quest (correction, Cailleen's quest), and she felt her protective instincts firing. Even bigger than the quest, Cailleen's heart was on the line. Jen was sure of that, although she didn't know if Cailleen had a clue yet. They all stood on new territory here. The line between assisting and interfering could not be easily discerned. No harm in doing a little reconnaissance, Jen thought.

Jen sank to the floor of her room and ran her fingers over the plush carpet. She then began to slow her breath down. She grounded and prepared to move into a deep meditative state. She would just poke around his cottage a bit, to see if she could pick up anything regarding James' intentions or agendas. As she began slowing her breath and moving into trance, she was interrupted by a sharp rapping at her door and then Lawrence's voice.

"You get right back here, Jennifer Rose," he demanded. "What do you think you're doing?"

"I thought I was ending the day with a little meditation," she said defensively, "but clearly you…"

"Bullshit!" Lawrence cried. "You're going to visit our neighbor and intrude into his privacy. You know that's not ethical. Just because you can, Jen, doesn't mean you should." He paced to the window and back while Jen remained calmly posed for meditation on the floor.

"I was not going to intrude into his thoughts," Jen claimed. "I was merely heading to the cottage to poke around a bit and see what might land in my lap, so to speak. And why aren't you attending to that beautiful woman in your bedroom instead of bothering me?"

"Yeah, well I happened to be doing just that when I felt you leaving the manor," Lawrence replied. "It's dangerous, Jen. We don't know who we're dealing with yet. We know next to nothing about this man. He has some power in him. I feel it. If he's trained, he'll know how to block you. If he isn't that could be even worse. If he senses you, he might psychically swat you simply out of instinct. You know that as well as I do. So, what's worth the risk? What are you after?" he questioned as he joined her on the floor.

"I just don't want Cailleen hurt," she answered with a catch in her voice. "He's important. I can feel that. But I can't see why? Without knowing why, I can't help or protect anyone. I can't protect Cailleen and she's vulnerable, very vulnerable."

"What do you mean?" Lawrence asked. "Has something else happened?"

"No Lawrence, a lot has happened already. In the middle of what may be the 'quest of her life,' Cailleen meets someone who may be the 'love of her life'. She's a generous and open woman. But most people do not see how very private she is when it comes to her personal life. Even with us, she doesn't share her more private thoughts or fears or wonderings. Besides, she may be a powerful Healer and Teacher, but in romance she's just a woman. And she's a woman who has always put everything else ahead of romance. I don't see her being able to do that this time. I don't think she wants to. I feel a sense of loneliness within her lately. Work is no longer enough.

"She doesn't like having us around as witnesses to this part of her life. At least she doesn't at this stage. We have to leave tomorrow and go back to the city," Jen continued. "Before I go, I'd like to know I did everything I can to check things out. And that's what I am going to do. You can leave me to it, or you could come along," she invited.

"I won't be able to concentrate on anyone else until you're back, so I might as well go with you and keep you out of trouble," Lawrence responded. "Besides, two eyes – I mean four eyes – are better than two." He took her hand and together they breathed, grounded and slipped into a deep meditative state.

They found themselves in the forest behind the bungalow. Together they simply checked the energy field surrounding the cabin and noted any feelings or resonances that might be helpful. "Sad and a little helpless," Jen sent her thoughts to Lawrence. The emotions pulled Jen closer to the cottage and she stopped just outside the window. Inside, James was looking at a photo of a little girl. The girl looked to be around nine years old and seemed sickly. He put the photo down, took a drink from a mug and then picked up a book from the stack next to him. They were all Cailleen's books. He opened her latest, "When the Body Speaks." As he read, the sense of helplessness dimmed a little.

Jen and Lawrence returned to their bodies and sat looking at each other across their joined hands.

"Not what I expected," Jen said quietly.

"Not sure what I expected, but it wasn't that," Lawrence agreed.

"Is he here to ask Cailleen to help that little girl?" Jen wondered. "She's so tragic with her sweet wise eyes and that beauty marred by dark circles and pallor. I want to find her right now and do whatever I can to help. I wish you wouldn't have let me go."

"I told you it was dangerous," Lawrence said. "It's like eavesdropping, you rarely find what you want to find. Still, I think it was worth it. The overriding sense I got from James was deep caring and a high degree of honor. He might hurt Cailleen, but he won't mean to. We have to leave it at that. Agreed?" he asked.

"Agreed," she nodded. "Go back to Yvonne. Kiss her for me and tell her I'm sorry to have pulled you away. See you at breakfast," she said as she rose and slipped under the covers on her bed. "Catch the lights on your way out, will you?" she asked as she closed her eyes.

"Sleep tight. Dream sweet dreams," Lawrence whispered as he turned off the lights and closed the door.

***

As James held Lily's photo, he let himself remember her laugh and the playful energy that had seemed to erupt from her, just a few months ago. How could things have changed so fast? He loved her in such a big way, not like a daughter he never had, but simply because of who she is. He wished his love was strong enough to wrap around her and protect her from everything and anything.

Funny, even after years of being a cop and learning that he couldn't save everyone, he still wanted to. Somehow, James had avoided the hardened heart that so often accompanied a career cop's life. He'd seen human horrors: children being sold as sex slaves, parents abusing their children, drug lords slaughtering anyone in their way. But he'd also seen incredible moments of hope and love.

Jenny Dierdron came to mind. She was only eight years old when he found her stealing potatoes from a neighbor's yard at four in the morning. Something about her tugged at his heart from the moment he spied her.

He'd intercepted an intruder call on his way home one night. He was in the neighborhood and took the call. It was a quiet neighborhood next to government housing. Backup was on the way, but he checked the perimeter to see what was happening.

Jenny kept looking over her shoulder as she quickly dug some potatoes in the garden. She looked sorry as she quickly put the potatoes in her pockets. As she looked around to make her exit, she noticed that a pot had been knocked over on the porch. The plant in it was wilting. Jenny quickly righted the pot and even took the time to give it water from the hose. Then she scampered off.

James decided he needed to know more about this little girl, who stole potatoes, but offered something in return. He tracked her across the street and to a small corner apartment in the government housing. The next day, he found out who lived there and tried to find out what the situation was.

Jenny was being taken care of by her grandmother after both of her parents had been killed in a car accident. James went to visit and inform the grandmother about Jenny's late-night activities. When he arrived, Jenny came clean with the whole story. Her grandmother wasn't feeling quite herself and hadn't had time to do the shopping. James met the grandmother and knew something more serious had happened. He called 911.

Jenny's grandmother had had a mild stroke a couple of weeks prior. It affected her mental abilities and had left her sight greatly diminished. Jenny had been afraid that if she asked for help, she'd be taken away. James knew that was a valid fear.

He sat with Jenny and they waited together to hear what was wrong with her grandmother. He could still feel her tiny hand sneak into his as the doctor came towards them with a sad look on his face. Once again, Jenny's life had changed drastically in a very short time.

James did everything he could to ease her way through the foster care system. Through it all, she'd kept a bright outlook and a sweet composure. It was simply who she was. She'd had her moments of fear and anger and she'd expressed them. But she just couldn't hold them for long. She'd see a sad puppy who needed a bit of love, or an elderly man who dropped his bag and she'd run to their rescue. She was lucky to find a foster home that was safe and loving. The family eventually adopted Jenny and moved out of state. James lost track of her after that.

James wondered how she fared now. She must be almost college age. He wondered if Lily would live that long.

With a sigh he put down Lily's photo and put aside his memories. He opened Cailleen's book and continued reading about preparing oneself to do sacred work.

***

James awoke the next morning with a stiff back and a crick in his neck. He'd fallen asleep reading. He was surprised to find Cailleen's book so interesting. She had a practical streak and it came through strongly in her books. He couldn't put her book down. When he fell asleep it seemed to have followed him to his dreams. He dreamed he was using her grounding exercises and trying her techniques to deepen his intuitive skills.

But now his body was making demands: bathroom first, then water and some movement to work out these kinks. Hard physical labor and then falling asleep with a book – not smart for a man in his early 50s. Stretching his stiff body, he made his way to the bathroom.

He decided to take a quick shower, then made a cup of lemon and warm water. A walk in the brisk morning air would wake him up and eliminate any need for caffeine. Looking out the kitchen window he noticed the sun was already melting the light frost on the ground. The day would be warm, but the morning was still chilly. He grabbed a wool sweater and his mug and left the bungalow.

He sat for a few minutes on the porch drinking his tea, watching the birds and listening to the morning sounds of his temporary home. The rat-a-tat-tats of a couple of woodpeckers gave counterpoint to the cry of a bald eagle in this morning's symphony. James inhaled the scent of forest, frost and wood stove. The sun rose over his bungalow and lighted the path that led to the grove. Why not go there, he thought to himself, and began a leisurely walk through the forest.

After about ten minutes James heard the crashing of a large animal moving quickly through the underbrush. He relaxed when he heard Rosey's welcoming bark. She smiled at him, then disappeared, only to reappear with a stick, which she promptly dropped at his feet.

"You're up early too, eh girl?" he asked as he scratched her behind the ears. She accepted his greeting then picked up the stick and dropped it at his feet again.

"OK, old girl," James said laughing. He threw her stick a short way up the path. Rosey looked at the stick and then back at James as if to say, "I'm not a puppy. How about giving it a real throw!" But she dutifully fetched it and brought it back. This time James tossed it as far as he could into the underbrush. Rosey barked with joy and set out after it. She returned and James gave the stick another throw.

This time just after Rosey's bark of joy, he heard someone swearing. A moment later Cailleen emerged with Rosey's stick in hand.

"Watch where you're throwing," she said as she threw Rosey's stick in the opposite direction. "It's all fun until someone's eye is put out."

"Sorry, I have a knack for interrupting your morning, it seems. Do you want the morning to yourself? I can head in another direction," he offered.

"No need. I was up at the Grove greeting the day. I recognized Rosey's bark and thought someone might need rescuing from her demands."

"You knew a game of fetch was underway. You should have been watching for flying sticks," he pointed out.

"Point to you," Cailleen smiled. "And thank you for the wood at the Grove. It was well timed, as none of us remembered to bring any along. You saved us a trip back to the barn."

"Happy to help. It was a peace offering. I behaved badly yesterday and wanted to make amends," he explained. "I wasn't sure if it was appropriate to enter the circle so I left it at the edge."

Cailleen nodded her acceptance and began walking the path in the direction he seemed to be heading. He made her nervous and she wanted to do something that didn't require looking at him. He walked along silently for a moment.

"Was it?" he asked.

His question interrupted her reverie. She'd been thinking about how fresh and sexy he looked in the early morning. It felt nice to walk with him in the quiet of a new day.

"Was what?" she asked blankly.

"Was it appropriate to enter the circle?"

"Oh," she said. The question pleased her. "What makes you ask that?"

"It feels sacred up there, and I don't know what the protocol is. I don't want to offend," he explained.

"You're correct. It is sacred ground. All the land is sacred, but the Grove holds an intentional sacredness. We often do circles there. What you feel in part is the natural power of the place. We've built on that power over the years," Cailleen explained. "We were not the first to use it so. We work there because it was clear to me when I first found it that it had been used for that purpose many times. It's like when a house becomes a home. The love and intention of those who use the space imbues it with an energy beyond its walls and windows."

"And you haven't answered my question. I'll keep clear. That's not a problem," he said, but his voice wasn't quite as warm as it had been. And Cailleen wanted that warmth back in her morning.

"You may certainly use the space and enter the circle. It's best to have a clear intention," Cailleen said. "Careless trespassers have reported branches swinging at them and even ravens dive bombing them. The Grove has its own protectors. They're generally defensive rather than offensive and they try to be very subtle," she laughed.

"Are you making that up?"

"Actually, I am not. I suspect the trespassers may have gotten carried away though. The feel of the forest shifts when someone unwelcome enters. It gets close and feels like someone is watching. Someone always is, of course. The trees have a consciousness and many have a protective nature. If they sense someone threatening – either actively or out of carelessness – they close ranks, so to speak. Then, I think perhaps the human imagination takes over. But I can tell you that what they say is certainly possible."

Cailleen looked at him to see his reaction to her words. She was testing him. Might as well see how he responded to her world now as later. He returned her look with curiosity. He showed no fear, disdain or mockery. She realized she'd been holding her breath, so she exhaled and walked on.

"I've seen gangs intimidate in the same way," James responded. "They don't actually have to do much but tighten their ranks and look tough. Trespassers will run and tell stories about being attacked. Patterns," he said, nodding to himself.

"Patterns," she agreed. "That's the core of my work - noticing and working within patterns. We're all subject to them and what we do affects them. Any healing we do in the circle radiates out and ripples through the patterns we have set."

"You were doing a healing last night?" he asked. "I heard drums."

"No, last night we were traveling between the worlds seeking information and advice. The sacredness of the circle helps to protect us and aids us in finding our way back when we travel," she explained.

"Was your trip successful?" he asked.

"How successful remains to be seen," she replied. "The messages are often challenging to unravel."

They arrived at the Grove before he expected it. Cailleen paused on the periphery.

"It's helpful to ask permission to enter and offer a gift," she taught him. "It's not necessary, but it does indicate your awareness of the sacredness of the space and your respect of its guardians." She pulled birdseed from her pocket and gave him some. Then she placed some on a rock and with eyes closed waited. After a moment, she opened her eyes and walked into the circle.

He did what he'd seen her do. After placing the seed on the rock, he closed his eyes and silently asked permission to enter. After a moment, it seemed that a door or window had been opened. He couldn't explain the sensation - maybe a slight shift in the wind - but he intuitively knew permission had been granted to him. He opened his eyes and stepped into the circle. The colors around him shone brighter now and the sounds seemed sharper.

"It's traditional to enter the inner circle from the East," Cailleen told him. "Then in a clockwise direction move around to each of the directions and make a small offering." She handed him more seed. "You can also offer a prayer, a song, tobacco. I often leave strands of my hair as a special gift to the birds, who watch the Grove. Truly, there are many ways. What's important is what feels significant to you. Sometimes, I simply offer gratitude."

Cailleen preceded him around the circle, making offerings at each of the directions and then waiting for him in the center. "The Center is the place from which all things come and to which all things return. Here in the Center, you also make an offering. I rather like to sing."

Cailleen closed her eyes. As he watched she seemed to sink into the earth and lengthen up to the tree tops. He rubbed his eyes and shook his head to see if it was real. He'd seen people on the street puff up and make themselves larger to intimidate others. But this was different. Although she did seem expanded, it felt more like she'd become more deeply connected to what was around her. She seemed both softer and more powerful.

Then Cailleen began a tone, which moved into another tone, and another. Her voice came from the earth and trees and rocks and everything around them. She was potent and glorious. What was in her flowed out to the earth and trees and rocks and everything around them. It flowed to James and he felt the tension and soreness in his body find release. His heart was soothed and his mind was cleared. He realized she'd stopped singing and he opened his eyes.

She opened hers at the same time and their eyes locked. Passion surged between them and they fell into each other. She traced his jaw with her fingers and moistened her lips. His hands went to her hips, pulling her in, then he tenderly bit her lower lip. She melted into him until there was no separation. She ran her fingers up his neck and into his hair, bringing him down closer to her. His hands glided up her back and grabbed handfuls of her hair, then his mouth plunged between her lips and devoured her.

He demanded and she gave. She demanded and he gave. Heat pulsed within and around them. They parted, gasping for breath, and looked at each other. She saw pain and shame enter his eyes.

"James," she cried softly.

"I'm sorry," he said. "I don't know what happened. I... I... I have no excuses. I've blasphemed sacred ground."

He was clearly very upset, yet he stood tall and erect – ready to meet whatever punishment was due him with as much dignity as he could muster. He bowed his head.

"James," she whispered softly. "That was a hell of an offering for a novice," she said, smiling tentatively. "It's OK. No harm, no foul."

"I don't understand what happened or why you're smiling?"

"I'll explain," she said, soothing him with her hand on his arm. "First let's sit. I don't really think I can stand."

Until that moment, James hadn't realized he was holding her up. He let her go for a moment, then took off his sweater and laid it on the damp ground. They sat.

First, I want to say I was not prepared for your openness here in the circle. That's not an excuse," Cailleen said, "but a reason. The Healer in me noticed the pain in your body as we walked. When I sing in a sacred space, I open myself to it. I offer what's needed to it and accept whatever I need. The song carries me.

"Because I didn't expect your openness, I didn't prepare you – or myself. I am sorry. I usually have more skill than that. As I sang you opened to me. Your pain called forth the Healer within and through the healing that happened we became deeply connected. That connection was still there when we opened our eyes, and well, our physical bodies took over. The energy we raised no doubt created energetic fireworks. It also fed the circle and everything around it.

"Listen to the birds and the trees and the chorus surrounding us. It's a symphony of pleasure. We were both consenting and I think I can safely say we both enjoyed the moment. In Earth-Centered practices we acknowledge the physical body as part of the whole. Sensual pleasure, a gift of our physical bodies, is as honorable an offering as anything else is. We blessed the land and the circle."

She waited for her words to register and his mind to accept or reject them. She kept her breath steady and took the moment to re-balance her system.

"Just to be clear here: I didn't offend anyone and you didn't bewitch me?" James asked shakily.

"I think you may have offended your own sense of propriety, but no one else was offended. As for the bewitching, I'm feeling bewitched myself," she said teasingly.

Cailleen jumped to her feet and then extended her hand to James. "Come on. After all those fireworks, a posse will be sent out if I don't get back to the house soon."

He took her hand and then pulled back at her words. "Are you telling me your pack up at the house knows what just happened here?"

"Not exactly. They probably just know *something* happened," she said.

"Probably? Probably? Your guard dog will be up here throwing punches at me!"

"What happens in the circle, stays in the circle," she said wickedly.

"In that case...," James said as he pulled her down on top of him and then rolled over on top of her. He gave her a quick teasing kiss and then kissed her thoroughly. Their hands explored each other's bodies and they lost any sense of time and place until a wet tongue and a happy bark brought them back.

"Rosey, stop!" Cailleen shouted.

"She's probably warning me of my impending doom," James said with a laugh. "Charles is likely charging up the hill."

"She seems pretty happy about your impending doom."

"Yeah, you throw a stick or two, you'd think you'd get some loyalty," James shook his head in mock disappointment. Then he stood and brought Cailleen up after him. He looked her in the eyes for a moment, then kissed her gently.

"How do I get out of this circle, teach?"

"In reverse," she answered. Then she led him out of the circle and back on the path to the bungalow. There she kissed him and walked away, back to her own home.

***

James watched her walk away then turned to the bungalow. He felt hungrier than he could ever remember and a bit wired. He needed to burn off energy so he ran back to his kitchen.

He cooked oatmeal with lots of fruit and made toast with some local jam he'd picked up yesterday. He ate with gusto. Everything tasted great and he felt particularly satisfied. Actually, he felt like a new man. He stretched with pleasure as the day grew and sunshine fell over him.

With some astonishment he realized Cailleen's song had indeed healed him. He felt vibrant. His methodical mind looked for reasons for his well-being beyond what happened in the circle. He was out of the city in beautiful country where he'd met a thoroughly interesting and beautiful woman. He noted that a satisfying physical relationship in itself released stress and tension in the body. In fact, he'd used sex more than once to find that kind of release, especially during and after a difficult case.

But the physical nature of his encounters with Cailleen hadn't exactly been satisfying. He wanted more and they'd been interrupted. The fact that she aroused his mind as well as his body probably made a difference, but not this much of one. He should be wound tighter than a drum at this point. Instead, he felt refreshed, vibrant and expansive. And the nagging worry about Lily shifted to caring concern. He seemed clearer about the situation and more certain about his role.

He couldn't deny something special happened this morning. He wasn't ready to attribute it all to Cailleen's healing abilities, but he was willing to allow they may have played a significant part.

Still feeling an excess of energy, James decided to go into town and chat up the locals. He threw the dishes in the sink and went to change his clothes. Dressed in black jeans and a black cotton shirt, he grabbed his keys and left the bungalow. At the bottom of the porch stairs, Rosey sat looking at him expectantly. She thumped her tail and whined.

When James scratched behind her ear, he noticed something stuck in her collar. She barked and put her paw up on his arm. "What have you got here, old girl?" he asked. It was a rolled-up piece of paper. As James unrolled it, he smelled Cailleen's scent: roses, incense and forest. Smiling, he read:

The pack leaves for the big city this afternoon. Dinner around 6? It will be something simple. Bring wine, if you like it. C.

"Looks like I've got a date, Rosey," he said as he put the paper in his pocket and headed toward his truck. Rosey barked sharply. "Oh, she's expecting a reply. Is that it?" Rosey barked in agreement. He went back inside to get paper and pen.

Dinner sounds great. I'll bring Irish Death. See you at 6, J.

He rolled the paper, put it in Rosey's collar and sent her on her way, then headed to town. On the 20-minute drive, James told himself he was not compromising his case. His mission was to check out Cailleen Renae to see whether she was the real thing, just well meaning, or perhaps a fraud. He felt that knowing her on a personal level would give him the answers he sought. There was no crime in enjoying one's work. He'd have to keep his perspective, of course. He'd built his reputation on personal integrity as well as his ability to get to the truth of things. He wouldn't risk ruining what he'd built. He'd get the job done and then see where things might go with Cailleen.

As he shifted gears to make a sharp curve, James caught himself. What was he doing thinking of where things might go with Cailleen? She was a subject of an investigation. He needed clarity and objectivity. Instead, he was acting like he'd never been attracted to a woman before. Again, a part of him wondered if she was using her powers to sway him. He shifted gears again and saw the town of Cle Elum ahead. He wasn't being fair to Cailleen, or to himself. One step at a time, he reminded himself. Stay in the present and observe.

In town James stopped at Pioneer Coffee, the local coffeehouse, hoping to strike up conversation and lead it to the Healer on the Teanaway. He had a knack for making people believe they opened the conversation. He targeted the older folks, but they seemed unaware of Cailleen, or simply didn't take his lead. He was about to give up when a young man in his early 20s asked him if he was renting the bungalow next to the healer.

"The healer?" James asked.

"Sure. Maybe there's a group of them, but I think only one actually lives there," the man said. "My mom goes up and drums with her about once a month. She always comes home happier than when she left."

"My aunt Jackie goes up to drum with her, too," his girlfriend added. "She also takes some classes to learn Reiki and Chakra balancing."

"She got a big happy dog?" James asked.

"That'd be Rosey," the girlfriend confirmed. "I remember her from when I did my coming-of-age ceremony. I thought it was going to be really silly - drumming and sitting around talking about what it means to be a woman. But I got a lot out of it and I'll make sure my daughters have their own ceremony. She, I mean Cailleen, does a lot for people around here. But she's pretty quiet about it. Kind of keeps to herself, but my mom says she'd do anything she could for someone."

"How do people know about her?"

"In a small town, mister, it's pretty much word of mouth," she said. "But she's also written a couple books so I guess she's kind of famous. The bookstore carries her books and she does a class for them once in a while. You should check it out."

"Thanks," James said with a smile. "Maybe I will. Can you recommend a restaurant that serves vegetarian food?"

"You're a vegetarian? So's Cailleen. You should check out the natural food co-op. They'll tell you where to find the best grub. We gotta go Jim. I can't be late for work," she said. "Nice talkin' to you. I'm Stacie, by the way. I work over at the newspaper."

"James. Thanks for the tips. I'll probably see you again." James shook both their hands and finished his coffee. Before leaving he asked the woman behind the counter where he could find the natural food store.

The drive to Roslyn reminded James of fishing trips with his dad. It had been almost 10 years since he'd been here, but it pretty much looked the same. He found the co-op easily and got some groceries while he checked the place out.

"Can I help you?" a man in his 40's asked."

"I'm James. I'm living on the Teanaway for a few months. I'm a vegetarian and a couple of kids in Cle Elum directed me to you. You carry a few things I thought I'd have to do without until I made a trip back over the mountains to the Westside - Field Roast and tempeh. I can live without them, but I'm glad I don't need to."

"I'm Doug. If there's anything you need that you don't see, let me know. If we don't have it, we can order it."

"Thanks. Do you carry any of Cailleen Renae's books?" James asked. "I was told she's a local and a healer."

"We don't. The bookstore in Cle Elum carries them. She's famous enough to warrant us carrying them, but since Book Nooks does, we don't. Kind of a small community, so we spread the wealth. She keeps a low profile so we don't get tourists asking for her books. They don't know she's local. It's not a scientific system, but it seems to work for us. I can order them, if you want. But you can get them in Cle Elum."

"Thanks," James said. "That's fine. I wanted to check out the local library and bookstores anyway. I like to support the local economy as much as possible. One last thing: can you recommend local restaurants with vegetarian options?"

"Sure. We actually have a list. We get that question a lot from the Seattle-area folks coming over for the weekend. Just ask when you're at the checkout," Doug said. "Welcome to Kittitas County."

"It's been a pleasure so far," James said, shaking Doug's hand.

James drove on to Salmon La Sac, where he'd fished with his dad so many years ago. The drive past Ronald and into the forest filled him with pleasant memories. It took him longer than he remembered to get past houses and into more forested land. Ten years brought changes.

But Lake Cle Elum still sparkled in the sunlight, and upriver, Salmon La Sac campground still waited for him. As he drove over the bridge, he remembered jumping off of it as a kid. He parked and walked down to the river. He found the same rock outcropping he'd sat on every summer, and as before, he contemplated the season ahead.

For James it was more than just a shift into the winter months. He was ready for a real change in his life. He'd officially retired last year, but ended up agreeing to consult on so many cases that he couldn't say he noticed much difference. He needed more balance. Twenty-five years on the force had given him plenty of time to develop patterns for loneliness. As an investigator he kept long hours and an unpredictable schedule. As a result, he had few real friends. Most of the guys on the force treated him with respect. But when it came to their personal lives, he sensed they feared he would see too much. A beer after work was one thing, but he was rarely invited to anyone's house for dinner. So, he worked and took his two weeks off to go fishing with his dad.

When his dad died, James stopped taking regular vacations.

It's time for a change in patterns, he thought. As the river flowed past him, James felt himself letting go of his life in the city. Nothing much there for him but work. Spending a couple of months in upper Kittitas County was good for him. He might even make a permanent move. He didn't need to make that decision now. He did intend to use his time well and check it out as a possibility. After the holidays he'd make a decision. Hell, he might as well winter here and decide in the spring.

With that he thanked the river and returned to his truck. As he got in the cab, he chuckled to himself. He'd just made an offering of gratitude to the river that ran through a spot, which was indeed sacred to him. Perhaps he was already changing.

He stopped in Cle Elum for lunch and then headed towards Ellensburg. He'd intended to check out the library and bookstore, but felt the need of the open road. He took highway 10 along the Yakima River and wished he'd brought his camera. He'd bought one last spring with the intention of getting a hobby. But he never remembered it until he was surrounded by breathtaking beauty. He made a mental note to put it in the truck so he'd always have it. For now, he'd just enjoy the ride.

He found the Iron Horse Brewery in Ellensburg with no trouble, and bought a bottle of their Irish Death - a dark, smooth ale. He'd had a glass a year or so ago when doing some research in Ellensburg. Since he noticed no wine racks or bottles in Cailleen's kitchen, he guessed she was not a wine drinker. If she'd wanted wine, she would have just asked him to bring a bottle. He wanted to bring something as a dinner guest and he thought flowers might send the wrong message. He was not looking for romance. Something from a local brewery seemed an okay choice. But now he hesitated. She said casual, but still a $5 bottle of beer might make him seem cheap. He knew it wasn't about the money, but still his male pride wasn't comfortable.

He drove through Ellensburg to get his bearings and a sense of what it offered to long-term residents. He also hoped for inspiration about his offering for dinner. Across from the university he noticed Vinman's Bakery and pulled in. He'd stopped here last year and practically moaned as he ate his Pain du Chocolate. He walked in and inhaled the scent of heaven. Yes! Double chocolate vegan brownies, an assortment of cookies, baklava, and more tempted him. As he didn't know Cailleen's preferences he chose a couple of vegan brownies, a lemon bar, a molasses cookie and some baklava. He mentioned he was a guest for dinner and they put it in a sweet little box. He drove home happily.

***

Jen, Charles, Lawrence and Yvonne had greeted her nervously when Cailleen returned from her morning walk. She hadn't missed Jen's elbow in

Charles ribs when he asked Cailleen if she'd had a nice walk.

"Beautiful morning," was all she said.

"Tea's hot and there's fruit and fresh biscuits on the table," Yvonne offered. "How'd you sleep?" she asked.

"I slept well enough. It's a new day and I feel hopeful after eight hours of uninterrupted sleep. How about the rest of you?"

Murmurs of "good" and "fine" moved through the room like an expectant wind. Then four pairs of eyes looked at her, waiting. When she looked back in silence, all four busied themselves.

"I see I'm not going to get a normal conversation out of the four of you," Cailleen said. "Yes, I ran into James. He asked about protocol in the grove. I explained about asking permission, making offerings, and we raised a little energy. He's informed. All is well. I am hungry."

She took her tea to the table and ate fruit and biscuits with gusto.

"That's a pretty hearty appetite for someone who's only raised a 'little energy,'" Jen quipped.

Startled, Cailleen stared at her and then laughed. "OK, you win. It was intense and we raised a lot of energy. I can't get anything by you and I should know that. I will be burning off excess energy turning over the garden for winter after you've all left to go back to the city. Any more questions?"

"We're good," Lawrence smiled. "And clearly so are you." He winked at her and poured himself a cup of tea. "Just be careful, will you?"

"I'm always careful," Cailleen said. "To a fault," she whispered to herself. Charles heard her but tucked the comment away. Jen was right, Cailleen did seem a bit lonely. His heart softened toward James, at least for now.

After reviewing their individual tasks for the week, the group left with plans to return either Friday evening or Saturday morning to see how things were developing for the quest. After they left, Cailleen changed into old sweats and headed for the garden. She loved the smell of compost and freshly turned soil. Humming to herself, she pulled up dying plants, mulched perennials, hoed, raked, and then planted winter beans.

Her actions were not just for the good of the garden. As she pulled up dying plants, she pulled out her resistance to allowing love in her life. As she mulched the perennials, she let the nourishment of her love for her friends strengthen their relationship. As she hoed, raked and planted – she sorted through her feelings about the events of the last few days and set her intention to stay open. She sang a song of gratitude to the land, wishing it a deep, restful sleep over the winter. "Merry meet," she whispered as she picked up her tools and headed to the barn.

She returned to the kitchen for a late lunch. She decided on split pea soup and a salad for dinner. She checked to see if she had another soup in the freezer in case James didn't like split pea. She found nothing, so decided to do a quick pot of lentil soup with spinach as well. She'd need variety for the week ahead anyway. And as she couldn't tell what spirit might ask of her, it was best to have easy food available. She started a loaf of oat bread and then went upstairs for a bath while it raised.

By 5:30, the soups were ready and the bread was in the oven baking. She hadn't thought about dessert. There was always sorbet if they had a sweet tooth. She tossed a salad and set the table. A few minutes before six o'clock she heard tires crunching in her driveway. She went out the kitchen door to meet James.

Wearing black chinos and a deep indigo dress shirt, James walked towards her like a man sure of his conquest. His assumption irritated her and she shifted into her regal bearing ever so slightly. He saw her friendly demeanor cool and slowed his step to give himself time to adjust. He offered her the dessert box and the bottle of Irish Death. She looked at him suspiciously, but accepted the gifts graciously and with warmth.

"What have we here?" she asked as she handed him back the bottle and opened the box.

"I'd say sweets for the sweet," he said, "but I fear it would insult us both. Too cliché for me and sweet does not describe you."

"I'll take that as a compliment," she said uncertainly. "Please come in."

"I didn't see any wine racks in your kitchen, so I figured you didn't imbibe," he explained. "If you don't fancy Irish Death, just keep it for another occasion."

"I might have a wine cellar in the basement," she countered. "A warm kitchen is the last place a wine connoisseur would keep wine. For an investigator you make a lot of assumptions. Or are you waiting for me to confirm or correct you as a means of getting information?"

She seemed hostile suddenly. He wondered what was up.

"Old habit perhaps. I'm afraid indirect questions go with the territory," he said. "Let me start again. Do you prefer wine or perhaps a hearty ale?"

"Actually, I'm quite fond of Irish Death. Wine tends to bother my sinuses and muddles my brain. Thank you for asking. And you, would you prefer split pea soup or perhaps a lentil soup with spinach and tomatoes?"

"You made two soups?"

"Yes, I did. I assure you it was quite practical; it only took another 10 minutes. I didn't know your preferences. Besides, I have a potentially busy week and I like to have healthy food easily available. If neither works for you, I have salad and I could throw a potato in the microwave and top it with steamed broccoli."

James put his hands up in surrender. "I quite enjoy both lentil and split pea soup. I should probably have told you I'm a vegetarian, though."

"I'm vegan, so you're safe in my kitchen."

"The brownies in the box are vegan, but I can't speak for the other choices."

"I claim both brownies, then," Cailleen laughed. "If you pour the ale, I'll check the bread. Shall we start with salad and then progress to the soup?"

"Sure." James poured the Irish Death slowly to avoid too much head. As Cailleen busied herself with the bread and salad he tried to read her. After their morning together in the grove he'd expected a warmer greeting and softer lights. She seemed to have forgotten the incident entirely. In fact, this meal had the feel of a business dinner. He could do business, yet he wondered what business she thought she had with him.

"I think that's everything," Cailleen announced. "Let's sit. May all who have given their time and talent to bringing this food to the table be blessed. Deep gratitude to the plants, who give us life. May this food serve us as we do our work in the world." Cailleen lifted her glass to him and nodded, "To neighbors."

"To new relationships," he toasted back. "Everything smells and looks great. You shouldn't have gone to so much trouble for me."

"No trouble at all. I'm simply sharing what I would have made for myself," she said.

"What time did the pack leave?" he questioned casually.

"They all drifted out by late morning. It was such a beautiful day; I spent a couple of hours preparing my garden for winter. How was your day?"

"Good. I went into Cle Elum and then found the co-op in Roslyn."

"Yes, they opened last year. Did you meet Doug?" she asked.

"Yes, quite helpful. Look is there a reason we're acting like almost total strangers, here?"

"James, we are almost total strangers," she said with a laugh. "I met you yesterday."

"The day before actually. And we sure weren't acting like strangers this morning in the grove," he said with a bit of irritation.

"Look James, I told you this morning that what happens in circle stays in circle. We were between the worlds. What's between the worlds is not affected by the worlds," she explained. "Here in the everyday world, we are relative strangers. That's a fact, detective."

"That's a very tidy little splitting of hairs you just did," James replied. "However, *what happens between the worlds affects the worlds*" he quoted from her book. Like it or not, we were playing tongue hockey this morning, and if Rosey hadn't interrupted us more would have passed between us. I'm not in the habit of being intimate with someone in the morning and pretending we're strangers eight hours later. "

"I'm sorry you're on unfamiliar territory. I'm navigating a new landscape here myself. I'm not playing with you or acting coy or being a bitch. I'm asking you to understand that the intensity of what happens within a sacred circle cannot be carried into everyday life outside the circle," Cailleen explained. "I am not Cailleen, the woman, in a circle. Cailleen steps aside and

I become priestess as I open myself to the needs of Spirit in that time and that space. There is a certain intimacy to the work. Attempting to maintain that level of intimacy outside the circle is not always appropriate.

"If you go to your doctor for an exam, it is appropriate to take your clothes off," she said. "If you have dinner with your doctor later that day, you don't do it in the nude. The level of intimacy does not translate into another situation."

"I'll have to let that settle in," James said. "I'll probably have questions for you later."

"Fair enough. Would you like lentil or pea soup?"

"Lentil with a pea soup chaser?" he asked with a charming smile. The tension between them eased and they finished their meal chatting about life on the Teanaway.

"I asked you here tonight for a specific reason," Cailleen shared as they ate dessert. "I like to be direct, and I hope you can be, too. I received a call from my publisher last night. He said he'd received a call asking for information about me as part of an investigation. I find it interesting that the call came within 24 hours of an investigator moving in next door. Are you investigating me, and if so, why?"

"I am not doing a formal investigation on you. I came here to get away from the city. I told you that yesterday," James said trying to deflect the direct question. He'd promised Ben he would not tell anyone why he'd come. "Is that why I'm getting the ever-so-polite-but-cool reception tonight?" he challenged.

"I just asked you a question," Cailleen countered.

"I answered it. Now I have a couple of questions. You spend time in sacred circle with your pack, yet outside of the circle you all remain very intimate. The depth and intensity of your relationships with each other are glaringly obvious. The textures between you all are different, but the intimacy remains. Why does *that* carry over into everyday life?" he asked calmly.

"We have worked together for years - Jen, Lawrence and Charles have all studied with me. Over the years we became close friends. Intimacy developed both inside and outside the circle. We trust each other completely. And we read each other pretty well. I don't know what I'd do without them. I depend on them as they depend on me," she explained. "And none of us has been romantically involved with any of the others. That's not always true in a circle such as ours. But that is our history. If necessary, any two of us within the circle could play the parts of the God and Goddess to heal, open or transform. It's powerful energy as you noticed this morning."

Cailleen gathered dishes and took them to the sink as James digested what she told him. Then he rose and helped her.

"So, while you were singing this morning you embodied your priestess self. Do I have that right?"

"Yes."

"And you were still in that role when we opened our eyes and passions flared?"

"True."

"And that has never happened in all the years you've worked with Jen, Lawrence and Charles?"

"Correct."

"So, when you then explained to me that I had not offended the spirits of the grove or anyone else, you were still the priestess?"

"Well, actually, I think I moved back into my teacher self at that point."

"So, you were Cailleen, the woman who teaches?"

"That's accurate enough." She sensed he was going somewhere with his line of questioning and turned to face him. He stepped closer to her and cocked his head in question.

"When Rosey interrupted us, it was Cailleen, the woman, who was rolling around on the ground with her hands wandering up and down my body?" As he spoke his voice got softer and he moved even closer, pinning her against the counter. He moved in to kiss her but halted just before their lips met.

"Cailleen?" he asked as he hovered.

"The woman," she agreed as she leaned into him and took his lips.

"You're very good at what you do," she whispered as she ended the kiss.

"Thank you. You're pretty good yourself," he said as he pulled her back to him.

"I meant at interrogation," she said putting her hands on his chest to push him back. "You didn't ask if Cailleen, the woman, had second thoughts because she didn't know or trust you. You didn't ask if she simply got carried away in the moment."

"Did she?" he whispered.

"Have second thoughts? Yes"

"Did she get carried away?"

"Yes."

"Will she again?" he asked sliding his hands up her back and into her hair.

She closed her eyes as she considered, then opened them and looked into his. She searched, asking if he could be trusted. He held fast and returned her gaze. Something told him that this moment was vitally important. He opened to her and let her search. As she drowned in the clear depth of his eyes, she whispered softly, "Yes".

They met each other with a fierce passion. They fell onto the table, sweeping dishes aside. When she welcomed him into her, he held the still point until the currents overtook them and they moved in the oldest and most sacred dance. Their breath and hearts slowed and James traced a path with his fingers from her jaw over the clavicle between her breasts to her hips, knees and back up to circle around her belly button.

"*This* is sacred space, isn't it?" he asked.

She rolled over on top of him, running her hands up his chest, across his shoulders down his arms and behind him to the small of his back, then down his hips to his knees and up his thighs.

"And this is sacred ground," she confirmed.

"Perhaps we should worship here again," he suggested.

"A delightful idea," she laughed wickedly. "But it's just as sacred upstairs."

Cailleen kissed James' hand and then led him up the stairs to her room. She left him standing at the door and went in to light candles around the room. James noticed that she lit them starting in the east and moving clockwise. When finished she stood in the center of the room just looking at him. Her radiance staggered him and he started towards her drawn like a magnet. But as he moved, she shook her head. He stopped where he was.

Cailleen slowly moved towards James, never taking her eyes from his. He felt her heat and watched as her chest rose on a quick breath. She stopped a few inches from him, inhaled and smiled.

Barely touching him, she unbuttoned his shirt and ran her hands up his chest and over his shoulders. His shirt fell to the ground. She continued running her hands down his arms, stopping to slowly twist the skin on his right forearm, then lifting it to kiss where she had just twisted. She turned into his arm and began kissing and licking her way to his fingers. When James moved forward to embrace her, she gently moved away. She wanted to explore without distraction. She licked up his fingers and sucked, then lay his hand on her soft belly. She leaned back into him for a brief moment and then away again. Picking up his left arm, she twisted, kissed, licked and sucked her way to his fingers. This time she put his hand on her left breast, leaned back into him, and sighed.

James enfolded her, eliminating the space between them. He let his hands explore her belly and breasts while kissing her neck and shoulders. Then he slid his hands to her hips, and turned her to face him. They stood inches apart, searching each other's eyes, wanting to take in everything – every flicker of arousal, every flash of emotion, every secret waiting to be shared.

James leaned forward, ran his finger between her breasts and down to her belly button. He rimmed her belly button and then stuck his finger in and out. Cailleen's breath caught and she trembled. James kissed her neck and bit his way down to her shoulder. He licked his way back up and she bared her throat in surrender.

He took her hands and led her to the bed. He kissed his way down her arms, to her hips and down to her toes. He bit his way along the edge of her foot and then sucked her toes one at a time. He turned her over and kissed and licked his way up the back of her legs. He stopped and ran his fingers lightly in small circles where her legs met her buttocks. His hands slid up to her hips and then straddled her. He used his thumbs to massage up her back on either side of her spine all the way up her neck to the base of her skull. He trailed his fingers down her back and stopped, resting his hands on her waist.

Cailleen was engulfed in sensations – every fiber of her being alive and hungry for his touch. She could hear James' breath ragged. She knew his stillness was an attempt for control. He slowed his breath, and whispering her name, he molded his body over her. His erection throbbed and she rose up to encourage him. He moaned and rolled off of her. As he started to pull her to him, Cailleen straddled him. She leaned forward rubbing her hardened nipples across his chest. He pulled her up and took her nipple into his mouth, gently sucking. He ran his tongue over her breast and massaged the other with his hands.

She rubbed and twisted his nipples, delighting in the flush that spread across his chest. She took James' hands, running them from her breasts down to her hips, and she lifted and arched her back. Leaving his hands on her hips, she reached back and ran her nails up his thighs. He bucked up. She repositioned herself over him. This time when she ran her nails up his thighs and bucked up, she was waiting to meet and enclose him. She took him deep into her center and linked her fingers in his.

"Sacred ground," she whispered.

"Sacred ground," he answered.

Together, eyes locked, they rode the energies to glorious heights. The alchemy between them took them beyond what they thought was possible. As they climaxed, light and sound exploded around them and radiated across the land.

The next morning, they woke in each other's arms, limbs entwined. Cailleen stretched, enjoying the loose and limber feeling of her body. She leaned over and kissed James.

"Good morning. I need breakfast. Do you want coffee or tea?"

"Whatever suits you, as long as it comes with a very hearty breakfast. I'm ravenous." He returned her kiss. "Can I jump in the shower?"

"Towels are in the cupboard. You've got ten minutes." She retrieved his shirt and threw on a pair of wool socks and headed for the kitchen. As she sliced potatoes, onions and mushrooms, she hummed to herself. She put everything into a skillet with coconut oil and added garlic. She sliced tomatoes and then tossed together a fruit salad. As the vegetables cooked and the coffee dripped, she thought of last night. She would not regret it. It might have been foolish, but even in the light of day it felt right.

She smiled as James walked into the kitchen in her purple bathrobe. "I believe my clothes are down here somewhere," he said, looking around.

"I tidied up a bit. Your clothes are in the bathroom. I'll trade you your shirt for my bathrobe."

"I like you in my shirt," he said, then went into the bathroom to get his clothes. He came back a minute later in black jeans, a t-shirt and bare feet.

She handed him a cup of coffee.

The phone rang and Cailleen answered it. "Hi Charles. Already? Sure, I'll meet you at two. Thanks." She hung up and turned to James.

"Ready for breakfast? There are biscuits and bread from yesterday in the breadbox. I've got everything else here, I think."

As they ate breakfast, cleared the dishes and washed up, James discovered they had already developed an easy rhythm with each other. He enjoyed watching her move about her own kitchen while leaving room for him. Some women – and men – overlooked the intimacy and comfort in these everyday moments. Even two years ago, he himself would have feared them. He was changing and he liked it.

"Do you have regular work weeks?" he asked Cailleen.

"Not really. I work hard most weeks, but each week has a different rhythm. In three weeks, I travel to Vancouver to give a workshop. Two weeks later I do a tour for my latest book. My publisher calls it the pre-holiday tour. I only do two tours a year. They're exhausting and do more for the publishing house than for me. In the winter months I concentrate on writing and doing local classes. I do another tour in the spring and travel to teach. Summer I stay here to tend my garden. Fall, more traveling. Throughout the year I do healing sessions and work with a handful of apprentices."

"Doesn't it bother you to not know what you'll be doing on a regular basis?" he asked.

"I do know. It's just that my frame is bigger than a week or a day. It's a more natural way to live. Nature changes with each season and within each season. I follow the seasons of Earth and the cycles of Moon. I go within when it's cold and dark; it's a time for introspection. I'm preparing for that time, now. I store food and prepare my garden for winter. Professionally, I do a last tour and turn over projects that need to lay fallow until spring, when they can support new life. It's a good and ancient way of moving through the Wheel of the Year, the wheel of life.

"When I was a kid," she mused, "I used to work hard in school, getting A's Monday through Thursday. On Fridays, I played with my hair and daydreamed. I knew even then that the Western rhythm of life was not for me. I found a way to be successful without catering to it. I would think being a detective, you would have worked outside of the usual 9 to 5 culture?"

"I've never thought of it that way," James said. "Frankly, it felt more like I worked *beyond* the 9 to 5 culture. I worked those hours and then some. Criminals don't generally punch a time clock. But I had my regular rituals of checking in and finishing the day with paperwork."

"You must have noticed monthly patterns, more crimes during the full moon, more suicides during the holidays, that sort of thing?" Cailleen asked.

"Sure. Precinct Captains scheduled manpower accordingly. And beat cops always knew the rhythm of life on their beat. But police work is a paramilitary operation and carries expectations of regular shifts and check-ins. They like to know where you are and what you're doing. It wasn't like I could take a week off to plant my garden."

"I don't suppose you could," she agreed. "But now you're retired and still young and virile. What's your week look like?"

"I'm just learning to figure that out. Right now, I'm investigating the upper county to see what kind of a fit it might be for me on a more permanent basis. I thought I might plan my strategy today. I like to have a plan of action and follow it. I just have more wiggle room now. Maybe I'll take up ranching?"

"You're a vegetarian."

"I could ranch tomatoes and sweet peas," he suggested.

"Why not," she laughed. "I have to ranch my week into shape or I'll get nothing done."

"Busy one?"

"Might be," Cailleen agreed. "It's a bit difficult to tell until I get some research done. That's what Charles called about. I asked him to put together some information and he has it all compiled. I thought it would take him another day or so."

"He probably wanted an excuse to drop by and growl at your new neighbor."

"Charles doesn't need an excuse to drop by. He's welcome here anytime and he knows it. I'm meeting him in North Bend at two o'clock. And I should get some things done before I head over."

"I'll leave you to it, then," he smiled. "Thanks for dinner… and breakfast. It's been nice getting to know you, neighbor." He walked over, planted a kiss on the top of her head, grabbed his jacket and let himself out the kitchen door. He glanced back at the house as he opened his truck door. She was leaning against the door watching him. She flashed him a warm smile and waved.

Cailleen only had about an hour before she had to leave to meet Charles. She tidied her room, took a shower and then sat for fifteen minutes in her study to consider what she needed to do in the next few days. She'd go over the notes Charles was bringing her and see if any new information or action suggested itself. She'd need to take some time this evening to sort through her conversation with Elan and her dreams. And she'd consider James and what he might have to do with the quest. Frankly, she didn't have a lot to go on in terms of an action plan. She was smack dab in the middle of unknowing - a place she found challenging, especially when a deadline loomed.

Chapter Eight
Strategies

Early afternoon found James in the grove. He wanted to go and experience the trees to see if he could feel the energies Cailleen spoke of without her being present. A part of him needed to know if she was messing with him in some way. He couldn't deny she had power. He wanted to know if what he experienced yesterday was a result of her power alone, or if something more existed. On a personal level he needed to know if he was just tagging along in her wake or if he brought his own power to their encounters. He brought along one of her books for reference. If she was the real thing, he should be able to use her exercises without her and get results.

He told himself it was just research, but in his heart, he knew that this new world she'd opened intrigued him. He wanted to play and explore. Lily's face appeared in his mind. He felt guilty about wanting to play when she was hanging on to life by a thread. He could hear her chastising him. "Uncle James," she'd say, "you wouldn't expect me to be sad if you were sick. You'd want me to play."

"I will play," he said to her in his heart. "I'll play and learn, so that I can make sure whether Cailleen will be of any help to you. I'll do anything to make her trust me, so I can see if we can trust her."

As he approached the grove, he remembered Cailleen's warning about clear intentions when entering. He felt a bit guilty about how he handled her question regarding his investigation. He had not lied; he was not doing a *formal* investigation. He was casually checking her out for a friend. He was just splitting hairs and he knew it. Yet he felt bound by his promise to Ben.

The cry of a raven brought him out of his reverie. He looked into the grove. The raven sat on the stone where they had offered birdseed yesterday. Her head was cocked as if in question. A crow cawed, circled the grove clockwise and then settled next to the raven. He couldn't help but wonder whether they had come to welcome or to judge him. Perhaps both.

He stepped towards the grove, pulling a bag of trail mix from his pocket. At his approach, Raven and Crow hopped to the center circle. James put trail mix on the rock and then asked permission to enter. He felt the same shimmering of the air as he had felt yesterday and the sense that a door had opened. With a sigh of relief, he entered.

He went to the gateway in the East and made his offering - then proceeded around the circle. Crow and Raven hopped and flew around the circle ahead of him. As they proceeded, he became more comfortable with their presence. When he came to the Center, they flew to cedar branches nearby. It seemed to him they were settling in for a chat. They both cocked their heads in listening poses.

James spilled his story before them. He told them about Lily and his long friendship with Ben and his wife Camille. He admitted the doubts he had about Cailleen and her work. He told them about his promise to Ben and then about his answer when Cailleen questioned him. He continued speaking about what he was learning from her books and directly from Cailleen. He told them about what he was beginning to learn of himself, including a sort of aching for a new direction.

As he spoke, more crows settled on cedar branches to listen. As his story concluded and silence hung in the air, James became aware that the trees were listening too. As he sat in silence, he felt another presence. A buck had entered the grove and now looked directly into his eyes. He was stunned. Several feet from the buck an elk entered the grove, looked at him, and then munched on some grasses. James let out the breath he was holding. The sound startled the buck and elk and they disappeared into the forest.

His heart beating fast, James knew something important had just happened but he didn't know how to interpret it. He remembered Cailleen talking about animal medicine in her book and pulled it out to reread it. She had a short list of animals with definitions of the medicine they carried. Deer carried gentleness. Elk offered stamina.

James found his ability to make connections very helpful in this new realm. Deer asked him to be gentle with himself as well as with others. Was elk telling him to pace himself. Did he have the stamina he needed, or did he need to gather new reserves? Crow and Raven were also on the list. Crow taught that spiritual law is different from manmade law. James considered his situation and determined that his actions were in line with what he believed to be right. That might be the spiritual law. And in that moment, he knew that in fact, he would not do anything he could to gain Cailleen's trust. He had to be true to his own honor, whatever he chose to do.

Raven carried the medicine of magic. In reading Cailleen's book, James was letting go of his misconceptions about magic and about those who said they used it. Still, he didn't quite understand how it worked. At that thought, Raven called to him and flew down to join him in the circle.

Laughing at himself, James said to Raven, "Yes, I get it. What's happening here and now is pretty magical. Now what?"

Raven flew back up to her perch. The crows all traded places and then settled in again, listening. The trees listened and waited. James felt their invitation but didn't know what to do with it, so he waited too. The grove grew very silent and expectant. James grew uncomfortable. Finally, his discomfort made him break the silence.

"Look, I don't really know what to do here. I've said my piece and I feel better for it. I thank you all for listening, for offering me your medicine. I thank you for it. I wouldn't mind your help as I find my way through all of this. In fact, I'm asking for your help (and, remembering Cailleen's teachings, he added) if it harms none and serves my highest good."

A gentle wind moved through the grove. Raven and the crows talked between themselves for a moment, soared from their perches toward James, then circled the grove and flew high with a lot of commotion. It seemed to James that they accepted his request and were getting to work on it. When he could no longer see them, he felt that what he'd come to do was complete. He retraced his steps around the circle thanking the trees and each of the Elements.

James returned to his bungalow feeling lighthearted and surer of himself again. He still felt a bit lost in this world. He'd need to keep his moral compass close and use it often. Even as he thought this, he knew he was making things more complicated by his own attachment to old ideas about magic and power. He needed a way to simplify the process of navigating everything. Why, he wondered, was he treating this case different than other undercover cases?

He already had a protocol for doing undercover work. Observe. Keep your head and trust your instincts when you're unsure what's happening. Move like you're comfortable in your own skin; fear will alert everyone that you're not who you say you are. Keep an open mind; things are not always what they seem. Keep an open heart.

No, keeping an open heart was never on his protocol list. He was more use to hardening his heart and not getting personally involved. He suddenly realized the real reason he'd retired. He was in mortal danger of losing his compassion. He did not want to live a life where his compassion could kill him. Or worse yet, live a life where his compassion could lead to someone else's death.

This case was already personal. Lily was already dying. He'd never really admitted that to himself. Lily is dying. It broke his heart, yet he could never close his heart to Lily, just because it pained him to see her wasting away. Whether he liked it or not, his heart was on the line and lives were at stake.

He understood in this moment that his own life, or at least the way he chose to live it, was at stake. Keeping an open heart might be the biggest challenge. For Lily, he could do it.

Another thought inserted itself. For Cailleen, he was willing to risk it.

***

Cailleen returned home just as the crows were flying from the grove. She made a mental note to go to the grove tomorrow and check things out. Tonight, she planned to heat up some soup and bread, then settle in to read through the notes Charles gave her. After that she'd consider James and his part in everything.

When she checked her messages, she found one from Deacon and called him back immediately.

"Cailleen, my favorite author. Thanks for calling back. How are you this fine afternoon?"

"I'm just great, Deacon. As you're calling me your favorite author, I suspect you have found out more about the investigation and are relieved. Or you want something from me," she laughed. "What's up?"

"So suspicious, my dear. Actually, I do have more information about the investigation. They, of course, would not reveal who hired them, but they did tell me it was someone considering using your services. 'As the services are not of the *normal* sort, the client understandably felt the need to check your credentials.' I told them you had the highest integrity of anyone I'd ever worked with and that I had more unsolicited testimonials regarding your work than I could ever hope to use. In fact, I have enough to fill the back cover of at least ten more books. You are working on something new over the winter, aren't you?"

"I see I was right on both accounts," Cailleen teased. "You're confident that the investigation is nothing to be concerned about?"

"I can't say for certain, of course," Deacon responded. "Everything they told me could have been a ruse. But I can say that I don't feel concerned. Can't you pull a card and meditate about it, or something? You know, use those brilliant skills you write about. I'm sure you can get more accurate information than what I just told you. "

"Yes, I can. I just wanted to get your take on it. As for another book this winter, you know I won't even contemplate the possibilities until early November. I've got a lot happening here at the moment, so don't push it, Deac."

"No pressure," he reassured her. "Just want to know as soon as you know so we can prepare the media for your tour. I'll be sending you an itinerary at the end of the week, by the way. Keep me posted and I'll do the same."

"Thanks Deacon," she said and hung up.

Another thing to add to the list, Cailleen thought as she made tea and an early dinner. After eating she decided to pull a couple of cards about the investigation situation and then see if it warranted any further attention. She went to Mellissae's deck and pulled two cards: *Gathering* and *Recognition*. As they were in line with what Deacon shared with her, she let it go. It made sense the client would want to gather and discern before recognizing her abilities enough to ask for her help. The cards suggested the client would likely seek her out.

She thought back to the cards she pulled about James, remembering the *Gathering* card had come up then as well. She wondered about that. Was James connected somehow, or was this potential client also connected to the quest? She sensed no other information was available at this time, so she put the cards away.

She went to her desk and pulled out some paper. James was on her mind now, so she might as well explore what his role might be. *Gathering, Awakening* and *Commitment*: these were the cards she'd pulled for James. Elan told her James would bring Chancha to her. Was that all he would be gathering? How was he acting as a gatherer so far? His presence certainly rallied the pack in a new way. She'd rarely felt such protective energies from them. Did he threaten them or did they fear he threatened her? She'd have to explore that question with them at some point.

Being an active neighbor carried a texture of gathering with it. He'd forced her to gather her wits several times. Of course, he was the one who made her lose them. She lost focus too often when he was around. For a moment she got lost in the memory of his eyes and of their time in the circle. They certainly could gather and raise energy between them with an ease that usually took more experience. Still, that could be simply sexual. As she jotted that down with the other notes, she immediately crossed it out. No sense in trying to fool herself. There was more between them than sex and she knew it.

When she asked about James, Elan had told her to look to the past to heal the present and future. She focused and slipped into a light trance to return to their conversation and remember the words Elan had actually said.

. . . the path has found you. He brings you the third and offers you the opportunity to heal the past and balance the present . . . Learn from the past, but look to your present and future to heal it.

She wrote Elan's words down and read through them several times. "Balance the present" seemed to stick out when she read them. So she circled those words in red.

Balance the present . . .fulfill the quest . . . redefine her relationship with Charles . . . deal with the new neighbor . . . go on tour in a couple weeks . . . prepare the land for wintering . . . consider a new book – it was suddenly all too much. She needed to do something active.

She considered walking to the grove, but recognized it was the chance of encountering James that drew her there. As enticing as it sounded, time with James right now seemed more like a distraction than a solution. She decided to walk in her gardens and make note of what needed to be done before fall turned cold. She got up and walked to the kitchen to grab a sweater and her gardening notebook.

It was dark. Where had the time gone? She wouldn't get much gardening done in the dark, but she could still walk. She put on the comfy wool sweater she brought back from Ireland and grabbed a wrap to keep out the wind.

The night air suited her mood perfectly: cool and brisk with a stirring wind that would gain momentum in the next hour or so. Wind had become her ally when she first moved to the Kittitas Valley. She remembered her first quarter at Central Washington University during the spring of 1979. The wind blew fiercely. She quickly traded in her full skirts and long hair pulled back with combs for overalls and a ponytail. Her mother had been horrified by the transformation. She smiled to herself at that. That had been one of her first steps in rejecting others expectations for what was practical for her. She thanked the wind for that gift and for teaching her how to enjoy engaging with nature, instead of resisting it.

She loved the feel of wind against her skin and the way it danced through her hair. The fierceness of the Ellensburg wind was undeniable, so she'd learned to surrender to it. One just had to let go to enjoy it. She did that now, turning directions to invite the wind to cleanse her of confusion, expectations and fear. Her Aunt Bonnie called it "blowing the stink off you". Although the wind blew cold, Cailleen could no longer stand the binding of clothes and pulled them off to give herself fully to the wind. She raised her arms and turned around and around counterclockwise to release everything that did not serve her. She became lighter and lighter as she let worry and feelings of being overwhelmed blow away with the wind. Then she laughed and began moving with the wind in a playful ecstatic dance.

The wind died for a moment and Cailleen became aware of the chill in her body. Still smiling, she pulled on her clothes. The wind picked up again. Cailleen faced it and listened. "Live your life more fully, more joyfully, and with more freedom from assumed responsibility. Don't miss the forest for the trees or the trees for the forest. Dance more." The wind continued to move, but his voice grew silent. Cailleen twirled around in gratitude and goodbye, then walked into the warmth of her kitchen.

Charles was waiting for her with a warm cup of hot chocolate. She danced into his arms and let his bear of a body take the first chill off of hers. Then she stood back and smiled radiantly up at him. He put the hot chocolate in her hands and smiled back.

"What brings you out at this late hour?" Cailleen asked

"The wind, of course," he replied cheerily.

"He is glorious tonight. We just had a chat and a lovely dance."

"I see. And what did the wind tell you?" he asked?

"Uh-uh. That's between me and the wind," she countered. "Did you come with a particular purpose or did you just miss me?"

"Of course, I missed you," Charles said cheekily. "Actually, Elan sent me."

"Oh, what for?" Cailleen asked.

"I don't really know. But I've learned the wisdom of following her lead over the years. So here I am," Charles answered.

"I see. Well, I was going to go upstairs, take a hot bath and then make an early night of it. But I can postpone it, if something is up. Should we go into the study, light a fire and try to connect with Elan?"

Charles considered for a moment. "No, I don't see why you should change your plans. A bath and an early night sound good to me. Why don't you go up. I have a few things to prepare for a meeting tomorrow. I'll have my bath in about an hour and then sleep."

Cailleen kissed his cheek and headed upstairs with cocoa in hand.

The hot bath after the exhilarating dance in the wind relaxed every muscle and soothed every nerve in Cailleen's body. She slipped under her flannel sheets and fell into sleep with the comfort of knowing Charles was here. It was good, she reflected, to have a man in the house. With that she sank deeply into a restful sleep.

Chapter Nine
Reckoning

She dreamed of meadows and mountains and clear running rivers. She had nothing to do but breathe and swim and enjoy the bounty of late summer when she grew hungry. Bees were buzzing. The wind blew gently carrying the sweet scent of apples, clover, and wild berries; the sharper scent of pine and juniper; and the earthiness of wild mushrooms and lichens. Heaven!

She began to doze off in the heat of the afternoon when she heard a quiet hum and the soft sounds of someone approaching. She opened her eyes and turned to identify who came to join her. She recognized the humming and the pace of the gait, but couldn't quite place it. The sun shifted and Cailleen saw her emerging from the trees. She watched as the woman moved toward her through the tall grasses. The brightness of the sun hid her features until Cailleen could almost touch her.

"Grandmama, how nice to see you! Come sit with me and enjoy this lovely meadow," Cailleen beckoned.

Grandmama reached out her hand to Cailleen. "Thank you for the kind offer, my dear. But I'm afraid we must make a journey. And the time to begin is now."

Cailleen took her hand and rose. Grandmama led her across the meadow and into part of the surrounding forest. They walked along a path, which Cailleen had not seen before. Grandmama continued her humming. Cailleen walked silently.

The bubble of a stream in the distance seemed to add counterpoint to Grandmama's humming. Then a third humming voice eased into the song — a voice Cailleen recognized immediately. Elan met them where the stream crossed the path. She held her hand out to steady Cailleen as she crossed over on the slippery stones.

"Merry meet," Elan said as she kissed Cailleen and then Grandmama.

"Merry meet," Cailleen said with joy. As Elan's eyes moved to Grandmama, Cailleen looked behind Elan.

"Charles won't be joining us on this journey," Elan stated.

"Oh," Cailleen said in confusion. "I understood you asked him to come tonight, so I expected him, I guess."

"He will be busy as watchdog tonight," Elan commented.

At the term watchdog, Cailleen knew that Charles and James would meet tonight. Her mind sought them out immediately. She just glimpsed them facing each other at her kitchen door when Elan called her back.

"You must trust them on their own. If you cannot do that, our journey tonight is useless." Elan turned to walk down the path, not waiting for Cailleen. Grandmama put her finger under Cailleen's chin and raised her eyes to meet her own. "Choose, child." Then she too walked down the path.

"You want me to choose between the Spirit world and the flesh and blood of men? Is that what you're asking? I chose that once already," Cailleen said in a faltering voice. "I lost my home, my children, my passion – and it killed my . . ." She couldn't finish the sentence. With tears in her eyes and resignation in her heart, she turned and followed the women. Elan and Grandmama looked at each other with knowing and nodded. Silently they led Cailleen down the path.

***

Back at the manor, Charles stood in Cailleen's kitchen doorway facing James. They tried staring each other down but neither would budge. Still making eye contact, Charles broke the silence.

"As you've dragged me out of bed in the middle of the night, I assume you want something. How can *I* help you?" Charles asked dryly.

"It's only 10:30," James countered, "- late, but certainly not the middle of the night."

"I'll concede that point. What can I do for you?" Charles repeated.

"I don't have a fucking clue," James said.

Charles stepped back a half step in confusion as he took in the fear and concern in James' eyes. A second ago they'd shown only challenge and arrogance. Now, shoulders slumped in defeat, James closed his eyes a moment. When he opened them, Charles saw pleading rather than a challenge.

"You better come in," Charles said as he walked toward the stove and put the kettle on for tea. He watched James out of the corner of his eye. James looked like he too had been roused out of sleep. He had no socks on and one leg of his sweats was pulled halfway up his calf. His bare chest could be seen under his jacket. James looked around the room anxiously as he tried to dig his hands deeper and deeper into his jacket pocket.

Part of Charles wanted to let James suffer. The better part of him had to do what he could to relieve James' pain.

"What's happened?" Charles asked as he put chamomile, oat straw and mint in the teapot.

"Don't you know?" James demanded. Before Charles could reply, he pleaded, "Just tell me if she's OK."

"Who? What's this all about?" Charles asked in a calming voice. "Sit down and tell me what's happened."

At the calm in Charles' voice, James drew a deep breath and released some anxiety. He shook his head and looked at Charles sheepishly. "That's just it, I don't know. I was sleeping and I heard Cailleen screaming. It woke me out of a dead sleep and I ran over as fast as I could. Look, I need to know where she is and I want to know right now!"

Charles began to sense Elan's fingers in the situation and smiled to himself. James nearly erupted when he saw the smile and clearly misinterpreted it. He grabbed Charles and demanded, "Tell me where she is, you son of a bitch!" Charles' face turned implacable. "I'll find her myself," James growled and ran to the stairs.

"Hold on," Charles shouted and ran after him. He tackled him at the foot of the stairs. James fought him and began shouting obscenities. Charles was able to hold him still for just a second and said, "Stop! You are endangering her." At that, James yielded. He was out of his depth and didn't know the rules here. When in doubt, trust your instincts, he reminded himself. Charles would not harm Cailleen. James held his hand up in surrender. Charles let go and they both sat, breathing hard.

"Give me a minute to check in on her," Charles asked as he slowed his breathing and sent out a quiet inquiry. "She's sleeping and dreaming very deeply, probably journeying." He opened his eyes and saw the doubt in every fiber of James' being.

"Look," he explained, "if she's deep into a journey and we go busting up there to see if she's alright, we'll pull her out of wherever she is too quickly. At the depth's she can go, that's dangerous. You were just awakened from a deep sleep. Remember how disoriented you were? To bring her back quickly from what is likely to be an out of body experience can do irreparable harm." Charles watched as James tried to process what he was saying.

"I see you are having trouble trusting me," Charles said. "I suggest we quietly peek in to be certain she is in no danger. Then we can come back down and I'll try to answer any of your questions. Agreed?"

"Agreed," James concurred as he sprinted quietly up the stairs with Charles at his heels.

Together they peered in to find Cailleen breathing deeply and soundly. Face and body were at ease. They closed the door again and walked down the stairs. At the bottom step, James sat down and bent over to put his head between his knees. His whole body shook. Charles left him returning a minute later with two glasses of whiskey. He handed one to James.

"Slainte," he toasted and took a long drink.

"Cheers," James replied, shaking his head. He drank down the whiskey, took a deep breath and walked to the kitchen.

"Three days with you folks and I find the thought of a cup of tea more comforting than just about anything I can think of. What the hell have I walked into?" he laughed nervously.

Charles poured the water over the tea leaves and then rummaged through the refrigerator looking for some hearty food. He gathered items for a manly sandwich. As he built the sandwiches, he encouraged James to talk by giving him a little bit of information.

"You walked into our lives in the middle of a unique week," Charles began. "I am not able to tell you details. I can tell you that Cailleen is traveling through past lives and present circumstances in quest of some very important information. She has some very strong spirit guides. One of them called me here tonight. I thought it was because Cailleen would need my assistance. I suspect she also called you here tonight, although not as gently. As she called us both here, there must be something we are to do together. Any ideas?"

"Me? This is your terrain, man. I'm just a visitor," James responded.

"Tell yourself that if it makes you more comfortable," Charles said.

"What the hell do you mean by that?"

"I mean," Charles said, "that spirit guides don't tend to mess with visitors – at least not in this way. Much as I am reluctant to admit it, you and Cailleen seem to have a deep connection. I felt it the first time we met you and I could see she felt it too. You, I wasn't so sure of. You're an arrogant son of a bitch."

"Nice to meet you kettle, I'm the pot," James said with sarcasm. "You weren't exactly warm and welcoming that morning. And yes, I felt it. Pissed me off. One look at her in wool socks and a purple fuzzy robe and I was shaken. Damn inconvenient it is. And it's not just her, it's this world she lives in that I know nothing about. How am I supposed to keep my bearings? It's frustrating as hell, especially as she seems surrounded by strong men, who she clearly loves. What am I needed for?"

"Well now, that's a question we've all been asking. What are you needed for? Why have you shown up at just this time? And what part, if any," Charles paused for emphasis, "do you play in this quest of hers?"

Charles cut the sandwiches and put them on plates. He held one out to James. When James took the plate, Charles held it until James looked up at him. "Why," he asked, "do you hide the real reason you came here?"

At that, James lowered his eyes. No sense in pretending what Charles said wasn't true. He took a breath and looked Charles in the eyes. "Like you, I am not at liberty to tell you the details of my arrival in your neighborhood. I can tell you I have no dishonorable intentions and that I mean no harm to any of you. I know nothing about this quest, so I can't see as I have a part to play in it. As to why I am needed, all I can say is that I feel drawn and bound by something I can't fathom. I am Alice down the rabbit's hole."

They ate in silence except for grunts of "good grub" and "guess we worked up an appetite." They let each other wander through their own thoughts and questions until they were drinking down the last dregs of tea.

"Who is this woman you said called us here tonight?" James asked.

"Her name is Elan. She guides travelers along the path. Often comes when you're at a crossroad. She always waits for you to ask for her help," Charles explained.

"I don't even know her. How could I have asked her for help?" James asked.

"Have you generally asked for help with anything of late. You know, the kind of general 'damn, I could use some help' or 'God, help me' kind of thing?

"No, nothing," James said and then stopped abruptly with his mug halfway to his lips. "Damn! I was in the grove today and asked for help. What the hell, does that mean I'm now fair game for any spirit guide who may have heard me?"

"Sometimes, it can feel that way," Charles conceded. "But no, there is always a rhyme and a reason for such things. It can take years to see the interweaving, though. With practice, it gets easier to trust and easier to interpret. Tell me about what happened in the grove."

James hesitated. He didn't want to seem foolish and he didn't want to share the nature of his discussion with the birds. It was one thing reading and talking with Cailleen about this new world he'd wandered into. It was quite another thing to share intimate details with this man - who saw him as a threat.

"Look," Charles said, "I've been where you're sitting right now. After my wife died several years ago, I came here to heal. Cailleen is a longtime family friend. Something about Whitney's death opened my intuitive skills. Blasted them open, actually. Without Cailleen's guidance as my psychic abilities opened, I would have gone crazy. She saw the signs and put me in a place where I could safely explore and develop my gifts. We have since uncovered several past life connections between us. We have worked together before in many lives – that's the source of the deep loving connection you feel between us.

"But more than anything," he continued. "Cailleen is *mother* to me in this lifetime. You will no doubt hear lots of rumors and conjectures about our relationship from the town's folk. But I give you my word of honor that our relationship has never had nor ever will have a romantic or sexual aspect to it - not in this lifetime. What I mean to say is that our relationship is well defined and we share a lot of history. That does not preclude either of us entering into other relationships. It does mean though, that we're part of each other's lives.

"For my part, I can say no one will prevent me from continuing to learn and grow in our relationship and in our work together. I believe she feels the same way, which means we must allow for new relationships in the other's life and make room. I do not stand in the way of any relationship you two might choose to enter. But I will stand by her and protect her if I feel the need, just as you did tonight. You have shown courage and loyalty. I won't forget that."

Charles took the dishes to the sink and returned with the cookie jar and a fresh pot of tea. He took one and offered the jar to James.

"I feel a purpose in our meeting tonight," he told James. "We've challenged each other. We've both acted to protect Cailleen this evening. It does not matter if the threat was real or imagined. We both showed up. We also both put aside our personal feelings to make sure she was safe. We shared a meal. We fought and drank whiskey. I think we've had an evening of male bonding. Let's not stop here if we've more to do. You're still sitting here. So, I figure you recognize we're not quite done either. Tell me about the grove. Whatever you say stays between us and I promise not to judge you."

"It calls to me - the grove I mean," began James. His words were calm, but Charles saw his discomfort in the way he fidgeted with a cookie as he talked.

"You know, I was there with Cailleen yesterday. " James rose, ran his fingers through his hair and then rubbed his jaw as he processed what he was trying to say. "The power I witnessed and experienced was incredible. I've been reading her books. The cottage has a shelf of them," he explained, "and since meeting her I feel the need to know as much about her as I can. So I read about the kind of thing I experienced yesterday.

"I don't know if you can understand this, but I felt a need to discover if the power and magic was just Cailleen's." James sat again and leaned toward Charles. He looked both excited and confused. "I wanted to know if I could feel it on my own. I needed to know if I had any part of it or was simply a handy tool. Even more, a part of me wanted to see if I could connect with the grove and with the spirits of the forest on my own."

James hesitated. When Charles smiled and nodded in understanding, he continued.

"Another truth is, I wanted to see if she's the real thing. If it was all just sexual tension and/or tricks or suggestions that had led me to believe I'd seen something, I figured I wouldn't be able to recreate it in any way. So I went up to the grove when Cailleen left to meet you. I brought one of her books in case I needed a reference."

James stood and walked about the kitchen as he continued. The tension was leaving his body as he committed to telling Charles everything. Charles relaxed in response as James continued his story.

"Yesterday, she showed me how to enter sacred space with intention and to ask permission. I followed what she'd shown me and I was able to create a similar experience today. I felt the door to another world open and welcome me. A raven and a crow joined me. That would have sounded weird to me two days ago." James paused and shrugged. Charles nodded in understanding.

"As I reached the center of the circle, I didn't really know what to do. Raven and Crow perched themselves up on a couple of branches, then looked at me and cocked their heads as if listening. I took it as a sign and I spilled my guts. Other crows gathered for my story, and as I spoke, it seemed that the birds and trees actually *were* listening to me. I felt it, like I can feel when a perp is lying or holding something back, or telling me the absolute truth. It was cleaner, though. I don't know if that makes sense. Are plants and animals always easier to read than people?" James looked to Charles to verify this new concept.

"In my experience, except for a few rare people, yes. Nature is cleaner and easier to read. Nature has no need to hide anything," Charles explained.

"Cailleen asked me a question earlier that I answered evasively. I was honoring a confidence of a friend, yet I felt uncomfortable with my inability to be totally honest with her. I told the crows and the raven about the entire situation and that my loyalties felt torn. It felt good to speak it out loud to witnesses. Then we sat in silence. Suddenly a buck came out of the forest and looked right into my eyes. Then an elk walked into the circle and huffed at me. I couldn't believe they came that close. They were fuckin' gorgeous." James stopped talking as he remembered the beauty of that moment. Charles smiled as he remembered similar moments in his own life.

James cleared his throat. "I remembered Cailleen spoke about animal medicine and I looked them up in her book. The elk and buck were startled away when I gasped in surprise, but I felt they'd already blessed me with their presence. Cailleen would say they'd given me their medicine."

Charles nodded in agreement.

"Then I didn't know what to do again," James said with frustration. "I sat there watching the birds and feeling the trees waiting for me to do something. All I could think of was to thank them for listening and to tell them what a help it was to have told my story. I asked them to continue to help me – if it harmed none and served my highest purpose. At that, they all flew up and circled the grove several times, and then flew off. It seemed they were accepting my request and, I don't know, getting started on the task."

James smiled to himself, then raised his eyes and shared the smile with Charles. He sat again. Charles waited.

"And here I am a few hours later, sitting alone in a room with you telling my story again. And I do feel better for it. I thought I'd feel silly sharing what could easily be interpreted as the ramblings of a man with an overactive imagination. Instead, telling the story makes it feel more real somehow." James drank some tea in silence.

"Thank you," Charles offered, "for trusting me with your story. You can be assured that what happened is as real as that mug in your hand. You revealed more to me tonight than you know. I caution you not to share at this level with everyone. I encourage you to not share beyond Cailleen and myself at this time. There will be others you can trust, but two is plenty until you learn more. Clearly, you're a fast learner. You protected yourself well enough by asking for help *if it harm none and it serves your highest purpose*. Those are not just words.

"I would like to share something with you now, but I need your word that you will not share it with anyone else. Cailleen knows, so you may speak freely with her about it. Do I have your word?" Charles asked.

"Will you trust my word?" James asked.

"I will," Charles stated firmly.

"I will not share what you tell me with anyone other than Cailleen and yourself. You have my word," James agreed.

"Did you read about or has Cailleen spoken to you about personal totems?" Charles asked.

James nodded. "I read about it in her first book. It made sense to me immediately. I used to apply animal characters to the people I met undercover. It helped me keep them straight and helped me to size up their character. There were a lot of weasels, always changing their color; rats eating off anything and everything; and more sheep than you can imagine. I understand now that I was assigning the shadow side of the animal, or totem, to the people I met. Then again, I was usually deep in a shadowy world. My fellow cops call me, the wolf. That's my totem. It fits. I can be a lone wolf, but I'm happiest in a pack that I trust."

"Yes," Charles agreed, "wolf does fit you. And we cannot always hide the totem allies that we carry. Like the rats, weasels and sheep you met, the characteristics are sometimes, obvious."

"To reveal one's totem is to reveal an aspect of one's personal power," Charles continued. "Crow is one of my power totems. I believe Crow, with Elan's help, brought you to me tonight. I have carried Crow medicine through every lifetime. I am crow, part of the murder. Flocks of crows are called murders," he explained at James' questioning eyes. "When the crows accepted your request this evening, I, by association, accepted it as well. I will help you in any way I can as long as it does not interfere with any prior promises and commitments I have made."

"I don't know what to say," James claimed. "Seriously, I don't know what's appropriate and I'm pretty sure I don't fully understand the depth of your offer. But I thank you for it. May I ask a question?"

"You may always ask a question. I may not be able to answer, but if I can, I will," Charles replied.

"If you are crow, why did the crows not go directly to you? Are you unable to communicate directly or over a certain distance?" James asked.

"An astute question. Not much gets by you, does it?" Charles considered James for a moment and then answered. "Yes, Crow could have communicated directly with me. Crows do have boundaries in the physical world and cannot cross into another murder's territory without being in danger. But on the psychic plane those rules do not hold. It is significant that Crow did not come directly to me. Again, I feel Elan's hand in this. It suggests to me that you and I are to walk a path together."

"Aren't we on the same path right now, here in this kitchen?" James asked.

"Not necessarily," Charles said. "Our paths have certainly crossed. But to walk a path together means we are allies with a common purpose. It suggests we will be better for having walked together."

"Oh." James paused in thought. "I admit to feeling like I walked into some alternate reality. I have no experience on which to make decisions," he admitted with frustration.

"It might not be so unusual" Charles suggested. "You did, consciously and willingly, set in motion a series of events when you asked for help. But you probably did that on a daily basis as a cop. Every time you had someone checked out you affected their lives and yours. Every time any of us choose to turn left or right we set in motion a series of events over which we have varying degrees of control.

"In the Western world we like to think we have control and that we know what will happen. There is truth in this thinking. For what we intend and what we envision happening tends to create that reality. You have simply entered an unknown world where you don't know the variables or possibilities. But you do have tools.

You've worked undercover." Charles reminded him. James nodded. "This isn't that different. You just need to recognize that different rules apply here and you need to learn them. You have keen observation skills and a high degree of intuition. You also learn quickly. These are traits that will serve you well in any world. It's important neither to under nor over-estimate yourself. You followed your intuition when you asked for help. As a result, you have a guide at your service." Charles bowed to ease the tension and bring a smile to James' face.

"You know," Charles continued. "I could complain that I have unwittingly been landed with you just because I'm a crow. A couple of hours ago I might have resisted helping your arrogant ass. But Spirit went and threw us into our earlier male bonding experience. That led me to open and begin trusting you. Then I learned I was committed to helping you, which is probably the very reason that Elan choreographed the whole thing. You see? The rhyme and the reason – or at least one of them."

James shook his head as if it was all too much to process. Charles looked at the clock. It was 1 AM.

"I think we might call it a night," Charles suggested. "I have a meeting tomorrow morning, which I can do via conference call. I'll hang out here in the afternoon and maybe even stay until the next day. If you need me, you know where to find me. Are you good to go home? You look done in. There are two other rooms upstairs. Why don't you crash here tonight?"

James wasn't sure if he accepted the invitation because he was exhausted or because he wanted to stay close until he actually had a chance to talk to Cailleen. The two men walked upstairs together. They both paused at the top of the stairs, wanting to turn left and check on Cailleen one last time. With a shared glance and a shrug of their shoulders they went to her door and peaked in. Cailleen was still sleeping deeply and had not changed positions since they'd looked in on her a few hours earlier.

***

Cailleen followed Grandmama and Elan down the path with more reluctance than she'd have admitted. She didn't like walking away from Charles and James. Something had shifted in her. Choosing the spirit realm over the physical realm no longer seemed so easy. This knowledge made her uncomfortable.

She looked ahead and saw that Grandmama and Elan were waiting for her. She quickened her step. They stood by a large sacred pool. It steamed and smelled of sulfur. In the middle of the pool several hundred feet away was a very large stone. A raft was tethered to a tree near them. Elan whistled what sounded like an ancient bird call, then waited. Within minutes a young boy came towards them.

"Merry meet," he greeted.

"Merry meet, Jacques," Elan answered. Grandmama and Cailleen nodded and greeted him too.

"Will you be scrying tonight, then?" Jacques asked.

"Yes indeed," Elan responded. "Has everything been made ready?"

"Yes, my lady," Jacques agreed with a smile.

"Carry us to the center then, Jacques." Elan indicated to Grandmama and Cailleen to step on the raft and then to sit quietly while Jacques poled the raft to the center rock.

When they arrived, the sun was setting. The rock was larger than it appeared from the edge of the pool. Cushions, robes and blankets had been set in a triangle. In the center, stood a small table with three cups and a matching carafe. The triskele, a Celtic symbol of balance, was inscribed in both the cups and carafe. The women wrapped the fine woolen robes of forest green around them and fastened their buttons, also engraved with the triskele. The deep brown cushions of wool filled with down and the corner of each blanket were embroidered with golden thread also in the shape of a triskele.

The women sat cross-legged in their robes on the cushions with the blankets tucked around their knees. They waited in silence. Just as the moon began rising Elan began humming. The others joined in. As they grew strong in voice, Elan nodded to Grandmama, who added a low descant to the melody line. When the two lines settled together and grew strong, Elan added a high descant. As they sang, the moon rose and the cold night air met the steaming pool, creating a swirling mist around the women. The nearly full moon rested at its apex and the women moved into silence once again.

Elan poured crystal clear water into each of the cups. In one she added a powdered mixture of herbs and handed it to Cailleen. They drank slowly, one sip at a time until the cups were empty. The mists grew heavy between them and Cailleen could no longer see either of the women. She called out to them but heard no answer. Sounds became distorted and Cailleen feared they had left her alone in the mists. She stood and tried to walk to them, but she couldn't get her bearings and didn't want to leave the cushion, which was her only hold on the physical world. She began to panic, but her training reminded her to breathe, to ground herself and center.

As she calmed herself, she heard her grandmother's voice.

"Child, come with me. We have much to see and learn."

"Where's Elan?" Cailleen asked.

"She is resting. Her task was to lead us here. Our work begins now." With a brush of her hand Grandmama parted the mists and led Cailleen to the edge of the rock. The moon shone like glass on the water. As she gazed into it things began to shift then settle.

Cailleen saw herself in her parent's basement. The family was looking at slides from their childhood. The screen showed Cailleen at about two years old sitting on Auntie's lap. She remembered Auntie whispering something to her, but didn't remember what. The scene shifted to that moment. Her father had just yelled at her for doing something he didn't like. She felt Auntie stiffen with disapproval. Then Auntie relaxed and pulled Cailleen closer. Auntie rocked her back and forth. As her father walked away, probably to take the picture, Auntie whispered, "Remember who you are. No matter what, remember who you are."

The scene shifted.

Cailleen saw the moon's reflection again. She turned to Grandmama, but her grandmother shook her head and pointed back at the water. Cailleen returned her focus and the scene shifted.

The familiar scene of the camp ground at Salmon La Sac in the upper county appeared before her. She walked along the river down to Lake Cle Elum. She was 33 years old and felt lost in her life. She'd been betrayed by family and had to cut herself off from them. She longed for the mother she needed, one who loved and accepted her, one who would cradle her and protect her, one she was not separate from. She'd come camping all alone. It was scary because she'd never done it. She'd never allowed herself as a woman to be alone like this. It wasn't like she was in the wilderness, but she felt very alone as she walked along the river where it flowed into the lake. The hot August sun beat down upon her. Nobody else was in sight and Cailleen let her tears flow and the child who needed her mother was set free.

Cailleen had left her family. She'd left the Catholic Church. She'd left her job as a youth minister. She had no idea what lay ahead of her, but she kept on walking. She asked for help. She took another step and sank into mud almost up to her knee. She wailed. "I ask for help and you sink me? I'm stuck!" In her fury, Cailleen struggled and pulled to no avail. "This is getting me nowhere," she croaked in frustration. She was just exhausting herself at this point, so she stopped struggling and surrendered. She wiggled her toes, and noticed how delightful the mud felt. It was cool, silky and sensual. She took another step so both feet were in the mud and she felt herself ease into its embrace.

It felt so good not to struggle and to simply rest. She stood for a long time in the mud.

She was no longer sinking. The ground beneath her felt solid enough and the mud felt so nurturing.

"I am always with you," she heard. She looked around and saw no one. "You can never be separated from me, daughter." The voice seemed to be coming from the earth and water and sky all at the same time. "I claim you as my own." The voice was comforting and soothing. "Do not fear. I am with you always."

Tears flowed in rivers down Cailleen's face, while at the same time laughter bubbled from deep within her. "Mama," she cried as she stripped off her clothes and covered herself in mud. Mother Nature was speaking to her, directly. She longed to feel her arms holding her. The mud was the Mother's touch.

She grew tired and floated easily out of the mud. She dried herself by the river. With the sun's heat, the mud dried, tightening around her like the protective arms of the mother. In that moment, she understood where she belonged. No human could be the mother she expected. She was Nature's daughter and always had been.

Memories of talking to the clouds and dancing with Faeries flooded her mind. She'd been asking her human family to support her in ways they could not understand. It was time to return to the ways of Nature.

The scene before her shifted again. She was now twelve years old, out in the field alone, planting seeds for the summer garden. The rhythm of planting took her into a trance. No, it was more than a trance. She'd entered the world of the Fey. The essence of light was different here. The air hummed, colors pulsed between the edges of plants, animals and the Faeries – showing the deep connection between them. A sweet sadness hovered over everything.

In the world of the Fey, Cailleen learned to heal, to observe and to listen. "How do I know how to get here?" she asked.

"We taught you of course," she was told.

"But when?" she asked.

"You were six years old back then." A beautiful Faerie woman walked toward her from behind a tree. Cailleen recognized her as the queen. "You were in an car accident and had to stay in what you call a hospital. It's a terrible place not suited for healing, so we brought you here. We taught you our ways as best we could and gave you the secret of how to return."

Cailleen shook her head. "I don't remember it," she complained.

"Well certainly you must or you would not have been able to return to us. It's not that you don't remember, it's more that you don't usually remember to remember. And you won't remember this for many long years, I'm afraid. But there will come a time when it will be safe for you to remember. You will be able to use the skills we've taught you, but you won't remember where you've learned them. Try not to let that bother you too much."

She walked for a while in the Fey world, letting herself remember.

"It's time for you to go now," the wind whispered. "You won't remember us in your head for a very long time, but you'll never forget us in your heart. Be joy, beloved."

The scenes shifted rapidly now. She stood outside the high school band room with Gerry O'Reilly. She was madly in love with him, but never acted on it. Then she stood at college talking with Kevin. She'd been so subtle in her pursuit of him, he never knew she was interested. Greg and Bob's faces flashed before her —unavailable men. She poured her heart into friendship. Stan, a promising prospect she rejected because of political beliefs. Felx, her fiancé, who turned out to be gay. Long years of focused study with no time for men broken by short relationships with weak men, who could not meet her. They tried to make her smaller to fit who they were.

Now, she was back with Grandmama. "It would have been better to become a nun," Cailleen said in despair.

"Certainly," Grandmama agreed, "if you'd been called to that lifestyle."

"Sometimes, I think I have been called to it," she answered sadly. "My work has been my priority all my life. And, the truth is, I haven't really met a man that was a match for me. I actually don't regret walking away from any of those men. When I was open to a relationship, I seemed to only draw weak or unavailable men to me."

"Look again," Grandmama invited.

The same scenes moved before her, but this time she saw angels and spirit guides stepping in to guide and protect her.

"I don't understand. Did Spirit block me romantically?" Cailleen queried. "Seems rather cruel."

"Yes, your angels and spirit guides blocked things. They did so at your request. You asked before you incarnated in this lifetime that distractions from your work and purpose be removed."

"But why not just remove my desire for a partner? That would have been easier."

"No doubt," Grandmama agreed. "However, that would not have served you. Just because it hasn't served you yet to be with a long-term partner doesn't mean it will not serve you at some point."

"I have to keep choosing?"

"Granddaughter, that is the nature of things. Each experience offers its lessons. You learned something about yourself and relationships with every choice you've made with men — and women.

You have turned away from possible relationships with several women, even if you don't recognize that. Consciously or unconsciously, we define who we will be in every potential relationship.

In your relationship with Everett, you learned what it was like to be in an intimate relationship with an alcoholic. That has served you in your work and in your ability to empathize with others in that situation.

You chose against it and you now have the ability to sense the desperation of that sort of addiction. The angels stepped in to help you see the truth sooner rather than later. They're not playing with you. They're helping you as you asked them to.

"I have been sent to you tonight to help you see patterns and to encourage you not to limit yourself by them. Patterns play out and evolve. Don't restrict yourself to those of your past. Choose what will serve you now. And please, granddaughter, remember we are not given desires to torture us. We are given them to propel us to our purpose. When we dance with them in balance, they help us understand who we are. Always remember who you *really are."*

Elan approached and told them it was time to return. Jacques took them back to shore and they walked back through the forest. When Cailleen emerged into her meadow once again, she was alone. She felt exhausted and wanted only to sleep. She lay among the grasses and the warmth of the sun helped her slip away.

***

Jen and Lawrence agreed to meet on Tuesday evening and attempt a journey. Jen's meditation and dreaming room fit their needs. Small with clean lines and warm colors in brown tones, it spoke of Jen's simple and uncluttered approach to her spiritual life.

A dreaming couch with a side table sat along the north wall. Each wall featured a small single shelf that served as an altar to its prospective direction. Between two small windows on the south wall, a shelf held an assortment of candles of various heights. In the west a large chambered nautilus rested on sea foam colored fabric. In the north a ceramic pot held five bamboo stems. The east featured a quirky little sculpture of a stylized cat. The cat had a third eye and its tail suggested perpetual motion. It resembled Coal, Jen's large male cat, who always joined her for dreams and journeys.

Coal had his own basket in the northeast corner of the room. Its elevation and style suggested a throne. In the center of the room a very plush round rug covered the hardwood floor.

Jen and Lawrence sat back-to-back on meditation pillows, and as their breathing synchronized, they fell into an easy trance. Jen would journey first to her past life to see if she could reclaim the memory of the family secret. Then, if possible, she would attempt to connect with Raneck. Lawrence would act as recorder of any information Jen found, and as a guardian.

They began by setting sacred space and casting a protective circle. Jen called on Isis, with whom she worked most closely. "Isis," she called, "come to my aid as I seek to piece together clues from the past. Join your creative and persistent spirit with my own as I travel. Guide and protect me. Blessed be."

They breathed together allowing Jen to integrate the energies of Isis into her own. When she felt centered and strong, Lawrence called his own guides. "Brother Elk, I call forth your spirit of stamina that lies strong within me. Help me to be strong and to give strength where it is needed this night. Lend me the antennae of your antlers to perceive clearly that which is ours to know. And I call on Hermes, God of communication. Help me to stay connected with Jen, yet emotionally distant enough for clear and easy communication. Blessed be."

They breathed together, allowing Lawrence to integrate the energies of Elk and Hermes. As he centered, Coal came and curled up in his lap. "Thank you, Coal," he whispered, "I accept your help."

With that, Jen set her intention and followed her breath into the past. She used the memory from her dream of how she felt sitting by the river. She felt the cool night air and Neville's arm around her shoulders. As she was being pulled in deeper to the emotions, Jen heard Lawrence's caution, "Don't try to re-live it, watch it as if it were a movie."

Jen began to pull out of the body she had known in this earlier life. She wanted to be there as an observer. As she pulled out, she felt Neville's hand tighten around her shoulder and she glanced over at him. She immediately sensed something strange, a hunger and urgency flooded through Neville's body. She wanted to flee from it, but was held fast by his eyes.

"Stop, do not leave me. I have only a short time."

Jen felt the weakness underneath the intensity of emotion that came at her. She realized it was not Neville who had spoken.

"Who are you and what do you want?" she asked.

Back in her meditation room, Lawrence's body had gone rigid and Coal's tail was twitching. He immediately sent Jen both support and courage, then he hesitated about whether to draw her back to her own time. He sensed before Jen did that Raneck was speaking through Neville. Coal was not hissing, only on alert. Lawrence decided to trust the cat's instincts and simply stand ready.

"I think you know who I am," Raneck answered.

Just then a small barking dog ran up to them followed by a harried looking woman. "Please excuse us," the woman said, "Poppins was alone a bit longer than usual today and he's now behaving badly." She reached down to scoop up the dog and looked Jen straight in the eyes. It was Elan. "Surprises along the path can be startling, but this one at least has not been harmful. Have a lovely evening, Miss."

Jen could only assume Elan was encouraging her to stay and assuring her she was not in any real danger. She turned back to the man next to her.

"Raneck, I presume?"

"Presumptions got us into this situation. I no longer have time for them. Calleigha must stand firm with Chancha *and* show him compassion. He despises not knowing. It makes him feel weak and impotent. Tell her to help him listen to his adviser. Tell her I'm sorry."

"Shall she stand firm with you as well?" Jen challenged. "Will you allow the others to choose for themselves?"

"There is no choice," Raneck sneered, "only duty."

"What is your duty?" Jen asked.

"To call the others to their duty."

"I guess you failed me in this lifetime, then," Jen countered. "I didn't perform my duty. I didn't even try."

"You did your duty; the story was passed on. It could only have been passed through you. You did your job then. See that you pass my message on now."

"I have one more job it seems," Jen said. "Raneck, I call you to let go. Release your grasp on the regrets of the past. You have strained your thread in this tapestry and it is unraveling. If it breaks, your line can never be healed. You must pass over and return to the source."

"You're a child. Don't presume you know more than I do."

"A five-year-old was once strong enough that she did not need you. She has trained me," Jen countered with a cool voice.

Raneck's unbalanced emotions flared into a psychic rage, Coal hissed and Lawrence threw his love for Jen up as a shield. Raneck staggered back with a cry and retreated. Jen's compassionate nature reached out and caught Neville as he fell forward.

"I feel a bit woozy," Neville said in a surprised voice. "I'm not sure what's come over me." Jen rubbed his back to soothe him. "Thanks; I think I'm fine," he said in a stronger voice, "It's so odd. I was trying to comfort you one moment and the next I'm falling out of my seat." Jen smiled. "Let's sit here for a bit longer," she suggested, "then you can walk me home."

To be certain Neville had not been harmed, Jen stayed within the body of the woman she had been. As they sat, the woman relived the events of her day and the story her grandmother passed to her. Then with a sigh, Jen left her and journeyed back to her own time.

Coal's purring brought Jen back to her own time and place. The cat now sat on Jen's lap. He nuzzled his head under her hand to be petted and began pressing his paws into her legs in delight and welcome.

"Welcome back," Lawrence sighed. "That was a bit intense on this end. How'd it go for you?"

"We got what we needed and no real harm was done. I think it went quite well. Did you catch Elan's appearance?"

"Elan?!"

"Elan."

Jen took Coal's lead and began stretching her limbs and reacquainting herself with her body in this lifetime. "Give me a minute," she said. Jen grabbed a journal from the table and jotted down notes. "Shall we close the circle and retire to the kitchen to compare notes?"

"Sure." Lawrence released the directions and they each gave thanks and released Isis, Hermes and Brother Elk. They extinguished candles and set the room to rights.

"I think I smell Yvonne's zucchini bread. She was baking it when I left her."

"She's a gem. If you don't marry her, I will!"

Over tea and zucchini bread, they compared notes, typed them into Jen's laptop and emailed them to Cailleen and Charles.

Chapter Ten
Rearrangements

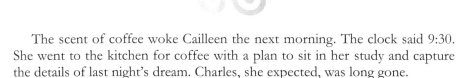

The scent of coffee woke Cailleen the next morning. The clock said 9:30. She went to the kitchen for coffee with a plan to sit in her study and capture the details of last night's dream. Charles, she expected, was long gone.

Charles' jacket was on the back of a chair and his briefcase on the table. On top was a note:

> "*Was up early for a conference call. Taking a mid-morning nap.*
> *Charles*
> *P.S. James is in Lawrence's room.*

Cailleen had no idea what happened last night. Still, she needed to get the details of her dream written down before she lost them. She grabbed coffee and went to her study.

She re-emerged an hour later to another surprise.

James was cooking breakfast while regaling Charles with some fishing story from his childhood. Charles sat at the table, laughing in genuine amusement.

"Have I entered the Twilight Zone?" she asked the two men.

James exchanged her coffee mug for a cup of tea, kissed her and handed a basket of muffins to Charles as if they'd all lived together for years.

"If you're in the Twilight Zone, you're in good company," James said wryly. "Now sit, you're just in time for breakfast."

"I see you've made yourself at home," she observed quizzically.

"Oh. Do you mind?" James asked uncertainly.

"No. No, I don't mind in the least. I'm surprised, but I don't mind." She kissed him and sat down for breakfast.

"We have news," Charles told her.

"No kidding," she agreed. "What happened while I slept?"

"Elan arranged for our paths to cross," Charles explained, waving a fork between James and himself. As they ate breakfast, they told her the whole story. Cailleen didn't know whether to be amused, intrigued or annoyed that the two almost came to blows over something that never happened.

"I don't understand why you came running over here in the middle of the night, James." Cailleen started clearing the table as she waited for him to answer.

"I heard you scream," James said.

"So, you were dreaming about me? What was happening in the dream?" she asked.

"Actually, I wasn't dreaming about you. I was dreaming about this undercover case I had about ten years ago. At the time, I was investigating a guy who ran a gambling ring. He was rumored to have a cruel streak. His favorite event was cock fighting. I worked my way into his inner circle. Along the way I met the sister of one of his underlings. I always tried to avoid any romantic relationships when I was undercover. I knew going in it would end badly and hearts would be broken, so I had a personal rule against it. But this woman was persistent and it came to a point where avoiding her would look like rejection and that would be dangerous for me and could blow my cover. So, I entered a lighthearted and casual relationship. It turned out that's all she was really interested in. We became friends. Well, my cover story and she became friends.

"Her brother wasn't too bright and he decided to skim some money off the weekly takings. He thought if he took just a little it would be OK, even if he got caught. The boss didn't see it that way. He considered it disloyal and he ordered quick and severe punishment. Like I said, this guy was cruel.

"Instead of punishing the brother directly, he decided to take his rage out on the guy's sister. I was on my way to meet her when I heard her pleading. I ran up the stairs to help her, but I was too late. I opened the door in time to see someone in black throw acid in her face, and then slip out the window and down the fire escape.

"Last night I was in the middle of that horror, only instead of Suzy's voice, I heard you screaming. I jumped out of bed, grabbed a jacket and ran over here. It was the longest ten minutes of my life. And if Elan sent me that dream and then put your voice in it, she's no friend of mine," James ended with anger.

"James. I'm so sorry about your friend." Cailleen sat next to him and covered his hand in comfort.

"James," Charles said, "I have known Elan for years, probably lifetimes actually. She would not be so cruel as to send you such a dream. She may have inserted Cailleen's voice into the dream you were already having. She may have used it to get your attention, and have you come over and check things out. I can't believe she would have known the depth of your reaction. Or, perhaps she guessed and thought it was important for you to recognize that depth. She is not afraid to do the difficult things to get our attention when necessary, but I've never her seen her be cruel."

"Well, I guess I'll have to trust you on that for now," James said.

They all started clearing the table. They moved together in silence allowing each to have their thoughts. When they finished, Charles handed James his coat.

"We're heading up to the grove unless you need us here," Charles informed Cailleen.

"More male bonding?"

"Crow lessons," James quipped. "I'll do up the dishes first."

"You boys go along and play," Cailleen teased. "I'll take care of the dishes."

They both kissed her on the cheek as they headed for the door.

"Rosey, my girl," Cailleen said as she scratched behind the dog's ear, "I fear I may soon long for the days when they didn't like each other."

Doing the dishes helped Cailleen clear her mind of extraneous questions. With each dish she cleaned she let more distractions go. The action and intention grounded her and put her in a calm reflective mood that felt productive.

She headed to her study to take care of business concerns. She made final notes on the class she was teaching next week and checked her itinerary for the upcoming book tour. The class she was teaching, "Courting the Hag: Understanding and Developing Your Intuitive/Psychic Gifts," was thankfully scheduled in the middle of the week at the Northwest Metaphysical Conference in Seattle. She also agreed to be part of a panel discussion the evening prior to her class. The conference staff arranged for her to stay at the same hotel and Jen had a guestroom ready for her if she needed more space. She planned to stay with Jen after her class ended and then return home the next day. That gave her two days before the Samhain celebration for her students. A more private celebration would take place later in the same evening.

She made a note to connect with Jen, Lawrence and Charles about Samhain. They still needed to create a ritual. She wondered about inviting James to be part of one or both of the celebrations. She'd pull Charles aside before he left this afternoon and get his thoughts. All four of them would have to agree to his presence for the later celebration. James would make them a circle of five, a representative for each of the Elements.

She began considering what Element(s) James would carry most comfortably. Perhaps Earth or Fire would suit him. He certainly demonstrated an ability to carry them well. His stocky, muscular build gave him the solid reliable feel of Earth. His passion and the genuine warmth when he played with Rosey or relaxed at her kitchen table showed a depth of fiery expression as well as a playful spirit. His analytical mind and quick wit indicated comfort with the Element of Air. Water and its association with the emotions may be the least comfortable for him. Then again, she thought that might not be a fair evaluation. His work of the past 20 years had trained him to keep emotion out of the equation at work. Yet, her experience of him just in the last few days included wide variations of emotional expression, and ease in traversing them. The story in the dream he shared showed he was sensitive to the emotions of others and had deep emotions himself.

Spirit, perhaps, was the Element he was weakest in. He was opening to its challenges and demands with incredible grace and a healthy dose of discernment. It would be a joy witnessing his journey. She wondered how James and Charles were doing in the grove. Sitting back and closing her eyes, she imagined them among the trees. She smiled as they moved together around the circle. She felt such joy in seeing them working together. As she took in the scene that surrounded them it became clear that what she saw was not the circle in fall, but rather in springtime. A closer inspection showed that both men were older by at least a couple of years.

She was projecting a long-term relationship and that was dangerous. She didn't know James that well. She didn't even totally trust him. She didn't distrust him, but she did feel he was holding something back. Until she discovered what that was, she had no business thinking about a future.

The man was in flux. He didn't even know where he would be living or what he would be doing in another six months. Did she really want to deepen ties and risk an emotional connection that might only end in pain?

Yes, she did. But would she act on it?

She didn't want to deal with this right now. The timing was off. She had so much to consider without the distraction of an attractive, seemingly balanced man who might be able or willing to meet her in every way. She had her quest. She had generations past, present and future depending on her current abilities. This was no time for a dalliance.

Of course, James was not a dalliance and she knew it. That was the crux of the problem. Thoughts of him kept intruding on her work. She turned her chair to look out the window in the direction of the grove.

Charles walked toward her alone. She felt disappointment that James wasn't with him and then shook her head in frustration. She expected that he would return with Charles and tell her his experiences over lunch. She felt deprived at missing out on witnessing his response to whatever work he and Charles had done in the grove. She'd hoped he would be excited to share his experience with her.

"Well," she said to the room as she rubbed the tension out of her shoulders, "at least I'll have time to chat with Charles. And I could use the time away from James to re-establish my equilibrium, adjust my expectations." Maybe a dalliance *was* the best approach. After all, she wasn't a 16-year-old with no control over her hormones or emotions. She could keep things in perspective.

She'd go over her notes from last night and this morning - and not even think of James. With determination she gathered pen and papers and moved to the table on the floor. She lit a candle and silently asked for Elan to guide her as she sought clarity and discerned what actions she should take at this time.

She glanced through the papers looking for patterns and anything that pulled at her or seemed to stick out.

He brings you the third and offers you the opportunity to heal the past and balance the present.... Learn from the past, but look to your present and future to heal it.

She'd circled that earlier and it still seemed important. Elan believed James was part of the quest. What part was he to play?

She went back to what Grandmama shared on that first night of the quest.

Do not let yourself be overwhelmed by this task. I will look over you as best I can. I see that several will come to help you. I also see you will be offered more than one version of this story. Use your heart and intuition more often than your head. Remember your task is ultimately to re-balance power. Do not get lost in the personal aspects of this story. Whatever you do will make a difference. Act from love as you wield your power. Know that your actions will ripple into the past as well as into the future. May you walk in beauty."

Contradictions lie in her words. *Don't get lost in the personal aspects. Act from love.* Love is personal!

The phone rang, bringing her out of her reverie.

"Jen, how lovely!"

"Hi," Jen said. "I have just a moment before getting to work. I sent you an email. Lawrence and I journeyed last night. We ran into an old friend of yours. I've emailed our notes. I think we should all get together pretty soon. I can't get a hold of Charles, but Lawrence and I can be there tomorrow around dinner time, if that works for you."

"It works for me, I'll make a stew or something. Charles has been in the grove with James most of the morning."

"Doing what?" Jen asked with incredulity.

"'Crow lessons,' was all I got from them. They had a transformative male bonding experience last night. We'll share the details tomorrow. I'll let Charles know. Have a good time working. I'll see you tomorrow. And thanks, Jen."

"Just doing my part. Bye!"

Cailleen's stomach demanded lunch and she found Charles making sandwiches in the kitchen a few minutes later. She told him about her conversation with Jen and asked him how the Crow lessons went.

"He's a natural. I didn't expect it," Charles said of James. "He's tentative, but that seems centered around his desire to not offend more than anything else. Do you know he's read three or four of your books since he's arrived? The man's a sponge.

"James actually quoted that bit in your first book about science and technology being relied on in our culture, as if they contained all the answers. Said he loved it and that he often ran into that bias in his work as a cop. The techies and CSI folks often forgot to look beyond their machines. How did he put it? Something like, *they look at me as if I'm a bug in their microscope when I ask questions based on human tendencies. Then when my hunches solve the case, they dismiss me as lucky.* Like I said, he's a natural.

"Our James is already pretty comfortable with setting sacred space. I'll be interested to see what gifts he might have and how he'll develop them."

"Charles, aren't you getting ahead of yourself a bit?" Cailleen asked.

"I don't see your point," he replied. "What am I getting ahead of?"

"We've known James for a handful of days and you're seeing gifts and his development of them. He may be walking out of our lives in another few weeks or months. Should you really be investing so much in him?"

Charles walked over to Cailleen, put his hands on her shoulders and looked her in the eyes. "Are you talking about me or about you and James?" He paused, searching her eyes. "For my part, I have been directed to guide him and will do so until such time as it seems unnecessary or inappropriate. It's a call I cannot refuse. A promise has been made." He saw the tears form in Cailleen's eyes and gathered her in his arms.

"I will tell you what I told James about us. I fully intend to continue to learn and grow and celebrate life with Cailleen. Her relationships with other people cannot change that. We both know how vital it is to make room for other people in each other's lives. I will not stand in the way of whatever relationships she pursues and I will not give up ours."

"Thank you," Cailleen said and smiled.

"The same goes with my relationship with James. My role as teacher/guide does not include or preclude relationships with anyone else."

"Oh," Cailleen said, feeling as if she was somehow being reprimanded.

"That being said," Charles continued, "if he hurts you, I'll have to hurt him! Not as his teacher of course, but as his friend and as your friend, son, colleague, confidante, etc. etc. etc." He said the etc. as if he was the King of Siam. "Shall we dance? Shall we dance? Shall we dance?" He twirled Cailleen around the kitchen table until they were both laughing.

An hour later Charles left for Issaquah. Cailleen walked through her gardens taking note of what needed to be done. The sound of tires on gravel brought her around to the front to see who was visiting. Rosey gave a welcoming bark and ran to greet Cailleen's two nieces, Jennifer and Willow, who were pushing each other to get to Rosey first. The three of them had their usual love fest and went running off to the gardens.

"Don't wander from the gardens," Emily called after them.

"Mom, we're not babies," they whined in unison and ran off giggling at Rosey's antics.

"I think they mean, *Mother we're old enough to know not to wander off.* But can we find a nice quiet place to sit where I can keep an eye on them?" she requested, "just in case I misinterpreted their whine." This last bit was said with a whine that perfectly imitated the two girls. Cailleen and Emily laughed as they walked arm in arm to the sun porch.

"It won't be warm in here for much longer," Cailleen mused. "Can I get you a cup of tea?"

"Do you have any cookies to go with it," Emily asked in another imitation of her girls.

"Only if you say please," Cailleen teased.

"Oh, pretty please!"

Cailleen arrived back in a few minutes with tea and cookies. She watched Emily's face as she watched her daughters' ramblings around the garden. Pride, joy, love, and genuine liking flitted across her face. Emily sighed in contentment then turned at the sound of Cailleen's footsteps.

"Sometimes I think I missed out by not having children," Cailleen told her. "You look like you're in heaven just now."

"Yeah, they're pretty great and I wouldn't trade them for anything. Well, this morning I would have paid you to take them far, far away," she laughed. "Contrary to what you see now, they don't always play well together. I told them I would simply not be able to risk taking them to their favorite auntie's house later today. I then added that their favorite aunt had mentioned something about pumpkins in her gardens. I suggested that same aunt might be willing to part with a couple and might even want some help carving what was left. So be forewarned. And yes, I know it was a not-so-subtle bribe. I just couldn't stand hearing "Mom, she's looking at me!" another time. Please tell me you have enough pumpkins to share."

"They can each choose one of their own. I'm not sure I'll be able to find time to do pumpkin carving before Halloween. My schedule suddenly got very busy," Cailleen explained.

"Busy?" Emily asked with a sly glance. "So, what was on that cassette tape?"

Cailleen considered for a moment. Although Emily coordinated delivering the tape into her hands, she wasn't at liberty to share the contents of it with her. She felt awkward about it, but had to put her off. Perhaps after the quest was finished, she could share the entire story.

"Can I tell you about it some other time?" Cailleen asked. "I'm really too tired to get into it right now."

"Are you sure he's not the reason you're too tired?" Emily asked pointing at James who was striding across the lawn towards them. Rosey yelped in greeting and ran to James with a stick in her mouth. The easy way he greeted the dog suggested he was very comfortable at the manor. Cailleen blushed and Emily noted her eyes softening. But then Cailleen squared her shoulders for some reason.

"You're complicating things again, aren't you?" Emily accused. "He's gorgeous, well-liked by both dogs and children…" Emily ran out the door as both Jennifer and Willow jumped up and started hanging on James. "Girls! Show some respect. You are climbing on a total stranger. Stop that at once!"

James, both girls and Rosey stopped in their tracks at the tone in Emily's voice. Rosey hung her head. Jennifer looked down with a guilty demeanor. James looked startled and confused. But Willow looked straight at her mother with her chin in the air.

"He is not a stranger, Mama. Rosey told us he was a friend. You said we could trust Rosey's reaction to people because she was wise." Then Willow's lip trembled and she burst into tears. Cailleen made a mental note to start paying attention to Willow's communication. Was she reading Rosey's body language or was she talking psychically to the dog?

Emily walked to Willow, knelt down on the grass and took her in her arms. "You are quite right, my darling. Rosey can be trusted. I just forgot you knew that. I'm sorry about that. However, it is still not appropriate to be jumping on someone you just met. He might have an injury you don't know about or he just might not like little girls jumping on him."

"Mama, I'm wise too," Willow said. "He's not injured and he likes little girls. I know it."

"Well then, perhaps you could introduce me to your new friend," Emily suggested.

Willow looked up at James with eyes that begged him to help her save face. "This is my momma," she said to James. "Mama, this is . . . ."

Before she had a chance to complete her sentence James stuck out his hand and said, "James. Nice to meet you." Willow reached up and squeezed his hand in thanks. James squeezed it back.

"It's gonna be like that, is it," Emily said with a smile and a shake of her head. James shrugged, then looked down at Willow and winked. "Perhaps James will help you two ragamuffins pick out a pumpkin? One each," she said to them. "Then we have to go pick up Daddy."

The girls grabbed James' hands and ran off. "I get first pick!" "No, I get first pick!"

"As I just saved you both from what could have been a lot of trouble, I think I should get first pick," James added to stop what he knew would be an enduring argument.

"That'll teach 'em," Emily laughed as she returned to Cailleen. "OK, quick! We've got about five minutes before they return bearing treasure. Who's the guy and how long has he been living here?"

"He does *not* live here," Cailleen said flatly and with some vehemence. "He's renting the bungalow down the road. He just introduced himself a couple of days ago."

"Well then," Emily mused. "You work fast. You're in love with him and he doesn't mind in the least."

"I am not in love with him. I hardly know him. He's a neighbor. James and Charles have developed a bond," Cailleen explained. "He probably came over to talk to him."

"Hmm? Charles isn't here, is he?" she asked. "And you, dear sister, are positively crackling with sexual tension. You're not the only one with gifts in this family, you know."

"You noticed what Willow just did?" Cailleen asked trying to shift Emily's attention?

"Willow? What do you mean?" Emily answered, taking the bait.

"Willow just demonstrated what is possibly the beginning of some psychic abilities. She talks to dogs and read James pretty well. We'll have to watch her a bit and see where she takes it."

"What do I watch for?" Emily asked with concern.

"Just keep your eyes open. Depending on how strong her gifts are, we might need to teach her that other people don't always take kindly to knowing that she knows things they've never told her. We might need to teach her to use shields so she can control what information comes at her. Don't worry, she's young and her abilities might come and go. Just stay aware and let me know how often it seems to happen."

The girls were running toward them with pumpkins in hand. "James got first pick," Willow explained, "then he let us both have second pick. He left his on the vine because he just lives next door. He said we could come visit him. Can we go now, Mama?"

"I'm afraid we'll have to make it another time. Your father awaits us. Thank James and say *hello* to your Auntie Cailleen. Next time you might do that on your arrival," Emily suggested. Both girls threw themselves around Cailleen and hugged her hard in apology for the lapse in their manners.

"Now," Emily instructed, "give her a hug goodbye and thank her for growing such wonderful pumpkins."

They gave both Cailleen and James hugs, then headed to the car discussing the merits of their respective pumpkins. Emily hugged Cailleen and whispered, "Wear that black negligee we picked up in Wenatchee. He'll love it!" Cailleen blushed. Emily shook James' hand then followed the girls to the car.

"I like the way your sister thinks," James said, smiling.

Cailleen decided to pretend he had not overheard what Emily had just said. "Yes, she dotes on the girls. They really like each other. It's good to see and to be a part of it. Charles has left for the Westside," she said gathering the tea things.

"I didn't come to see Charles," James answered.

"I've got a couple minutes before I get back to work," Cailleen said politely, "What can I help you with?"

"What's with the ever-so-polite treatment?" James asked guardedly. "Are you upset that I went to the grove with Charles?"

"What?! No. Why would that upset me?"

"So, you are upset about something?" James queried.

"Stop it. I am not a suspect being interrogated here. I'm not upset. I am just busy." Cailleen stood with her hands full of the tea things and looked at him expectantly.

"I won't keep you then," James said with cool politeness and turned on his heel.

"James," she called, dropping the polite veneer, "would you like a cup of tea?"

"Tea would be nice," he accepted.

"Are you and your sister close?" James asked.

"Yes, and no. We love each other dearly and would do anything for the other. On the other hand, our lives have taken decidedly different turns. I can't truly understand the demands of mothering small children. She can't truly understand the work I have been called to. But we find ways to stay connected and we watch out for each other. I truly like her and her family. They bring a normalcy to my life. I'm not sure exactly what I bring to theirs?"

"Magic," James told her.

"Magic?"

"Yes," James explained, "Willow told me when we were in the pumpkin patch. *Mama has love. Auntie Cailleen has magic.* I believe those were her exact words." Smiling at the memory James looked up at Cailleen and saw the tears rolling down her face. "Oh damn, what did I do now?" he cursed as he walked over and wrapped Cailleen in his arms.

She leaned into him for a few moments, registering how wonderful it felt. Then she sighed and pulled herself together. "You didn't do anything. No, actually you did. You played with my nieces in my pumpkin patch. That was very nice of you. Thank you."

"I enjoyed it. That made you cry?" he asked.

"No, that made me smile and be grateful. Willow's words just struck an odd chord. I think I must just be tired. I'm over it now," she said, looking away from his eyes that saw too much.

He decided it was time to shift the topic. "I came down to share a bit of what we did in the grove today and ask you a few questions. But as you're tired and it's almost dinner time, why don't I take you to dinner instead and then you can make an early night of it if you want to."

"You know what I'd really like to do? Get in my pajamas, raid the fridge and watch a movie."

"Another time then," James said and headed for the door.

"Another time," she agreed. "Or you could join me. I'll let you pick the movie?"

"Best offer I've had in days," he teased.

They stared into the fridge together.

"Soup's too healthy."

"Salad's too cold."

"Sandwiches?"

"Charles has fed me sandwiches three times in the last two days."

"Pizza!"

"Pizza? I don't even see pizza," James complained.

"Tsk, tsk," Cailleen shook her head. "A full morning of Crow lessons and you can't see a pizza? Look," she said as she piled his arms with items, "mushrooms, onions, olives, zucchini, vegan cheese and marina sauce."

"What about the crust?"

Cailleen threw a package of yeast onto the counter behind him and pointed at the flour canister. "Crust!"

"Pizza!"

James chopped and grated while Cailleen made dough. They shared stories about the children in their lives. James talked about Lily. Cailleen spoke of her nieces and some of her students' children.

"Did you ever want your own children?" James asked.

"Yes, when I was in my twenties. At least I thought I wanted children. Truth is I've always been good with them and I really enjoy having them in my life. I get kid time through friends and family. But I've never really missed not having them myself. I have moments like today when I saw the look of pure love and joy on Emily's face as she watched her daughters. But then I think of how much of her time and energy they take. I know I couldn't be a mother and do my work. I love my work. I'm called to it and it satisfies me deeply. I don't know that Emily can understand that. Other women in my family have come right out and asked me if I'm punishing myself for some reason by not choosing to get married and have children.

"I can get pretty angry at that," she admitted. "Then I think about my Aunt Bonnie, my mother's sister. She never married nor had children. When I was a kid, she was the only adult I knew who seemed to have fun. Her presence in my life gave me permission, I think, to not do the married with children thing. I remember my mom saying once, 'Poor Bonnie doesn't have a husband or any children.' I thought to myself, 'she seems happy enough to me.'

"Can you crush another clove of garlic for me?" Cailleen asked. James did so and handed it to her.

"Thanks. What about you? Ever longed for children of your own?"

"I guess when I was young, I thought I'd eventually get married and have kids like everyone else did. But my job is probably less conducive to having kids than yours. I always pictured spending lots of time with my kids. That's hard to do when you're undercover or tracking criminals across the state. I'm good at my job and I like it.

"And I always had kids in my life, too," James continued. "My partners had kids. And Ben, my best friend from college, has Lily. I've become her Uncle James. Kids don't expect the same things from uncles as they do from fathers. I'm a really good uncle. And I find that fills my need for children quite nicely."

"This pizza needs a bit more cheese and then about 20 minutes in the oven. I'm off to get into my pajamas."

"Try the black ones," James called after her.

She stuck her head back through the doorway. "Tonight, I'm afraid is made for flannel jammies with stars and moons, a fuzzy purple robe and warm wool socks. I could see if Charles has anything for you to wear?"

"I'm good in my own clothes. Don't want you confusing me with Charles."

Cailleen headed back to the stairs. James called after her, "Are we going to drink tea with pizza?"

"There's beer in the fridge on the back porch," she called back.

James got the beer and poured a couple of glasses and left the kitchen to find the TV and movies. Cailleen found him standing between the living room and the study looking confused.

"Crow lessons seem to have failed me again. I cannot find your TV."

Cailleen turned him and pointed to a door behind him.

"I thought that was a closet. I've never seen it open." He walked in after her and stood staring at the large plasma screen and the comfortable couches and pillows. "This is a man's room; it's most men's dream room. I expected a small TV installed in an antique stereo or something. This is high tech."

"Mr. McEwen, I have been meaning to talk to you about your assumptions," Cailleen laughed. "You seem to make a lot of them." He glared at her between half slitted eyes and took a deep breath. Before he got started with whatever verbal onslaught he had planned, she took her beer from him and held it up in toast. "To teaching tools," she drank and then explained, "I use DVD's as teaching tools. Sometimes the class is a dozen people. A big screen can be quite compelling when you're trying to make a point."

"The ever so practical, Ms. Renae. To teaching tools," he toasted back.

"I shall leave you to sort through the movie selections and no doubt add to your ever-expanding profile of me via my collection. I'll check the pizza and get napkins, plates, etc." With that, she breezed out of the room.

James was thrilled to be left alone with her collection. He noted not only the titles, but also how they were arranged. Several versions of the Cinderella story, Disney's "Beauty and the Beast" and "The Little Mermaid" sat next to "Shirley Valentine", "Girl Interrupted" and "Miss Potter". She had a collection of Cary Grant movies, which did not include the more manic stories like "Arsenic and Old Lace". An assortment of movies with magical themes – "Harry Potter", "The Golden Compass', "Roan Inish", "The NeverEnding Story"– did not surprise him. Romantic comedies (lots of Sandra Bullock and Colin Firth) he expected. TV series – "Dead Like Me", "The Vicar of Dibley"," Monk", "Charmed", "The Bob Newhart Show", "Friends", "NCIS" – intrigued him. "Super Size Me", "What the Bleep Do We Know", "Bowling for Columbine", "Home", "Food, Inc." – not fun movies, but important information. He saw no Westerns, no "party" movies, no thrillers or slasher movies. "Matrix" was the only one with any violence to speak of. "National Treasure", "Pirates of the Caribbean", "Indiana Jones" made up the action movies section.

Just as she walked back into the room, he discovered her collection of erotic movies but didn't get a chance to check out the titles.

"So detective, any surprises?" she asked.

"You know the answer to that. Overall, I'd say you don't like to be typecast."

"Charles said you were a fast learner!"

"He did?" James asked eagerly. Cailleen was touched by his response to a mention of approval. His shoulders went back and his chest popped out ever so slightly. It seemed the work they'd done had been as important to James as it had been to Charles.

"He did. Now, what movie did you choose?"

"Hadn't gotten that far," James said. "Research takes time, you know. What are you in the mood for?"

"Something easy. A comedy maybe?"

"You could have a comedy, romance, adventure film with something for everyone," James said in TV announcer voice. "I know I saw it. Yes, Madame. For your viewing pleasure, I present, 'The Princess Bride!'"

"Before Madame agrees to this classic cult film," Cailleen said, playing along, "she must warn you: she used to be able to recite most of the dialogue, and frankly, she can't help doing it while the movie is in play. Can you deal with this extraordinary skill? Or would you prefer to choose a gentler film for the evening?"

"Madame, your extraordinary skill not only fails to intimidate me, but forces me to reveal that I may be able to surpass your skill. For I carry the uncontested title of 'Greek Geek of Sigma Nu.' James bowed and put the DVD in the player. Then turned to her and explained, "I was undercover at the University of Washington. We got what we thought was a reliable tip about a prostitution ring operating out of a fraternity. Turned out to be a hoax. It was my first undercover assignment. It was pledge week and one of the tasks was to memorize the "Princess Bride". As an undercover eager pledge, I gave it my all. The undercover assignment lasted a week. The nickname "Frat Boy" lasted somewhat longer."

He grabbed the remote and made himself comfortable next to Cailleen. Then he turned to her with a smart-ass look on his face. "And to what do you owe your skill?"

"Actually, I have a similar story but it has a bit more danger," she joked. "When the movie came out, I happened to be working with teenagers. That's right, no frat boys, I was working with hormonal junior high and high school kids! Actually, they were great. A couple of rather nerdy junior high boys started quoting the movie. The dialogue was so absurd around the Youth Center that it evolved into 'cool.' It was a big shift for these boys to be included in the group, so I encouraged it. We watched the movie like 20 times in one month – sometimes three times in one day. I, of course, used the lessons within the movie to make a point whenever possible – like the power of friendship and not getting stuck in roles you've outgrown. I found the movie impossible to forget. Every couple of years I pull it out. It brings back good memories.

"So, press 'play' already. No, wait. I think I heard the buzzer. Our pizza is ready. I don't want to miss the intro. It's been years since I've seen it."

"You can't mean it!?" James rhymed.

Ninety minutes later the Princess Bride and her Pirate finally kissed.

The cheesy, yet romantic, end notes to the movie spoke of love's purity and passion – and a really great kiss. The hero and heroine rode off into the sunset with a musical fanfare.

"That kiss didn't seem so special," Cailleen said, turning in James' arms. "I think we can do better."

"We have before," James smiled and lifted her chin, meeting her lips with his own. The kiss was sweet and pure, and then heated into a fiery passion.

Cailleen eased away and ended the kiss. "Thank you, James. I've had a wonderfully silly and rejuvenating evening. It's been good to laugh and play. I appreciate you not pushing to ask me questions about your time in the grove with Charles. I really needed the break."

"It's been fun for me too. I'll go home and let you have an early night," he said without a trace of disappointment. He got big points for that.

"Oh, well. If you want to go, I'll see you to the door. I wasn't actually trying to end the evening. I just didn't want to forget to thank you. We can talk in the morning about the grove. If the commute is too much for you, you could stay here tonight," she invited.

"As you desire," James smiled slowly, kissed her hand, tucked it into his elbow, and escorted her upstairs.

The next morning after breakfast, just as Cailleen and James were heading to the study to talk, her phone rang. The convention committee had never received Cailleen's prep material for her class. Information needed to get to the participants by tomorrow and they needed her to re-send all her documents.

"I'm sorry James. I need to attend to this now. Can we talk this afternoon?"

"Sure, I have some errands I need to do in Ellensburg. It will take me a couple of hours. Why don't you come to the bungalow any time after two?"

Chapter Eleven
Arrivals

While James was headed to Ellensburg, his friend, Ben, was heading to Cle Elum. Things were getting desperate with Lily. Camille had cried in his arms this morning after raging that there must be something they could do. Ben had been trying to reach James for two days without any response. In his own desperation to take some action, he canceled all his appointments and headed to Cle Elum.

Ben hoped that by the time he actually reached Cle Elum, he would have talked to James, but he couldn't get through. He was in Cle Elum now. Not knowing what to do, he stopped for coffee. He'd call again in fifteen minutes. *Pioneer Coffee* was busy that morning. It was clearly a local favorite and at mid-morning it was full of people on break. It had the usual stuffed chairs by a fireplace and scattered tables and chairs. Local crafts were displayed on shelves here and there. By the time Ben used the facilities and got his coffee, the fifteen minutes had passed.

Ben was a man who caught people's attention. He dressed well and carried himself with an inner authority. People moved aside for him and they listened when he spoke. In the business world he used this to full advantage. Outside of it, he seemed unaware. He didn't realize how his voice carried in the coffeehouse.

"Damn it, James, where are you?" he said into his phone. "If you get this, I'm here in Cle Elum. I don't know where the hell you're staying and I need to talk to you ASAP. I need to know what you know about this woman, Cailleen Renae. Call me," he almost barked.

A young woman at the next table spoke. "Excuse me, I couldn't help overhearing you. Are you looking for James McEwan and Cailleen Renae?"

"I'm sorry if I disturbed you," Ben said trying to calm his voice in apology. "Who are you?"

"I'm Stacie. I work across the street at the newspaper so I'm in here every day," she explained. "I met a James McEwan a few days back. He lives in the bungalow next to Cailleen's place. I'd be happy to give you directions. My mom goes over to Cailleen's at least once month. I was there myself a couple of years ago. She's a wonderful woman and I guess she's pretty famous. She keeps kind of quiet and to herself. It's best to make an appointment if you want to see her."

Ben interrupted Stacie. "Thank you, I would appreciate the directions. I'm in a bit of a bind and need to get back to Seattle soon." With directions in hand, he practically stormed out the door and nearly ran over a woman entering.

"Bye," Stacie called after him. The woman he'd nearly run over was scowling.

"Do you know him?" she asked Stacie.

"Not really. I overheard his telephone conversation. He was leaving a message for James McEwan. You know, the man I told you I met last week? Lives next to Cailleen in that bungalow? Well, this guy," she said pointing at Ben as he drove off, "was trying to get a hold of him and needed some information about Cailleen. I just helped him out and gave him directions."

"Stacie," the woman exclaimed, "you work at a newspaper! You edited a column last week about safety and taking note of strangers poking around your neighbor's property. You actually gave a stranger someone's address – two people's addresses? What were you thinking? You don't know anything about that man."

"He dresses well, he's highly educated and he smells really good!"

"So did Ted Bundy. You're a danger to yourself and others," the woman said as she stomped off.

***

James was running late. He had to start remembering that in a small town, people often liked to chat. He'd spent a very productive hour with Milt, the library historian in Ellensburg. He simply wanted to check out some history of the Kittitas County to get a sense of how the community had grown and where it was headed. James liked to investigate a city like he investigated a person. Without past and present one couldn't create a good picture of the character of a place or a person. He left with a head full of stories, a bag of books and an open invitation to use the historic files.

He enjoyed his time with Milt and would plan better next time. By the time he finished his other errands, he was running about a half an hour late. He didn't know Cailleen well enough to know if she'd be put out about his tardiness.

When he pulled up to his bungalow she was sitting on his front porch with a cup of tea in a relaxed reverie – and no lines of tension in her posture or face. As he stepped out of his truck, she turned to him and smiled.

"Sorry I'm late," he offered in greeting.

"No worries," she said. "It gave me a chance to sit quietly with a cuppa. I helped myself. You left your back door open. I took it as an invitation to make myself at home. Hope you don't mind."

"No, I don't mind a bit. That is if you don't mind paying the fare," he said taking her in his arms and kissing her thoroughly.

Ben drove up to see James wrapped around a soft woman. They looked like they were made for each other. Ben was torn between joy for his friend and annoyance that this new woman might be the reason he couldn't reach him. He hated to interrupt them. But Camille's look of pleading trumped James' romantic life. He slid out of his BMW and shut the door with enough force to get the couple's attention.

"I hate to interrupt, pal, but the situation is becoming urgent," Ben began. As James moved away from the woman and turned towards him, Ben saw Cailleen. He froze in mid-sentence and stared.

Several things ran through his mind at once. James had betrayed him. She'd bewitched him. What was she doing here? Why did she seem so familiar? Why was his stomach churning at the sight of her? Why did he feel guilty and annoyed at her? And yes, he felt fear. A part of him feared this woman and the potential of her powers.

By the time James reached him, Ben was in a cold sweat. He reached out to grasp James' extended hand and anger surged. "You son of a bitch," he gritted out. "My daughter grows weaker every day and you're here having a holiday fling with the very woman I asked you to investigate!" Ben clenched and unclenched his fists several times. He wanted to hit something. James was a very handy target, but he was staring at him with a pained and startled expression.

James waited for Ben's initial reaction to cool. He was hurt by Ben's words, yet he also knew the tension and fear Ben had been living in for months. When Ben's shoulders softened, James spoke.

"Let's get you a cup of tea and have a chat. You can tell me what's going on with Lily in a moment after you've calmed down a bit." With that James turned to go in the bungalow. Cailleen met James' eyes. She deliberately let him see the hurt, and then she turned on her heel and walked away as regally as he'd yet seen her.

"Damn! I'm between a rock and a hard spot here," he muttered to himself. He looked up in the trees. At the sight of a crow he said, "I could use some help here." With a sigh he let Cailleen go and went inside to make tea for Ben.

He heard the door slam a few moments later. Ben found him in the kitchen. "I really don't want a cup of tea. Don't think I've ever wanted a cup of tea. Don't remember ever seeing you drink a cup of tea. What the hell's going on over here? I trusted you when I had nowhere else to turn. I thought I could count on your professionalism and your ability to stay objective. What the hell am I supposed to do now, James?" Ben sat at the table with his head in his hands. James placed a cup of chamomile tea in front of him.

"Ben, my friend, you can trust me. I have checked Cailleen Renae and her friends out pretty thoroughly actually. I did not get involved with her until after I discerned that she is the real thing. I have been learning about what she does and how she does it so I could be of more help to you and Camille and Lily. I needed some experience and language to explain how everything worked. I think she can possibly help Lily. I trust her, Ben."

"James, you'll have to forgive my doubts, but I drove up to see her wrapped around you and steam rolling off the two of you. Can you really tell me you have a clear head in this matter?"

"Yes, Ben. I have a clear head. I've never been more certain of anything in my life. Drink your tea." Ben automatically took a drink at James' command.

"Why didn't you call me, Ben? I'd have come to you and brought Cailleen if you wanted me to."

"I've been calling you for two days," Ben said letting the exhaustion and fear show in his voice. "Two days trying to calm Camille and be cheerful for Lily. Two days of hoping you would call back and give me some hope."

James pulled his phone out of his pocket. "No bars. I'm sorry, Ben, I must not get reception here. I don't get a lot of calls when I'm not on duty, so I didn't think anything of it. I'm sorry."

"You have anything stronger than this tea?" Ben asked.

"I do indeed. But why don't you tell me what's been happening while you finish what's in that cup and I'll find the whiskey later." Exhaustion, temper and whiskey were not a good combination for his friend, particularly if they needed to take some action quickly.

***

Cailleen's hurt transformed to anger by the time she reached her own kitchen. He'd lied to her. She asked him if he was investigating her and he said, "No." She thought back over the conversation. He hadn't said, "no." He said, "I'm not doing a *formal* investigation."

Splitting hairs! That was a lie by intention, wasn't it? She'd let him into her personal life, her professional life, her intimate relationships, her heart. Damn him! Why did he do it? Who was his friend? Seems like he betrayed him too.

Cailleen wanted to heap up grievances and faults, but she couldn't find enough to satisfy her. She was so angry, she needed to do something. She decided to head to the barn and organize the potting area. That would give her an opportunity to throw things.

As she sorted through the bags of soil, tools and pots – she also sorted through her feelings. She let herself list his few transgressions several times and with vehemence. But after the third time, her heart wasn't in it. James as the betrayer simply didn't ring true. Something else was going on. When it came down to it, she knew she could trust him. But apparently, he couldn't trust her. She sat on a bag of potting soil and wept. She'd done nothing untrustworthy. A bit of anger returned at the thought that he didn't trust her.

She wanted to know what was really going on and she wanted to hear it from James. She went to the house, washed the tears and smudges of dirt from her face and took a moment to compose herself. Then, she grabbed her coat and walked back to the bungalow.

Charles, Lawrence and Jen pulled up in time to see her stomping into the forest toward James' bungalow. "Trouble in paradise," Lawrence predicted.

"Hush!" Charles and Jen said in unison. They each sent out their antennae to feel the energies.

"Trouble, and not just with James," Jen said.

"The players have been gathered," Charles stated and headed toward Cailleen and the bungalow. Jen and Lawrence followed.

Cailleen reached the bungalow to hear Ben shouting, "I'm not letting that witch touch my daughter!"

Cailleen pushed the door open and faced him. "What makes you think this witch would agree to touch your daughter?"

"Cailleen, Ben. Ben, Cailleen." James muttered. "Where are the crows when you need them?" he asked under his breath as he glanced out the window.

"What are you talking about?" Ben fumed.

"There they are," James said with satisfaction as he looked up and saw Charles and company heading their way.

"James, what is this about?" Cailleen pleaded. "You lied to me," she accused. He opened his mouth to protest but she silenced him. "So, you didn't technically lie; but you evaded the truth in a way that led me to an untruth. That's pretty close to a lie and I deserve to know why."

"The truth was not mine to tell," James said. "It's as simple as that. I gave a promise to my oldest and dearest friend. And I will not break that, for anything. I'm sorry it hurt you, but I would do the same thing again."

"Whose truth is it to tell?" she asked turning to Ben.

Ben simply stared down at her.

"Another impasse, I see." Even as she said it, Cailleen wondered at it. She'd never met this man before, how could it be *another* impasse? Just as she was working out a possibility, Charles walked in.

"Charles, Lawrence, Jen – this is my oldest friend, Ben Hodges," James introduced.

"Ben, glad to meet you," Charles greeted. "We just stopped by to see how you were doing and make sure you're all settled into the bungalow. I hope your first week has been a good one," he inquired.

"Fine, yes. Good. No problems at all," James said with irony.

"Ben," Charles began, "you remind me of someone. I can't quite place you." Charles looked at Jen, Lawrence and Cailleen. "Aha, I've got it. You look like our friend, Frank. Doesn't he, Cailleen?"

"Frank? Um, Frank who?"

"What was his last name? It's been ages since we've seen him, just ages. Chancha! That's it. You remember - big guy, great leader."

"Chancha," Cailleen coughed to cover her surprise. "Yes, I remember now. I guess he does look a bit like him."

"I don't remember him," Jen added.

"Way before your time," Charles laughed.

Ben sensed something was going on beneath the conversation and it made him feel helpless and angry. He looked all four of them over slowly and with a hint of contempt. When he got to Charles, he raised his eyebrows in surprise.

"You're Charles Murphy. I've seen your picture in the paper. You were married to Whitney Dooley. You're a highly respected businessman and supporter of the arts," Ben said with confusion and dismay.

"You seem surprised and bothered by that," Charles observed.

"Um, no, it's just that I would not expect you to be mixed up in all this," Ben explained waving his arms disdainfully to include Cailleen and the general area.

"All this?" Charles asked in a chilly voice.

"All this *magic* and deception," Ben answered condescendingly.

Lawrence and Jen took a step away from Charles. Cailleen and James stepped forward to separate Charles and Ben. Charles raised his hand to halt them. He looked directly at James and, in his teacher's voice, spoke.

"We'll leave you to your friend. Perhaps you can educate him about *magic* and encourage better manners in him."

Charles left the bungalow after shooing Jen and Lawrence out through the door. He turned to wait for Cailleen. Cailleen looked at James to be sure he would be alright. James nodded and she followed Charles out the door.

After they left, James looked at Ben for a long couple of minutes. He wasn't sure how much Ben could handle at this moment. He also wondered how many more moments Lily had. He sensed Ben was close to being out of control and decided a firm touch was needed.

"Ben, I love you as a brother. And as a brother, I'm telling you, - you're being a total ass. I know you're going through a lot. I know you feel a bit helpless and maybe even a little desperate and you don't like either of those feelings – especially when it comes to the two people you love most. I also know you need to tread a little more carefully.

"Every one of the four people who just walked out this door has gifts and skills beyond your reckoning. You don't understand those gifts or skills. But do you understand the gifts or skills of a surgeon any better? Or are you simply more comfortable because those words are familiar to you? Technology and modern science do not have all the answers – as you have cause to know. Other than tests and dashed hopes, what has the allopathic medical profession done for Lily in the last nine months?

"You've tried everything they have to offer. Lily is no better. She is wasting away before our eyes and it breaks my heart. I would never jeopardize her well-being for anything. I have been not only investigating these people, I've been studying what they know and what they do.

"I have personally experienced their healing powers. Some of their skill comes in the form of tea, or talk, or simple, yet profound, observation. In their company I have begun to understand my own gifts. I've only begun to scratch the surface of them it seems.

"They approach their work in similar ways to mine. We observe. We feel into the character of those involved and try to understand the system at work. In understanding how the pieces fit, one can understand the path to healing – or in my case, justice.

"Cailleen is the most adept. She has the most experience and has taught the others to develop their own gifts. She did a healing on me just a couple of days ago. I was in pain from chopping wood and then falling asleep on the couch while researching who these folks are and what they do. I met Cailleen by chance in the forest and among the trees she sang and energetically offered healing. Afterwards, I felt better and more vital than I had in years. She is a gifted and talented healer. And she is a practical and careful woman.

"I would trust her with my life. I would trust her with Lily's life. I don't know if she can do anything to help Lily, but I wouldn't hesitate to ask for her assistance. She'll be straight with you."

"It's too weird," Ben replied. "I can't just hand Lily over to some woman who does things that cannot be explained. And there's something about her – like a memory tugging at the back of my mind. It's too much. I feel fear and resistance in her presence. I don't think I can even talk to her about Lily. I can see that you trust her – and because of that, I want to trust her. But it's beyond me. I just can't do it. I can't raise Camille's hopes or expose Lily to something I don't understand or feel comfortable with. I just can't. Look, I have to get back. Camille probably can't reach me here," he said pulling out his own phone to check for bars. "I gotta go. Could you call me every day and check in? Please? I don't need to be worrying about you or how I'd get a hold of you if I needed you."

"Sure Ben. I'll call. I'll find someone local with a land line so you can get me if you need me. Are you safe to drive, brother? Do you want me to drive you home?"

"I'm good," Ben said and gave James a quick hug. "See you soon."

"See you soon. Ben?" James called after him. "Is it OK with you if I share Lily's story with these folks? They might have some other ideas or suggestions. I'll make it clear you don't want them to do anything."

"I trust you to share what you think is best, James." And Ben drove off into the darkening sky.

***

On the way back to the manor, no one said a word. All four of the friends were wrapped in their own thoughts and working to ground their emotions so they could stay clear.

At the manor, Cailleen put on the teakettle, Charles grabbed his briefcase, Lawrence and Jen brought in groceries.

"Do you have a cigarette?" Charles asked.

"On the shelf above the coat hooks. Matches are in the pack," Cailleen offered.

"Do you want one?" Charles asked.

"No, I'm feeling pretty centered and don't feel the need to be smudged. You go ahead. We'll wait to talk until you get back."

Charles walked outside. Lawrence and Jen emptied their bags and very enticing smells wafted towards Cailleen.

"Is that..?"

"Yes, we brought you Judy Foo's noodles and dumplings and an assortment of her vegetarian dishes. We'll have to heat them. Do you have chopsticks? I don't see any in the bag," Lawrence explained.

"You two are the best," Cailleen said with tears in her eyes. "It's been a hard afternoon, but the evening's looking very promising. Chopsticks are in the top drawer. Jasmine tea?"

"Do you have a nice green tea?" Jen asked.

"I'll make a pot of each," Cailleen answered.

Charles walked in the kitchen.

"Can we eat and then talk?" Jen pleaded.

"Judy Foo has been teasing me all the way from Seattle. We should let her cuisine sooth our souls and fill our bellies. Then, we can face anything," Charles declared with just a little too much enthusiasm!

They sat at the table. Lawrence raised his cup, "to Judy."

"To Judy!" they all toasted.

As they finished the last precious morsels, James knocked lightly and stepped into the kitchen.

"You're too late, we've eaten it all," Cailleen said a little coolly.

"I didn't come for food," James answered politely.

"What can we do for you?" Charles asked with just a tiniest bit of distance in his voice.

"Come in, James. Have a seat," Lawrence offered. "You look like you've had a hard day."

"You're in time for dessert," Jen added as she handed him a cup of tea.

"No thanks," James refused. "I'm guessing you all have some work to do tonight. I came to apologize."

They all sat watching and waiting for James to continue. They offered neither encouragement nor judgment. James needed to work his way through something and they waited.

"Look, I know you have no reason to trust me at this point," he began, and then paused again, seeking the right words.

"Our trusting *you* is not the issue," Cailleen stated quietly in an attempt to move him beyond whatever hesitation he had and to suggest to him the real issue – at least how she perceived it.

"What?" James turned to her slightly and then forced himself to turn away. Cailleen saw in him the detective refusing to be distracted by something not pertinent to his current pursuit.

"I'm struggling here," he blurted out in frustration. "I want to sincerely apologize for the subterfuge of the last few days and yet, I cannot say that I wouldn't do the exact same thing again. I am truly sorry at the way Ben treated you and I took him to task for it. I also requested and received his permission to tell you the whole story. In an effort to redeem myself at least a little and to clarify the extent of the subterfuge, I would like to share that story now."

The four looked at each other, everyone nodding consent. Jen stood up with hands on her hips in an attitude of annoyance. James dropped his shoulders in defeat. Jen had always seemed most supportive of him.

"It is incredibly rude of you to come here and interrupt our dinner," she began. "But," she sighed and then winked at him, "if you'll stop keeping us from dessert, we're all ears." She kissed him on the cheek, pulled out a chair for him and then went to the counter for dessert.

"Sit," Lawrence commanded and passed him the tea he'd refused earlier. James sat and looked at them with relief and consternation.

"It's a bitch, ain't it?" Charles mocked him. "You get set for judgment and alienation and instead you get tea and dessert. If we're going to work together, you will need to trust *us* a bit more. Our work is not so different from yours, you know. At times, you simply are not at liberty to share everything you know." Charles looked at him to see if he understood. James nodded. Charles nodded back.

James took a drink of tea and picked up his fork to taste the fresh peach tart on the plate in front of him. He put the fork back down slowly, then pushed back his chair and stood up. Anger flared in his eyes.

"This is not the same as my work. In my work, I deal with criminals and strangers. I am not withholding from people I care deeply about, people I wish to earn the right to call friends. And I do feel alienated. I can feel right now that you are all sharing some knowledge for which you don't need words. You are a circle - a tight, loving intimate circle. I stand here on the outside looking in. And for the first time in my life, I feel really tired of my post," James finished quietly. He stood looking embarrassed and turned slightly toward the door.

"You feel better now?" Charles asked.

"Marginally," James agreed.

"Then get on with your story. Jen's right," he smirked, "these interruptions are really interfering with our enjoyment of dessert."

James looked around the table. Everyone had stopped eating, except Lawrence, who was putting the last bite of tart into his mouth with relish. All eyes were now on Lawrence.

"What?" he complained. "I'm the one who doesn't get so emotionally wrapped up. That's an asset. You said so yourselves just a few days ago. And currently it gets me closer to the last sliver of tart left in the pan!" As Lawrence intended, this broke the tension and everyone laughed.

James took a recovering breath and began his story:

"Ben is my oldest friend. We went to high school together and have managed to stay connected ever since. We roomed together in college and I introduced him to his wife, Camille. They got married right out of college. After Ben got settled in his career and opened his own investment company, they decided to have children. Lily was born within a year. They have led what most people would consider a charmed life. They set goals and achieve them with seemingly little effort. Of course, the truth is they work very hard at it. They also allow themselves to enjoy the fruits of all their work. They have all the money they could ever want and a strong, satisfying marriage. Lily was the cherry on top. She's a delight. Smart, compassionate, funny – she matches Ben and Camille quite well. They all adore each other.

"A year ago, Lily caught a bug that turned into pneumonia. She was quite ill. She never quite recovered from it. I mean, she doesn't have pneumonia anymore – but her energy and vitality didn't return. Camille talked to her doctors and they simply said some children take a while to get back on their feet. But weeks and months went by and Lily didn't change. Camille finally got her doctor to take another look. He did a blood workup and found some suggestion of cancer.

"They put her through a series of tests. Everything came up negative. By this time, it had been nearly a year and the doctors were also concerned about her 'failure to thrive.' For the last nine months they've run that sweet little girl through all kinds of tests, some of them not pleasant. They've found no reason to explain her condition. A couple of weeks ago, they told Ben and Camille there was simply nothing more they could do.

"Camille heard about your work, Cailleen. She told Ben she thought you should be called. Ben is not the most imaginative guy. He likes numbers and charts and predictable, understandable outcomes. He was dead set against it.

"Last week, he came to see me. Camille had collapsed in hysterics in his arms. She's really been a trooper in all this. She's been the rock. She hasn't faltered when hope after hope was dashed by doctors who were certain they could make a difference, yet failed.

"'We can't just do nothing,' she said to Ben. He'd never seen her eyes so desperate and pleading.

"He was still set against asking you for help. He asked me to come check you out. He believed I would find that you were some crackpot or charlatan. Camille's hopes might be dashed again, but at least Lily would not be exposed to another round of being poked and prodded, even metaphorically.

"He couldn't say 'no' to Camille without at least checking you out. I don't do this kind of work, but I couldn't say 'no' to Ben. He's a brother. He made me promise not to reveal why I was here. He didn't want you to know you were being investigated.

"As you saw, he's pretty attached to his beliefs about your work. They're totally outside his way of looking at the world. I told him he was an ass and gave him a few things to think about. He agreed that I could tell you the story and that I could ask if you have any suggestions about where else they might turn. He made it clear he did not want you to interfere with any of your *magic*."

James drank some tea and let everything sink in. Then began, "I know it's a lot to ask, but *do* you have any suggestions?"

Cailleen looked at him with pity and sorrow. "A child's life is in the balance. It's not too much to ask. Have they consulted a naturopath, acupuncturist, herbalist, psychiatrist?"

"I'm sure they have. Camille would leave no rock unturned, but I'll check. Thanks. One more thing: Ben can't reach me on my cell here. He asked me to call him every day to check in, but also to see if I could find someone with a land line that he could reach to get in touch with me if he needed me. Do you have a land line?"

"Actually, I do," Cailleen answered. "I rarely use it and don't usually have the phone plugged in. I can certainly plug it in. I don't even know the phone number, but I can look it up on a bill. Or Charles probably knows it - he uses it for business when he's here sometimes. I'll go plug it in and you can call Ben. Oh, I forgot. I'll be out of town for three days next week, so I won't hear the phone. Well, we'll figure something else out by then. Charles, do you have the number?"

"It's in my cell phone. I'll get it." He wrote the number on the back of one of his cards and handed it to James. James followed Cailleen to the phone and called Ben.

"Well, I left him a message. Thanks everyone. I'm going to leave you to your work and go see if I can get some rest. I feel tired suddenly." Charles squeezed his shoulder in reassurance and James walked back to his bungalow.

He stopped at the grove on the way to thank the crows for all the help they'd sent him that day.

Chapter Twelve
Tapestries

Thirty minutes later, the four were gathered in Cailleen's study around the fireplace. They sat lost in their own thoughts for another fifteen minutes.

"There are too many threads to follow," Lawrence declared. "I need paper and colors. Do you still have that big easel pad and markers, Cailleen?"

"In the AV room in the closet," she directed.

Lawrence came back in a few minutes with easel, pad and markers. "Let's see if we can get a big picture put together on one sheet and then follow the details of the various pieces on other sheets. Can we get some Post-its to write down pieces we don't know where to put?"

Cailleen went to her desk and came back with Post-its for Lawrence and paper and pen for herself and the others.

"OK," Lawrence began. "The three are gathered." He drew three circles in the middle of the pad. He put Cailleen's name in the top circle. "Our focus is her quest, so I'm putting her at the top." Below and to the left, he wrote Raneck's name in that circle. "Not corporeal, but still a player." In the third circle he wrote 'Ben/Chancha.' "James has indeed gathered Chancha into the quest – at least from our perspective."

Lawrence drew lines from each of the circles to a meeting point in the middle. "The crossroad of potential Elan spoke of," he said, pointing to where the lines met. "The time seems to be upon us."

Lawrence now drew a curved line between each of the three circles creating a circle of connection. With a yellow marker he drew concentric circles around the group of three circles. "The original actions of the three have rippled out in time. Up 'til now, those ripples have carried with them what?"

"Pride unbalanced, refusal to claim or use gifts, imbalanced sense of responsibility, not meeting potential, inability to ask for help, distrust of love, distrust of power," Charles offered.

"Desire to right things, inheritances of power and story, integrity; ability to gather allies," Jen added.

"Leadership and helping community," Cailleen added.

Lawrence wrote madly around the last ripple of yellow. "Did I get everything?" They nodded in affirmation. "Now what?" He walked back and forth in front of the easel. "We're not trying to shut the whole works down. At least I don't think so. It's more about bringing things back in balance. It seems to me each of the players has something specific to do to bring back the balance."

"Not all of the players are on the board yet," Jen observed. "Hand me those post-its." Lawrence tossed them to Jen with a marker. "At least one or two of the other players have dual roles – so I think we should put them all on stickies. That way we can move them around as needed. We could also make more than one sticky for them, I guess. But let's start with one each. She scribbled names on post-its.

"James." She offered the post-it to Lawrence. "He should be put on the line between Ben and Cailleen at this point. He's brought them together and seems to have a role in both of their lives. He'll probably end up as two stickies, but we don't really know yet. His role may now be finished in terms of the quest."

"Charles." Jen stood up and placed his sticky where the three lines intersected. "I want to put him here at this point. He is the link between the three and he has worked with Elan the most intimately. He may well end up with three other stickies," she said shrugging her shoulders.

"Lawrence," Cailleen asked, "can you put Charles' name at the top of a new sheet? And do the same with James' name. I sense that the activities of the quest – regardless of the outcome – will influence their lives almost as deeply as the central three. Both Charles and James are at critical crossroads in their own lives. Charles, you are finally getting a chance to confront and resolve your own emotions around that first life. You have chosen to face that square on with me. But Raneck hangs in the balance. You are also coincidentally stepping into the new role of Teacher." Cailleen held her hand up as both Jen and Lawrence started to interrupt.

"James is also at a crossroad. He's beginning to suspect that the intuitive gifts on which he's built his reputation as a top investigator, may have deeper and more far-reaching applications. He's also just told us 'he's tired of his post'. He's looking at changing the way he lives his life and perhaps even defines himself." She stopped for a moment and closed her eyes. The others knew not to break the silence.

"From the perspective of the quest, I can't see whether it's any of our business how either of them makes choices. I just think we need to acknowledge the timing and keep their stories at least on the periphery. Jen, I can feel you bursting with questions. Let's hear them."

"What about Lawrence and me? We have already been affected by the quest ourselves," she said.

"Yes, I asked myself the same thing a moment ago. I can only offer this: the quest is training and experience for you and Lawrence. You will grow in your abilities, but mostly in your confidence with them. However, it is not a major life crossroad. You have significant parts to play. I do not doubt that. But in the larger scheme of things, this quest will not stand out as overly significant in your life paths. At least that is my sense. I could be persuaded otherwise."

"I concur on my part," Lawrence said. "This quest is helping me define my role in this circle. It allows Yvonne to get a sense of the demands of this aspect of my life before I ask her to marry me." Everyone smiled at this admission. "It also gives us a chance to set and test boundaries around the work and our relationship. But the truth is any big project the four of us do together would serve the same purposes. Begging your tolerance here, but yeah, this quest isn't particularly special in my life."

"That all makes sense," Jen agreed. "We have both been involved in the story through our other lives, but only in small ways. I wonder if these ripples are what brought us together? I mean all of us, not just Lawrence and I. The common link between us?"

"That," Cailleen agreed, "and our psychic, intuitive and empathic gifts. Or maybe that's the glue that holds us together? As a teacher, I love seeing how they all develop in you." She smiled fondly at them.

"So, what's this about Charles stepping into a role as Teacher?" Lawrence asked.

"Yes, it's been a busy couple of days. I'll tell you the details later," Charles promised, "but for now suffice it to say that Elan stepped in and brought James to me as a student. We worked together yesterday for several hours. He's quick. And Cailleen's right. He's only beginning to guess at the depth of his gifts. We don't have to decide now, but I'd like to suggest we include him in our Samhain celebration."

Jen and Lawrence looked at each other and did their wordless communication. They both nodded. "We were going to wait to say this," Jen proceeded, "but now seems a good time. In the kitchen earlier, when James said he didn't like being outside our circle, I – well, we – thought how odd that was. We don't know when it happened but we both feel he's already stepped inside and been embraced by our circle. We would welcome a chance to work with him in ritual and see how that feels."

Cailleen nodded in agreement, but Charles noted a small moment of pain move across her eyes. He looked at her in question.

"Yes, please invite him to join us. We can leave it to you to discern how big of a role he will play," Cailleen instructed.

"OK," Lawrence said, moving back to the easel. "Let's put me and Jen around Cailleen at this point."

"Put Jen between me and Raneck," Cailleen added. "She's made a significant connection with him from what I sensed in your email. We can leave Lawrence where you have him, but he may very well be moved to master of the crossroads with Elan. And let's not forget to put her on the board." Cailleen took the fresh post-it from Jen and put Elan at the crossroads with Charles.

"Yvonne?" Jen asked.

"No," Lawrence answered. "She's not really part of this. It does feel like someone's missing. Camille?"

"Let's put her at the edge of the paper on Ben's side. I don't sense she will play more than a very minor role, but we don't really know. Let's not dismiss her entirely. Who does that leave?" Charles asked.

"Lily. I've felt her significance from the first moment I saw her," Jen explained. "She's important. She's very important."

"What do you mean?" Cailleen asked intensely. "When did *you* see Lily?"

Jen glanced at Lawrence, then back at Cailleen. "The night before we left last week, I did a journey."

"A journey to a kid you've never met? You'd better tell us everything."

Jen hesitated. Lawrence spoke. "I was just getting comfortable with Yvonne last Saturday when I feel 'Elvis' here," he pointed at Jen, "leaving the building. I went to her room to find her half gone sitting in the middle of her floor. I called her back and chewed her out."

"I knew what I was doing," Jen objected.

"Well then you're not very smart or you're just reckless. We knew next to nothing about James at that point except that he was clearly hiding something. And as Charles has just told us, the man has gifts. We had no idea if he had them, if he was aware of them, if he was dangerous. You had no business doing it," Lawrence accused.

Jen looked at Cailleen with apology and pleading. "OK, it may not have been the most well thought out act. I was worried about you. It was clear that James had some pull on you. You were drawn to each other. It seemed mutual and unexpected for both of you. Still, I wasn't about to leave you alone with the man without checking him out a bit. It was a risk I was willing to take – and it turned out OK in the end."

"Lawrence stopped you, but you went anyway?" Charles asked.

"Don't you start on me too," Jen said stubbornly.

"Jen, we work together, often. I need to know what kind of risks you are inclined to take. I'm not too excited," Charles reprimanded, "about working with someone who's reckless. And," he said, softening, "we need as much information about the different aspects of this quest as we can get."

"Her impulse was reckless," Lawrence said defensively, "but she didn't go alone. She gave me no choice but to go with her. Which, I see now, was her intention all along. We'll talk about *that* later." Jen shrugged her shoulders at him.

"*Anyway*, I journeyed with the intention of simply going to the bungalow and palpating - you know, feeling out the energies. I already wanted to like James and I didn't want to be intrusive or unethical. Lawrence came along as back up. We got to the bungalow and it felt clean and clear, strong and honorable – and then I felt his sadness. So deep," she reflected with teary eyes. "I saw him through the window and moved closer. Actually, I don't remember moving so much as being pulled closer. He was sitting on the couch, bent over a framed picture. From his description earlier, I'm sure it was Lily. When he spoke about her tonight, he had the same sadness as I felt from him last week. She's lovely and sweet and – waning. I could almost feel the life force slipping from her. I also felt she has some knowledge about what's happening to her. She can't find the words and no one around her can help. She's lost and looking for someone to help her. She just doesn't know who it is. Doctors can't help her, Cailleen. I'm pretty sure we can."

Cailleen wrote Lily's name on a post-it. "Where should we put her?"

"Jen?" Charles asked. "I know this might sound odd, but is it possible she's been kidnapped?"

"Kidnapped? You mean sometime today? Are you asking me to try to find her?"

"No. I have a bad feeling about something. I want to know if she *feels* anything like someone who's been kidnapped. I want to know if someone took a part of her – a vital part."

"Charles, I don't know how to answer that or how to go about checking it out," Jen replied.

"Charles," Cailleen asked, "what are you thinking?"

"Raneck. He may have a hand in this," Charles explained.

"You think he may be using Lily?"

"I don't know. It's just that as Jen spoke about Lily, I caught his scent, so to speak. Remember, I know my grandfather well – particularly in his less balanced years. I can tell you he was never above using anyone as a tool to whatever he thought was the thing to do. He used all of us repeatedly. If someone was harmed, he brushed it aside as the cost of working with the Spirits. He never wanted to hurt anyone – with a few exceptions," he looked meaningfully at Cailleen. "But collateral damage never bothered him. He used one of Rasia's daughters once and it almost killed her." He turned to Jen and Lawrence. "Rasia was my sister. She married Chancha's eldest son. Her daughter was his granddaughter." Charles looked back at Cailleen.

"Ben may have a residual memory of that. It would explain his reluctance to let anyone with our gifts get near his daughter in this lifetime. How did he respond when he first met you?" Charles asked Cailleen.

"I wouldn't say we met, so much as bumped into each other. I walked in as he was saying something nasty like: *I'll never let that witch touch my daughter.* I responded with a haughty, *what makes you think this witch would be willing to do so?* Not my finest hour and I'll allow it may not have been his either. But I would agree that at some level we recognized each other and took defensive stands. Poor James!"

"Ben was confused at meeting me," Charles offered. "Makes sense. We became quite close when he was Chancha. He treated me like a son, a trusted son. He seems to have been aware of me in this lifetime and he couldn't reconcile whatever idea of me he had formed with this aspect of my work." Charles looked at Lawrence. "Shouldn't you be writing this on your board, these are threads that might be important?"

"Right," Lawrence said, standing. "How to do it is the question."

"Start another page for Ben. Put this all on his page. We can then link the pages to get different views," Jen suggested.

Cailleen sat quietly while they put everything down on paper. She preferred a 3-D view and was arranging the connections in her mind. She'd used this technique many times. She imagined each person as a ball. She let the balls and their connecting strings float before her. She waited until one of the balls or strings spoke to her. When she connected Raneck with Lily she wasn't sure the thread would hold. She wasn't sold on Charles' theory. But it did hold. There was a connection - a strong one and it was currently twinkling. That was the thread she wanted to tug at a bit. She opened her eyes and found three pairs of eyes looking expectantly at her.

"I truly treasure that you all know to leave me be when I'm deep into it. It's comforting." Cailleen stood and began pacing. She hadn't found the way to unwind this thread.

"Charles is right. There is some connection between Raneck and Lily. I can both see and feel it. I can't discern it, however. Let's assume for a moment that Charles is correct. What would be Raneck's motivation? What would he gain by making a little girl ill?"

"A larger question," Lawrence suggested, "might be what is it that Raneck needs to do to resolve this story?"

"OK," Cailleen agreed, "let's consider both questions. Anyone?"

"He failed in two ways," Jen said with certainty. "The first he is aware of. He didn't go to Chancha and advise him when he banned Calleigha. Chancha expected it and felt betrayed when it didn't happen. The second failing is that he didn't let go. Once he acknowledged the first failing, Raneck took all responsibility upon himself. That, in its own way, has bound all three players and prevented them from clear action. All the other players are continually responding to Raneck's manipulations. It doesn't leave them free to right their own paths."

They all looked at Jen with a little surprise.

"What? I can pull threads together as well as anyone. And I seem to connect more easily with Raneck than the rest of you."

They looked at her doubtfully.

"OK, I channeled Elan a bit with that - but only the very last part. I didn't see that his actions were binding the others."

"So Raneck needs to let go and also to advise Chancha?" Lawrence asked. Jen nodded. "How do we help him understand and do that?" he asked.

"I read the notes you sent about your journey," Cailleen said. "It doesn't seem likely that Raneck will let go at this pivotal time. You said he seemed like he was weakening. Can we use that in some way?"

"What you perceived may be exactly what he wanted you to perceive," Charles added. "He is an expert at misguiding people. One minute he can seem like a weak and simple old man. The next he's attacking. I advise we stay on the defensive where he is concerned and not let our guard slip."

"Charles," Lawrence countered gently, "he *was* an expert. He may still be, but we don't know that. I was with Jen on that journey – remotely, but I saw what she saw and felt what she felt. He does not know I was there. Could he really have put a glamour on both of us?"

"If he didn't know you were there, he is slipping," Charles told him. "Making someone believe he didn't see them was one of his best tricks," he added bitterly.

Lawrence walked over to Charles' page and wrote 'forgive Raneck.' He blocked what he had written with his body.

"Cailleen, how is it that Raneck exists?" Lawrence asked. "He's not here and he hasn't passed over. What sustains him? How can he have any power at all?"

"Excellent question," Cailleen said. "He certainly took as much with him as he could when he died. I'm not sure how long that lasts in the in-between place. Beyond that he would need another source, I guess. Charles?"

"Exactly what I was thinking," Lawrence said excitedly.

"That he would need another source?" Cailleen asked.

"That it's, Charles!" Lawrence explained.

"I wasn't suggesting Charles," Cailleen corrected him. "I was asking Charles if he had anything to add. You're suggesting that Charles is Raneck's source of power?"

"Not Charles generally. But I wonder if he feeds off of Charles' feelings about him." Lawrence turned to Charles. "Each time you refer to Raneck, the energies radiating from you increase intensely. Bitterness, frustration, regret and loathing are pretty strong emotions with pretty high-energy outputs. Could Raneck be feeding off of that energy? Could he even be sending you dreams or otherwise interfering in a way that keeps your feelings fresh and active? And maybe it's not just Charles. Maybe all these years he's stayed connected to the players not just to guide them in resolving this story. Maybe he's been staying connected to survive on the energetic planes. Am I off base here?"

"No, you could be on to something," Charles admitted. "The easiest sources would be from strong connections he had when he was alive – blood connections. Which makes me wonder, who is Lily? We tend to reincarnate in our own families over and over. Is Lily a reincarnated relative of Raneck?"

"Jen," Cailleen asked, "can you key into Lily's energy signature enough to be able to recognize it in another lifetime?"

"I can try. It would help to have something of hers – maybe her photo would be enough? How do you propose I surf through to get to other lifetimes?"

"I believe Charles can provide you with all the data necessary," Cailleen said. "My guess is that Lily is one of my grandchildren and one of Raneck's and one of Chancha's. She may be the physical manifestation of this crossroad."

"Wouldn't it be simpler," Charles suggested, "for me to look at Lily's picture and get her energy signature and match it with my own memories? I recognized Chancha immediately."

"That *would* be easier on Jen and certainly no more difficult for you," Cailleen agreed. "It may also be easier for you to get James to let you see the photo. Can you do that first thing tomorrow?" Charles nodded.

"Once we have that info, we can make plans for how to help Raneck see what needs to be done." Cailleen stood and paced back and forth before the fireplace. "I wonder if we aren't doing exactly what Raneck has been doing. Making plans for other people's lives and thinking we know best. We have to tread very carefully here. Very carefully."

"An innocent child's life is in the balance here," Jen said comfortingly. "We have to take whatever action we can to help her."

"We don't know she's innocent. We don't know if her purpose is already met and she's not intended to live much longer. We cannot interfere in her life without her permission – or in anyone else's. 'Do No Harm' – that is our creed. As a Healer, if I have any doubt, I will do nothing. I want you all to know that now. I'll listen to Spirit with my heart and mind and I will follow where I am led and do whatever I can for anyone. But we cannot abandon our principles because the face of an endearing child is plucking our heartstrings. We cannot abandon the protocols of our work because we fear for the safety of a friend or a Teacher," Cailleen said looking at Jen pointedly. "We must lean on our principles and our protocols when we are emotionally involved. We cannot clean up one mess only to leave another in its place. Am I clear?"

They all nodded in agreement. "Should we take a break and look at some other aspects in an hour, or call it an evening and start early in the morning?"

"I vote for a break and then another session. I'm not fond of early mornings," Jen offered. No one objected. "Great! Do we have any popcorn?" Jen led the way to the kitchen.

"I need some air," Cailleen said as she grabbed her wrap and walked out into the night. James kept coming into her mind anytime she wasn't focusing hard on something else. She needed to clear him out by reflecting on the afternoon and evening events around him. She walked to the edge of her gardens in the direction of the bungalow. As she looked over her land, she saw a fire glowing in the grove. She knew James would be there and walked to him.

He met her at the edge of the outer circle. "Merry Meet?"

"Merry Meet," she offered and kissed him in the traditional way. They walked together to honor each of the directions. In the center by the fire were two blankets. They sat on one and wrapped the other around them for warmth.

"How are you?" Cailleen asked.

"I'm calm and ready to face whatever's ahead of me," he answered. "You?"

"I'm uncertain. We're in the process of puzzling through the weavings of many lives and lifetimes. It's tricky because it seems to involve a lot of other people's lives too. I guess it's like a cancer. It's hard to tell the healthy cells from the ones out of control."

"How can I help?" James asked.

"You just did," Cailleen smiled and leaned into the curve of his shoulder. "I'm trained for this, you know. And the truth is I feel ready for it. Even in the moments of most doubt, I know that I'm in the right place. And I feel pretty confident that I'll do the right thing. I've been doing this for a while, but I rarely have someone to put his arms around me and offer comfort and support simply by his presence." James pulled her more securely into his arms and laid his head on the top of her head. Together they sat in silence.

Grandmother Moon shifted above the trees and her light poured into the grove. Cailleen stirred. "I need to get back. We still have work to do tonight. Thanks for the fire and the shoulder." She rose to her feet and James rose to meet her.

"I'm sorry about not trusting you more to understand my predicament," James said.

"I'm sorry for storming off and then returning and brandishing words with a guest in your home."

"He did start it," James offered.

"Still, it wasn't my best moment."

"Here's to better moments to come – and lots of them," James smiled and they kissed.

Cailleen walked back into the kitchen looking refreshed and happy.

"The *air* seems to have done you good. You look great," Lawrence winked at her.

"A girl does what she can," Cailleen quipped. "Did Jen save any popcorn for me?"

"No such luck, but we did make tea. I found some graham crackers. So I made some chocolate frosting and made a special treat. There's also fruit and nuts. It all awaits you in the study."

They walked into the study to find Charles and Jen on the floor making notations on everyone's pages.

"Nothing is sacred!" Lawrence raised his hands in mock disgust. "Away you two. I am the master of the crossroads and only I can wield the markers."

"You shouldn't leave them unattended then," Jen retorted as she hurried to write before he took the marker from her. "We were getting antsy so we thought we'd add info from the journey with Raneck." She wrote next to Chancha, "Doesn't like not knowing."

"We put his words in green so we could differentiate our perspectives from his," Charles pointed out.

Lawrence took the markers and set the pad back up on the easel. "I think that for consistency we should ask the same questions of all three players: what is their motivation and what task is theirs to resolve the story? Since you were just working with Chancha, shall we continue with him?" They all nodded.

"From what I recall," Lawrence began, "Chancha was a leader who acted on behalf of his tribe but over did it a bit because his personal pride was injured. He knew he couldn't allow two Senechals in the tribe, as it would upset the balance of power. He banished Calleigha, but probably anticipated that Raneck would offer him a different option that would protect the people and also allow Chancha to save face. It seems to me that except for the severity of his action, the guy was acting in good faith for the welfare of his people.

"James said earlier of Ben that he's not very imaginative. I wonder if that was also true of Chancha." He looked at Charles for confirmation.

"I never thought about it in those terms, but I'd have to say yes. Chancha was a decision maker and had the ability to stand by his decisions. But he almost always leaned on others to help him come up with options. His brilliance as a leader was his ability to listen to the ideas of others and to appreciate their value. And more than once when he went with his gut instincts, he needed advisers to help him back out without appearing weak. He knew the tribe needed to see him as strong and sure. He was right."

"So, welfare of the tribe is his primary motivation?" Jen suggested.

"Yes," Charles agreed, "and in the fullest sense of it. He looked after their physical, mental, emotional and spiritual welfare. He always looked for balance in the community."

"His tasks?" Lawrence asked.

"Listen to his advisers?" Charles offered.

"Allow me to do my work AND feel that he doesn't lose his power in doing so," Cailleen said.

"I know Ben Hodges by reputation," Charles began. "He is highly respected not only as an investment manager, but for his business acumen. His company has been featured more than once as a model of balanced work ethics, financial stability, and employee satisfaction. He has a gift for hiring people to create a very balanced team. He makes final decisions, but he leans heavily on the expertise of his staff. When he fires people, he helps them in any way he can."

"Are you suggesting his part in the quest is more personal?" Jen asked.

"Yes. He seems to have learned to listen to advisers in his professional life. We can talk with James. I wonder if he listens as well in his personal life? Or maybe he does well with it unless he's in crisis. Perhaps in crisis he reverts back to earlier patterns."

"But Charles," Jen interrupted, "you said he had those characteristics back when the story began. Is it possible that he carries with him this one big mistake and that when the stakes are high his fears about making it again get triggered?"

"Or," Lawrence continued, "that the characters who have shown up this time are the same characters. He knows that at some level. It throws him back into the same feelings, but he doesn't know how to reconcile it all. His daughter being endangered through it all can't be easy."

"I think it might be about me, specifically," Cailleen offered. "We have to make amends, to heal the past between us. When I look back at that lifetime, I keep wishing I had another chance to do something different. I want to speak less confrontationally to Chancha or to apologize and ask for pardon. I keep feeling there's something I could have done. Maybe he wishes the same thing? For me it seems not about Chancha, the Headsman, so much as Chancha, the person. I want to make amends to the person."

After a few minutes Cailleen added, "and I want to know who his daughter is, or was."

"I wonder," Jen asked, mostly to herself?

"Give her a minute," Lawrence suggested when Charles turned to ask Jen what she meant.

"What I sense most from Raneck," she continued to herself, "is regret and, I think, shame. Yes, I think behind his arrogance and manipulations there lies a thread of shame, and definitely regret. He needs to redeem himself – perhaps just in his own eyes – before he can let go and move on. We can use that! Yes, we can all use that and benefit."

Jen turned to the others for confirmation and then realized she hadn't connected the dots except in her own head. Lawrence smiled and nodded but the other two looked at her with confusion.

"Sorry. Look, here's how I'm putting this together: Raneck failed to advise Chancha when he banned Calleigha. Chancha knew he overreacted, but didn't know how to fix it. Raneck, much later, realized he could have shifted things by going to Chancha and suggesting some alternatives. So, they both screw up and the one who suffers greatly is Calleigha.

"They are both honorable men. It must have been difficult for them to watch Calleigha wither and finally disappear, knowing they could have changed things. Raneck responds by becoming more controlling and watchful – much to Charles/Chalic's discomfort. Chancha responds by making a promise to himself to seek out advisers and to listen to them. Chancha makes some reparations by adopting Calleigha's son as his own. But he has not resolved his mistakes with Calleigha/Cailleen."

Jen takes a breath and looks to make sure everyone is tracking what she's saying. She nods and continues.

"So, here's what we do: I journey again with the specific intention of connecting with Raneck, and with getting him to advise Ben/Chancha in regards to letting Cailleen/Calleigha take a look at Lily. Yes, I know. Raneck is not about to take an order or plea from me. But I can give him all the threads of story along with a plaintive and even desperate wish that someone could do something to edge Ben into accepting Cailleen's help.

"Hmm? Yes, I think it would work," Jen said again to herself.

Then looking back at the others, she said, "I'll tell Raneck I'm seeking him out to see if he can help me enter Ben's dreams. I'll say I don't have much time, but that I hoped an experienced shaman like himself might know a trick or two that could be learned quickly. I'm pretty sure he wouldn't think of letting me do something he could do himself."

"If he doesn't take the bait, you could always come to me," Charles said bitingly.

"Dear Charles," Jen said, trying to placate him, "I would actually like you to teach me a few things in that arena. But we don't have time. But I'll take your suggestion. If Raneck doesn't bite, I'll tell him I'll just have to see if you can do it."

"Aren't men fun?" Jen said to Cailleen. "Across time and culture, they still like to compare whose is bigger."

"Careful, Jen," Cailleen warned. "We're going to need these men. Best not to antagonize them."

Charles and Lawrence looked at each other in solidarity and shook their heads at the two women. "Can we get back to work now?" Lawrence asked.

"Your idea has merit," Charles agreed looking at Jen. "Just remember that Raneck is wily and often a couple of steps ahead. But as you said, your plan will serve everyone. He won't likely reject it even if he sees through you. But he might 'slap' you. Be sure you have one of us with you when you journey."

"Of course," Jen agreed. "Just in case I do get slapped, I'd like to see what I can find out about Lily before I journey to Raneck. Any objections?"

"Seems like a sound plan to me," Cailleen affirmed. The men nodded their ascent.

"OK, that's two players down – which leaves only me," Cailleen said. "No holds barred here guys. I need you to be as honest with what you see as my tasks as you were with the other two."

Charles looked down. Lawrence and Jen looked at each other. Cailleen waited.

"Elan already gave you tasks," Jen reminded Cailleen. "Be compassionate with Ben and give him information – he doesn't like not knowing. You also already discerned that whatever you need to do to balance things with Chancha is personal."

"Grandmama told you to let your heart lead the way," Charles added.

A pregnant silence sat heavily in the room. Cailleen could tell there was something else and that nobody wanted to say it. She waited. She learned long ago that people become so uncomfortable in these silences that the idea of saying difficult things seems less and less difficult.

Lawrence cleared his throat. "Cailleen, we're hesitating because this takes us into the very personal realm. Over the years we've worked together we have always kept a line. We've become friends as well as colleagues, but we're not intimates. You keep your more personal life very private. Charles crossed it last week and the two of you were speechless for at least an hour." He held up his hand when Cailleen started to speak.

"Let me get this out. I know that what you and Charles went through was also lifetimes of emotion suddenly released. When Jen and I walked in, we were pretty shaken. Not only was it obvious that something drastic had just happened, but we were suddenly in the position of needing to take care of you on a personal basis. We didn't mind in the least – kind of enjoyed it actually."

"Enjoyed it?" Jen questioned. Lawrence ignored her.

"I believe it was important in the quest. It shifted things. Jen and I stood – no, we stand more comfortably in our roles now. We've grown up and we know we can handle it. We also got to see through your power, confidence and efficiency. We saw the woman you are. Then James shows up and turns up the volume.

"Cailleen, I believe your task is to let go of your Priestess/Teacher/Healer self," Lawrence continued. "Not entirely, but significantly. You reclaimed your gifts in this lifetime. That is not your task. I think it would be easier if you thought it was. And, I could be wrong. But Calleigha gave up both her gifts and love. You have reclaimed the gifts. Where is love in your life?"

Cailleen looked at each of them and felt their strength. They stood like soldiers willing to take whatever came from her. They stood steadfast and allowed their love for her to flow freely.

"Here," she pointed at them. "Here is the love in my life. I would be lost without you. Each of you means so much to me, more than you will ever know."

"Thank you," Charles spoke for all three. "But, that's not what we're talking about. Where is the romantic, can't think straight, 'work isn't everything' kind of love?"

Cailleen walked to the window and looked in the direction of the bungalow. "'Can't think straight' isn't a very good position for a Priestess/Teacher/Healer. I have responsibilities. I've needed space to develop my gifts. It's not enough just to have them. You all know that," she said quietly. She was unaware that as she spoke, she squared her shoulders.

Charles came up behind her and placed his hands on her shoulders. "How long has it felt like such a burden?" he asked compassionately.

Cailleen wiped the tear from her eye and turned to face them. "Honestly? It's become more burdensome over the last couple of years. There's just so much to be done."

"A wise woman once told me, 'You can't work 24/7. You've got to shut down, rest and rejuvenate,'" Jen offered.

"She also said, 'there's always more work to be done. The question is, is it *your* work? If not, let it go,'" Lawrence added.

"It's a great irritant for a Teacher to have her words thrown back at her," Cailleen complained. "I'm probably going to need your help, you know."

"You've been training us to do it for *years*," Jen pointed out with exaggeration. "And," she said, kissing Cailleen on the cheek, "we like seeing you in love."

Cailleen looked at her sharply. "He's hot, he's smart and he's handy – that is not a recipe for love. Our relationship has involved secrets on both sides. And it's only been a few days. I am not in love with James."

"You've got a great start on it, though." Lawrence kissed her other cheek. "Jen and I are going to make more tea." He grabbed Jen's hand and they walked out.

"This is all a bit much," Cailleen objected.

"Quests are not known for being easy," Charles commented dryly. "We love you and we'll follow you pretty much anywhere you need to take us. But we'd feel more comfortable if you were as balanced as possible." With that Charles walked out.

"That's playing dirty," Cailleen whispered to the closing door, and then she let the tears fall. Last night's dream ran through her mind. She was not being asked to choose between Spirit and love, but to find where the balance of the two was. Charles was right. She wasn't balanced as just a Priestess/Teacher/Healer. She needed to allow herself to also fully embrace herself as a woman. She was just a woman, after all.

Cailleen steadied herself as a flash from the past came through. Raneck was standing over her as she breastfed Chalic. He was trying to convince her to take up her training again and was telling her he wouldn't live forever and that someone needed to take over for the tribe's sake. She had told him she was just a woman of the tribe now and nothing more. "You will *never* be just a woman," he shouted bitterly.

She'd resented that, even now. In many different lifetimes, she'd wished to be just a woman. She didn't want to be special; she wanted to be included in the everydayness of community life. And sometimes she resented loving her gifts. She couldn't give them up and yet, they separated her.

Had she been wrong all these years believing that she couldn't have both? She couldn't even picture a life with both.

The first morning with James in the grove came to mind. She'd been both then. No, she hadn't - at least not at the *same* time. She was Priestess. Then, in James' arms she was just a woman. It felt wonderful, she remembered. To let go and let passions take her into territory that may not be wise, was wonderful. James was very good medicine for her.

But she couldn't count on it to last. She could enjoy whatever they had while they had it. Would that be enough for the quest? As Lawrence said, it was a start. She looked at the papers scattered around the room. They'd made a very good start this evening. Her three apprentices had done very well. She acknowledged how difficult it must have been for them to be so honest with her and smiled at the depth of love they showed. "And that," she thought, "is a good note to end the day on."

Chapter Thirteen
Confluence

Charles went to see James early the next morning. He sent a thought ahead to let James know he was on his way. He did it in part as a teaching, but he also wanted James to have a few moments to prepare. Yesterday had been a big day for them all.

"Coffee?" James asked, pointing to the mug waiting for him on the deck railing. "Used my small supply of tea on Ben yesterday. Need cream or sugar?"

"This'll do," Charles said as he sat. They drank in companionable silence for a few moments.

"How is everyone this morning?" James asked.

"Fine. Asking for any particular reason?"

"Felt some disturbances last night," James mocked himself with the Star Wars reference. "Thought something else might have come up in your work."

"Several somethings, actually," Charles said. "A couple involving you."

"Oh?"

"We wondered if you would be interested in joining us for our private Samhain celebration next week. Seems that the group is interested to see how you would work within our circle. We do consider you part of it. We discussed that after you left. None of us felt your statement about being an outsider rang true for us. Of course, we weren't sure how the others felt so we had to talk after you left.

"It was a quick decision to invite you to the celebration to see how you'd fit in a working capacity. We've never felt totally complete with just the four of us. Occasionally we invite someone to join us."

"Is this like a test? Do I have to do some preparation?" James asked.

"Yes and no – to both questions. It is not a test for you as much as a test for all of us. We've invited people before whom we all trust and enjoy. Yet, in the workings of the circle, the energies didn't merge well. Sometimes that's obvious right away. Other times it takes time to discern. There's no pressure. It's an invitation. Including you in our circle of friendship is not contingent on whether you accept the invitation to join our sacred circle.

"If we have time this week, I can take you through some exercises so you know what to expect in the circle. Otherwise, we'll walk you through it at the time. We're not planning anything complicated this time year. There's too much going on already."

"Can I accept conditionally?" James asked. Charles raised his eyebrow. "I'd be very interested in joining you. Yet, if Ben needs me, I have to go to him. Lily's getting critical."

"Of course, we understand that. I'll let everyone know. What's happening with Lily?" Charles asked.

"Ben said they've had to take her to the ER several times a month lately. Shortness of breath sometimes or she won't eat, so they take her to get an IV. It's heartbreaking. I have a picture of her taken at her last birthday. She's got half of her usual vitality in the photo. Now, she's a shadow of that." James hung his head in defeat. "It's terrible not being able to do anything to help her."

"Do you have the photo here?" Charles asked.

"Yes. I keep it in my bag. I don't want to forget her in her fullness. It might be silly, but I feel like it would be giving up on her ability to recover."

"If you'd like, I can teach you to use the photo as a focus to send her energy," Charles offered.

"What kind of energy?"

"Love is the easiest," Charles answered.

James went to get Lily's photo. "Do we need anything else?" he asked before shutting the back door.

"Nope. Just you and the photo. Come sit down. Take a few breaths to center yourself and clear your mind." Charles waited until he saw James' breath deepen and his body relax.

"Good. Now go to a time when you felt most connected with Lily – perhaps a special time the two of you shared. Let yourself feel your love for her. Gather that love. Now, hold the photo of Lily and imagine gently offering that loving energy to her. See her soak it up. Visualize her being fed and nourished. Be certain to simply offer her the energy without forcing it on her. Let her take it in and use it as she will and can. Continue to gather love and feed it to her as long as she takes it in.

"Good. Now press your feet into the deck, then relax. Remember you are still yourself. You are standing here on this deck in the morning sunshine. It is only your love for Lily that is being sent forth. Your love is part of the endless supply of Universal love. You are simply tapping into the endless supply, flavoring it as it passes through you, and sending it to Lily. You are maintaining your own energy while you do this."

James settled back in his chair and took a cleansing breath. He slowly opened his eyes, squinting at the brightness of the sun.

"Nice job. Bring yourself totally back into your body in this time and this space. Stretch. Take a couple of deep breaths. Rub your hands together. In time you'll choose what works best for you. How do you feel?"

"Refreshed, actually," James said uncertainly.

"That's a good sign. If you do it right you get energized too. Do you have any questions?" Charles asked.

"Can I send her too much?"

"Yes. But if you hold the intention to simply offer her the energy, you allow her to take it in as she can and will. It frees you from the burden of having to decide, and, it honors her free will. The truth is, James, we don't know what Lily's path holds. To interfere can do harm, so remember to *offer* your love without strings or agenda."

"Can I do the same for Ben and Camille?"

"Yes. What you're doing is offering an active prayer. If you would pray for them, you can send them love. It's just semantics, James, and a slightly different frame of reference."

Charles gave James a few moments to take in everything. He had avoided looking at the photo of Lily so he wasn't distracted while leading James through the exercise.

"Tell me about Lily," Charles encouraged.

James turned the photo so Charles could see her. "She's a funny kid. In some ways she's very serious and focused. And, she's also delightfully silly. I was thinking about the day she invited me to a tea party. 'Formal,' she said. 'And don't forget to shine your shoes, Uncle James.'

"I show up in my Sunday best and find them out on the lawn. Camille and Ben are also dressed to the nines. Lily is dressed like a princess. Behind her come the butler and her nanny with very serious looks on their faces except for the laughter in their eyes. The nanny sets down the bag that she is carrying. Lily opens it and it's full of hats. She puts a top hat on her own head and then proceeds to give us each a hat. Ben gets one that Carmen Miranda would envy, Camille is given an admiral's hat, and I am awarded a dress hat my grandmother would have worn. It had lots of flowers and netting that came over the eyes. When we all have our hats on, she says, 'These formal affairs can be so tedious if we take ourselves too seriously. Shall I pour?' Best tea party I ever attended!"

As James spoke, Charles looked at the photo. He gathered the resonances of the photo and the girl James spoke of. He felt he'd known her. Yes, there was a familiar resonance. He took that resonance and went back in his own memories to see if he could find a match.

"Charles, are you alright? Charles," James called again.

"Sorry," Charles said shaking his head a bit. "I guess I drifted away. Your story reminded me of someone and I was trying to place it. I hope I get to meet Lily someday."

"Do you think it's too early to go over to the manor and call Ben?" James asked "I'd like to call early so Ben knows I'm available."

"Everyone was up when I left. It shouldn't be a problem. Shall we head over?"

Jen saw them coming and greeted them at the door. "Charles, I need your opinion about something. Do you have a minute?"

"Sure," Charles answered. "James came to call Ben. You know the way," he said to James.

"What's up?" he asked Jen as they walked towards the study.

"I wanted to know how it went. Did you find out who Lily is?"

"I know that I know her, but James interrupted me before I could define who she is. Do you want to have a go at it with me?"

"Thought you'd never ask," Jen answered. "How shall we go about it?"

"Let's link and then I'll share my impressions of Lily. You can add them to your own. Then I'll take you with me down memory lane and we can both look for a match. Shall we tell the others what we're doing?"

"I'll give Lawrence a heads up. They won't disturb us unless we're gone too long. Ready?"

Fifteen minutes later Charles and Jen emerged from the study.

"James said to tell you he's on his way over the mountains. Lily had a bad night. He'll keep us informed," Lawrence said. "Any news from you?"

"Yes, as we expected, Lily is involved."

"How?" Cailleen asked as she came into the hallway where Charles spoke.

"She's your granddaughter and Chancha's. She's the one Raneck used before. He's using her now too, probably – although I couldn't feel him."

"Well that's confirmed. It doesn't really change our plans. Jen," Cailleen began, "you'll connect with Raneck and suggest he send Ben a dream. Be careful and remember he's old but probably has enough power to be difficult. Lawrence, you'll travel with her?"

Lawrence nodded. "I'll also play a bit with our work from last night and see if anything else emerges that we might have missed. Speaking of which, I was remembering this morning that you said your Grandmama said it was your 'task to re-balance power.' At the time I thought it meant power between the three. I wonder now if it is more about re-balancing the powers of love and your esoteric gifts?"

Charles nodded and looked at Cailleen. "You did teach me the importance of that as Calleigha after you died and then came to me on my year of separation from the tribe. It makes a lot of sense."

Cailleen took in their comments and nodded her acceptance.

"Charles," Cailleen asked, "will you continue training with James this week? Did you ask him to join us at Samhain?"

"If at all possible, yes. And James accepted our invitation as long as we understand that Lily comes first and he might be called away."

"Shall we do a bit of planning for Samhain before lunch?" Jen suggested.

After lunch, Jen, Lawrence and Charles prepared to get back to Seattle. At the car they made last arrangements to meet at Jen's house on Thursday evening, after Cailleen finished with her workshop.

"Charles?" Cailleen yelled as they headed down the drive. She ran to catch them. "I don't have James' phone number. Can you tell him he is welcome to stay in the manor while I'm gone so he has access to the phone? He may not even come back this week, but just in case?"

"I could give you his phone number," Charles suggested.

"Just the message. But give him mine when you talk to him. Thanks."

Chapter Fourteen
Commitments

Her hotel room featured the usual impersonal luxury, which served to make Cailleen restless and unsettled. A more relaxed workshop schedule would have allowed her to stay with Jen. But the tight schedule required Cailleen to begin at 9 am and teach until 6 pm. She'd be exhausted and need the alone time a hotel room afforded.

Her past travels taught her to take a bit of home with her. The first thing Cailleen did was pull out a colorful sarong in purples, golds and greens. She draped it over the dresser and placed the Elements on top. Her "travel kit" included a candle, shell, wolf carving, incense burner and a stone with a spiral carving. She lit the candle and some incense. She moved counter clockwise around the room, using the incense to clear it of unwanted energies. She put a purple scarf on the table along with a photo of her nieces and a card they made her last week. She brought several wraps with her for the workshop. These she draped across chairs and the settee. As she personalized her room, she sang. In just a few minutes the room felt warm and cared for.

Now Cailleen could relax for an hour before meeting members of the Conference Committee for dinner. She decided to take a bath and focus her mind on the material she was presenting tonight. She neatly tucked away the quest and its intrigues so she could be present with the participants of the conference. She enjoyed teaching how to develop intuitive and psychic gifts. And from experience she knew she had to keep her shields up – the topic tended to draw at least a few unbalanced personalities.

As she dressed, she noticed the many ways in which she put together her Teacher self. Relaxed business attire – a pantsuit with some flow - became the base, which let participants know she was credible and professional. She did not want to be considered an "airy fairy, woo-woo, guru." She was too practical for that and she felt that such an image would isolate her work from those who might need it most. Jewelry created the next level of presentation. Her power ring and amulet were always present. She added other rings, necklaces and earrings. Each piece held a story and most carried helpful energies for the task at hand.

Hair was the final physical tool for the Teacher. Tonight, she'd wear it up. She discovered a few years back that committee members liked to know they could count on their presenters. If they were uncertain, they tended to micro manage. She found that if she put her hair up just before she met them, they were comforted by her no-nonsense appearance. As time went by, however, her hair would slowly loosen on its own. Within an hour she would have a warm, friendlier look, which made her seem more approachable to participants. She smiled to herself as she thought of Deacon. He was the one who pointed out the effects of her hair. He'd thought she'd done it intentionally. She let him believe it.

Tonight, she dressed in chocolate browns and wore amber jewelry. She added a warm wrap in autumn colors for meeting the committee. In her bag she had brought a painted silk scarf to wear for her talk and for meeting participants. She decided to take her frame drum just in case she wanted to offer a chant during her talk.

Before she left her room, she wrapped herself in what Deacon called her "glamour." This was the energetic piece to her Teacher self. Deacon described it as one part diva, one part queen, two parts Earth mama, four parts confident knowing and just a pinch of remoteness. "It makes people want more and keeps them at a safe distance," Deacon told her. He assumed she did it for marketing purposes, but that was his job so he would appreciate it as such. Her real intent was to magnetize the people who needed her teachings with her confidence, to encourage them with her earthiness, and, to require them to make an effort before getting access to her. When she first began teaching, she made herself very available and learned that people also expected her to do their work for them. A little remoteness along with a carriage of importance tended to weed out the folks who were just playing at making life changes.

At the conference, as Cailleen was being introduced, she became distracted by an unidentified sense of desperation. She sensed it was coming from someone in the audience, but she didn't have time to follow it. As she spoke, she tried to find the source, but without the proper focus, she failed. She searched faces at the end of the evening, but came up empty handed.

It wasn't unusual for Cailleen to feel strong emotions coming from audience members. Often she would be approached after an event. Tonight she was thanked and asked questions about her workshop the next day. Nobody approached her asking for help.

When she returned to her rooms, she felt someone watching her, but again, no one approached. In her rooms she took a few moments to check out the energies she'd been feeling to make sure they were non-threatening. She felt no sense of danger, so she went to bed.

The next morning as she went to the conference rooms, she again felt eyes watching her. She wondered if she had a stalker. It had never happened to her, but many writers and public speakers had dealt with stalkers. She considered calling James and asking his advice, but dismissed it as premature.

At lunch she felt nothing unusual and began to relax a little. Perhaps the quest was getting to her or maybe Raneck was watching her. She eliminated both ideas. She was handling the quest well and she felt pretty certain that she'd recognize Raneck's energy.

***

Jen arrived for her appointment with Ben Hodges dressed in a cashmere suit that made her look like a member of the elite class. Her hair was styled in a sleek up do. Her feet were in a short boot with a four-inch heel. She looked like a force to be reckoned with and she knew it.

"Jennifer Arante to see Mr. Hodges," she offered at the reception desk. "I have an eleven o'clock appointment."

"Yes, Ms. Arante, Mr. Hodges is expecting you. Please have a seat; he'll be with you momentarily." The receptionist phoned Ben's office to say she had arrived and a minute later an elderly woman came out to receive her.

"Ms. Arante, I'm Beverly Finch. I'll take you to Mr. Hodges' office now. Can I get you coffee, tea or a Perrier?"

"Coffee with soy creamer if you have it, please." Jen followed Beverly to Ben's office.

Jen had made the appointment for the first thing Monday morning. She'd been meaning to invest some of her money anyway, but this gave her an opportunity to observe Ben in his natural habitat, and if the opportunity presented itself, to talk to him about Cailleen. She'd felt compelled to come. No one knew she was here. She just had a hunch and she was following it.

Beverly led her into a small conference room. She poured the coffee and brought her a small pitcher of soy creamer. A plate of fruit, nuts and muffins sat in the center of the table. Beverly looked around the room to see that everything was in order, and then walked to the door. "Mr. Hodges will be right with you."

A moment later Ben walked through the door. "Ms. Arante, it's a pleasure to meet you. I've seen your work at the Seattle Art Museum as well as your larger pieces at the Arboretum and I think a park in Bellevue?"

"Yes, thank you. I've been lucky to have the commissions."

"I'd say it's got less to do with luck and more to do with talent, Ms. Arante. My daughter is a fan, as well. She likes the whimsy that is so characteristic of your work. But you probably didn't come here to talk about your art. What can I do for you?"

"Well, actually, I did come to talk about my art, but not the art we were just talking about. I do work in some other arenas. I may be an artist, Mr. Hodges, but I have a very practical streak. I have some significant savings that need to be invested. Some of my finances, of course, need to be put back into my art. I have $20,000 I'd like to put into some investments."

"I'd be happy to help you with that." Ben pushed the intercom. "Beverly, could you bring me a new client packet, please?"

"If you don't mind Mr. Hodges, I'd like to ask you some questions."

"Certainly, Ms. Arante."

"First, could you please call me Jen? I feel so old when someone calls me Ms. Arante. Second, why should I trust you with my investments?"

"We've been in business for fifteen years, Jen, and have a steady and happy clientele. I can show you industry figures and how we rate against other companies."

"Mr. Hodges," she interrupted.

"Ben."

"Ben, I've already seen the figures. As I said, I'm quite practical. I researched your firm before I made the appointment. I chose you not just because of your track record in investments but also because of how you do business. What I really want to know is how do you choose where you put my money? How do you know it will pay off?"

"I'll be honest with you, Jen, we don't know – at least not absolutely. Investments are not a science, but there are observable patterns that help us get a read on the market. Depending on what your risk/security inclinations are, we invest your money to give you the best return."

"If the patterns are observable, why does your firm have a more impressive track record than other investment firms? What makes you special?"

"Jen, I have a knack for interpreting those patterns and a gift for hiring others with the same knack. We also are very good at discerning the needs and desires of our clients. There are no guarantees. But we're good at what we do, we follow strict ethics and we really care about our clients. I don't know what your situation is, but many of our clients trust us with their life savings. We take that responsibility seriously. We understand it's more than money we're handling. You've worked hard for what you have, Jen, and we know you're trusting us with your future."

"What I'm hearing is that you have a lot of skill, good ethics and clear intention. I'm also hearing that you understand the client is in charge. It's the client's desires and needs that focus the investments. It also sounds like you have a bit of magic when it comes to investments."

Ben smiled. "I see you've read the article in the Times about the firm."

"Sorry?"

"Oh, I assumed you were quoting the article. They used the same line "a bit of magic when it comes to investments," he explained.

"Really? You've been written up in the paper as having magic. That's interesting."

At the end of the hour, Jen had filled out all the paperwork and written a check for $20,000.

"Thank you, Ben. Use your magic well for me. You know, I do a bit of magic myself. It's a true art. Goodbye."

"Goodbye," Ben said. As she walked away her gait triggered his memory. Jen was the woman who came to James' bungalow with Charles Murphy. He wanted to be mad, but she'd been so charming and forthright. She felt what James would call "clean." She came to give him a message. Of course, she might have come to make an investment and simply used the opportunity to make a point. He guessed she made it. He could see why James liked her.

James had never let Ben down, ever. He'd shown up within two hours of Ben's call yesterday. Lily had a bad night and they took her to the ER early in the morning. She kept talking as if James was in the room. When James arrived, they were just getting ready to leave the hospital. Lily's heart rate and breathing returned to normal rather suddenly while they were waiting for tests. When James walked in, Lily thanked him and asked him why he had been hiding.

"I told Mummy and Daddy you came to heal me, but they said you weren't here. But I saw you. You were reminding me about our tea party. Your hat was the silliest, Uncle James."

After they got home and Lily went to take a nap, James shared what Charles had taught him to do. James said he thought Charles was just giving him something to do so he wouldn't feel so helpless. He knew in theory it could support Lily, but he had no idea it could actually make such a difference. James told them he was actually a bit shaken by the knowledge that such a simple act of love could truly make a difference.

Camille felt some hope returning as James shared his experience. Some days she felt like the only thing keeping Lily alive was her love. Now she thought it might have some truth. Ben was less impressed. He certainly welcomed the ease it seemed to have brought to Lily. Of course, it may have just been a coincidence. After all, both he and Camille have been loving Lily as much as they possibly can. In the back of his mind, he heard Jen's words mocking him, ". . . sounds like you have a bit of magic."

***

Lawrence suspected Jen was up to something. She'd blocked him. He couldn't feel her at all. He could locate her by other means, of course, but that would be an invasion of her privacy. He and Jen had been connected since childhood. He remembered the day his family moved next door to hers. He saw her and wanted to say, 'that's where you are.' He didn't know something was missing until they met. He could breathe better and felt more at ease in his own body. When she shut him out, it felt like a window had been closed on a gentle breeze. It unsettled him a bit.

They weren't lost without each other exactly. They both had full lives and were whole balanced individuals. They simply brought each other a higher vibrancy, or more vitality. They just worked better, together. Jen mirrored Lawrence back to himself. That's what he'd told Yvonne. In that mirror he couldn't hide and he couldn't miss his own significance. She saw his higher self. Jen told Yvonne that he was like a monitor for a musician. It wasn't that she needed him to sing. Rather, she needed him to hear herself sing.

Yvonne embraced Jen from the beginning without any hesitation or jealousy. She understood that Jen and Lawrence were a package deal and seemed to enjoy getting a sister as a bonus to their relationship.

He heard a car door shut, then a quick knock and Jen came through the door.

"I'll tell you everything in a moment," she said apologetically. "I just need a moment in the bathroom."

"Come have a bite to eat," Lawrence invited when she returned. "I wasn't sure but I suspected you might have had a busy day. I want you energized before we journey." He poured her a short glass of Chardonnay and brought out a platter of hors d'oeuvres.

Grilled asparagus, hummus and pita bread, olives, grape tomatoes and fresh cucumber slices had Jen's mouth watering. "We don't usually have wine before a journey," she said as she nibbled on asparagus.

"That's why I gave you a short glass. I thought you might want a bit to relax. So, how was your day?"

"I'm sorry Lawrence, I had to do it. I couldn't risk having you in my head."

"Jen, you don't need to apologize. You have a perfect right to privacy. If it wasn't that we were in the middle of this quest with Raneck's unpredictability, I wouldn't have worried at all."

"Damn, I didn't think you'd be worried, just annoyed. I'm sorry I worried you."

"You're forgiven. Just give me a heads up until this thing is over. You might give Yvonne some flowers, though. I think I bit her head off this afternoon."

"Hmm, there's something wrong about me taking responsibility for you treating Yvonne badly," Jen said with a laugh. "You get the flowers. I'll get her chocolate in exchange for pulling your attention away from her."

Jen told him about her meeting with Ben. "That was brilliant," he said. "A bit subtle for you, but brilliant. I never thought about investing as another avenue for using our gifts. Of course, I wouldn't be interested in putting the time in to learning the system. I might give Ben a call myself."

"I'm beginning to feel like a valuable and appreciated member of the team these days. Feels good."

"About time you caught up with how the rest of us see you," Lawrence said, giving her a hug. "Ready to journey?"

"Ready."

They went to Lawrence's study this time. A very masculine room, it reflected his strength and subtlety. Jen thought it felt as if one walked into a tree. The room seemed round. No harsh angles were evident. The furniture itself was dark in greens and browns. Lawrence had painted the walls with texture in a soft mushroom color. Textiles in tans and greens softened corners of shelves and desk. A philodendron plant wove its way around the top of walls, eliminating the harsh line where they met the ceiling. Earth poles, walking sticks and plant stands filled the corners of the room. The walls featured Lawrence's photographs from his own travels: an elk in the Cascades on the north wall; doves snuggling on a pine branch on the east wall; a sunset in Santa Fe on the south wall; and, on the west wall, a view through tree branches of a whale breaching the water.

Candles and soft lighting added a mystic quality for tasks such as journeying. Lawrence lit the candles as he walked clockwise and honored the directions. The two of them sat across from each other in comfy leather chairs. Jen called again on Isis. Lawrence called on brother Elk for stamina and Hermes, the god of communication.

Jen wasn't sure how to connect with Raneck. He sought her out the last time. She decided the first approach would be to simply call him. If that didn't work, she'd gather Ben, Cailleen, Charles and Lily in her mind and try to use their combined resonances to attract him. She intended to shift from placating him to an attitude of not really needing him. She'd show him both her strength and her need. She wanted him to be uncertain and therefore careful with her.

She connected more deeply with Lawrence and then sent out a call to Raneck. As soon as she began, she felt the presence of Coal. "Hello, love. I'm so glad you came. I should have stopped by the house and brought you with me. But I see that wasn't necessary." Coal meowed and then began walking down a path. Jen followed.

The path led through a rather barren landscape. A cave nestled 50 feet above a dry river bed. Coal was picking his way toward the cave. As they approached, Raneck emerged from the cave.

"I presume you need me for something?" he said arrogantly.

"Presumptions are what got us in this situation," Jen quoted back to him his first words to her. She then waited until he invited her to sit. It took him several long minutes to do so.

"It looks like you intend to stay, so you might as well sit." Raneck handed her a cup, which she accepted. Coal jumped onto her lap and knocked the cup from her hand.

"I'm sorry, he doesn't always travel well," she apologized as she righted the now empty cup and sat it down in front of her.

"Raneck, you have wisdom and the experience of ages. I hope you might consider helping me with something. What I propose will, I believe, help to resolve this story and bring in a new balance." Jen waited.

"I *may* help you," he said with doubt in his voice. "Continue."

"Thank you. As you probably know, Cailleen and Ben have now met. From what we know from the past, Ben needs to allow Cailleen to use her healing abilities – in this lifetime - to help his daughter, Lily. She's quite ill, you know?" Jen watched for a response. Raneck merely nodded in acknowledgment.

"It also seems highly probable that Ben/Chancha needs an adviser in this situation. He doesn't trust our skills because in this lifetime he has no frame of reference for them. Most people today consider our skills to be tricks and diversions."

Raneck spit and rose to his feet. He paced in irritation and mumbled about loss and foolishness. Then he seemed to become aware of Jen again and sat back down.

"I believe that through a dream, Ben might be less resistant to receiving honest information about our gifts, and he might be able to open to the idea of allowing Cailleen to help Lily. I don't know how to enter someone else's dreams. You've entered mine so I know you have this skill. Will you teach me?"

"Bah! You expect the honor of being taught by one of the most powerful shamans? What do you bring to me in exchange? Why should I waste my energies on a weak one like you?"

Jen looked around and then waved her arm to encompass the landscape. "I don't see anyone else asking to be taught," she challenged. "It would be a foolish loss to allow your skills to simply vanish."

Raneck rose again and paced. She was using his own words to manipulate him. He didn't like being outmaneuvered. He stopped and considered her through a distasteful glare. Jen knew it was time to placate. She dropped her shoulders in defeat and began trembling slightly.

"I'm not even sure if I can do it. Charles, I mean Chalic, probably can, but he gets on his ethical high horse sometimes and I don't know if he will. I suppose I could get him to teach me. It might not be in time, but it is a hope." Jen rose as if to leave him.

"Sit," Raneck commanded. "I have not told you whether or not I will help you." He paced about again, then, coming to a decision, he stopped directly in front of her forcing her to look up at him. She allowed him his power positioning. Coal twitched his tail in warning.

"I will not help you by teaching you this skill. We don't have time. Chalic was always too careful and overly concerned about others' feelings. He will not move quickly enough. I will send Chancha the dream myself. I will come to him as Raneck and remind him of the days when he trusted me as his adviser."

"Are you strong enough?" Jen asked with great concern.

"I am Raneck. I always find the strength." Then he allowed himself to sag a bit and put on a glamour of weakness. "I may need your help. I am quite old, you see."

Jen pretended not to see through this ruse. Her eyes got big. "I hadn't thought of your age. What do you need, grandfather?"

"A bit of your strength is all. My source of strength has grown weak," he explained.

Jen took a gamble. "Lily is just a small child," she offered.

"Quite," Raneck agreed, not catching how Jen had just maneuvered him. He was too intent on getting a fresh source of power.

Before he could instruct her on how to allow him to feed on her power, Jen stood up. "I will send you some energy tonight. I'll tap into the Universal source and channel some your way. I think about ten minutes should do it. Lawrence and I will raise power together within our circle and then focus it your way. Take what you need from what we send you." Coal nodded in approval and began picking a path back down to the riverbed.

Lawrence threw an extra shield behind Jen's back. She had just dismissed Raneck by turning her back and walking away. She couldn't see the fury on his face, but Lawrence did. He watched as Raneck fought to control himself. It was clear he had little choice and he didn't like it. Lawrence wrapped his love around Jen and brought her back to his study surely and safely. When she was back he took a moment to put extra protections around them.

He got a blanket and a glass of brandy. He pulled Jen onto his lap and into the physical warmth of his arms. "Drink," he encouraged. Jen shook herself a little and took a sip.

"I'm fine, Lawrence. A little cold, but fine. I think that went well."

"You walked a tight rope, but I think you're right. It did go well. I think he'll do it. I also think he'll try to find a way to get more from you. So, don't take any foolish risks. Don't journey without me and don't shut me out until this story is resolved," he commanded. Then he added, "Please?"

"I promise to be quite careful. Should we raise energy to send to Raneck now or have some dinner and come back to it?"

"Dinner. Let's refuel first. And I think we should consult Elan before we raise energy. I'm thinking we route it through her."

"What?"

"Computer geeks can route an Internet connection or a cell phone through a series of towers so that it becomes difficult to locate the true source. It's modern technology, but I don't see why we can't adapt it. And Raneck is unlikely to expect it. I remember Charles saying he doesn't know where or when Elan is from. So, I wonder if she has a bit of magic in that area."

"Makes sense, but you're the one who's going to explain it to her. And I think we should connect with her now in case we have things to do to prepare."

"Good idea. It's also twilight right now, the crossroad between day and night. She does guard the crossroads; it will be easier to connect within one. Let's call on her and see if she's willing to have a chat." They held hands, forming a small circle.

"Elan of the Crossroads," Jen began, "we need your assistance. We stand in the twilight hours, be welcome here now."

The air shimmered between them and took Elan's shape. "Hello dears."

"Merry meet," Jen and Lawrence chorused.

"Merry meet," Elan returned. "Do you need assistance?"

Lawrence explained the idea to her. Elan shook her head in understanding and smiled.

"You are right to be concerned Lawrence. Raneck believes he is fighting for his survival and won't abandon the hopes of an energy source. He doesn't understand that he has become stretched too thin to hold any form of energy for long. Without a boost he will not be able to connect with Chancha through the dreamland. I have a way to give him the power he needs and motivate him to let go and pass between the veils to the other side."

"We're open to suggestions," Lawrence invited.

"In Raneck's understanding, power from the Land and power raised through the act of sexual love are sacred. If you can give him that, two things will happen. First, the sacredness of the energy will remind him of his own sacredness and prevent him from trying to manipulate the energies to bind you to him. Second, the energy raised between lovers will give him a taste of what it is to have a physical body again. That taste may just tip the scales and help him to let go.

"Jen, come to me at midnight. I'll be at my cottage," Elan said. "Lawrence, invite Yvonne to help you raise the necessary energy. If you can add the energy Cailleen and James can raise, that will be helpful. Charles might be of use at the grove. If Lawrence and Cailleen can send the energy to Charles at the grove, Charles can channel it, along with energy from the grove to Jen. Together Jen and I will send it to Raneck.

"It will surprise Raneck to get such a potent form of energy and I believe prevent him from tethering onto Jen's field. I'll step in to prevent it if he tries. We can only hope the experience will encourage him to cross over so he can incarnate again."

"See you at the crossroads," Elan whispered as she shimmered away.

"I'll tell Yvonne she needs to have sex with you tonight and call Charles. You can call Cailleen," Jen ordered.

"Not on your life. I'll be speaking to Yvonne. You've got Cailleen. I'm willing to call Charles, too."

"Fine," Jen moped. "I'll do the hard part."

Lawrence walked counterclockwise around the room, extinguishing candles and releasing the directions. Then they each made their calls, after which Lawrence took Jen to the kitchen where Yvonne was waiting with dinner.

After dinner, Jen headed home to get some much-needed sleep. As Yvonne cleared the dishes, she started humming. Lawrence knew that hum. It meant she was worried about something and needed to talk, but she wasn't quite sure how to approach it. He knew Yvonne well enough to give her a bit of time and space so she could get her thoughts together. When she was ready, she'd talk.

"I'm going to throw some laundry in the washer," Lawrence said and left the room. She gave him a distracted grunt and he smiled. These little rhythms and understanding of one another were surprisingly sweet to him. He loved knowing what she needed and loved being able to give it to her.

Ten minutes later, she found him in his study deep into something on his laptop. She leaned into the door jamb and just watched him. When he resolved his thought, he would become aware of her. She liked to watch him sense her, and then see the smile bloom on his face. She hoped they'd be able to share these moments for a long, long time.

Yvonne was worried about her role in tonight's activities. She'd never been invited into his magical work. She didn't really feel called to it. He didn't exclude her in that part of his life. He talked about it, and she asked some general questions. But they both knew it was about making conversation and not about any burning interest she had in the work. She was charmed and pleased that he asked her to participate tonight. She just didn't know what it meant.

Lawrence closed his laptop and saw her standing there. A slow smile spread across his face and his eyes twinkled. "What a lovely sight you make, darling," he said as he walked across the room to her. "Have you figured out what you need to talk about, yet?"

"I have, indeed," she said and kissed him gently. "I have a pot of tea that should be ready. Shall we have it in the living room and get comfortable?"

"Sounds like a long conversation," Lawrence said.

"It may be. I'm not really sure. But as we have a couple hours before the working tonight, I thought we might as well get comfortable." Yvonne walked through the kitchen to get the tea tray and then led the way to the living room.

She'd started a fire and the room looked cozy and comfortable. Lawrence poured their tea. Yvonne snuggled into the corner of the couch and turned toward him. As he handed her her mug, he shifted toward her. As he moved his leg, she tucked her bare feet under it. It was a dance they choreographed a long time ago. They each took a moment to sip their tea as they gathered their thoughts, and then looked into the other's eyes. With their dance complete, Lawrence gave her an encouraging smile.

Yvonne took a deep breath. "What does participating in the magic tonight mean?" she asked. "Is this a one-time event? Is it some kind of initiation? What will be expected of me and," she took another deep breath, "if I'm going to play, I want to know what it's about."

"Fair questions," Lawrence nodded. "We haven't ever really talked about my magic work, and what your part might be in it. I've never sensed that you had a particular interest in it other than to be supportive of something that's important to me. Do I have that right?"

"Very well put," Yvonne said. "Go on."

"Yes, this is a one-time event. Although, I can't say that other such events might not arise. But it is always an invitation, which you may accept or not – without any pressure from me or the rest of the group. It's very important that you understand that." Lawrence gave her a moment to let that sink in.

"OK. Thank you. I didn't feel pressured, but it's nice to hear the words," Yvonne said touching his arm.

"As it's your first time, I suppose that in a sense it is an initiation. But not a formal one. All that will be expected of you is to just be together with me, like we've been together many times before," he assured her.

Yvonne cocked her head and gave him an intense look that challenged his statement.

"You're right, it won't be exactly like before. It might just be better," he teased. "Here's what will happen. I will create a sacred circle calling to the five directions – north, east, south, west and center. You might feel a bit of a tingle or a shimmer in the air. It will be important for you to stay inside the circle until I take it down after we're finished."

"Is this dangerous," Yvonne asked a bit nervously?

"No, it's not dangerous. We create the sacred circle to keep interfering energies out and also to contain the energy we will be raising together. If you walk outside the circle, it tends to burst it, like a bubble. It weakens the container and can cause a loss of focus for the energy we raise." Lawrence took her hand and gave it a comforting squeeze. "It's nothing you have to worry about and I think it will make more sense to you, when we actually do it. This is the initiatory aspect. You're a newbie, but I have no doubt that you will be just fine."

Yvonne said nothing. She drank more tea and watched him over the rim.

"Yvonne, this is not so very different than our first time together. Do you remember how we both wanted it to be special? We picked the place and the time. I brought flowers and you had champagne and strawberries. When I arrived, you walked around the room lighting candles. Then, I'll never forget how you walked to the center of the room, dropped your robe and gave me a come-hither look. I nearly fainted from the power you sent toward me." He leaned over and kissed her gently.

"You're a very good teacher," Yvonne smiled and kissed him back. When he deepened the kiss, she drew back. "You still have some teaching to do. A couple of my questions remain unanswered."

***

"James, it's Cailleen. I'm sorry to bother you," she began. "Are you in Seattle by any chance?"

"You aren't bothering me and yes, I'm still in Seattle."

"Do you think you could meet me at my hotel room around eleven tonight?" Cailleen asked.

"Best invitation I've had all day, but I'm guessing this is not a booty call," James laughed.

"Um, well actually it sort of is. I need you to make love to me tonight around midnight," Cailleen said matter of factly.

"OK, but why at midnight?"

"Can I explain when you get here? A hotel is not the best place for this, but it will have to do."

"What would be the best place?"

"The grove would be ideal, but anywhere outside would be a great improvement," Cailleen answered.

"I'll pick you up at 10:30," James offered. "I have friends who live near the Arboretum. They have a very private back yard. They're out of town and I'm watching the place for them for a couple days. Will that do?"

"Quite nicely. I'll meet you out front at 10:30. James? Thank you."

"Anything for you," he whispered.

***

On the way to his friend's house, Cailleen explained to James the strategy as Jen had explained it to her. She explained further that she would make a light link with Charles before they began and then as they climaxed, she would focus that energy through the link toward Charles."

"Should I send a link to Charles as well?" James asked. They decided to send a link together and both focus their energies through that link to Charles.

"I have a few other questions. Will the others be able to see us? Will it be like having a big orgy? Will this change our relationships?" James paused to consider. "I think that's all of them."

"Those are totally fair questions. You've taken everything in with such ease, that I forgot that it's all rather new to you." Cailleen squeezed his hand to calm and comfort him.

"Please understand that this is not a performance of any kind. It will be just the two of us, in a sacred circle, raising energy. Yes, we will be having sex and celebrating our deep connection." She leaned over and kissed him. "No one will see us. The sacred circle protects and contains what we will be doing. Lawrence and Yvonne will be doing the same thing, but we will not be participating with each other. Our intention will be to send the energy we raise to Charles at the grove. He will send it to Jen. Jen and Elan will send it to Raneck. It's like a river damn creating electricity. The electricity travels to each home and business, but the river doesn't come along for the ride."

"That's a good metaphor, teach," James said. "Staying on that metaphor, do we need to be cautious about surges? Will Charles and Jen be able to receive the energy without getting fried?"

"I love your quick mind," Cailleen said. "Yes, those are concerns. Charles is adept at working with such energies. Jen is not, but she has Elan with her to help. Also, Charles will send her a steady flow – gentle at first, and then growing as she adjusts to it. It will be a lot of work for Charles. We should check on him after all is complete.

"Yes, my dear, this will change our relationships," she continued. "Magic never happens without ripples. Rippling out is, in fact, magic's nature. That is why I spend so much time teaching about intention and focus. Still, we cannot truly predict the rippling effects of magic any more than we can totally predict the effects of our everyday actions and words. What I can tell you is that none of us have done this particular kind of magic together. Any new venture together in magic brings with it, new levels of intimacy. And, we're human. As with all new intimacies, fears can come up and with them misunderstandings. I believe that the foundation of relationship we have can handle that. How do you feel about that?"

"We don't have a long relationship, Cailleen. But it feels rather solid to me. We've already made it through one trust issue. I think we can risk another level of intimacy between us. But it's not just the two of us you're talking about, is it?"

"No, it will bring a new texture into all of our various relationships. It's a risk, one that has the potential for some truly lovely outcomes. Any other questions?"

"I think I've got it. I'll ask if anything else comes up."

***

Charles finished his meeting around 8 PM, drove home to get Rosey and headed over the mountains. He arrived at the grove around 11, which gave him time to build a fire and create sacred space. By 11:45 he was deep in meditation and calling on the trees and rocks and all the land for support and energy.

***

Just before midnight Jen went to her meditation room, with Coal following after her. After creating sacred space, she went to the crossroads and followed the path to Elan's cottage. When she arrived, Elan saw her look of anxiety.

"Come child, you will be able to do this. You've grown as a practitioner in the last few days. Time to put your doubts away," Elan chided.

"It's not just that," Jen admitted. "I've never been connected to Lawrence while he's making love. We always shut each other out for privacy. And the idea of participating even remotely is just odd. And then there's Cailleen and James, which is also weird. It seems like it will change things."

"It most certainly will, my dear. Your vulnerability to each other tonight will strengthen you in ways you cannot imagine. However, my dear, you will be much too busy to look in on them in any way. You need to focus on staying grounded and connected to the land. And the sexual energy you will be working with directly will be your own and Charles'."

"Please explain that?" Jen asked.

"Channeling the energy of arousal and release is very arousing. Charles' arousal will arouse you and there will be a climax. It is that energy that you will send to Raneck."

"Oh, sort of like Spring Fever run amok."

"I certainly hope not," Elan chided again. "You will need to be focused and controlled. That doesn't mean you can't enjoy it – just stay focused."

Elan pulled an earthen jar from her shelves. "Please disrobe, Jen. I will massage this balm into your body. It will help you relax now and will ease your muscles after. I will continue to massage you throughout to help you stay grounded and to boost your capacity for carrying the energies. Deepen your breath now and prepare yourself."

***

Charles stood now in the center of the grove with his roots connected to the trees. He gathered the energies being sent to him first by Lawrence and then by Cailleen and James. He channeled them into his own body and pulled energy from the Land up to meet it. He slowly sent a gentle stream to Jen and then let it build. His own arousal took shape as the tension of the energies grew, until he could hold it no longer and let go with a cry, sending the full potency toward Jen.

Jen caught her breath as the first waves of energy came toward her. The richness and power were intoxicating and sensual. She remembered to ground herself as she opened to and gathered the energy from Charles. It was delightful. She could taste the Land and feel the separate textures of Lawrence, Yvonne, James, Cailleen and Charles. When she could take no more, she cried out and sent the energy to Raneck in his cave.

She saw Raneck lift his arms to receive the energies in triumph. His eyes met hers and began to form a link. But before he could establish it, his eyes widened in shock at the qualities in the energy he was receiving. Fear - then acceptance and joy, and, finally, sorrow - moved across his face. With a sigh he let go and allowed the energies to fill him.

It had been so long since he had any real taste of the physical world. He perhaps had underestimated Calleigha and her students. He could taste earth and trees. He could almost feel the moonlight. And although he had no ability to actually feel it, he remembered the feeling of being sexually aroused. He couldn't resist any of it. It was water to a man dying of thirst.

For just a moment, Raneck felt the horror of his own denial. He felt thin and stretched and incapable of holding anything. But as the energies boosted him, he forgot all that and only remembered the duty that he needed to serve. Yes, he was hungry. And, yes, he would find satisfaction.

Before he could think about creating a permanent link to Jen and the energies that she provided, the flow was cut. The very best part of him was not sorry.

***

Jen became aware of hands moving across her body. She was exhausted beyond belief and her entire body was sore. "Drink this," Elan commanded. Jen drank thirstily from the cup Elan handed her. It was slightly bitter, but tasted mostly green with a touch of honey. Elan handed her another cup, this time spring water. Jen drank that down too. In a few moments her limbs began to feel warm and tingly.

While she was recovering, Lawrence arrived at Elan's cottage. "How is she?" he asked

"Ready to go home and have a good night's sleep," Elan proclaimed.

Lawrence picked Jen up and carried her down the path to the crossroad and back to her own meditation room. He laid her on the dreaming couch and tucked her in securely. He left a protective circle around her with Coal as guardian, and then went home to Yvonne.

Charles lay oblivious in the middle of the grove. The fire had died down and his body began to tremble. Three crows circled above him, cawing. When they got no response, one went to get Rosey and the other flew down and pecked at Charles' ear. Several minutes went by before Charles batted the crow away. He opened his eyes and tried to reorient himself. He was cold, very cold.

"Damn," Charles said to the air, "I let the fire die." He grabbed a stick and tried to rouse the embers, but they were too far gone. He grabbed some newspaper and matches, but his hands were too cold to hold the match. He could feel the temperature dropping with every breath he took. He was in danger and he knew it. He told himself not to panic. He took a couple of deep breaths to build his inner fire and rubbed his arms and legs briskly to bring himself fully back into his body.

He tried to light the match again, but he still couldn't hold the match. A crow cawed behind him. He turned to see Rosey running fast toward him. The dog knocked him over and started licking his face. The crow cawed derisively. Charles imagined he was saying, "Stupid dog should have been on duty to begin with!"

Charles put his hands under Rosey's front haunches to warm them. In a few minutes he could feel them heat up. He lit the match, then threw a few small logs on the fire. Between Rosey's body, the fire, and his blanket, Charles was feeling almost normal.

Now that he was out of danger, he could feel Cailleen calling to him. He tuned in to her and sent her a message saying he was all right. He could feel James in the link too. "Brandy in a flask at the base of the north tree," James sent him. Charles smiled and went to get the flask. "Thanks, brother," he toasted and took a couple of swallows.

When his limbs felt strong enough to walk, Charles put out the fire and walked back to the manor. "Come on Rosey, let's go get some food. I'm hungrier than I can ever remember." Rosey barked her agreement and led the way home.

Chapter Fifteen
Questions & Challenges

James dropped Cailleen off at her hotel early the next morning. She showered, dressed, and sat down to go over her notes for the day. This was the last day of her workshop. The participants had been a pleasure and she anticipated several of them coming out to the manor for other workshops. She considered adding a new focus class to her curriculum. Healing the past seemed to be a common issue for the women in this workshop. And she certainly was gaining a wealth of personal experience in the last few weeks.

Cailleen stopped what she was doing to consider Charles as a teacher. Although she never pushed it, she did hope that all three – Charles, Jen and Lawrence – would soon consider teaching. It challenged Cailleen to teach the same courses again and again. Yet the basics must be taught to everyone. Of course, each class offered its own rhythm and needs. So she did get variety. Still, it would be nice to have more time to focus on some new material.

Maybe she'd talk with Jen about it this evening. She'd be glad to leave the hotel today. As beautiful as it was, it didn't feel like a loved home. Tomorrow, she'd be in her own home and she truly did love it. She missed the trees and the birds and her garden.

Thinking of home brought her back to Charles. She wanted to check in on him to make sure he recovered from the work last night. She called as he was reaching his office and was assured that he was good as gold.

Cailleen gathered her things for class and left her room. As she stepped out of the elevator, she felt eyes on her again. She continued to her conference room as if she hadn't noticed.

The morning went by quickly. Just before noon Cailleen felt those eyes on her again. She glanced up and looked through the doorway. A smartly dressed woman stood there. When she noticed Cailleen's glance, she stood straighter, met her eyes, and nodded. Then she turned and walked out of view.

Cailleen announced a lunch break. When she left the room herself, the same woman was waiting. At the sight of Cailleen, she squared her shoulders, took a deep breath and extended her hand.

"Hello. My name is Camille Hodges. I'm terribly sorry to intrude. I wonder if I could take you to lunch. I understand perfectly if you can't, or choose not to. But I truly hope you will accept my invitation. "

Cailleen noticed the dark circles under her eyes beneath the expertly applied makeup and the desperation in Camille's voice. She considered declining. She usually needed her lunch break for down time when she was teaching. But the need emanating from Camille was so strong. Cailleen could feel distress radiating off the woman.

Camille saw her hesitation. "I will confess that I have something to ask of you. And, again, I understand if you wish to have this time to yourself." She smiled and Cailleen saw a brief glimpse of the warmth and charm that was characteristic of Camille Hodges. Although she would have preferred to put Camille off until after the conference, she knew she would accept the invitation because of James. And, she found she liked this woman very much and immediately wanted to help her.

Cailleen took Camille's hand in both of hers. "I will have lunch with you and consider whatever it is you have come to ask of me. However, I do need fifteen minutes alone before class begins again to prepare for the afternoon. Can we manage that?"

"Of course," Camille agreed. "Shall we eat in the hotel restaurant? I called ahead and made reservations. I also made certain they could offer us some vegan options. Jeff, the chef here, is a friend of the family," she explained. "And James mentioned that you eat a vegan diet."

"Seems we'll be well taken care of then. Shall we?"

They were shown to a very private corner where hors d'oeuvres awaited them. Cailleen ordered a spicy sweet potato soup. Camille ordered a salad.

"James speaks very highly of you," Camille began. "He's clearly smitten."

"Oh?" Cailleen replied tentatively. She expected that Camille was here to talk about Lily. But perhaps she came to check her out on James' behalf. She looked at Camille questioningly. Was she making small talk to establish rapport as a good hostess? Or was she establishing a shared link to draw her to her cause? Cailleen decided Camille was primarily being a good hostess. And she also understood the benefits of establishing a strong link with Cailleen. Cailleen appreciated the practicality and relaxed a bit.

"Yes. It's not what he says, but how he speaks of you. It's clear that he greatly respects you and your work. It's also pretty evident that something special and more intimate has passed between you. I'm glad for him. He's been alone for a long time. He's an unusual man. It would take an unusual woman to capture his interest on so many levels.

"I want to apologize to you for the way my husband has treated you. I did not know he coerced James into investigating you. I hope it has not caused you any harm or too much inconvenience."

"I understand he's going through a difficult time," Cailleen offered.

"Yes. James said he told you our story." Camille reached into her purse and pulled out a photograph. "This is our daughter, Lily." Camille's eyes teared up and her throat tightened in an effort to control her emotions. "I just want her back. I want to be able to hold her in my arms again and feel that she's present, instead of feeling that a part of her is missing." She looked Cailleen straight in the eyes, allowing her to see the pain and frustration of the last year. Then she closed them and took a shuddering breath.

When she opened them again their food was set before them. She nodded, indicating to Cailleen that the ball was now in her court. She ate a few bites of her salad and asked Cailleen how she liked her soup.

They ate for a few minutes in silence. Camille held herself with assuredness and grace. Her soft strawberry blonde hair and big brown eyes were captivating. Something about her made one want to do whatever she asked. Yet there was no manipulation in it at all. She asked for what she wanted as clearly as she could. Then she simply allowed whatever response that came back to her. Cailleen could sense her desire but felt no expectation from her.

"What is it that you think I can do for your daughter?" Cailleen asked of her.

"Honestly, I don't know. Something tells me that you can direct us to an answer. I think it's possible you can heal her. I don't want you to think that I'm grasping at straws here and that I'm to a point where I'll try anything. I don't consider you a last-ditch effort. I wouldn't insult you or your work in that way." Camille hesitated for a moment and then continued. "I wanted to contact you months ago." She tapped her fingers on the table in agitation. "Despite all evidence to the contrary, Ben still has more confidence in doctors and hospitals. They can't do anything. They've told us there is nothing they can do. Ben has trouble with things he can't understand."

"Most of us do," Cailleen said gently. "It's quite difficult placing the life of someone you love in the hands of someone or something you can't understand. It's unsettling."

"That's kind of you," Camille allowed. "I've come here the last three days with the intention of talking to you." When Camille saw Cailleen nod she was taken aback. "You knew?"

"I knew someone was here for the last three days. I didn't know it was you."

"The first two days Ben didn't know I was here. I didn't speak to you because I couldn't go behind his back. It just didn't seem right. I was torn between my daughter's needs and my husband's beliefs. We've never hidden anything from each other, and despite the circumstances, I didn't want to start now. This morning at breakfast I told him I was coming to see you. I expected a fight. I didn't get one.

"He simply said, 'I can see you need to do this. Be careful.' Then he kissed me on the top of the head and left for the office. I don't think he's changed his mind about you. I'm sorry about that. I think he simply couldn't say no to me."

The photo of Lily lay face up on the table. Cailleen picked it up. She could see that Camille was right. Not all of Lily was present; something in the girl was missing.

"I would like to meet with Lily. I think it would be important for both you and Ben to be present. Can you arrange that? I'll be in town only through tomorrow, but I can return next week."

"Thank you. I'll talk with Ben directly. Can I leave a message at the hotel?"

"Yes. Camille?" Cailleen paused to be sure she had Camille's full attention. "I don't know what I can do for Lily. A lot depends on her and her own fate and choices. You need to know that I will not do anything to interfere with her purpose or her choices. You need to understand that. But I will do anything I can to help her along her way."

Camille nodded, understanding that Cailleen was telling her Lily might not be meant to survive this. She knew Cailleen was telling her to prepare herself and to prepare Ben as best she could. But Camille had already been on the roller coaster of hope and despair.

Every time the doctors offered another treatment, Camille let her hope grow. And with every failure, she slipped into despair. She only had to look at Lily to face the truth that her daughter may not be with her much longer. And, as much as she wanted to hold her close and never let her go, Camille could not fathom a Lily who was only half there.

Her Lily was a naturally vibrant and active child. Her Lily had been gone for quite a while. Camille was at the point of wanting whatever was truly best for her daughter, even if that meant losing her.

Ben had not come to that place, not yet. He was still holding on, but Camille did feel something shifting in Ben. Neither of them would ever let go of the hope that their daughter would be made whole again. However, other possibilities were hard to deny.

"I need to return to my class now," Cailleen said. "I'll look for your call. Thank you for a lovely lunch. It was truly a pleasure meeting you, Camille."

***

Three hours later Cailleen returned to her hotel room for a short rest before she headed to Jen's. The red light blinking on her phone got her immediate attention. She had a message. She called the front desk. Camille had called, inviting her to visit them at home anytime this evening.

After calling Jen to update her and to revise their plans, she returned Camille's call and agreed to visit after a short rest. Camille told her that James offered to act as chauffeur since it was a bit of a challenge to find the house the first time. Cailleen was happy for the support – both for herself and for Ben.

At five o'clock, James and Cailleen pulled into the Hodges' estate overlooking Lake Washington. The setting sun flashed off the west windows as they stopped the car. Cailleen shivered, wondering if it was a sign from Spirit. The crossroads of twilight – she supposed it was appropriate.

James led her around back and in through French doors to a garden room. "Lily loves this room at this time of day," he explained. She nodded.

"Uncle James! You've finally come and I see you've brought me a visitor." A small girl with an old-world essence about her spoke weakly, but with love and laughter in her voice. She wore a simple ivory dress with lace at the throat and cuffs and a wide ribbon at the waist. On another child it would have seemed frilly and affected. But Lily wore it as a second skin, and its color hid her pallor somewhat. The circles under her eyes, however, could not be missed. She sat on a wicker sofa, her shoeless feet dangling, a blanket recently cast aside. She'd clearly been resting before their visit.

"Hello, Lily. Did you miss me?"

"Almost before you were gone, Uncle James." She grabbed his hand and lifted her cheek for his kiss. It was very regal and she was totally unaware of it.

"This," James said, pulling Cailleen close to his side, "is my very good and dear friend Cailleen. She has come to see you."

"I know. Mommy told me you were coming," she directed Cailleen to sit by patting the seat next to her. "She thinks it was her idea, but it was really mine. You don't have to tell her I said that."

James lifted his eyebrows. Cailleen sat down next to Lily on the sofa. "Your secret is safe. It's very nice to meet you, Lily. I've been hearing very good things about you."

"It's nice to meet you," Lily said formally. Then in a very childlike manner asked, "What have they been saying about me?"

"Well, I hear you like tea parties and have quite a fondness for hats. I wonder if you have any pictures of Uncle James in his fancy hat with the flowers and netting?"

Lily giggled with glee. "I shall ask Nanny if she can find them. He looked very..." she paused, looking at James with a teasing smile, then looked back at Cailleen. "He looked quite handsome, really. The flowers brought out his eyes." Lily laughed again.

"You seem to be feeling better. I can tell you two have become fast friends," James sighed. "I shall have to leave this abuse and go in search of your parents. Back in a minute, poppet."

"No need," Ben said, "the cavalry has arrived. Ms. Renae," he said, formally extending his hand.

"Cailleen," she offered, shaking hands.

"Thank you for coming," Camille greeted. "Can I get you a glass of wine or tea?"

"A cup of tea would be most welcome," Cailleen said. "A strong black tea with soy cream if you have it, please." Cailleen sensed that it would be easier for Ben if he could provide something specific and perhaps unusual for her. Knowing Camille had done her homework before lunch, she assumed she would have the same consideration in her home.

"Tea for five, Henry," Camille ordered.

"I'd prefer a sherry," Ben added.

Henry left and came back five minutes later with a tea tray and sherry. They sipped their beverages and politely asked each other about their days. Cailleen watched them all without appearing to do so. Ben was reserved and distant while being ever so polite. Camille was nervous but handling it well. James was a rock, and Lily, she saw, took comfort from that.

"Lily?" Camille said, getting her attention. "Cailleen has come to see if she can maybe help you get better."

"I know, Mama. She can, you know," Lily said with a reassuring voice.

At her words, Ben started. "What have you been telling her?" he demanded of Cailleen.

"I've been telling her I'd like to see pictures of James at her tea party, the one with the extravagant hats," Cailleen said matter of factly.

At the memory Ben smiled for a moment but he remained alert and on the defense the rest of the visit.

"Tell me about your illness, Lily," Cailleen encouraged.

"Well, I got sick. And when I had a fever, I dreamed I lost my dolly. I've looked for her everywhere but I just can't find her."

Cailleen looked at Camille, wondering if the doll had been thrown out because of germs or something. Camille shook her head. "We don't know what dolly she keeps talking about. She's never taken an interest in any dolls. We're not sure what she means. We think it was just a dream."

"Lily, tell me about your doll," Cailleen suggested.

"I had her forever. I didn't need a fake doll. They're not as much fun. Mummy and Daddy just don't remember. Do you remember my dolly, Uncle James?"

"I'm sorry, my sweet. I don't remember a doll either. What was she like?" James asked.

"She had golden hair and big eyes like me. She was a bit wicked at times. It was her idea to have the hats at my tea party. When I was sick, she sang to me. When I got sicker, she left to go find me medicine. And now I can't find her." She looked at Cailleen. "Where did my dolly go?"

"I'm not sure, Lily. But I'll talk to Mummy and Daddy and see if we can figure out a way to find her. Is that OK?"

"Yes, you must find her. She has the medicine I need. And Uncle James should help, too."

The Nanny appeared, and at Camille's nod, told Lily it was time for dinner, a bath and then bed. She gathered the blanket and Lily's shoes, then took Lily by the hand and led her from the room. Lily pulled her down and then whispered something in her ear. The Nanny nodded. Lily turned back to Cailleen.

"When you come back to help me find my dolly, Nanny will have a picture waiting for you. Goodnight," she said to everyone.

After Lily left, all eyes focused on Cailleen. Camille's held guarded hope. Ben looked skeptical. James's shone with support and love.

"There is no doll," Ben stated flatly. The room fell silent.

Cailleen considered what she could and should say. Lily had given her a very good clue. She decided to approach it from a psychological approach.

"Children are very good," she began, "at understanding metaphors. And sometimes they see the metaphor as real life. I believe the doll is a metaphor." She looked around the room for understanding.

"You see," she continued, "often with a very serious illness, a part of our psyche will separate. It's often the part of ourselves that can't survive whatever is happening to us. It's very much like when someone loses their memory in the wake of a trauma. They can't survive with the memory of the trauma so they shut it off and separate it. The part of Lily - the part that has a playful and wicked sense of humor – couldn't survive within the frame of the illness. So she went off to find a cure. This doll of Lily's is vital to her. Without her she can't maintain her energy. Without her she diminishes."

"So, you're saying Lily has a psychological problem. It's all in her head?" Ben asked accusingly.

"No, Ben. I think Lily's experience is very real indeed. It's not a mental problem. It's only secondarily a physical problem. Lily's condition is more accurately a spiritual condition. Her spirit has been damaged. And from what I've learned about her, Lily is not willing to exist without that spirit. It's vital to her. Without it she has no vitality."

"Without it, she's not our Lily," Ben whispered with a pained expression. He rose and walked to the window. He looked helpless, and angry.

"What can we do?" Camille asked. Ben turned and faced the group again. His stance was alert and a little antagonistic.

Cailleen smiled at Camille and then directed her answer to Ben. "We can go on a journey to find her doll." She held up her hand as Ben began to object. "A journey is a deep meditation. I could do a journey myself. But I don't think that's the answer. Lily knows what to do. She said, 'When you come back to help *me* find *my* doll'. That tells me that Lily believes she is the one to find her doll; she just can't do it by herself. She needs a guide on her journey." Cailleen paused to let the information sink in.

Ben turned and walked back to the window. He ran his hands through his hair in a gesture of considering something distasteful. Camille sipped her tea and glanced anxiously at Ben.

"We have several options," Cailleen continued. "I can do the journey on Lily's behalf. It's unlikely to work as I see it. But it's also unlikely to hurt anything. It will use up time, time that may be valuable."

"What do you mean?" Camille interrupted. "Lily has been much improved in the last few days, especially since James arrived."

"I've been feeding her energy, Camille." James reached over to cover her hand in comfort. Ben turned and raised a questioning eye at James.

"I've been sending her love and energy as Charles taught me to do," James reminded them. "It's a boon, but not a long-term fix. At least not as I understand it," he said deferring to Cailleen.

"It's not a long-term solution for Lily," Cailleen agreed. "She needs to find a way to build and maintain her own energy field. The loss of her 'doll' has created a kind of hole in her field. What goes in quickly drains out."

"The other options?" Ben asked tersely.

"Lily and I can journey together. I'll guide and protect her, and if needed, help her understand what it is she needs to do."

Ben turned his back and paced back and forth in front of the door.

"James can journey with us, if that makes you more comfortable."

"If James can journey, why can't he just take Lily?"

"He doesn't have the experience." Cailleen said bluntly. "And, Lily doesn't have the time to wait while he gets it." Then, more gently, "I believe Lily would like him to come along. She said, 'and Uncle James can help, too.'"

"Any other options?" Ben asked

"We could all go. But I would need to invite Jen, Lawrence and Charles to help. We would need their experience. Frankly, there's both danger and benefit in everyone going. Lily knows her parents the best and trusts them. That could make her more comfortable. But as parents, your emotional attachment and responses could inhibit the journey. I do not recommend this option."

"What do you recommend?" Camille asked.

"I suggest we take Lily's lead. I help her find her doll and James comes along - that is, if James is willing."

They all looked to James. James suddenly felt overwhelmed by the responsibility. He was new at all this. What if he screwed up and Lily died? Would Ben ever forgive him if he failed to bring Lily back safely.

He looked at Ben. Ben had his arms crossed, looking totally closed off to the whole idea. But then he caught Ben's eye and saw the pleading. He seemed to say, 'I need you there, brother. If you want me to trust Cailleen, I need you there.' Then Ben tightened his arms, indicating he had not decided to let Cailleen work with Lily.

James looked at Camille. She smiled her trust at him. James' resistance melted. He could not say no to either of them, and he could not say no to helping Lily. 'Man up', he said to himself. Then he squared his shoulders, smiled at Camille and nodded.

"Could I suggest Charles be invited?" James asked. "I don't mean invite him into the journey. I think it might be helpful for him to be here to explain what's happening so Camille and Ben are more comfortable."

"I'd prefer it to be Jen, if it's all the same," Ben put in.

"Jen?" Cailleen and James asked in unison.

"She came to see me a couple of days ago. Gave me some things to think about. I trust her."

"I'll ask her. She's got the experience, and apparently, a connection. That does make her a better choice," Cailleen agreed. She was happy to give some say to Ben in how they proceeded. She was also curious about why Jen went to visit him.

"When?" Ben asked.

"Early next week," Cailleen said.

"Why so long? Can't you do it tomorrow? Are you holding out for more money?"

"We haven't even spoken about money," Cailleen pointed out. "The truth is that we need the time. I've just had a couple of long exhausting days, and it's best to be fresh. It will make the journey shorter, and easier on Lily. Even minutes can be significant in these situations. I want everyone at their best.

"Also, I'd like James to get a bit of experience, so I don't have to look after him as well as Lily. I also need to check with Jen about her schedule. As I'm committed already this weekend, that takes us into next week. The extra time will give you a few days to be sure Lily is well rested.

"As to money, I don't do this kind of work for money. There are some excellent practitioners who do and I can refer you to them if you like. It takes a certain toll - a toll that doesn't leave a lot of room for teaching. That is the focus of *my* work. I do this particular kind of healing work only with my apprentices, and when Spirit brings someone to me. I believe Spirit has brought Lily to me. Or, more accurately, Spirit has brought me to Lily."

The room fell quiet again. Conflicting hopes and desires filled the room. It felt like the uncomfortable silence when a jury returns to court and the defendant waits to hear their decision. Everyone seemed to be lost in their own thoughts. After a few moments, Cailleen spoke.

"I'm going to leave now and let you talk about this between the two of you. I'll speak to Jen about her schedule and willingness to assist in case you decide to move forward. Camille, you know how to reach me. James, will you take me home now?"

"Thank you," Camille said as she walked Cailleen and James to the door. "I'll call tomorrow or the next day."

James drove off the estate and through the neighborhood a few blocks. Then he pulled off the road, stopped the truck and reached into the back seat. He put the blanket he retrieved around Cailleen's shoulders and pulled her into his arms.

"You're trembling, you know. Are you OK?" he asked.

"I'm fine," she said, but her voice was shaky. James kissed her temple and pulled her closer.

"I'm better, thanks," she tried to assure him. "Just a reaction to a few very long and eventful days."

"You'll tell me the real story later?" he asked.

Cailleen laughed. "I don't suppose you have a flask of brandy under a tree in the back seat, do you?"

"Be right back," James said and jumped out of the truck. Cailleen watched as he ran across the street and into a liquor store a half block down. He came out a moment later and ran back to the truck. He opened and handed her a little bottle of brandy.

She took the tiny airline size bottle of brandy from him and raised her eyebrows in question.

"I'm a retired cop. *I* can't drink. I'm driving. I didn't figure you'd want a full bottle, and I don't have a trunk to put leftovers in. So, drink up and then I'll get you home."

He held her in his arms as she drank the brandy. When she started feeling more herself, she sat up and kissed his cheek. "Thanks."

"You're most welcome," he whispered softly, then pulled out onto the road again.

They arrived back at Jen's, where Charles, Lawrence and Yvonne had joined her. One glance from James in his direction told Charles that he was agitated about something. He glanced at him again when Cailleen explained everything that happened with Lily.

"James," Charles said, squeezing his shoulder in support, "I've no doubt you'll do a fine job journeying. I can give you some time this weekend if you want to get a bit of experience. And we can do a journey as part of our Samhain work as well."

"Thanks, I'd appreciate the time. Perhaps we can go check our schedules now and see what works." James indicated they should leave the room to do so.

"What's up?" Charles asked him when they were alone.

"I don't know exactly. She made it sound like it was a normal conversation with Ben's family, but Cailleen was trembling when we got to the truck. I can't figure out for the life of me what triggered such a reaction. I thought you should know. And I want you to be certain I know what I need to know when we do this journey."

"You'll be prepared, and Cailleen will be fine," Charles assured him. "There's nothing to worry about."

"Bullshit! Things don't add up. I can smell it. There's something else going on. I don't like going into a situation unprepared or uninformed. As I understand it, I'm going in to this as backup. Don't send me in with one hand tied behind my back. I sense a level of danger that none of you are talking about. I *won't* go into this blind!" With that James headed for the door, then turned and gruffly said, "Call me tomorrow."

Charles smiled to himself as James shut the door. This might just be a bumpy ride, he thought to himself. He went back to the kitchen to join the others.

"Where's James?" Jen asked. "Isn't he staying for dinner?"

"I'm afraid he's left it to us," Charles explained.

"We were just talking about Jen's visit to Ben a few days ago. Apparently, she used his work and his company's PR to open him to the idea that we weren't just crackpots."

"Just shared some common sense with him, that's all," Jen replied to Cailleen. Charles noticed a significant decrease in the deference Jen usually paid to Cailleen. It was a welcome shift to see Jen standing more fully in her own power.

"It seems Jen is not the only one not telling us everything," Charles said. "James said you were trembling when you left Ben's house." Charles looked at Cailleen, waiting for an explanation. Cailleen looked at Yvonne to indicate she could speak about it when the four of them were working later.

"It was just a long day, particularly after our adventures last night. I'm fine. Let's eat."

After dinner, Yvonne went next door to Lawrence's home and the four of them sat at Jen's kitchen table drinking tea and talking about the events of the week.

"What happened at Ben's that you haven't told us yet?" Lawrence asked.

"Several things, actually," Cailleen began. "First, Lily is gifted and she knows it. She just doesn't know what to do with it yet. Ben will probably struggle with that. She told me that it was she who sent for me, not Camille. Although she said her mother thought it was her own idea. The child then went on to pretty much outline what needed to be done and who should be doing the work. I was left with the task of explaining it in terms that Camille and Ben could understand and accept.

"During the entire conversation, Ben and I were playing a chess game – one that spanned 2000 years. He's shifted his position, but I don't know if he will allow the journeywork. At the same time, I was scanning Lily. She doesn't have a lot of time. James is boosting her energy, but she can't hold that any better than her own.

"All in all, I was operating on about three levels for over an hour. When I got to the truck and could relax, I was more tired than I realized. The entire situation is fraught with strong emotions.

"By the way, Jen, if Ben agrees to the journey, he would like you to be there to help him and Camille through the process. I suggested Charles, but he trusts you. I thought Charles would be the more comfortable choice because he seemed to have knowledge and respect of Charles. I didn't know then that you had talked with him. Are you available early next week if Ben agrees to the journey?"

"Sure," Jen confirmed. "I can flex my schedule pretty easily next week. He said he trusted me?"

"His exact words," Cailleen said.

"We have a bit of a situation with James that needs to be discussed," Charles told them. "He knows there's more going on than he has been told about. He doesn't like being uninformed, especially when he's being asked to go along as backup. The man was twitching in agitation. We need to discuss bringing him into the story a bit more. I agree with him, he needs to know."

"I was going to bring this up myself," Cailleen sighed. "I didn't like using him last night to raise energy when he didn't know what it was about. It was necessary and I didn't ask him to do anything he wasn't willing to do, but I still didn't like it. He trusts us enough to know our intention to do no harm, but I think asking him to go on this journey without giving him vital information will do *him* harm. And if Ben senses any hesitation from James, he may very well refuse to allow us to do the work."

"Take him to see Elan," Jen suggested. "Elan can give him a perspective we can't. That's my sense, anyway. And you'll have to journey to get to Elan, which will give him experience and boost his confidence. It will also introduce him to an ally."

"Good idea," Cailleen said. "Makes it somehow less personal and shows him we do trust him. Do you want to take him, Charles?"

"I certainly can, but I wonder if Jen would be a better choice. That way when you do the journey, he will be comfortable with her energetic touch. And if Jen has familiarity and comfort in working with James, she'll be able to connect with him more deeply and therefore be better able to know what's happening on the journey."

"Jen?"

"Sure, if James is open to it."

"Good. Jen, do you know if Raneck has sent the dream to Ben yet?" Cailleen asked.

"No, he hasn't. He was a little overwhelmed with the energy we sent him and with the choices we presented to him. Elan was pretty smart. Anyway, I think it will be tonight."

They talked for another hour, making plans for the Samhain celebration.

Then Charles left and everyone else went to bed.

Chapter Sixteen
Journey to the Crossroads

Raneck entered Ben's dream later that night. Ben found himself standing on a slight hill overlooking a dozen or so simple shelters set in a circle around a communal fire. People were beginning to gather around the fire. Ben knew they were waiting for him.

He watched as they gathered. He couldn't miss the murmuring and the glances up at him. He knew they waited, but he was waiting for someone, too. But nobody came. So, Ben went down to the tribe and faced their fear and discomfort.

They needed to feel his strength and certainty. He felt neither, at the moment. The crowd parted and Raneck stood before him. Chancha – yes, that was his name in this time. Everyone looked to him, waiting for words that would make everything all right. But he couldn't remember what was wrong.

Raneck spoke. "Calleigha has left us and is now on her own in the wilderness. She has honored your ban of her." Raneck's words brought back Chancha's memory. Raneck had announced, not that Calleigha would be offered to him as a mate, but that she was now a fully initiated Senechal. As a mate, she would make the tribe stronger. As a second Senechal, she upset the delicate balance between chief and Senechal. Raneck should realize this. When he, Chancha, refused to accept her in this role, she challenged him and confirmed that he was right to fear her power. He didn't know what to do to ease the situation.

"Take it back," a voice within Chancha cried. "Tell Raneck to go get her and return her to the tribe." Another voice spoke in his head. "You will lose face and the tribe will not know who to follow; stand your ground. She has too much power. She dared to challenge you, twice."

Chancha couldn't dismiss the picture in his mind of Calleigha all alone in the wilderness. Yet, if she was such a powerful Senechal, she should be perfectly safe. He could not let a young woman challenge him, twice, without consequences. How could he have thought she would be offered to him as a mate? She was only interested in her healing work and power.

Why did Raneck not offer a solution so that he could bring her back and save face in front of the tribe?

Suddenly, Ben was himself again. The tribal scene before him disappeared and he stood alone on the small hill. He heard a rustling sound behind him.

"I let you down," Raneck admitted as he drew close. "I was a blind old man and I didn't see your need or your pain. I am truly sorry. You were the nearest thing to a friend I had and I respected you greatly. I am here now and I see more clearly. It is time, Chancha, to heal the past. Allow Calleigha to help Lily. Allow her at last to use her gifts in service of your tribe. It will serve us all."

Raneck then left Ben to his sleep and wandered again between the worlds. He felt very old and thin. Having finally met his duty to Chancha, he now felt lost. He longed to sleep and eat and walk the land again. It had been so long. But he had a duty to fix what he broke, to make up for his own blindness. He knew what he needed to do, and he was happy that one way or another, it would all be over soon.

***

Something woke Camille in the early hours. She listened to the monitor for a sound from Lily's room, but heard only her gentle breathing. She turned to Ben. He was up and standing by the window. He sighed heavily and sank into a chair.

"You want to talk about it?" Camille asked.

"I'm sorry, did I wake you?"

"What's on your mind?" Camille encouraged as she walked to him.

"Lily, of course. I thought that maybe she was getting better, you know. She's been laughing more these last few days. I hoped to avoid this whole idea of letting Cailleen work with her."

"What bothers you so much about it?"

"That's just it. I don't really know. It's like I remember something about her. I sense her power and feel threatened by it somehow, but I can't place the details. I also feel guilt, like I've harmed her in some way. I'm afraid she'll retaliate. I'm afraid I'll lose face. None of it makes any sense and I feel like a babbling idiot."

"But?" Camille prompted.

"I just had a very strange dream. I time traveled, sort of. At first, I was a clan leader. Cailleen was there and also someone else. And then I moved forward in time to Lily being ill. I can't remember any details, but I feel like I need to allow Cailleen to help Lily.

"I fear it - too many things seem hidden. But I can't quite shake that I need to allow Cailleen to help - and not just for Lily, but for all of us. As strong as I feel that, I have no understanding of what it's about. And it seems like I've been given a second chance, but I don't remember for what.

"I'm sitting here wondering if I've gone over the bend.

"If I have, then can I trust my own judgment? I can't help sensing that Lily is a pawn in some outrageous game, and I just want to get her the hell off the board. I don't know how to do that. Does Cailleen? Or are we just taking some last desperate chance?"

Ben's hair was going in all directions. He tended to run his hands through it as he sorted through things. His hair reflected his mind and heart. His eyes registered his fear that he was making the wrong decision. The rest of his body, however, was oddly relaxed. There was some tension left, but his shoulders were soft and he looked comfortable in his chair.

"Hmm? Would you like to know what I see, Ben?"

"Of course, love."

"I think you've already made the decision to let Cailleen work with Lily. You know I'm in favor of it — even though I can't say for sure why. It's just a gut feeling. Lily clearly wants to do it. She's very comfortable with Cailleen, and she totally trusts James. James also favors it. Whatever has been holding you back from agreeing, I wonder if it has been resolved for you through your dream."

Camille sat on Ben's lap and leaned into him, tenderly. "I know you, Ben Hodges. You're wound up tighter than a drum while you consider things. When you make up your mind, your entire body relaxes. Actually, my dear, the entire room relaxes. That's no doubt what woke me up. The release of tension in the room is palpable. I feel the tension moving out of my own body.

"Not only is it the right decision, Ben, it's also the only option I see left to us. Even if it doesn't help Lily, I truly believe it will not harm her in any way."

Ben hugged her close for a minute. "And what if it doesn't help her, Camille? What if it makes no difference at all?"

"Ben. We might lose her. We need to prepare ourselves for the possibility. I think we need to prepare Lily for it."

"Yes, I know." His voice cracked with that admission. They clung to each other, their grief washing over them. "I didn't want to face that, but here it is." He kissed the top of her head and carried her to the bed.

"I need you to promise me something," Camille demanded. "Promise you'll stay with us until we know one way or another. I think I will very much need someone to hold my hand."

"Where else would I be, except with my girls? Sleep now in my arms. When Lily gets up, we'll talk with her. And then we'll spend the next couple of days doing special things together. Sleep now, my heart. And dream sweet dreams."

They held each other until the sun rose.

***

Cailleen left to go home around noon the next day. Jen and Charles would join her around dinnertime. Lawrence and Yvonne were due the following morning. This would be Yvonne's first Wheel of the Year Celebration. She'd be joining them for the public circle early on Saturday evening. The deeper work of Samhain would be done at midnight with just the five.

Feeling rested and enjoying the beauty of the drive, Cailleen let herself anticipate the ritual to come. When it came to the public rituals, she felt like a kid anticipating a festival. Several drummers always showed up, which made the singing more energized. She kept the celebrations light and playful while providing a significant teaching within the ritual. Samhain tended to be more solemn than the others – at least at the beginning.

Samhain was a time to connect with the ancestors and to honor the dead. The veil between the living and the dead was thinnest at Samhain. The anticipation of communication across the veil brought an excited nervousness to some, and sorrow to others. Allowing space for both without dwelling on either was important.

Traditionally, participants brought their ancestors' favorite food for the potluck that followed. They also placed pictures and other items of remembrance on the altar. During the ritual they read the names of all those who had passed on during the last turn of the wheel.

She hoped that Lily's name would not be among that list next year. She wondered about Lily's purpose in this lifetime. She had already served as the magnet that brought Raneck, Chancha and Calleigha together at this power crossroad. She fervently hoped that Lily was not required to sacrifice her life to aid in the resolution of the story. It was a possibility and Cailleen understood the need to honor that, if it was Lily's path. But Cailleen really wanted to get to know Lily as the vibrant, active child that James spoke of.

Of course, even if they found her doll and reintegrated that piece of Lily, it didn't mean that Ben would welcome or allow a continued relationship. If he didn't, it would be hard to deal with, she admitted. Journeying together would bond Cailleen and Lily for life, and would strengthen both their bonds with James. But no use focusing on that possibility yet, it would only make it more likely to happen.

Cailleen was glad she had not given in to Ben's request for something to be done immediately. When she was younger to the work, she often gave into such emotion. But she'd learned, through some hard lessons, not to "push the river." Not only would everyone be more rested and more prepared for the journey on Lily's behalf, but the cyclical timing of the seasons would also be better. The thinning of the veil gave the ancestors more access to what was happening here on the earth plane. Cailleen would make an extra request for help from them.

It was so tempting to put aside the small and large rituals of life when a crisis was on hand. She'd done it many times when she was less experienced. Learning to wait for the right timing and for all the pieces to be in place before taking action could be quite a challenge. She wondered if James had learned this skill in his undercover work.

As she drove over Snoqualmie Pass and into Kittitas Valley, Cailleen moved her thoughts to the small rituals of this season. Doing them would not only ground her, it would clear her "things-to-do" list and leave her more focused for the Samhain ritual, then Lily's journey. "All things in their time and place," she chanted to herself.

This was the season of death, which always led to new life. Nature had drawn the strength of the waning sun into her leaves, squashes, herbs, and whatever flowers remained. Cailleen, like the plants, needed to draw the last of the sun's harvest into her own stores for winter. She had gathered berries and other fruit earlier in the season. They were now in her freezer or dried in jars on her pantry shelves. She'd take stock when she got home to make sure she had what she needed to last until spring. Herbs for cooking, tea, and healing were drying in her kitchen and on the sun porch. Pumpkins and other winter squash needed to be brought in yet. If the weather held, she'd have time to get up into the higher elevations and collect some healing plants. She'd already put most of her gardens to bed for the winter. She still needed to check the generator in the barn and her stockpile of wood.

These practical rituals were basic for a witch. There was nothing particularly glamorous about them, but they were quite satisfying. On Samhain morning, she'd do a private little ritual that she did every year. She'd run her hand along the jars of food thanking all the plants that would help her through the winter months. She'd make tea with mint harvested from her own garden and thank the sun for the summer's gift. Then she'd walk the land appreciating the beauty of the bounty it still offered. At the grove she'd sing the earth to sleep.

Sun wanes and the earth now sleeps,
Days grow long and cold.
The Wheel does turn and its promise keeps
from the ancient stories told.

Cailleen hummed her winter sleep chant through the Teanaway and up her drive to the manor. "It's good to be home again," she whispered.

***

James drove back to the bungalow early Friday afternoon. He'd spoken to Charles, who explained the importance of working with Jen before doing the journey with Lily and Cailleen. They'd arranged to do a journey later tonight with the three of them.

James still felt uncomfortable about what was being kept from him around the journey with Lily. But he looked forward to learning how to journey. He was eager to gain as much experience as possible before next week. James felt pretty confident that Ben would allow the journey. He'd felt a shift in him when he joined them in the garden room last night. And as Lily talked with Cailleen he could feel Ben's resistance dissolving. She was a child, but Ben had always trusted Lily's instincts. It sometimes took him a while to let go of his protectiveness of her, but he always managed it. The only doubt James had, came from the strong reaction Ben seemed to have regarding Cailleen. He seemed to have taken an instant dislike of her.

No, he thought to himself. It wasn't dislike. Ben rarely disliked a person, and when he did it was because they were intentionally dishonorable. No, what Ben felt toward Cailleen was a much stronger and more complicated emotion. And Ben didn't seem to understand it any more than James did. Perhaps it was a past life thing, he thought.

James laughed at his thought. Ten days ago, he would have raised his eyes at the idea of past life connections affecting the present. He'd simply never considered it. He liked the idea that he was opening up to something new. Rigid thinking was a hazard for cops. It could be easy to close oneself off as a response to the waste and horror one sometimes saw on a daily basis. His mentor had encouraged him to maintain some connection to normal life while he was a cop. It was too easy to forget that the folks who vice and homicide cops dealt with were only a small percentage of the population. Most folks were good intentioned and worked hard to make a good life. Ben, Camille and Lily served that role for him through the years. He felt blessed to know them.

A past life connection would explain a lot. It would explain why Cailleen had that reaction last night. She might be aware of it. He'd already noticed Cailleen was good at controlling and masking her emotions when the need arose. He considered what the interview with Lily might have been like for her. He could tell she'd fallen for Lily instantly. He knew how difficult it was to love Lily and to see her failing. Camille as the heartbroken and brave mother pulled at one's heartstrings just as strongly. Ben was difficult and yet it was hard not to have compassion for him in the situation. On top of the emotional soup, he didn't doubt that Cailleen was scanning Lily as a Healer. He remembered how she had done that with him their first day in the grove.

"Damn, she's a pretty tough cookie!" he said aloud to himself. And he loved her. There it was. He knew it the first day he met her, but held himself in check because of the situation. He just felt the last string of reserve snap. He loved her.

He'd already learned the power of love as a healing tool with Lily. Every day he sent his love to her and every day he felt stronger doing it. It was a tool that grew in strength with practice. Something told him that loving

Cailleen was important, and that acknowledging it was vital.

James began to feel quite hopeful. If he carried all this love into the journey with him, maybe, just maybe, they could help Lily. James felt a burden of fear and dread lift. He decided to be hopeful. He couldn't wait to talk to Charles about all this. He wanted to ask questions about the power of different emotions and how to focus them. Would they have time before the journey with Lily?

He decided to stay focused on today. He'd go over to see Cailleen at the manor if she was home. He'd check on her and see how she was after last night. He'd stop and get her flowers. He was a man in love. Men in love brought flowers!

He stopped in town for flowers and went to Pioneer Coffee for a couple of sandwiches. If she was home and hadn't eaten lunch, he'd suggest a picnic. Sunny days would soon be rare when winter set in.

James went straight to the manor and was delighted to see Cailleen's car. Gathering flowers, sandwiches and a bottle of sparkling water, he jumped out of the truck and headed for the kitchen door. On the way he caught sight of her in her garden. She walked around slowly, reaching out to touch dying leaves and leaning corn stalks. She plucked one of the last blooms off a small chrysanthemum and tucked it behind her ear. She looked a little sad, James thought. He hesitated. Perhaps she'd rather have some time alone. While he paused in indecision, Cailleen turned and smiled at him.

"Are you coming or not?" she asked with a tilt of her head.

"I wondered if you might prefer time alone right now. You seem sad. Shall I leave you or do you want company?"

"I love you for asking," Cailleen said, and then sighed. James' heart beat faster at her use of the word, love. It didn't mean she was in love with him, but it was a step in the right direction. "I'm always a little sad as I walk through my dying garden. I've got to get the pumpkins in and cleaned for tomorrow," she said shifting the subject. She walked towards James. "Next week I'll plant a winter cover crop and put the garden to bed for the season. It's my personal goodbye ritual. I sing a sleepy time song and then I settle in for the winter. But 'til then, I let myself be sad. A little melancholy is good for an Irish soul. I actually enjoy it."

She slid her hands around his neck and pulled him to her for a kiss. "A little smooching is also good for this Irish soul." She kissed him again. "Did you come bearing me gifts?"

"I did," he said, looking bemused. The everyday woman in Cailleen intrigued him. He realized he'd become so focused on the magical and powerful sides of her that he felt stunned by the everydayness of her. He wanted to dance with the magic and power. He wanted to hold and protect the everyday woman. She was perfect. He came out of his reverie to see Cailleen looking at him questioningly.

"You seem rather attached to them," she whispered wryly.

"What? Oh, sorry. I guess I got distracted." He bowed and presented her with the flowers. "For you."

"Thank you. They're lovely. It's always nice to get flowers." She took the flower from behind her ear and put it through a buttonhole on his shirt. "For you."

James pulled the flower from his buttonhole and smelled it. "Thank you." Then he tucked it behind her ear again. "I can see it better here," he said. "It brings attention to your ear," he nibbled her earlobe, "and your neck." He kissed her at the base of her neck, then her chin and then he claimed her mouth. He pulled back and looked at her. Her blue eyes twinkled and laughed. Her full lips turned up slightly at the corners in a knowing laugh. "The many faces of Cailleen," he whispered. Then he stepped away from her. He needed either to step away or to slowly ravage her. He was reconsidering when she spoke.

"What's in the bag?"

"A picnic. I brought sandwiches, fruit and sparkling water. Is it warm enough or should we go in the house?"

"Let's enjoy the sun while we can. Winter approaches. Look at the snow on the Stuart Mountains." She turned north and pointed. He put his arm around her and they walked over to a bench on the south side of the garden. Cailleen must have been sitting there earlier. She took the blanket off the bench and spread it on the ground. They ate their lunch snuggling together for a little extra warmth.

"The sun grows weak and I'm officially cold," Cailleen announced when their sandwiches were gone. "Let's go into the kitchen and have a cup of tea. We can talk a bit about tonight's events, if you want." They spent the next hour talking. Then James went to the bungalow to take a nap and get ready for the evening ahead. Cailleen asked him to come back and join everyone for dinner around seven.

Cailleen was putting the finishing touches on a couple of pots of soup and homemade bread when Jen and Charles arrived.

"Feeding an army?" Jen asked as she hugged her hello.

"Just us. Thought it would be good to have some easy to heat food in the fridge for the next couple days."

"Jen, it seems, had the same idea," Charles added as he hauled in six tote bags loaded with food. "And she's forgotten we're in a new millennium - one where men are NOT expected to do all the hauling." He kissed Cailleen on the cheek after he sat the groceries down. Then he tossed his keys to Jen. "Grab my bag when you get yours, will you?"

"I'd be delighted," she said sweetly. Then to Cailleen, "no one asked him to carry in the groceries."

After dinner they finalized plans for the public Samhain celebration, which

Lawrence would lead. The format stayed pretty constant from year to year, but within the framework were variations in songs and in who played which roles. A jack-o-lantern parade always preceded the circle celebration. So the group worked steadily to clean and carve thirteen pumpkins. Charles took the job of separating and roasting the pumpkin seeds.

By eleven o'clock an assortment of jack-o-lanterns grimaced, smiled, leered and winked at them. They took them out to the sun porch and placed them on ledges and in corners in readiness for tomorrow's circles. The parade would begin here and end up at the grove.

Charles and James prepared a tea tray for after the journey they would take tonight. Jen and Cailleen prepared the study. They lit a fire and several candles around the room. They placed the representatives of the Elements on the small center table. Cailleen smudged the room while Jen placed pillows in the directions around the table. They smudged themselves with sage and, taking the tea tray from the men as they entered, smudged James and Charles in turn.

"James, if you're comfortable, we'd like to invite you to call in one of the directions. It doesn't have to be formal, just something from the heart." James nodded his assent. "Is there a particular direction you'd like to call?"

"I'll take East," he said.

"Lawrence, will you take West across from him?" Cailleen asked. Jen nodded agreement.

"Charles?"

"I'll take North."

"That leaves me with South. Jen you're leading the journey tonight, will you call the Center?" Jen nodded again.

"We're still in the season of fall; shall I begin in the West?" Jen inquired. Charles and Cailleen both nodded. Jen looked at James. "Ready?" James nodded.

Facing the West, Jen began. "Guardians of the West, powers of Water we invite you into this sacred space and thank you for your gifts of death and rebirth. Tonight, we seek clarity for the journeys ahead. Give death to all that stands in our way, including ignorance and hesitation. Help us rebirth our circle as we explore this new alliance with James. Help us flow together in common purpose. Be with us now. Blessed be." The others responded, "Blessed be."

Facing North, Charles began. "Guardians of the North, powers of Earth, winter beckons and we prepare for a long journey. We invite you to join us, bringing your rooted and steadfast energies. Let us ground ourselves in your endless knowing as we grow together in action and spirit. Be with us now. Blessed be." The others responded, "Blessed be."

Facing East, James began. "Guardians of the East, powers of Air, please join us here in this circle. Blow away indecision and doubt." He paused.

"Inspire in us shared trust as we take these beginning steps together. Be with us now. Blessed be." The others responded, "Blessed be."

Facing South, Cailleen began. "Guardians of the South, powers of Fire and transformation. We stand here on the cusp of the new and the unknown. Bring us the ease of transformation and the warmth of friendship and caring as we light the torch of our journeys together. Be with us now. Blessed be." The others responded, "Blessed be."

"Guardians of the Center, Spirit" Jen began, "we call you to witness our connection with each other and we welcome your flow inside us and among us. Help us in this circle as we seek to deepen our connection and build our capacity to be one with all. Be here now. Blessed be." The others responded, "Blessed be."

"Hecate, Dark Mother," Jen called, "we call on you as we prepare our way through the crossroads. Lend us your compassion and fierce dedication as we make our individual choices in approaching this crossroad. Hail and welcome, Hecate."

"Hail and welcome, Hecate," the others echoed.

Jen looked to Lawrence in a silent request to call on the God. "I call to Eros, God of love, to be with us in this circle," Lawrence began. "Let your arrow of loving intention guide us as we make our choices and step through the crossroad ahead. Hail and Welcome, Eros!"

"Hail and Welcome, Eros!" the others echoed.

"Join hands," Jen instructed. "Breathing deeply, find your center and ground yourself here in this space." She waited until everyone's breathing had synchronized. "Become aware of the hand on your left offering you energy. Open to and accept that energy. Become aware of the hand on your right receiving the energy you offer. Open to the flow and joy of giving. Feel the circle of energy moving through our linked hands. Let it calm and connect you." She waited until the energy going around the circle found a steady pulse, flowing consistently as it moved from hand to hand.

"Send your grounding cords down through your hips and legs and feet. Let it move through this floor and into the earth below. Feel Earth opening to welcome you. Allow your cord to take root and send those roots out to each person in this circle so that together we form a web below us. Allow this web to expand up around us and to connect with the circle of energy flowing through our linked hands. Bring the energy up again, this time through your entire trunk and head and out above you. Let the energy flow out into a canopy above us and flow down joining our linked hands and merging with the web. We stand now in a sacred sphere. Together, we'll take three breaths and on the exhales we will gently expand the sphere to reach the walls of this room. One, two, three. Good.

"We stand now between the worlds. What happens between the worlds is separate from and cannot be affected by the world. But what we do here will flow out into the world to heal and strengthen. Blessed be."

"Blessed be," the others responded.

"Please sit," Jen instructed. "We will now send out two cords of light. James in the East and Lawrence in the West will connect a line of energy to be the first cord. Charles in the North and Cailleen in the South will connect a line of energy to be the second cord. They intersect in the center, creating a crossroad. It is twilight and we now sit at another crossroad, between one day and the next. Focusing your inner eye on where our two energy lines cross, follow the song to Elan's forest." She chanted:

> *"Lady of the Crossroads, teacher and guide*
> *Elan of the Ways walk by our side*
> *Help us prepare for the journey at last*
> *Help us stay true to our fated path."*

The song carried them to the bridge over a stream and onto the path to Elan's cottage. Charles led the way down the familiar path. Jen, holding James' hand, walked behind. Cailleen and Lawrence followed in the rear. At the clearing in front of Elan's cottage, Charles stepped aside and let Jen walk forward.

"Merry meet Grandmother. May I present James?"

"Merry Meet," James said looking Elan in the eyes. He waited for her to *see* him with her inner eye. It felt to him, like a warm comforting breeze as she looked into his soul.

"Merry meet," she said with a smile to James. "It's good to greet you here in my home."

James stepped aside as Charles came forward. Charles kissed Elan's cheek and then knelt for her blessing. Elan placed her hands on either side of his face and then kissed Charles on the third eye. "Merry meet," they chorused to each other.

Cailleen held back. This was Jen's journey and James' initiation into journeying. But Cailleen and Elan's eyes met in greeting and acknowledgment.

"Charles, you will find a pot of tea and honey cakes in the cottage. Please help yourselves. James and I will take a walk." With that Elan hooked her hand under James' arm and began heading into the forest.

"I see you have love, James. Do you have patience?"

"Yes ma'am, I believe I do."

"Good. Don't forget that. Now, I am to tell you some pieces of a story. I am afraid I cannot tell you the entire story, for it is not mine to tell, or yours to know at this time. As I am sure you have guessed, your friend Ben and Cailleen are tied to one another. Their lives crossed many lifetimes ago. In that time, through their actions, an imbalance was created. A third person, Raneck, was also part of that imbalance. He exists between the worlds and has affected them greatly. Two nights ago, the six of you gave him power to do one last task, which he has promised to do. He was bound by sacred Land and love to follow through with this task. He did so last night. His task was to send a dream to Ben reminding him of the past so that he may be guided by it here in the present.

"Charles and Lily are also part of that past. Charles was once Cailleen's son. Lily is the grandchild of all three – Cailleen, Ben and Raneck. She has served as the magnet to draw them together at this time. Her role has been met and she must be released. Raneck has drawn energy from her on a regular basis for a long time. Her energy can no longer sustain him – and will not be able to sustain her for much longer if the connection is not broken and her soul reintegrated.

"Please understand that Raneck is not evil – unbalanced perhaps, but not evil. He sees himself as the one most responsible for the original instance of imbalance in the lifetime where this all started. He has risked much to make amends and bring about balance once again. Lily has also taken on a responsibility, knowing that it came with risks.

"In the time you live," Elan explained, "the people do not understand how vital meeting one's purpose is. Raneck understands it intimately. Cailleen was prevented from using her gifts and meeting her purpose in that first lifetime, and it has had grave consequences not only for Cailleen but for her entire line, for every generation of the tribe since, and, for the world. Raneck knows that each individual matters. He knows that Lily has come to play a part in the re-balancing. I don't believe he looks beyond that or to the possibility that Lily might have other work to do in this lifetime.

"She may not, James. She may be here only for this purpose and her time on the planet may be coming to an end. You must remember this and not interfere." Elan paused.

"Are you telling me," James asked, "that this journey we're taking may be fruitless?"

"I am telling you just the opposite. Whether or not Lily has further work in this lifetime, her soul still needs to be reintegrated. You must do the journey and help her find the piece she is missing. Do all you can to help her find and reintegrate herself. When that is done, she will have a choice to stay or to cross over. Do not interfere with that decision. I am asking you to support her in making the decision she needs to make for her own life contracts. It may be difficult and she may look to you to make the decision. It is not yours to make, James. You must remember that."

"She is just a little girl," James said in confusion.

"Yes, she is a little girl – a little girl with a powerful purpose. Do not underestimate her power or her ability to choose," Elan warned.

"She's just a little girl," James repeated to himself. He couldn't fathom how such a responsibility would be laid upon her.

"Your friends are waiting," Elan said pointing to Charles, Jen and Cailleen. "Merry meet, James."

"Merry meet Elan," James said respectfully.

As they walked back to the bridge James let his thoughts stew. He would not play by these rules. He would do everything he could to keep Lily safe. He would not let Elan's or anyone else's ideas of purpose stand in his way. She was too little to know what to do.

Elan was waiting at the bridge. She spoke to Cailleen but her eyes never left James. "You must speak to him about the babies. And you must write about them so others will also know." With that she turned and went back into the forest.

At the bridge they all joined hands. Jen directed them to focus again on the crossroad and on their breathing. "Follow your breath back to your body and to our circle. Feel your hands and feet. Squeeze the hands you are holding. Return more fully to your body. Feel your breath moving in through your nose and out through your mouth. Become aware of your roots and how they connect with everyone else's. Rotate your shoulders and neck. When you're ready, open your eyes and return fully to this room and this time."

James' anger and frustration shifted the energy in the group. As more experienced travelers the other four adjusted. Jen walked them through opening the circle and releasing the directions. She bent down laying her hands flat on the floor.

"It's important to release excess energy after the circle is open," she explained to James. "In love we take the circle down, returning power to the ground. Take a couple of breaths and send any excess energy build-up down into the earth." Charles and Cailleen were doing the same.

They drank cold tea and ate sandwiches in silence, each lost in their own thoughts. James' anger had not cooled.

"James," Cailleen called and gently touched his sleeve. "What did Elan say? Why are you so angry?"

"She's just a baby," James said shaking his head. "I won't sacrifice a baby and I won't let any of you do it either." He looked at them with hurt and shock.

"What are you talking about, James? None of us are going to sacrifice anyone. I think you must misunderstand," Cailleen said gently.

James looked at her as if he was seeing her clearly for the first time. "I'm going to the bungalow." He was running away and he knew it. He just couldn't sit there and talk about the possibility of losing Lily. He wasn't built to stand by and watch while someone he loved died. He wouldn't do it.

Something told him he was overreacting. Something else told him he was missing a significant piece. But another voice told him he'd been conned and that hurt his pride. He felt the eyes of the forest watching and mocking him. "Coward," the crow said as it flew away from him.

Cailleen went to bed after James left. She needed time to process his reaction. She should have expected it. It had happened before. Men had been charmed and attracted by her power but ran when they saw a glimpse of the pain and sorrow that often came with the work.

They always seemed to blame her. His eyes had been so cold and accusing. She heard the words he wouldn't say: "Ben was right. Keep your hands off of Lily."

Why did she think it would be different with James? She thought it would be different because she wanted it to be different. She wanted it badly. She could feel her heart breaking. But she didn't have time to dwell on a personal crisis. So, she steeled her heart, calmed her breathing, told herself she was all right alone, and closed her eyes for sleep.

She didn't sleep well, of course. She woke in the early hours just before dawn. She rolled over and curled up in the warm covers, but it was too late. Thoughts of James came. She threw back the covers and decided to get up and take an early morning walk. She refused to lay about, nursing a broken heart. She could indulge herself after Lily was taken care of; best to keep busy until then.

She put on coffee and then bundled up and walked outside. It promised to be a beautiful day. The wind coming off the hills smelled faintly like snow, but the sky overhead was clear and the air crisp. She walked down to the river in the quiet of early morning. Fox walking, so she made very little sound, rewarded her with sightings of rabbits, a fox, and as she turned round the bend, a deer with her fawn. Mother and baby both looked up at her. She stopped in her tracks. They went back to their morning drink. After a moment, the deer turned to go back into the trees. Then she stopped, took a half step towards Cailleen and just looked at her with gentle eyes. The fawn peeked around her mother and looked with questioning eyes and a tilt of the head. The mother turned and walked back into the trees with the fawn following.

Crow flew down and settled on a rock ten feet from Cailleen. "Tell Charles I'm fine," Cailleen smiled. The crow cawed. Another crow answered and flew off. The crow on the rock hopped to a higher vantage point and sat looking at her in an attitude of waiting. "I will not send a message to James," Cailleen stated. The crow flew to where the deer and fawn had stopped to remind Cailleen of their medicine of gentleness.

"Yes, alright. Let James know I'm fine as well." The crow cocked its head at her as if waiting for more. "And tell him I'll wander his way in a bit," she sighed. She had promised Elan she would to speak to him of the babies. She didn't understand the point, but Elan had never led her astray. The crow flew off.

Cailleen walked along the Teanaway and found the path leading to the grove. She might as well check it for tonight's celebration while she was out and about. From there she'd go to see James. As she climbed the hill to the grove, she considered deer's message: carry gentleness.

It was much easier for Cailleen to be fierce and formidable when she felt judged and rejected. Gentleness required a softening. She'd felt attacked by James' words. She'd heard them often enough coming from ignorance and fear about her work. Some people came right out and asked her if she sacrificed babies. They didn't understand. And why should they? The church and the media have done a very good job of spreading misinformation about psychics, healers and pagans.

Misperceptions were common, but they didn't usually come from someone as close as James had become. How had she let that happen so quickly? She'd let her hormones override her better judgment. And she'd allowed it to happen in the middle of a quest. She should have known better. She should have kept her distance until things were resolved.

Of course, everyone seemed to be pushing her into allowing love in her life instead of doing the work she knew to do. And now she had to pay the consequences. How was she going to get through the next few days working so intimately with James? She'd find a way. Lily was depending on her – on them.

Cailleen was almost to the grove and still didn't feel ready to talk to James. She stopped and sat on a log to get more time. What, she wondered, happened when he was with Elan? She had said something that upset him. She had said something he didn't want to hear.

Cailleen decided to approach James' reaction as if it came from one of her students. What would she say to a student?

She'd share one of her own experiences as a novice to the work. She'd talk about how doubts and fears kept finding her until she learned the lessons she needed to learn. Maybe that's what's happening now, she smiled to herself - not just for James, but for herself.

At every point of deepening or initiation in the work, one met fears and doubts. Resisting them usually made the journey longer and more difficult. Facing them took courage. She had the courage to stand her ground. She'd done that with Ben.

But did she have the courage to change, to shift her perceptions about how things worked? She wanted to believe she could have love *and* do her work. But the first time they butted heads she wanted to put up the walls and go back to what was comfortable and familiar. Yes, she had to admit, she had made a cowardly retreat.

"That won't do," she said to the forest. "I might fail miserably. I might be rejected and scorned. But I will not be a coward!"

She felt better. And she could also feel that she'd softened. Perhaps James needed to retreat and find his bearings as well. With a lighter step now, she skirted around the grove and down the path to the bungalow.

***

James berated himself all the way home last night. He didn't want to hear that Lily might not make it. The thought of him allowing that to happen was inconceivable. It wasn't right. Lily was too young. But he knew in his heart that Elan spoke truth. Up until then, he had never once admitted to himself that Lily might not survive this.

He wanted ignorance and he wanted somebody to blame. Cailleen provided a perfect target. She started this whole thing. He wasn't clear how, but it was enough that she was there. And on top of that, she'd brought him into this world. She introduced him to Charles and Jen and this whole way of opening to the Universe.

Sure, it was wonderful to explore the world in a new way; it felt great to develop gifts he'd never recognized he had. Making a difference in Lily's life by sending her love and energy compared to nothing else he'd ever experienced. He felt useful and so grateful to be able to do something to ease her.

To go on the journey to help her reintegrate her soul parts frightened him a bit. He feared he wouldn't have the skills he needed to help her. But to hear that he had the skills but shouldn't use them, felt like betrayal. He loathed the whole situation. He didn't understand how it could be true.

But did he ask questions? No. He made accusations. He attacked the woman he loved. He ran. Things got tough and he ran from it. The shame he felt overwhelmed him. He'd always stood steady as a cop. His partners could always depend on him.

He was simply out of his league here. He had to admit it and face the circle with the knowledge. He only hoped that if he faced them honestly, he could still be considered a friend.

The crows made a racket letting him know he had company. He glanced out the window to see Cailleen walking toward him. He thought she'd be angry and disappointed in him, but her gait and body language suggested neither. He walked to open the door with a flicker of hope beating in his chest. He'd face her and see what happened next.

She stopped a few feet from the door. He leaned against the door frame. They looked into each other's eyes, searching. Cailleen looked for the loathing and accusation she'd seen last night. James looked for the disappointment and anger he expected. Neither found what they were looking for.

"Coffee?" James offered.

"Does it come with breakfast?" Cailleen asked.

"Oatmeal?"

Cailleen nodded and poured herself coffee while James filled a pot with water. She took a sip and leaned against the counter facing him.

"Several years back, when I worked more with individual clients, a lot of infertility cases came my way," she told him. "At first I hesitated to work psychically with them. It was such an emotional issue and I didn't feel qualified to cope. But Spirit kept sending me these clients who were trying to get pregnant or ones who got pregnant, but miscarried.

"I expected sorrow and disappointment. What was surprising was the self-blame these clients brought to my table. 'What's wrong with me?' and 'what have I done to deserve this?' were commonly asked. I couldn't answer those questions, of course. But I had the sense they were the wrong questions.

"One day I was working with a couple who had been trying to get pregnant for over a year. The woman had been a student of mine so I felt a bit more comfortable checking in psychically for them. The spirit of the baby that would eventually come to them connected with me immediately. She told me that she was waiting to come to them, but that they had to work a few things out first in their relationship. She was ready, they weren't. The baby's communication helped them shift the question from 'Why aren't we getting pregnant?' to 'What do we need to do to make room for this child?' They identified several issues in the next couple of sessions and worked through them. They became pregnant quite soon after.

"From then on I allowed myself to open to the spirits of the children trying to come through. Often the spirit needed something in order to come through: the timing wasn't right, the parents needed to be better prepared for their arrival – that sort of thing.

"Miscarriages and abortions presented a different approach. The information I received from the spirits of the babies that had passed on challenged many of my assumptions and illuminated some fascinating strategies.

"I'd heard from my teachers that we come to this planet by agreement. We choose our parents for the lessons we need to learn and we come with a purpose or life contract to fulfill. I didn't realize I had always assumed it required a long time to fulfill it.

We become so distraught when a young person dies. We say things like, 'what a waste' or 'she never even got to live.'"

"Cut down before their time." James added, nodding in shared experiences.

"Well," Cailleen continued, "it's not the story I got from the spirits of those babies. I remember one woman, who had been blocking herself from getting pregnant because she'd had an abortion when she was quite young. She never stopped grieving for that unborn child and she believed she didn't deserve one now, since she'd rejected one before. We agreed the first step was to help her move through the grief of having the abortion. During our session the spirit of that baby came to us. First, he asked his mother not to grieve and said he was coming back to her when she was ready. Then he told her that he chose to come to her before, when he knew she wasn't ready, because he wanted a peek into what it would be like to become incarnate.

He'd never been born before and was afraid. He also told her that he'd come to try to turn her from a path of destruction. She'd been using sex to feel loved and accepted. The consequence of pregnancy and the guilt of the abortion made her take stock and changed her life.

"Another woman came to me shortly after that. Her 18-month-old had died in a car accident. Her husband left her after the girl died. During the session the little girl's spirit spoke and assured her mother she was well and happy. The child explained her purpose had been to experience love and to open her mother to true love. She accomplished both. Her death released her mother from a very unhealthy marriage and opened the way to a nurturing love.

"James, I can go on with these stories. What I learned from all of them is that we can meet our purpose in a very short time. I learned that age is not an indication of a fulfilled purpose. And I learned to not see a short life as a tragedy. Spirits becoming incarnate sometimes need a run through. Sometimes they get scared and choose to leave again. Often, they come back to the same parents. Most importantly, I learned to not anticipate another's journey. We simply do not know their purpose and must allow them their path – even if it brings us pain."

Cailleen took the bowl of oatmeal from James and sat at the table. He sat across from her and they ate in silence for a moment.

"I don't know why Elan wanted me to share the baby stories with you, but I hope it helped."

"She told me," James paused as his throat closed with emotion. ". . .she told me that Lily might not live. She told me not to interfere. She said even if I could, I shouldn't influence Lily to stay. She said Lily had to make the choice and I wasn't to do anything but support that choice. How can I do that? How could I ever look Camille or Ben in the eyes knowing I allowed their daughter to die? How can this be asked of me?" he demanded.

Cailleen squeezed his hand in understanding. He remained tight fisted. Cailleen sighed.

"James, no one expects you to harm Lily or to allow her to come to harm. Elan was trying to prepare you for a very real possibility. You've told me how full of life Lily always was and how painful it is to see her now as a shadow of herself. If her purpose has been met and it's time for her to cross over, she must be allowed to make that choice. If she chooses to stay because your love holds her here, she will always be a shadow of herself."

James remained silent but Cailleen could see he was listening to her words.

"I remember," Cailleen paused as the pain of the memory moved through her, "I remember what it was like to live without purpose. I moved through the motions of life. I married. I birthed and raised children. But I always felt removed from everything. This invisible barrier kept me from falling in love with my husband and with my children. A beating heart does not make a life,

James.

"I knew a woman once whose life centered around her dog. The dog grew old and became quite ill. Even though she knew the dog was in pain, she kept him alive because she couldn't imagine life without him. The dog eventually died, of course, and the woman survived it. It took a very long time for her grief to pass, not just because she missed her companion. It took her a long time to forgive herself for selfishly keeping him alive, when it was clearly his time to go."

"I get it," James said. "How do you do this work? How do you handle the pain and loss?"

"You learn to see the joy in helping someone do what they need to do. You learn how significant it becomes to the other person to have someone willing to witness their pain, struggle, joy, victory, sorrow, sacrifice, etc. We have a great need to be witnessed in our lives. I consider it a privilege to be that witness, to offer encouragement, to lend support."

"Do you ever feel alone?" James asked.

"Yes. I often feel alone. Few see the beauty of the work. Many run from the horror it can seem to be. Sometimes those who are left to mourn blame me for what passes. It can be very lonely work," she agreed.

"I'm sorry I ran," James apologized. "If you think you and the rest of the circle can find a way to trust me again, I'd like to follow through with the journey. I understand if you don't think that's appropriate. I promise not to run again."

Cailleen looked through James' eyes to his heart and smiled. "I don't think you ran, James. You retreated and that's quite understandable. Lily needs you and I see no reason to change our plans. But that's a couple of days off. You should be sure you're rested for this evening's events. Come up to the manor around six."

"Thanks," James said, and rose to walk her to the door. He wanted to touch her, to hold her so he could feel if everything was really all right now. But she opened the door ahead of him calling, 'Thanks for breakfast' over her shoulder on her way out.

Cailleen ran down the steps with teary eyes. She could trust him in the circle. But she wasn't sure she could trust him with her heart. And suddenly she felt lonelier than she'd ever felt before.

Chapter Seventeen
Samhain

By six o'clock Cailleen's kitchen was full of adults and children bringing in food for the potluck after the ritual. Some came in costume. Some brought jack-o-lanterns. They began in the study where a large table sat in the north as an ancestors' altar. Everyone brought something to put on the altar and informally shared stories of ancestors.

The lights dimmed and everyone grew silent. Lawrence invited everyone to ask their ancestors to meet with them up at the grove. Then he directed everyone to the porch to gather jack-o-lanterns for the procession to the grove. They walked in silence to the grove and entered the circle, each person stopping at the cardinal points to make an offering. Once the circle was complete the drummers played a call to gather and invited the ancestors in. Then the Elements were called in and a protective circle cast.

They sang. Lawrence led them through a visualization. They did a litany, naming all those who had passed in the last year. They sang again, giving thanks for the harvest they'd gathered. Then they raised energy and sent it to the Universe with the intention that what they had harvested would sustain them through the winter.

They closed the circle and Lawrence led a procession back down to the manor, this time with drums and song and dancing. A potluck dinner followed with lots of laughing and sharing of stories.

"So," Lawrence said to James, "was it what you expected?"

"I guess it was, at least in form. I didn't know it would feel like a warm and loving family reunion. And my body seems to be pulsing in an interesting way."

"Sure. When 25 people get together to celebrate and raise energy it's a bit electrifying. It's one of the reasons we ground the energy at the end of the ritual. A nice little energy buzz is one thing, but too much can be unsettling at best. And we *are* a family, James. A few of you are newcomers, but most of us have been celebrating together for at least five years. It's good to have you with us," Lawrence said, and then moved off to the kitchen when someone called his name.

James had played hard with the children and had eaten heartily. He was pretty sure he'd met everyone so he sat back and just watched for a while. Cailleen, it seemed, was avoiding him. She'd smiled briefly at him across the room when their eyes met. But she didn't seem to be particularly aware of him. He, on the other hand, knew where she was at every moment.

He probably screwed things up with her last night. He'd let it go for now. But when Lily was taken care of, he fully intended to do whatever he needed to do to win her over again. He smiled at Jen as she walked over to sit with him.

By ten o'clock everyone had left, the kitchen was clean, Yvonne was in bed and the five of them sat talking in Cailleen's study.

"Have you heard from Ben?" Charles asked James.

"Not yet. He'll take the time he has. I expect we'll hear from him on Sunday." He paused in reflection. "I guess that's tomorrow."

"It is indeed," Lawrence said. "But we still have tonight. I think we should do something in our circle to celebrate our new addition – our new harvest. It would also be a good time to ask for any assistance you think you might need," he suggested to Cailleen and James.

"I could use some help understanding where the boundary between supporting and interfering is," James offered. "And how the hell do you get enough distance to be clear?"

"It's an issue of the heart," Lawrence suggested as he walked behind Cailleen and put his hand on her shoulder. She understood he was talking to her as well as to James. "A friend of mine is a singer and was asked by a friend to sing at her baby's funeral. She was fine until that little tiny coffin came down the aisle. She was in the middle of a song and tried to hold back her emotions, but her throat began to close. The only way she got through it was to allow the tears to run freely while she sang. Her emotions empowered the song, she told me. We think emotions just get in the way. I think we should use their power as a tool more often, instead of trying to deny them or put them off until later when it's more convenient."

"But how do I do that?" James asked.

"Why don't we do it in circle tonight?" Charles suggested. "It would be a good way to clear the field for the work with Lily. What shall we focus it on?"

"We could use it to cut away whatever might stand in our path to completing this quest and bringing healing to Lily. I could use clarity and a cleared path," Cailleen said.

"Sounds like sword work," Lawrence grinned. "I brought mine."

They talked for a short while longer, creating a form for the ritual. Then everyone went their separate ways for a half-hour to prepare in whatever way they needed. Jen took a fifteen-minute catnap. Charles walked in the moonlight and did breathing exercises to energize him for the ritual. Lawrence spent the half-hour watching Yvonne brush her hair and moisturize while she shared her experiences during the earlier ritual.

Cailleen sat gazing into the fire. She contemplated Lawrence's words. Was she lying to herself about the need to put the personal situation with James aside until after the work with Lily? Was it simply habit to put her personal life second? There were times when one's personal life clearly came second. It was simply part of her work. But was this one of those times?

She got up and paced in front of the fire for a few moments, then paused and turned to the fire as if they were having a conversation. She'd never done work that seemed more critical. A young girl's life was in the balance. The quest of many lifetimes was in the balance. And love came walking into the middle of it. She knew she was being tested. Whatever choice she made would frame the next stage of her life. She turned her back on the fire and found James watching her intently.

"I didn't hear you there," she said. "Do you need something?"

"No," James shook his head. "You seem restless and I meant to ask if you needed to be alone. But then I didn't want to disturb you."

"You're fine, James. I'm going to go change," she said, giving him a distracted smile, and left the room.

James went back to the window and stared up at the stars. Their vastness made his situation seem smaller and less intimidating. The earlier celebration had been fun, and even profound in the warmth of sharing both within the circle and during the potluck afterward. He knew it would be different in the ritual they planned to start in a few minutes. He didn't know how. But he did know he would no longer be just one in the crowd. He wondered whether he would feel the same sense of intimacy he had whenever he'd worked with the other four so far. Would the cool distance Cailleen had been offering him all day continue or drop? He wasn't sure which would be more difficult. If she dropped it he'd see how she truly felt about him. The pain of rejection or the joy of acceptance would each be distractions in their own way.

There was nothing he could do about it other than hope he could handle whatever came with grace. Whatever it brought, he was committed to follow through. He considered if there was anything he should be doing to prepare. Cailleen was changing her clothes. No one mentioned a dress code to him. He looked down at his black jeans and burnt orange brushed-cotton shirt. He'd dressed for the holiday and he was comfortable. No one told him anything about how to dress, so he shrugged his shoulders and decided not to worry about it.

While Cailleen was changing, someone knocked at her door. She'd just slipped into black wool pants and a turtleneck sweater. She called, "Come in," as she went to her bureau. She threw a pair of warm wool socks on the bed and then moved to the carved wooden box that held her ritual items. She wound a sacred cord around her waist and slipped a silver bracelet engraved with a triskele onto her wrist. She pulled all the rings she'd worn earlier off her fingers except for the amber stone. Her hand went to her amulet that was tucked under her sweater. Then she peeked into the box again.

Charles watched all this silently. It made him feel like a little boy watching his mom get dressed for a night out. The rhythm of it comforted him.

"I thought you might need this tonight," he said, walking toward her. He pulled from his pocket the silk bag that held Calleigha's necklace. The necklace spilled out into his hand and he held it in his palm. Charles wanted this moment between mother and son to last. This quest would change things. He admitted to himself that he was gathering memories before the changes happened. He rubbed his finger over the engravings and looked closely at the disk that held them.

"Is it bone?" he asked.

"Elk antler," Cailleen answered. "Elk was chosen for its gift of stamina. On one side a Wood Pigeon hovers over a thistle next to a stream. In the background you can see a bear, our clan totem. The other side holds three small spirals with an acorn in the center of the three." She took the necklace from Charles. Smiling, she ran her fingers over the engravings.

"It used to have feathers," Cailleen explained outlining where they hung. "And a delicate bead in the shape of an otter, and also a whistle made from a wood pigeon's leg." She held the necklace with eyes closed and a reminiscent smile on her face.

"It's time," Charles stated as he took the necklace and slipped it over her head settling it just above her breasts. "Fulfill your vows – balancing love and power, woman and priestess." A surge of shared power enfolded them and they smiled in memory of another time when it was Cailleen who had placed an item of power around Charles.

Charles sighed, kissed Cailleen sweetly, and held out his arm gallantly. "Shall we?"

"I need socks and shoes. Hold on." She pulled on socks and shoes then took Charles' arm. They walked downstairs together.

James walked out of the study as they descended the stairs. The two of them sparkled. He closed his eyes and then reopened them to have another look. The air around them seemed to shimmer. He caught his breath at the beauty of their connection. He also experienced pangs of envy at the ease they shared with one another.

"They do that sometimes," Lawrence said as he threw his arm over James' shoulder companionably. "Freaked me out the first time I saw it. Did a double take myself," he said, grinning. Then he handed James a heavy wool sweater and a scarf. "We'll have a fire, but it can still get cold up there – and definitely gets cold on the walk back."

James looked at Lawrence and Jen behind him. They both had warm clothing on. Lawrence wore a purple long sleeved heavy tee shirt under a flannel shirt of forest green. He'd tied a wool jacket around his waist. More elegantly dressed, Jen wore a high-necked cashmere dress in cerulean blue. It molded to her breasts and hips and then flared out as it made its way to her mid-calf. Underneath she had black leggings. Between her breasts nestled a large moonstone. A matching bracelet circled her wrist and, on her finger, she wore a star sapphire.

"You look like the most beautiful night sky I've ever seen," James stammered.

"Yea," Lawrence winked at Jen. "*She* does *that* sometimes," he directed to James.

"Look, it twirls!" Jen spun in the middle of the hall to show off her dress. Her girlish delight reminded James of Lily.

"And it twirls," he agreed laughing.

Charles wore casual wool pants and a black hand-woven tunic with an embellished crane design on the sleeves. Underneath the tunic a Hikenbiker merino wool tee shirt would keep him warm. Under his arm he carried what looked like a wool poncho.

Noticing the sweater already in James' hands, Charles remarked, "I see someone has already brought you something warmer. I'll take this along anyway in case someone needs it," he said, motioning to the poncho.

Cailleen grabbed a bag as she walked out the kitchen door and the rest followed her. James decided it was time to take a risk. He causally caught up with Cailleen, reached out and took the bag from her. She gave him a distracted smile and walked with him up to the grove. Her response wasn't what he hoped for, but she hadn't dismissed him.

They each entered the circle on their own, leaving gifts as they moved clockwise around the circle. As James faced East and offered birdseed, a crow landed directly in the boughs in front of him and spoke encouragement. James nodded and walked on feeling like he was not even close to alone in this. He felt the entire murder was with him.

Each person had picked up a couple of logs on their way into the inner circle and they offered them to Lawrence to add to the central fire. Once the fire was going again Lawrence gathered everyone's attention.

"The Wheel has turned and we stand at the New Year with the winter before us. Let's begin the circle in the North. Jen?" he prompted.

Jen raised her arms and faced the North. "Guardians of the North, powers of Earth," she began in a strong clear voice. She howled the cry of the wolf. "Brother Wolf with your thickening coat of winter," she called. She raised a small branch to the sky saying, "Sister Rosemary with your sharp scent that calls us to remember." She ran her hands across the branch of rosemary releasing its pungent smell, which sharpened their senses. "Join us in this circle on this Samhain night and bring to us your blessings. We thank you for connecting us to Land and the wisdom of the North. We thank you for teaching us when to stand alone and when to walk with the pack. We thank you for helping us remember who we are and from whom we come. Honored teachers, allies and ancestors BE WITH US NOW!" Jen threw the rosemary into the fire and the scent enfolded them.

They all turned to the East. Charles raised his arms, his tunic flapping in the wind. "Guardians of the East, Powers of Air," he began in a deep baritone. A crow came and settled on his shoulder as he called, "Crow, keeper of the laws of spirit." He raised a bunch of herbs tied in string saying, "Lavender, ally of breath and inspiration." He crushed the lavender, releasing its sweet scent. "Join us here as we celebrate the turning of the Wheel. We thank you for winds bringing us clarity of purpose. We thank you for guidance as we follow spiritual law to our "good road". We thank you for inspiration and ease along the way. Honored ones, BE WITH US NOW!" Charles threw the lavender into the fire and the scent enfolded them.

They all turned to the South. James lifted his arms, beginning tentatively, "Guardians of the South, Powers of Fire." His voice gained strength as he called, "Mother Snake, healer and transformer." He raised a string of peppers, "Pepper, ally of heat and passion. Be welcomed. Join us in this circle of power and love. We thank you for igniting the heat of our convictions. We thank you for helping us transform and focus our passions. We thank you for teaching us not to fear the power and heat. Fiery ones, BE WITH US NOW!" James threw the peppers into the fire and their heat enfolded them.

They all turned to the West. Cailleen lifted her arms and sang, "Guardians of the West, Powers of Water." She let her toning move from the sound of the ocean to that of a bubbling stream, then sang, "Father Salmon, wisdom of the ages." She raised a handful of dried seaweed, "Seaweed, nurturer of land and sea. Sweet allies of death and rebirth join us as we pass between the veils. We thank you for teaching us the wisdom of ebb and flow. We thank you for showing us the way up the rapids and back to the sea. We thank you for nurturing us through all the stages of life. Sacred ones, BE WITH US NOW!" Cailleen threw the seaweed into the fire and the smell of the sea enfolded them.

Lawrence stepped into the circle and everyone turned in to face the Center. He lifted his arms and turned in a circle as he called, "Guardians of the Center, Powers of Spirit." He held out the arms of the sweater he'd tied around his waist as well as the ends of his long scarf and stood so the moon cast a shadow of an eight-legged being. He posed and intoned, "Grandmother Spider, keeper of the web of life." He raised his hands in the moonlight, illuminating the slice of apple cut cross wise to reveal the natural pentacle within and called, "Apple, ally of love and balance. Keepers of the crossroads that connect us all, join us in this sacred circle as we seek balance, understanding and focus. We thank you for walking with us always. We thank you for tugging on the strings needing our attention. We thank you for the gifts of love along the way. Beloved ones, BE WITH US NOW!" Lawrence threw the apple and a handful of dried apples into the fire and the scent of sweet comfort enfolded them.

Jen stepped forward across the fire from Lawrence and their eyes and hearts linked. Together they spoke, "God and Goddess, Creator and Birther, Male and Female, Strong and Weak, Yin and Yang," they paused, "Sweet Fibonacci, Goddess of balance, step into our circle as we seek balance on all levels. We thank you for the gifts you bring to us individually and as a circle. BE WELCOMED!"

Jen stepped back into the circle. Lawrence picked up his sword from near the fire and walked clockwise to the north and behind Jen. Holding his sword straight ahead of him, point out, he walked clockwise with his back to the others creating an energetic circle with the point of the sword. Passing Jen again he stopped and made a figure eight with the sword to secure the circle. He handed the sword to Jen. Then he brought his hands to the level of the circle he'd just created and, using his breath to empower them, expanded the circle below and above to create a sphere of sacred space. He reclaimed his sword from Jen and walked into the circle.

"The circle is cast in perfect love and perfect trust. Only beings of the highest good embraced are within. We stand between the worlds. We are not affected by what happens in the world; but what we do here will flow out into the world to heal and serve. Blessed be."

"Blessed be," they responded.

"Cailleen, please lead us in a toning meditation and into SpiritSong."

"With knees slightly bent," she instructed, "send your roots down into Mother Earth. Feel her heart beat and let it echo up through your roots and up through your body. Listen to the Mother's song and the tone she offers to you. Feel that tone move up through your roots, through your legs and hips, and belly and trunk, and chest and throat. Sound the tone and let it flow into the circle.

"Now, take the sound of the tone back into your body through your ears; let it flow over you like warm honey, slowly over and down your body and back to the earth. Now pull it back up through your body, through your throat and out into the circle – now, back over and down through your body. Continue this cycle, allowing the tone to shift as it moves through your body. Sound your body - let it become flow. Sound the resistance, sound the flow. Allow your body to move in its own rhythm within the flow of sound."

They each toned and moved in their own rhythm for several minutes until their bodies vibrated and the sound found its rest. They remained in silence allowing their bodies to pulse and find balance as a unit. At the still point, Lawrence nodded to Cailleen to continue.

Speaking softly, she instructed, "We will enter the song again as we just did, this time with the intent of releasing our emotions and singing them into balance and focus. When we reach balance, Lawrence will raise the sword and we will each focus the power of our controlled emotions to the blade. Lawrence will then direct the gathered power. Are there any questions?"

No one spoke. "Let us begin once again with the heartbeat of the Mother." They began toning. When Cailleen sensed that each of the others was in their flow, she began a SpiritSong. She sang the love they shared in wordless tones. She sang their hopes, their fears, their frustrations. She sang whatever emotions they offered and they sang with her.

James was astounded by the SpiritSong technique. While in the flow of the sound, his emotions seemed to simply make themselves known one by one. The toning and the flow of the song that came forth held no judgment. The tone shifted with the different emotions. Some tones were not what one would call pleasing to the ear, but it didn't matter. The overall sounding - the SpiritSong - was beautiful.

It allowed him to identify his fears about failing Lily, the circle, his life. It gave him access to the feelings of boredom and discontent he'd been experiencing in the last year. It bathed him in the delight and joy he felt with this new work he was exploring – and with that, the undertones of fear and awe. Respect, curiosity, tentativeness, wariness, doubt, compassion - they all flowed and revealed themselves. Then came the anger and despair.

All the years of restrained emotion as a police officer freed itself. The moments of great hope, and the frequent let down when something failed. James saw the ways he tended to limit hope. But as the song continued to carry him, he released the restraints. The anger that someone might hurt Lily; the frustration of the inability of the medical community to help her; the pain of seeing Camille and Ben face it all; almost overwhelmed him. But he felt Charles behind him at that moment and Charles seemed to be singing him strength.

James let it all flow and allowed himself to truly feel for the first time. As he did, he began to understand that allowing the feelings to flow brought an incredible ease. He was able to continue to feel and yet he felt somewhat detached from the feelings. It wasn't that he didn't feel their power. It was simply that he began to see it all as part of the human condition. And in that, he saw the beauty. He saw how every emotion, even rage and anger, could facilitate a lesson or an action toward empowerment and balance. Emotions were not hindrances to clarity. He could choose to see them as allies in his life. He began to understand that pain, fear, anger, rage, pity, and frustration were not to be diminished, ignored or restrained. They could be used and focused to facilitate change. With this understanding his heart broke open and his capacity for love, joy, hope, delight and peace expanded.

And then James noticed that the wave of sound he was riding gently came to shore and dissipated. He felt both empty and full. As the song ended, he became aware of his physical body and surroundings. Charles stood behind helping to support him. He opened his eyes to see Jen sitting on the ground before him with her hands on his feet. As he shifted to stand on his own, Jen looked up with a gentle smile and Charles took his arms from around James and placed his hands on his shoulders until he seemed steadier.

James could feel a continued sense of deep focus in Charles. He looked up and into the circle in time to see a stream of energy moving from the three of them toward the sword that Lawrence held pointed to the sky. Cailleen stood with Lawrence, supporting him and singing.

Earlier, it had become clear to Cailleen that James had powerfully entered the song. As a trained Priestess she monitored him closely. When she sensed James beginning to feel overwhelmed, she moved clockwise around the circle to support him. Charles noticed her intentions and moved to James' side instead. Jen and Lawrence also became aware of the intensity of energies flowing from James. Jen went to James to help him ground some of that energy.

Lawrence, as facilitator of the circle, knew their original plan had just been diverted. The five of them would not be feeding the sword tonight. But they could use the energy James was raising. The others were helping James to ground the excess and contain the flow of what was passing through him. Lawrence raised the sword. Reflected fire flashed in the steel and drew Charles' and Cailleen's attention. They understood Lawrence's intention and nodded. Charles stood ready to act as a conduit to focus the energy as James released his emotional turmoil, and with it, the song. Cailleen stood ready to assist Lawrence and to send intention with the energy.

When James' heart broke open, Charles felt its strength and purity. Without interfering in the flow of James' song, Charles began sending some of that energy toward the sword. Lawrence stood strong, holding the sword up to send the energy into the Universe.

Cailleen began a chant of intention to send with the raised energy:

> *Pathways are cleared of all that defeats*
> *Balance is found for our quest to complete*
> *Air and Earth and Water and Fire –*
> *Spirit, hear our heartfelt desire*
> *All our emotions, we do greet*
> *Healing and balance, merry meet.*

As James' SpiritSong waned, Cailleen's chant grew. Jen and Charles added their voices to help contain and support the energy James had raised. Lawrence could feel the power in the sword intensifying, he joined in on the chant. James followed their lead, adding his voice. As the voices merged and blended into one strong force, Lawrence raised the sword higher, raised his own voice in command and repeated the last two lines.

> *All our emotions, we do greet*
> *Healing and balance, merry meet.*

With that Lawrence released the energy, which moved up out of the sword above the trees and burst forth flowing out in all directions. Charles, Jen and James had all joined Cailleen around Lawrence. When the energies burst forth high above the trees, Lawrence swayed and the four stood solid to support him.

After a few moments Lawrence steadied and opened his eyes. "Well, that was a surprise," he smiled. "I think I'm fine," he added when they continued to support him. "How about everyone else?"

They stepped away from Lawrence and looked around at each other. Everyone was nodding to affirm they were fine. "Let's have cakes and ale then and close the circle, shall we?" Lawrence asked.

Jen went to the other side of the fire and picked up the goblet of cider and bowl of pumpkin seeds, then returned to the group. She raised bowl and goblet.

"May the blessings of the God and Goddess infuse these gifts and may they sustain us on our journey, blessed be."

"Blessed be," they echoed.

Jen offered a few pumpkin seeds to the fire and poured some cider onto the earth. Then she turned to Lawrence, who was on her left. "May you never hunger," she said offering him the bowl of seeds.

Lawrence replied, "Blessed be," and then turned to Cailleen on his left. "May you never hunger." And so it went around the circle.

Jen offered the goblet to Lawrence. "May you never thirst." Lawrence replied, "Blessed be," and then turned to Cailleen to offer her the goblet. "May you never thirst." And so, it went around the circle.

They each moved then to their respective directions. Thanking the energies of Earth, Water, Fire, Air and Spirit as well as the Goddess Fibonacci, they dismissed the directions, took down the circle, and returned excess power to the ground. And they sang:

> *The circle is open and unbroken.*
> *May the love of the God and Goddess go in our hearts.*
> *Merry meet and merry part and merry meet again.*
> *Blessed be, Blessed be, Blessed be.*

Chapter Eighteen
Aftermath

James had questions. The ritual did not go as planned and he knew he was the cause, but he didn't truly know what that meant. He also didn't know what to ask. Some protocol needed to be met and they waited for him to meet it. He searched his memory for a clue to it in the books he'd read recently. But after the ritual he was having a tough time focusing on it.

Jen and Lawrence headed to bed shortly after they all returned to the manor. Charles and Cailleen stayed with James. Each had played a role as Teacher to him, but in different ways. It was clear he needed a Teacher in this moment, but which one? They waited for him to ask a question or make some comment that indicated who he needed in this moment.

Finally, James broke the silence, more out of discomfort than of any particular forethought. But then, Spirit worked that way often. "Tell me more about SpiritSong," he asked them. "I thought we were just going to do some simple toning. That was not my experience."

SpiritSong was Cailleen's arena, so Charles said goodnight and headed upstairs to bed.

"SpiritSong functions in many ways," Cailleen began. She used her teacher voice to give him some space from the more personal aspect. "I use it often when I'm writing and get blocked. It serves very well to get things moving and to shift one's perspective. I also use it when I feel strong emotions for which I have no explanation. I sing the emotion and it will reveal its source and often a necessary action. I also use SpiritSong as prayer, to express gratitude, or even just for fun.

"I teach a local SpiritSong circle as a spiritual practice. We use chants and different exercises like writing or drawing or movement. And several opportunities to do SpiritSong are included in the format.

"Most often, one person does SpiritSong while the circle holds space and acts as witness. Sometimes, like tonight, the song gets away from the body who is singing. Or, more accurately, the person gets away from the song. I usually touch the body to help the person ground the sound and stay in the flow," she finished.

"So, I lost control of the song tonight and that's why things went astray?" James asked.

"On the contrary," Cailleen told him. "You handled the song very well indeed. You fully opened to it and tapped into some very powerful emotion. That is what shifted the working of the ritual. And you should know that even the best planned ritual must allow for Spirit to move in its own way. That's what happened in the circle tonight. Through your openness to the song flowing through you, you accessed a deep source of power. When we sensed that, we simply shifted to accommodate what Spirit was offering. SpiritSong has its own wisdom. You listened and followed. We supported you, that is all. Our *intention* for the ritual was met; we touched into emotion, released blocks to find clarity and used the energy we raised to bless the journey ahead.

"Our plan was to do that more collectively, and I think we did each individually connect with our emotions and release our blocks. You taped into a deeper experience, one that was certainly more powerful than any of us anticipated. In SpiritSong circle, we say, 'Sometimes you sing, sometimes you are sung.' You did quite well tonight, James," she said, laying her hand over his.

James turned his hand and intertwined their fingers. "I felt a presence inside the song, like another living awareness. It came subtly. I'm not even sure if it was separate from me. I was in the song fully, and at the same time I seemed to be observing it and learning from it as if I was watching a training video. That's not really quite right either. All these emotions were flowing and I allowed myself to really be with them. They weren't all easy to embrace. And then I seemed to fall into this well of restrained emotions from being a cop. Once I opened that pit it seemed it would be endless and I would drown in it.

"But I felt Charles behind me and so I moved into it. At first it was intense, but as I let it flow and the song carried it, I began to understand things at a different level. Emotions can be tools for change. As I let them flow, it felt like my capacity for emotion grew. Ten days ago, that would have scared the shit out of me. As a cop, I always believed that emotions were a weakness, one that could get you killed."

He turned to Cailleen and took her other hand. "I sensed the detachment that I see *you* use. I get that it's not cold distance from them. It's allowing them, without judging them or attaching more meaning to them – or, being ruled by them. I understand now, how you can do the very difficult things with such compassion and steadfastness. I saw the beauty in allowing pain, anger, lust, joy, etc. I know how important it is to allow Lily her experiences, and even if it breaks my heart, I think I can do it now."

He lifted her hand and kissed it. "I respect what you do very much. I trust your skills and intuition. I love you." James paused. "I was going to keep that last one until after we did whatever we need to do for Lily. After tonight, I think it may very well be a tool. I wanted us both to know it was there." James kissed her other hand, then got up and left. "Sweet dreams," he called as walked out the door.

Chapter Nineteen
Healing

Cailleen woke the next morning to a strange ringing sound. It stopped before she could identify it. *I should recognize it*, she thought to herself. Before she could think more about it, someone knocked at her door.

"Come in," she called from under the warm covers.

"Ben just called. Lily took a turn for the worse last night. He wants you to come as soon as you can. Jen is dressing. Lawrence went to tell James. I'll have breakfast ready for you in ten minutes." With that Charles closed the door and left her to rally.

Cailleen wondered what could have brought about the change in Lily. Was it something that happened here last night? She wished they had a day or two so they could be fresher and have more of a plan. Well, they didn't. They'd do whatever they could and trust it would be enough.

She packed a bag of clothes and then gathered some ritual supplies. She didn't know if she'd need any of them, but she felt better having them with her. She took her ring, sacred cord, and the necklace Charles had returned to her. She still wore her amulet. She added Chakra stones, smudge stick, and a bottle of water from the Chalice Well in Glastonbury. Camille probably had candles but Cailleen added some to her tools just in case. Her athame, a short double-edged blade, might be needed to focus energy.

She looked around her study to see if anything else needed to be taken. Nothing spoke to her, except the notion that she was bringing all these tools to prove to Ben that she had them. She didn't really need any of them. But most people felt more comfortable with her skills if she gave them something to look at while she worked. Ben probably didn't need them. No, she thought, Ben would need something to do himself. Drums, she thought! She grabbed several drums and her rattle.

She was ready so she carried her bags to the kitchen. Yvonne was bustling about, feeding everyone and asking if they had everything they needed. Cailleen smiled. Everyone needed to know they could add something in an emergency. It pleased her to see Yvonne find a place for herself in the circle even though she was not called to work within it.

"Coffee or tea?" Yvonne asked holding up a mug. Cailleen walked over and kissed her on the cheek. "Coffee please," she requested. Yvonne blushed and a very pleased smile lit up her face. "Fruit and biscuits are on the table," she said directing Cailleen to a chair. "I have fried potatoes, onions, mushrooms and zucchini with sliced tomatoes on the side coming up."

Charles walked in at that moment. "Do I smell coffee?" he asked.

Yvonne said. "Sit Charles. I'll get you a cup. You can start with fruit and biscuits."

"I think we should marry her," Jen quipped with a wink at Lawrence.

"Stand in line if you want, but you'll never get past me," Lawrence said, kissing Yvonne as she handed him and Jen mugs.

James walked in the door. "I didn't know what to bring so I brought a thermos of strong tea with cream." He looked a little helpless and Yvonne took pity on him.

"Brilliant," Yvonne smiled. "I had one of coffee prepared but couldn't find a second one for tea. This lot tends to drink coffee the morning after a ritual, but soon enough they revert to their sacred tea. Sit and have some breakfast James."

"Bless you," James said, kissing her cheek. "I could barely manage the tea. But on the walk over here, I discovered I'm really quite hungry."

Charles looked at the growing pile of bags at the back door. "Lawrence, can you manage to take Jen's things home with you? I'm not sure how I'm going to get four people and all these bags into my hybrid."

"Are you coming with us?" Cailleen asked Charles. "How will Ben feel about that?" she asked, looking at James.

Charles answered her. "I told him I would deliver you all safely so that you would be rested when you got there. He's expecting my arrival. Elan encouraged me to be there, so I expect I am needed for something."

"I'm very happy to have you along," Cailleen assured him.

They pulled out of the manor fifteen minutes later and headed over the mountains to the Hodges' estate. On the drive they talked about strategies, but decided they couldn't really plan anything specific. Cailleen would guide the journey with James coming along for support. Jen would stay with Camille and Ben and help them to hold space with drumming. The rest they would see to when they arrived.

Cailleen settled back and leaned into James. He put his arm around her shoulders and pulled her more comfortably into his embrace. She moved into a light trance searching the interconnected web for signs of what was happening for Lily and what might be needed to assist her. She felt Elan's presence doing the same thing and felt comforted to have this ally.

Something elusive kept shifting on the web. It didn't seem to be able to hold its shape long enough for her to discern what it was. She'd feel a flicker of recognition and then it was gone. It was weak, hungry and a little bit desperate, but that's all she got. She sighed heavily and opened her eyes.

"No luck in your search?" Charles asked.

"Nothing I can get a hold of," Cailleen answered.

"I can't get a hold of Raneck either," Jen added. Charles and Cailleen both looked at her. "I've been keeping tabs on him ever since we sent him energy. I can usually find him pretty quickly. But now, every time I think I've found him, he slips away again."

Charles and Cailleen looked at each other through the rear-view mirror. Cailleen asked, "Do you think he's crossed over finally?"

Charles shook his head, "That's not his style. He'll want to see this thing through. It's more likely he has some other agenda he's trying to push and he doesn't want us to know about it."

Cailleen sighed heavily again. She was growing weary of the intrigue Raneck brought to the situation.

"There's not much you can do until we get there, Cailleen. Why don't you get a little nap in while you have the chance? Take James with you," Charles suggested.

"Charles, you've come a long way," Jen teased. "A week ago, I would have never thought I'd hear you suggesting they sleep together." As she had hoped, the other three chuckled and the atmosphere in the car relaxed. Jen tossed a blanket to the back seat. "Keep it tame, you two," she laughed.

Cailleen and James snuggled in and fell into a comfortable sleep. An hour later they felt the car slowing and heard Jen on the telephone. "Camille? Yes, it's Jen. We just got off the freeway and should be to your place in about 20 minutes. How's Lily? Uh huh. OK. We'll see you soon." Jen turned to Charles. "Lily is resting but not comfortably. The stress in Camille's voice is pretty high. Did you think to bring some of your magic brew?"

"I did indeed. I brought two different brews in fact. One I mixed especially for Lily to drink after the journey."

They pulled up in front of the Hodges' estate fifteen minutes later. Ben came to greet them, looking pale and just a little frightened. James jumped out of the car and went to him immediately with a wordless hug. They pulled away from each other and nodded in that way men do when they've shared deep emotion but don't want to talk about it. They cleared their throats and wiped their eyes casually as if they were removing a particle of dust that just flew in. Cailleen smiled at them.

Charles walked over and shook Ben's hand. Ben thanked him for driving everyone over. Jen stepped out of the car and treated Ben with her best '*Hi, you big hunk of a man'* smile. It had the effect of easing the tension in Ben's body and making him feel like a man in control again. He puffed out his chest ever so slightly and stepped toward Jen. "Thank you for coming."

Jen said, "Of course I'd come," then looked pointedly back to Cailleen, who was still in the car.

Ben nodded to himself and went over to the car. He opened Cailleen's door and offered her his hand to help her alight. It was how he would greet a high-ranking dignitary and Cailleen accepted it as the olive branch he intended it to be. "Welcome to my home. I'm so glad you came," Ben offered.

"I'm delighted to be of service," Cailleen said in a regal, yet warm way. They walked together to the front door, leaving the entourage to follow. Of course, everyone knew the other three would play vital roles. But in this moment, Ben needed to treat Cailleen with utmost respect and deep gratitude. And Cailleen must accept it from him. It was her due as Wise woman and Healer. Watching, Elan felt the strands on the web begin to shift.

Camille greeted them as they walked in the house. She hugged Cailleen and thanked them all for coming to help her Lily. "What do you need and what do you want us to do?"

"Can we sit in your garden room and talk for a moment?" Cailleen asked. Ben led the way. He sat next to Camille on the divan that Lily had been using when Cailleen first met her. They looked at her expectantly. Cailleen took a deep breath and looked both of them directly in the eyes – first Ben and then Camille.

"We do not know exactly what will happen today. I believe you are prepared for that?" Ben and Camille both nodded. "Much of what happens depends upon the choices which Lily will be making on the journey. You can help most powerfully in two ways. First, by absolutely not interfering. Second, by focusing on the love you share with each other and with Lily. That love will be a beacon for her to return to – IF she chooses to. If you stay in the room with Lily and us, it is very likely there will be times you will want to step forward to comfort or protect her in some way. You must not do this. Jen will be with you to prevent that. I want you to understand that by interfering you could very well jeopardize the success of the journey, and even Lily's life." She let that sink in.

"If you would prefer, you can wait with Jen in an adjoining room. You will see nothing of the process, but that may be preferable for you." She waited for them to consider this.

"We'd rather be in the room with you," they both agreed.

"Can you promise to not interfere?"

"Yes. Is there nothing we can do besides watch?" Ben asked.

"You can focus on your love for each other and for Lily," Cailleen reminded them gently. "And you could drum with Jen to help hold the space and guide us back to you." They both sighed with relief at having a physical job and nodded their agreement.

"Wonderful. Jen will guide you. Do you have any questions?"

"Will she be in pain? I won't interfere," Camille rushed to explain, "I just want to prepare myself."

"I can't tell you the effect of the journey. They usually have a challenging aspect in this kind of situation. She may very well be tested. Then again, the testing may already be in process. Each journey has its own pathway. I will do everything I can to make it easier on her, as long as it doesn't interfere in her process. James will do the same. Anything else?"

"Do you need anything? Water? Candles? Anything?" Camille asked.

"Water and candles would be lovely, Camille. And I wonder if you might have a shawl or a wrap. I seem to have left mine in the hurry to get on the road. I sometimes get cold without realizing it during a journey, so I usually wear a shawl," Cailleen explained.

"Certainly. I'll ask Henry to fetch something. He's prepared some sandwiches and other edibles for after the journey. Is there anything else? "

Charles stepped forward. "Would he allow me to brew some tea in his kitchen? I've brought some to prepare you for the journey and also some for Lily for after the journey. Each brew needs a specific preparation."

"Of course," Henry said with a slight bow. "Please follow me, sir."

"Good," Cailleen said rising. "Now, where shall we work?"

"I wasn't sure what you would need for space," Camille answered. "We could use the garden room if you like, or perhaps one of the guest rooms?"

"I think a guest room would be better," Cailleen answered. "Can I see them?"

Camille led Cailleen to the guest wing and showed her several rooms. Cailleen chose one that had a large bed with a settee and chair sitting across the room. An oak and apple tree grew outside the window. Camille left Cailleen and James to prepare the room. Jen took Camille and Ben to the garden room and explained how the drumming worked, so they felt prepared. Charles brought them cups of chamomile and oat straw tea, which they dutifully drank.

Everyone met together in the guest room. The nanny carried Lily in and laid her on the bed. She made no effort to hide her ill feelings about the healing they were about to do. Henry walked in behind her, carrying a special blanket for Lily. Camille dismissed the nanny immediately. When she left the room, Camille apologized for her behavior.

"Please forgive Nanny Sue's rudeness. She's not familiar with your work and has been raised to believe such things are from the devil. I have asked her to stay in her room until we are done."

"I think we need to take some stronger action, Camille. I remember how loving Nanny Sue was toward Lily and how attached Lily is to her. That's a strong connection. Nanny Sue's feelings could potentially interfere with our work. Is there an errand you could send her on, away from the house, while we work?" Cailleen asked.

"I'm not sure she'd leave easily. She feels very protective," Camille explained.

"Then can you send her for something that seems medically needed and ask Henry to escort her to make sure she goes?"

"Yes," Camille said, clapping her hands. "Nanny Sue said she was almost out of her inhaler. Henry, please ask her to go get a prescription filled and also to pick up something special for Lily that will entice her appetite when she feels better later today. You might also suggest a stop by her church to pray for Lily. Will that do?" Camille asked.

"Brilliantly done," Jen smiled. Cailleen nodded in agreement.

"Henry," Ben interrupted, "I need you to pick up several things for me. I'll write you a list. I'm afraid it might take you quite a while, as the items are at different places across town. I'll call you if we should finish here and need you back sooner."

"Yes sir," Henry said with evident relief. Nanny Sue was apparently a force to be reckoned with when it came to Lily.

While they were discussing how to get Nanny Sue out of the house, Cailleen went to Lily to say hello.

"Hello Lily," she said. "How are you doing this morning?"

"I'm better now that you're here and I know we shall soon begin. I'm getting very tired, you know, and I think if we don't get started I'll never find my doll," she said with her eyes still closed. Then she opened them and looked beyond Cailleen. "Is Uncle James with you?"

"Yes, dear. Uncle James is here and we'll begin very soon." She smoothed Lily's hair back from her face and noticed her over warm skin.

"You'll have to hold his hand," Lily told Cailleen.

"Perhaps *you* can hold his hand?" Cailleen suggested.

"It has to be you," Lily said and then slipped into unconsciousness.

Cailleen walked across the room to where the others were whispering. "We need to begin," she told them. "James, I think it would be easiest on Lily if we lie on either side of her. We can each hold her hand so she knows she's not alone. Jen, will you set the circle while we get settled? Camille and Ben, remember that you are brave, steadfast and a great source of love."

Jen walked to each direction, creating sacred and protective space. As Ben watched, a memory of working in sacred space was triggered and he felt safe and comforted. He relaxed. Camille felt the shift in the room, and in Ben, and she too relaxed. They were not aware that outside the room Charles had created a secondary protective circle and was serving as guardian for the inner circle.

On the bed, which had been moved to the middle of the room, Cailleen and James lay on each side of Lily with her hand in each of theirs. They focused their breathing until they were in sync. Cailleen walked them through the protocol of grounding to the present time and place. Although Lily was not conscious, Cailleen could feel her following her directions.

Jen, Camille and Ben began drumming just as Cailleen, James and Lily reached their roots out to each other linking themselves to the present. Then Cailleen took them to the crossroads where Elan waited for them. As they approached, Elan kneeled and Lily ran to her.

"Elan, you came to help us?" she asked falling into Elan's open arms.

"Where else would I be on such an important day?" Elan asked smiling.

"Can you tell me where my doll is?" Lily asked.

"I can tell you how to *find* her, Lily," she explained. Elan waved her arms in a great circle. "Behold the web of life," she commanded. All around them appeared silver strands. Some shimmered with sparkling light, others were dark or in shadow. "Be advised," Elan said, looking at James and Cailleen, "the strands appear different to each of you. The ones you see shimmering are ones that have greatest significance for you. This is Lily's journey. It is her strands you must follow and only she can perceive them clearly. However, there will be a point where hers will intersect with yours and with a fourth player's. You must all be able to identify the point where your significances meet. I cannot help you any further, except to send my love with you."

Elan walked off along the web and disappeared. James looked to Cailleen for guidance, but she simply raised her eyebrow at him. They turned together to look at Lily. One tear ran down her face and her lip quivered for a moment. Then she took a deep breath and lifted her chin.

Not running to her to help her decide what to do was the hardest thing James had ever done. But he did it. Cailleen reached out and squeezed his hand in compassion and comfort. He smiled weakly at her.

"This one, I think," Lily said, pointing along a strand.

"What makes you think so?" James asked to help her commit to the path.

"It just feels right," she answered.

"It's a very good choice, then," Cailleen told her, and walked forward to offer her hand.

Lily smiled and then reached her other hand out to James. "Off we go," she said. "Do you think Dolly is looking for me?"

"I would not be surprised," Cailleen answered her. "Try holding her in your mind and heart and see if the connection will bring us to her." Lily concentrated very hard for a moment, then nodded her head and stepped off onto the strand.

They were immediately taken into a new landscape. What had once been a lush environment now looked mostly dry. A few plants still held their green but were wilted on their stem. A mama deer with her doe scampered off as they approached. Down a stream they saw a mama bear and her cubs. The baby animals indicated it should be spring, but leaves were falling off trees. Smells of fall decay floated around them, but something was not quite right about it. The leaves that had fallen were not the reds and golds of fall, they were pale green.

"It feels very sad here," Lily said with big eyes. "It looks like I feel on the inside. I don't want to be here." She looked at James with the hope that he would take her away.

James knelt down to her level. "Poppet, I think this means you have chosen the right path. If it looks to you like you feel on the inside, then it seems to me you have chosen a strand that is significant for you. I wonder if we should try and see what clues it might have to help us find Dolly?"

"Yes, you might be right. Let's hurry and find her so we can leave this place behind." Lily walked ahead, pulling James and Cailleen along with her.

"Do you see a light ahead?" Cailleen asked them. They both shook their heads no. "I see a shimmering path leading into the forest. When we get there, I think we need to stop for a moment."

They walked along until they found a fork in the path. The path to the left shimmered in Cailleen's eyes and she felt a strong pull. Lily and James both looked at her. "I cannot make this choice. It is Lily's choice."

"What do you see, Uncle James?" she asked.

James looked down both paths. The one on the right appealed to him and he sensed sunlight as it wound its way upward. "I see a light, probably just sunlight, down the path on the right."

"Which path shimmers for you, Cailleen?"

"I'm afraid it's the path on the left, Lily. Which path calls to you most strongly?"

Lily closed her eyes again. She wanted one of the adults to make the choice. But since they didn't, she focused hard on Dolly. The path on the left pulled at her, so she headed down that one. The path rose up and then over a hill. From the top of the hill, they looked down. An old man drank hungrily from what was left of a dying river. As he drank, Lily began breathing irregularly and fell to her knees.

"Lily!" James shouted as he knelt beside her. "Lily, breathe slowly. That's it. Don't panic. You'll be alright," he soothed. While he talked, he let his love flow over her, offering her his strength. After a moment she seemed to recover. He held her in his arms, rocking her and making soothing sounds.

Cailleen focused on the old man. He was the elusive source she'd been trying to identify on the drive over. Now that he was before her, she recognized him. "Raneck. Raneck, the fourth player," she said, turning to James and pointing at the old man.

Lily looked to where she pointed and saw her dolly tucked through Raneck's belt. "Dolly," she cried and wiggled out of James' arms. She tried to run, but James held on to her and Cailleen commanded her to stop. Lily looked at her with rebellion in her eyes.

"Lily, you must still choose the correct path or you'll never reach Dolly. I'm certain of it. Look," she pointed. "See how many paths lead down the hill? They aren't large and they aren't obvious, but if you look you can see them."

James and Lily both looked at the hill leading down to the river. Lily whimpered, "I see three paths and they all feel the same to me, how do I choose?"

"I see four paths," James said. "Two of them feel right to me."

"I see many paths and several of them beckon to me pretty strongly," Cailleen offered.

Lily plopped down hard on the ground. "It isn't fair. We need to choose a path that intersects with everyone else's but we can't see each other's paths. I'm just a little girl," she sighed.

"Darling," Cailleen said, sitting down beside her, "you are a little girl, but there's no 'just' about it. You are a very important little girl. Many, many, lives ago you were my great granddaughter. And that old man you see down there was your great, great grandfather. And your papa was also your great grandfather. You, my darling, are the crossroads for all of us. You gathered us here today to heal a very old wound. I think that together we can do it."

"Sometimes," James added, "we're asked to do things that seem too big for us. But they aren't really too big. We just haven't realized we've grown. The thing we have to do helps us grow and also helps us to understand we've grown. And Cailleen's right, you are not 'just' a little girl. You are a wonderful, loving, sweet, brave little girl traveling with a very powerful woman and a man who loves you dearly. I shall be your knight and Cailleen shall be your sorceress. So, Princess, we wait to do your bidding."

"I shall be a queen," Lily said. "Queens know how to get things done better than princesses. My dolly shall be the princess and we will save her." Lily stood and looked down the hill again, considering what to do. Then she sat back down.

"I think that one of my paths crosses both of your paths and will meet with Grandfather's path. Uncle James, you have only two paths that call to you. Please describe how they wind down the hill. Cailleen and I will listen and see if any of your landmarks are close to our paths."

"Of course, my Queen. One path starts with that outcrop of three rocks and wanders off to the edge of those trees. Then it crosses back at an angle to a spot straight below us. From there it moves back toward the trees, over that big stump on the left and then straight down to the river, but it bypasses the old man and doesn't reach the river for another 20 yards or so. It crosses the river and then moves up into the trees on the other side where it disappears into the forest." James stopped and looked at the two of them.

"Two of my paths cross yours," Cailleen told them. One crosses at the stump and the one on the other side of the river."

"My paths also cross his but not at either of the points you said," Lily explained. "Describe the other path, Uncle James. Please."

"The other path begins far off to the right where that tall cedar stands." As he mentioned the tree, a crow flew off from it with a call. "That's the path," James said excitedly. "The crow is my totem. He is flying along the pathway now so you can see it. Thank you, brother," he called to the crow.

Lily and Cailleen watched the crow's flight and called out when he crossed a point on either of their paths. Two spots were intersections for all three. One spot was on the hill about 20 feet above where Raneck currently sat waiting for them. The other spot was much further down at a river bend.

"We have eliminated one of my paths. The other two take us to one or other of the intersections. How do I choose," Lily asked them?

"There are only two paths," James offered. "If the first one you choose is not correct, we can come back and then follow the other one."

Lily looked up at James with sad eyes. "Uncle, I don't have that much time."

James staggered back at this knowledge and for a moment was helpless in his grief.

"Only one of those intersections will cross Raneck's path," Cailleen said. Only he can tell us which one. And he knows that. I shall simply go ask him."

"I think we should stay together," James demanded. "I don't think I trust this Raneck exactly. Lily was fine until we saw him. She grew weak when he drank from the stream. Lily told us this landscape feels like her insides. I think," James gritted in a whisper to Cailleen, he's a parasite and has been draining her life force. He has her doll. What kind of a man is he?"

"A desperate one," Cailleen informed him. "But he was once a great and powerful shaman. He trained me." As she said this, Cailleen realized for the first time that it wasn't true. She knew how to use her powers before she apprenticed with Raneck. He helped her hone them. She learned from him. She also learned from Chalic and Chancha and the tribe and the Land. She'd given him too much credit and too much power.

"But it wasn't balanced training," she said aloud. "He showed me the craft of the work and helped me understand how to read the web of life. But he could not show me the force that would help me sustain my power and help it to grow. I knew all along. I passed it on to Chalic, but I'd forgotten until now."

"Tell him the queen commands him to meet her," Lily said weakly.

"Don't leave us," James pleaded. "I don't think it is safe for you to go alone."

"But I won't leave you, James, and I'll never be alone again. I love you. I love you fiercely and with my whole heart. I no longer fear having to choose. Love is my greatest power. I give mine to you and I accept yours with deepest gratitude."

She walked down the hill toward Raneck along the path that now shimmered most strongly for her. She stopped a few feet from him.

"I see you've finally decided to come to me and stand in your power," Raneck said. "I don't know why you wasted so many years. We shall do wonderful things together. Come cross over with me."

Cailleen shook her head no. "I have come to ask where you will meet us. Downstream where the river bends or on that small plateau above us?"

"We have met already," Raneck said with disdain. "We do not need *them* to do great things."

"Raneck, I will not leave them. And," she paused, letting herself expand energetically until Raneck was required to look up at her, "*I* do not need *you* to do great things. This healing will be your final chance to share our powers in a common cause. The queen commands that you reveal where our paths intersect." As Cailleen spoke in her most regal manner, she realized that Lily was telling her to be the queen when she approached Raneck. Such wisdom for 'just' a little girl, she thought.

"It is too late to heal the child and that man cannot match you in power," Raneck said. "I have brought you here to *me*. We must combine our powers and re-balance the web."

"Yes, we must re-balance the web. We have all played our parts. But now it is your turn, Raneck. You must cross over. I will not be going with you. We have all found our way to this power crossroad. I will be leaving with James. Before I go, we can work together to save this child, our granddaughter. You, Raneck of the Bear Tribe, have pledged your life to protect the tribe. I call you to release this child and to do all in your power to heal her." Cailleen expanded again and commanded, "Great Spirit, Creator of All, I call you to witness the final act of your servant, Raneck."

Raneck shook with anger, fear and defeat. He had miscalculated when it came to her, again. Calleigha would never have challenged him and called him to his oaths in such a way. He must do what she asked or lose all honor. Without his honor he would be lost forever.

"I will meet you on the plateau," he said with as much dignity as he could muster.

Cailleen returned to James and Lily. Lily was resting comfortably in James' arms. She opened her eyes as Cailleen approached. "Well done, sorceress queen. Shall we finish our journey?"

"We go to the plateau," Cailleen agreed. "Can you walk or shall James carry you?"

"I have been resting up," Lily informed her. "I will walk."

Lily led them along her path to the plateau where Raneck awaited them. As they approached, the power at the crossroads grew. Back at the estate, Ben felt the surge and began drumming more powerfully. As he drummed, he was pulled into the sound and found himself standing with James, Cailleen, Lily and an old man on a plateau above an almost dry riverbed.

"Well met Chancha," Raneck greeted him. Ben didn't know what was happening or what to do. He promised not to interfere so he just kept drumming.

"I will be leaving you all in a moment," Raneck said. He looked down at Lily. "Thank you for the use of your doll. As you see, I found it for you. Unfortunately," he said looking at Cailleen, "I've also become quite attached to her and through her to the child. If I cross over with the doll, the child dies. If I sever the connection with the doll, we both die. I'm afraid after all that I am just a tired and weak old man. I will cross over, but I have no power to heal any longer."

A door to the past opened when Ben saw the doll in Raneck's belt. "Little Rasia," he called in anguish. Then he looked at Lily and was confused as lifetimes bled together. "You will not take another child from me," Chancha said in a cold voice. "Calleigha, please do something."

"You still have a voice," Cailleen reminded Raneck. "Sing," she commanded. And with that command she began to sing. Raneck joined her and the song began to take shape. Cailleen was shaping the song into a sword and the sword vibrated and became crystalline. Cailleen took the sword in her hands. "Take your doll, Lily," she commanded. As Lily pulled her doll away from Raneck, Cailleen raised the blade to catch a flame from the sun. She brought the sword down and severed the doll from Raneck.

Raneck screamed, "Chalic!" Then he faded into the sunlight and was gone.

Ben kept drumming. Cailleen fell to the ground, unconscious. Lily collapsed with her doll safe in her arms and a peaceful smile on her face. James cried out in anguish at the sight of Cailleen and Lily on the ground. "Elan! Elan of the Crossroads, help me!"

Elan walked out of the forest. "Merry meet, James. The quest is complete."

"Complete?" he shouted. "It can't end this way."

"Actually, it can. But it doesn't have to," Elan explained. "You can do nothing more for Lily. But you can possibly call Cailleen back to you."

"Lily!" James sobbed. "I'm sorry, Ben. I'm so sorry." He touched Lily's cheek, which was so pale, though not yet cold. He kissed her forehead and then turned to Cailleen.

He held Cailleen's hand in his and kissed it. Then he kissed her other hand and then her lips. He held her hand to his heart. "You said you wouldn't leave me. I hold you to that promise. Come back to me, Cailleen. Come back and live a life with me. Come back." He imagined he felt her hand twitch but saw no other sign of her returning. So, he sang. He sang his love for her. He sang his anguish. He sang his broken heart and just as he let go of his own desire for her to return to him, she gasped for breath. He raised her up in his arms gently.

"We have to go back," she whispered.

"Back?" James was confused. Back to where? Then he remembered they were on a journey, an out of body experience. They needed to return to their bodies.

"Ben, keep drumming," he directed. James picked up Lily in his arms and carried her to Cailleen. He put his arm around Cailleen. "Ben we're going to follow the drum beat back to your house. Listen to the drum, feel it become your heartbeat, follow the sound of the drum. Follow it back to Jen and Camille. Yes, hear their answering drum beats. Oh, and there's Charles singing. Follow the song...."

They were now back in the guest room at the Hodges' Estate. Camille was rubbing Ben's hands and calling his name until he returned to her. "Lily!" he cried. "She found her doll. She looked so peaceful," he sobbed. Camille hugged him to her breast and rocked him.

Jen was attending to James and Cailleen. She'd been able to see what was happening, but could not get James' attention through his grief. If he hadn't brought Cailleen around, they would all have been lost. She called their names and massaged their bodies to bring back warmth and an awareness of their physicality. James revived first. "Merry meet," Jen said, smiling. As James tried to raise himself, she pushed him back. "Just lie still for a while," she told him.

Cailleen returned to consciousness a moment later. "He did it," she whispered to Jen, and then she drifted into sleep.

Charles had practically stormed into the room. He waited impatiently as Jen cut an energetic door for him to enter through. She closed the door and turned to him for an explanation.

"I was called," he said. He looked to the bed where James, Cailleen and Lily were lying. He deepened his psychic awareness and assessed their energy fields. Lily was almost gone. He walked over and gently lifted her into his lap. He began singing. He sought her spirit and followed the frail tether that still connected it to her body. Someone had called to him. But he wasn't sure it was Lily's path to return to them. He could see her hovering above her body, pausing in indecision. He kept singing to keep the path of returning open while she decided. She was whole again. The part of her soul represented by the doll was now intact, and Lily was filled with light.

Lily was looking for something. She turned and Raneck stood before her. "Thank you for releasing me," she said. "I forgive you for using me. I will not allow it again. Our contract is complete. Go rest and renew yourself. Perhaps we will meet again, but I think it will be a long, long time."

"Thank you," Raneck said, bowing. "Chalic will help you, if you want to return to your life," he said.

Lily turned toward the sound of Charles' voice. She hadn't seen Chalic in a very long time. She would like to sit with him and to talk about everything that had happened since she saw him last. But she felt so whole and wondrous at this moment, here in the light. She could be happy staying in it for a very long time.

She hesitated. She turned to the light and began walking deeper into it. Then she turned again. Her heart missed Chalic. Beyond him she sensed others who waited, hoping she would return to them. She couldn't remember them exactly, so she focused beyond Chalic, trying to remember those who waited. She heard a faint sob and someone whispering her name. Yes, Lily, that was her name. It was her mother calling. She smiled as she remembered being held by her mother and her father. It would be nice to smell her mama and papa again. She floated toward Charles and reached out her hand to him.

Charles shifted the song now to call her back. He opened his eyes, caught Jen's attention and looked pointedly at the drums. Jen began drumming along with his song. The sound brought Ben and Camille out of their grief. They didn't know what was happening, but hope seemed to fill the air. So they drummed, and they loved each other, and they loved Lily.

Charles ended the song. "Tea," he requested. Jen brought him the tea he had brewed for Lily. Charles opened Lily's mouth and poured a few drops on her tongue, then a few more until she swallowed. He sighed heavily and with relief. He looked up at Camille and Ben, who hovered nearby. He stood up and placed Lily in Ben's arms. He gave the cup of tea to Camille. "Give all of this to her as soon as you can, but don't force it."

They took Lily to the settee and fed her the tea, along with their continuing love.

Charles poured another cup of tea and handed it to Jen motioning to James. He poured another and went over to Cailleen and gently lifted her. She fluttered her eyes open.

"We need to talk about how often you try to leave me," Charles chided. "Drink."

"Lily?"

"Lily returned to us whole. She's resting now. I think she'll be running the household very soon. She will need a teacher, you know."

"We all need teachers, Chalic. How is your student faring?" she asked.

"Jen made him drink some tea. Now the two of you can sleep it off. No more adventures until you're rested. Promise?"

"Promise," Cailleen said with a sigh as she drifted into a restful sleep tucked in safely next to James.

Even in sleep they reached out to one another. As their hands met, they both smiled softly and sank deeper into dreams.

The End

An excerpt from Book 2,
In the Song of the Beloved

Celeste looked for someone to approach, but the crowd overwhelmed her. She reconsidered calling it a night and going home.

"They're not so bad when you get to know them."

A tall elegant woman stood next to her, looking over the crowd. She was confident, beautiful, and might have been intimidating except for the kindness in her brown eyes. "I'm Camille Hodges. I've never heard the songs you played. Are they original?"

"I'm Celeste Fallan. It's nice to meet you. Yes, I wrote them. I wasn't sure anyone heard me," she said with a smile.

"I'm terribly sorry," Camille said, "there was a mishap with the original sound system and we had to make do with a backup that, shall we say, is shadowed by the size of the crowd."

Celeste laughed. "Well, one person heard my music. That's more than if I'd stayed home."

"I not only heard it, I loved it," Camille told her. "Do you play anywhere regularly?"

"I've recently moved to Seattle and am just getting my feet wet. I play at a few small places. I'd be happy to put you on my mailing list. Or, you can find out where I'll be on my website." She handed Camille her card.

"Thank you. I'm surprised you're here at this event since you're new in town. You must know someone."

"I happened to be in the right place at the right time. I work at a restaurant in Bell Town and overheard a customer say someone had cancelled. I smiled brightly and told her I was available. One of my co-workers told her I sing like an angel and she offered me the spot," Celeste told her.

"Who's representing you?" Camille asked.

"No one, officially. I recently met a guy who has offered his services, but I'm not sure about him."

Camille considered the enchanting young woman in front of her. There was something special about her, something that made Camille want to take her under her wing.

She wondered if Charles Murphy would be interested in Celeste professionally, maybe personally. Charles was an agent, and single. She pictured the two of them together, liking what she saw.

"I know someone in the business. In fact, he will be at my home tomorrow for a New Year's celebration. It's more of a family gathering than a party, but there will be great food and I can guarantee you won't be bored. Why don't you join us?"

"Really? I'd be delighted, if you're sure I wouldn't be intruding."

Camille reached into her purse and handed Celeste her card. "Here's my number. We're gathering around noon. Call me in the morning and I'll give you our address and details. Everyone else is spending the night and you're welcome to do the same.

"It was nice to meet you Celeste. I'm afraid I'm being hailed by the committee chair. I have duties to attend to. I'll see you tomorrow."

And now, it was tomorrow! Celeste shut off the shower, dried off, and headed to her closet. She hoped the gathering wasn't too formal or upscale. She didn't have a lot of options.

She called Camille for details and was told to dress casually, but to bring a formal outfit and pajamas that she could be seen in. Celeste hung up wondering what she'd agreed to and hoping she could cope with what the evening brought to her.

She could hear her mother's voice warning her about rich people from the big city and the scandalous things they do.

But Celeste had a good feeling about Camille. She was a kind woman, and trustworthy. Celeste didn't have much to base that description on, except her own intuition. Besides, it was a New Year. A perfect time to take a chance and see where it led her.

She called her boyfriend, Josh, to tell him about it. He hadn't asked her to spend New Year's Eve with him, but was angry when she told him she'd made other plans for today. She explained it was an opportunity that she couldn't afford to pass by.

Celeste knew he had a selfish streak. But his lack of attention suited her; her music came first and she didn't really need a man in her life.

But she did need friends and hoped Camille's invitation was a step toward that.

***

What Celeste didn't know is that Hawthorn of the Fey had a hand in connecting her with Camille.

He'd offered an irresistible opportunity to the musician who gave up the spot in last night's benefit. He'd charmed the woman responsible for scheduling entertainment into having a drink with him at the restaurant where Celeste worked. He'd used magic to encourage her co-worker to speak up for her, and to get the woman to offer Celeste the gig.

At the event, he'd used magic again to make sure Celeste's voice was heard, specifically by Camille Hodges. He'd been prepared to use magic to make Celeste sing especially well, but hadn't needed to.

Finally, he'd used enchantments and subtle lighting around Celeste to draw Camille's attention to her; whispered, "she needs your help," behind Camille when they met; and, whispered "invite her to the gathering".

Once Camille had invited and Celeste had accepted her invitation, Hawthorn slipped back into the realm of the Fey.

"She will meet the circle, tomorrow," Hawthorn reported to his mother.

"Good. Will she need help to make a connection with them?" Queen Aoife asked.

"I'm not sure she needed much help to get the invitation," Hawthorn told her. "She's an enchanting young woman – and very talented. People like her and want to help her."

"Still, you should stay close. I'll reach out to Cailleen in a few days."

About the Author

C. Rhalena Renee catches the stories needed for our times. She writes in the Bardic Tradition of teaching stories. These teaching stories come from the land, ancestors, and other realms. C. Rhalena teaches us the importance of carrying our gifts into the world, believing this is specifically vital for psychics, intuitives, and empaths - who are awakening in a world that desperately needs them. C. Rhalena weaves her own personal experiences of carrying these particular gifts into her stories.

C. Rhalena lives in the beautiful Pacific Northwest, where she gardens, does healing circles, sings, cooks with friends and family, makes bitters, and drinks lots of tea. She offers spiritual healing, circles and rites of passage.

Her favorite spots include Shilshoe Bay on Puget Sound, the Wenatchee National Forest, and the desert steppe above the Columbia River.

She can be contacted at: **CRhalenaRenee@gmail.com**.

Other books by C. Rhalena Renee

Choices for Joy, 2015 - C. Rhalena Renee teaches us the secrets of embodying joy and dancing in the wild beauty and grace that joy offers. In "Choices for Joy", she shares 25 years of experience with clients and her personal stories of the gifts and challenges of stepping onto this incredibly transformative path. Through the tips, tools and inspirations in this book, expand your own capacity for joy; learn to play more; and, discover the wonder of living an ecstatic life.

The Spiraling Past Series:
2. In the Song of the Beloved 2021
*3. In the Chambers of the Nautilus (*Available April 2021)
*4. In the Dance of the Web (*Available Fall 2021)

Made in the USA
Middletown, DE
09 July 2024